Above Rubies

By Jaclyn M. Hawkes

Other books by Jaclyn M Hawkes

Journey of Honor
The Outer Edge of Heaven
The Most Important Catch

Other Rockland Ranch Series Books
Peace River

Above Rubies

By Jaclyn M. Hawkes

Above Rubies
By Jaclyn M. Hawkes
Copyright © December 2012 Jaclyn M. Hawkes
All rights reserved.

Published and distributed by Spirit Dance Books.LLC
Spiritdancebooks.com 1-855-648-5559
Cover design by Anna Young and Jeffrey Goodwin

Printed in USA

First Printing March 2013

Library of Congress control number 2013932329

ISBN: 0-9851648-2-9

ISBN-13:978-0-9851648-2-9

Dedication

This book is dedicated to my two lovely daughters. One blonde and one brunette, they are sweet and smart and beautiful, and I'm honored to be their mom. They are truly becoming virtuous young women worth far above rubies.

It's also dedicated to my good husband, whose patience is one of my greatest gifts. Knowing that he'll take whatever in stride is wonderfully empowering to an adventurous wife. Thanks, hon. You're the best.

Chapter One

Millions of lights on the Las Vegas strip streamed through the smudged bus windows like alarm beacons. It felt like hundreds of flashing cop cars at some freakishly huge accident. The glare made the hungry knot of worry in the pit of her stomach tighten. Before she'd even gotten off the Greyhound, Kit knew she'd made a disastrous mistake.

****

Girl, what are you doing? As Rossen Rockland began to fill his truck with gas, he shook his head as he watched a slender young girl walking alone in the dark carrying a guitar. She was anything but safe out by herself in Las Vegas at almost one o'clock in the morning. Down a side street he could see a number of teenagers hanging out in an unruly bunch. Even though he was from a part of Wyoming that didn't have a problem with gangs, he still recognized one when he saw one. They were making hand gestures to another group of youth who appeared near the rear of the station, not far from the young woman and he heard himself repeat out loud, "Girl, what are you doing?"

His best friend and roping partner, Slade Marsh,

had gotten out to double check the horses in the trailer they were pulling and wash the windows, while Slade's fiancée, Isabel remained in the cab. Even at this hour of the night, Las Vegas was just really getting going and she was more secure inside in this wide open party town.

The three of them had just come from the last round of the National Finals Rodeo, where the two men had taken top honors in their events. They'd reached their ultimate rodeo goals, but now, as tired as they were, they just wanted to go home. They'd been on the road rodeoing for most of the year, and it had been a great ride. But the season was over, Christmas was a mere ten days away, and they intended to be home on their ranches in Wyoming by morning. The entire National Finals had been a roller coaster of not just rodeoing, but several other troubling instances as well, and the three wanted to leave the hubbub of the City of Sin behind, and return to the peace and serenity of the mountains.

Almost as if Rossen's thoughts had started it, the girl was approached by a cocky youth from the gang hanging out behind the station. Even though Rossen's tanks weren't yet full, he returned the nozzle to the pump and jumped back into the truck. As Slade climbed back into the passenger seat, Rossen drew his and Isabel's attention to what was going on as the heavyset young gangster approached the girl. She immediately turned around and started walking in the opposite direction, but the youth simply turned and followed her. As he dogged the young woman, Rossen gunned the truck toward the girl, all three of its occupants tense at what they were watching take place.

The gang member followed the girl for a moment, then grabbed her by the arm and started dragging her toward the back of the station as Rossen and Slade slammed out of the idling truck. Rossen yelled, but it was only swallowed up in the music that issued from the station speakers and they started to run.

It all happened so fast they couldn't stop it as the girl slapped her aggressor and began to fight him. The much larger youth backhanded her, sending her reeling into the building. Her guitar was knocked away and shattered as it hit the pavement and the gangster jerked her arm up behind her back, turned her and slugged her full in the face. The blow knocked her backwards. She stumbled off the curb, tried unsuccessfully to put an arm back to break her fall and then slammed into the asphalt on the back of her head. Rossen was horrified when the young woman lay sickeningly still.

Arriving seconds too late, Slade punched the gang member, doubling him over, and then slamming his face into his raised knee, as Rossen bent to the still form on the pavement.

At that moment Isabel shouted and began to gesture at something around the corner of the building. She was pointing and yelled, "Get her inside quick, before they get here!" Rossen scooped the unconscious girl off the street and quickly climbed into the rear door Slade held for him, then Slade jumped into the driver's seat, pulled out of the station and onto the freeway, literally closing the door as he drove away.

Slade drove as fast as he dared with a trailer full of horses, while Isabel bailed over the seat to help Rossen try to stop the girl's bleeding. At first, they couldn't believe a nose could bleed that much, but it took only a moment to find she also had a two inch gash down the back of her head that was gushing blood. They quickly depleted the supply of napkins in the cab and went through a pillow case and then Isabel's soft jacket, before the flow even slowed. It wasn't until then that they noticed her left arm bent at a strange angle, and it felt like hours more before they sighted the hospital sign posted at the freeway exit, and pulled off the interstate.

When they got to the emergency room entrance, Rossen carefully carried the unconscious girl past the crowd in the waiting room and into a cubicle, her head and nose still dripping blood. He gently laid her on the exam table indicating her arm, and then the three of them stood back, as a doctor and two nurses began examining her all at once. They cut the oversized denim jacket off to reveal an obviously broken arm that was beginning to bruise and swell. They finally got the bleeding from the back of her head stopped, and were working on her bleeding nose, as both eyes grew black and swollen.

The doctor was instructing his staff to get her cleaned up and prepped for surgery when one of the clerks from the front desk came back to get information.

As Isabel turned and said that they didn't even know who she was, the whole room seemed to slow and back off. All of the staff looked up and paused at what they were doing.

Slade realized what was going on and said, "Is, dig in her pockets or through her back pack and find her ID."

Rossen wasn't happy with the instant slacking off and his tone was impatient when he asked, "What's the problem, Doctor? I thought she needed immediate surgery."

"We can't just operate on someone you don't know."

Disgusted, Rossen asked, "Why not, if she needs it?"

"There are legal ramifications. It's not all that simple."

Shaking his head in disappointment, Rossen asked, "This is about money, isn't it?"

The doctor finally looked up angrily. "This is about it's illegal to treat her, especially with surgery without a parent's consent if she's under eighteen. The only way I could do this was if her condition was immediately life threatening."

Typically easy going, Rossen was completely disgusted, and said, "Of course she's eighteen! Look at her!"

Without backing down, the physician insisted, "She doesn't look eighteen to me and even if she were, someone still has to sign the releases."

Isabel stepped between them with a calming hand on Rossen's chest, "Perhaps if I personally guarantee the bills, would that help? I'd be glad to." She extended a dainty hand and smiled up at the doctor. "I'm Isabel."

He turned to her, glancing at her up and down and changed his demeanor instantly. Still holding her hand he reiterated, "I'd be happy to take your information Isabel, but I really can't operate, or even treat her further without some verification."

Slade rolled his eyes. "Which we can't get because she's unconscious, and has no ID. Great!" He looked pointedly at the doctor's hand still holding Isabel's, and then met Rossen's eyes. They were good enough friends that they could all but read each other's minds and Rossen knew he was wondering if they'd encounter this same situation if they tried to simply take her to a different hospital nearby. They both knew they probably would. Slade gave him a minimal nod and said, "Okay. Plan B. We're taking her with us. We'll take her home to our personal physician."

The doctor half-heartedly objected, "You can't just pick a juvenile up and take her with you. That's technically kidnapping."

Rossen all but snarled, "Does she look like anyone here is taking a particular interest in her?" The room was quiet because the neglect was so obvious.

Slade addressed the doctor, "Can you at least tell us she isn't in imminent danger if we have to drive for awhile?"

Reluctantly, the doctor let go of Isabel's hand and turned back to Slade. "She does have a concussion, but it isn't life threatening now that the bleeding is stopped. She should come to anytime, but I'll give her something to help her sleep, and numb the arm for the duration. How long is awhile?"

"Hours. Several hours."

The doctor looked hesitant, but then shook his head and said, "She should be fine. But, one of the main concerns with concussions is they often cause patients to be horribly ill. There's a very good probability she'll vomit in your vehicle on the way. Other than that, she should be all right." He started hustling around the room again to splint her arm. "You know your own doctor legally shouldn't work on her either."

The hospital staff was obviously glad to be free of the responsibility and was, in fact, very helpful after all. They splinted the unconscious girl's arm, injected it for pain, and supplied them with bandages and ice to try and keep the swelling to a minimum. They even provided them with blankets to transport her. Rossen, Slade and Isabel were completely disgusted, but felt they were doing the right thing and loaded back into the truck for a fast run up I-15 to Wyoming.

For the next seven hours, Rossen cradled the slight, injured girl on his lap in the rear seat of the cab with Isabel beside him. They struggled the entire way to keep ice on her arm and her face, and elevate her head which, even with pressure on the wound, bled intermittently. As they drove, Rossen prayed. This girl seemed so young and fragile. She was so thin she was almost emaciated, and he was pretty positive from the distinctive rounded tummy, that she was a few months pregnant.

Her clothes were faded and threadbare and didn't come close to fitting. And they certainly weren't warm enough for mid-December, even in the desert. Her backpack had contained almost nothing. A spare change of worn clothing, a hairbrush, a toothbrush, a squashed peanut butter sandwich, and a sandwich bag of something that looked like modeling clay. In the back pocket of her cut-off Levis, they found four dollars.

Her appearance alone in the street in Vegas late at night, her condition, and now her terrible injuries, all combined to fill him with a deep sense of pity. He thought of his own younger sister and vowed to himself he would help this girl.

At just after six the next morning, Slade placed a call to their own orthopedic surgeon who practiced out of Evanston. Dr. Sundquist had worked on Slade and the members of the Rockland family enough to be considered a family friend. When they explained the situation, he agreed to be at the hospital waiting for them with an operating room available and an anesthesiologist on call. Slade closed his phone and they all three breathed a sigh of relief that their decision to bring her home had worked out at least this far.

Rossen in turn opened his phone to touch base with his mom, Naomi, and sister, Joey. They were the only ones of the family who hadn't been in Vegas with them. The rest were coming home the next day.

About an hour outside of Evanston, Rossen realized the injured girl was starting to come around. He and Isabel retrieved the bags the hospital had sent in case she threw up, just in time. He pulled her long, dark, now bloody, hair back from her face and helped her wipe her mouth with a tissue. When she looked up at him through black and bloodshot eyes, her fear was greater than her obvious pain. She pulled the light blanket they'd wrapped around her tight to her neck apparently in an effort to cover and protect herself.

He could feel her heart race as he held her and kept his voice low and gentle to keep from frightening her any more as he asked, "What's your name?"

"Kit." She winced in pain.

He moved to smooth her hair out of her face and she pulled back in fear as he asked, "Kit what?"

"Just Kit." Her voice held a deep sadness.

He tried again. "Where's your ID?"

She barely shook her head. "I have no ID."

The ice slipped off her elbow and he slowly retrieved it. "Are you from Vegas?"

She looked from him to Isabel, then lowered her eyes. "No."

Using a gentle voice, he asked, "Where are you from?"

She didn't answer immediately. Finally she sighed deeply. "It doesn't matter. I'm never going back." She closed her swollen eyes for a few minutes, then opened them to ask, "Did I lose my guitar?"

He was hesitant to tell her, "I'm afraid so."

The cobalt blue irises of her eyes deepened within the bloodshot whites and filled with tears. She closed them once again, and a single tear drop slowly slipped out to trail quietly across her thin cheek bone and into her hair.

At length, he knew she was asleep again, but this time it was shallow and restless. When she moved around, she would grimace in pain. She pulled her legs up and curled with her good hand over her belly.

Even with medication the hospital had given her, she was unable to settle down again. After watching her struggle for half an hour, Rossen placed his hands on her head and silently gave her a blessing. She was finally able to relax again and rest. As she slept, he contemplated what he'd felt prompted to say. He'd blessed her to be healed in body and spirit and to know when she found security. He'd also said she would learn with a surety that she was a daughter of God and of infinite worth. He smoothed her bloody hair back from her face, wondering what that knowledge could do for her young life.

****

Dr. Sundquist was as good as his word, and upon their arrival, took Kit straight into radiology without even waking her up. They carefully draped several lead shields around her to protect her baby and filmed her elbow. They also did an MRI on her head before they brought her back to the ER and began to clean her up.

He carefully examined her, grumbling in disgust

that the Las Vegas hospital had ever let her leave in the shape she was in. When the x-ray came back within minutes, he confirmed the shattered elbow and prepped her for surgery. He explained to the three of them that they would set and pin her arm, stitch her head and splint her nose while she was under, and that it would be a minimum of two hours in the operating room.

Rossen stood beside her bed watching as they inserted an I.V. and drew blood samples. The grimace of pain that flickered across her face in her sleep somehow touched his heart. A nurse came in with some forms and Rossen signed them, uncaring about the legalities for the time being.

As they wheeled her off, Slade and Isabel left to get the horses home to the ranches, and Rossen settled on a couch in the lounge near the recovery room to wait. It was nine-thirty on Sunday morning. He'd been awake over twenty-eight hours and felt like he had gravel in his eyes. He desperately wanted to sleep, but worried the hospital staff wouldn't wake him when she came out of surgery, and he felt strongly that she shouldn't be alone. The appearance of his mother several minutes later in the lounge was exactly what was needed.

He stood to give her a hug. "Mom, what are you doing here?"

Stepping back to examine him before she answered, she asked, "Are you as hammered as you look?"

He glanced down at his rumpled rodeo shirt, the sponsor patches spattered with blood, and ran a hand through his hair with a sigh. "It's been a long night. How did you know I was just wishing you were here?"

They sat down on the couch, and he stretched his long legs out in front of him, realizing for the first time that he still wore his spurs from the rodeo the night before. What a hectic time.

Smoothing the hair back from his forehead with a gentle hand, his mother smiled and said, "Moms just know. Joey and I decided that at the very least we ought to meet you and bring the horses. We figured none of you got much sleep, so Joey's driving Slade and Isabel home. And from what little you told me about this girl, it sounded to me like she'd need someone to sit with her. Plus, you'll have to sleep sometime. On top of that, I'm dying to hear all about the rodeo. It's not everyday your son becomes a world champion roper. I'm still mad I couldn't be there."

Rossen smiled tiredly, thinking about the night before. "It all felt surreal, even before I was this much of a zombie." He yawned. "Honestly, I haven't had much chance to think about it. The mess with Isabel's father and the FBI, and Slade's bull ride, then picking up this girl have all kept us busy. It hasn't even sunk in yet that we really did make it. We've wanted it for so long, but in the mix of life and death situations, it kind of takes a back seat.

"I don't think Slade has even stopped to consider his buckle yet. He realized they'd grabbed Isabel just as he settled onto his bull. It's a wonder he even made it through that ride. I guess Dad filled you in on it all?"

She nodded. "We talked until two. It must have been quite a night!"

With a long sigh, he leaned his head back against the top of the couch. "Isabel's finally safe and they'll get married now. It feels great to be the best, but I'm really looking forward to coming home and moving on." He rubbed the back of his neck. "The rodeo was just the beginning. I have no idea what this girl's story is, but she's in a mess. I'm so glad we were there when we were." He went on to tell her the details of what had happened, and ended with simply, "She needs us, Mom. She was desperately sad in the truck. I don't know what's going on, but she needs some help. Her name is Kit, by the way. That's all we know about her."

He got up to move across to another couch where he stretched out full length on his stomach, spurs and all. "Do you mind if I have a short nap?" Naomi shook her head and smiled, and he mumbled, "I think I'm well into the killing brain cells realm. Wake me when she's out." He was sound asleep in seconds.

****

Smiling, Naomi thought, if he had put his boots and spurs on her leather couch at home she'd have crowned him, but today it was all okay. Rossen was her oldest child at twenty-six and she couldn't have asked for a better son. Oh, he'd been a normal teenager and at times had given her fits, but he'd become everything a mother could ask for as an adult and they'd become the best of friends. As she sat and watched him sleep, she was grateful for the fine man he was.

She sat beside him and read her Book of Mormon, then went over her Christmas lists until Dr. Sundquist came in almost two hours later, pulling off his rubber gloves and surgery mask to toss them in the waste basket.

"Naomi!" His smile caused his eyes to almost crinkle shut as he took her hand in his. "I should have known you'd be here watching over everything."

He plopped onto the couch beside her with a sigh. "What have these boys gotten you into this time? I don't know anything about her, but it would appear she's in quite a fix. You're exactly what the doctor is going to order! More than anything, she just needs good old fashioned care and you're the perfect remedy."

The young doctor's words made her smile as he continued, "Rossen and Slade look good. Came home from the big rodeo all in one piece, apparently. Heard they both took world champion! Makes us all proud. I told my wife I get all the credit, because they couldn't have done it without me putting them back together from time to time."

Chuckling to himself he added, "I wasn't sure Slade could pull it off after that bad wreck last summer, but he did. Shouldn't a doubted him. He's a good man. All of your family are good people. You're obviously a wonderful parent!"

"Thank you." She enjoyed his compliment as he wound down, but she had to add, "Although it's not my parenting. They're just good kids and a lot of that is

Rob's doing. I think he teases them until they behave. I swear sometimes it's like raising an extra child. And Slade I can't take any credit for. He's always been good and has helped raise the whole bunch. If you ever get a chance to have an extra kid like him, better jump on it."

The doctor sobered somewhat. "Well it looks like you may have another extra kid for a little while. They couldn't tell me much about her, but I can tell you she's been neglected and abused. And I see no signs of drug use, not that I can always tell, but there's nothing overt.

"The surgery went well. She's got three pins under her cast, but her malnutrition is more of a problem than anything. She has a rather serious concussion and I put twenty three stitches in her head and Noah Grady came and set her nose. She is also about three or four months pregnant. I don't know how old she is, but she's young and obviously hasn't had much care.

"She needs food, love, probably counseling-- depending on what her background is, and prenatal care. She'll have the cast on her arm for eight to ten weeks and the nose splint on for eight days or so at least. I'll keep her here for another day or two, depending on how she's feeling. Her concussion and the pain medicine will keep her pretty out of it, and head injuries often cause extreme nausea, so this might be quite a project." He patted her hand as he stood up. "But, like I said, you're the perfect motherly person for it. And I'll do what I can to help.

"By the way, under the circumstances, I'll donate

my services and see what I can do about the hospital costs. I'm assuming from her condition that there is no money for medical bills."

Naomi nodded. "Thank you. I don't know anything about her either, but we'll do the best we can to help her."

Dr. Sundquist went to leave. "She'll be in recovery for a while, then they'll come and get you when they put her in a room.

"Care and food and she'll be fine." He indicated Rossen. "Tell him he did a good job getting her here. He's a good man." With that, he went back through a set of double doors, leaving her to contemplate the next while. She mentally began to reorganize her life to fit in an extra person who may need a lot of care. The fact that this was the third time in four months that she'd sat beside the hospital bed of someone who was not her biological child never even registered. To her, they were all God's children, and as long as her own family was okay, she was happy to be able to help.

Forty-five minutes later, when a nurse came to tell her they had moved Kit to a room, Rossen still hadn't moved a muscle, so Naomi left him, and followed the nurse into a dimly lit hospital room. Alone, and lying on a steel hospital bed, was a pale girl with almost black hair, two black eyes, and a nose splint. Her hair was a mess of tangles and looked like it had been chopped with a butcher knife, and the hand that lay on top of the light blanket was so thin it was hardly more than skeletal, the vein that held the I.V., large against the small bones.

The low light and neutral walls, combined with white linens and beige electronics, made the room positively dismal and her heart went out to the patient before her. The first thing Naomi did was call the hospital gift shop and order two bouquets of flowers and a bunch of balloons sent up, hoping that the color and smell would lighten things up a bit before she came to. Then, with infinite patience she settled into a chair beside the metal bed to watch over the girl, going back to her book and planning. Occasionally she walked down the hall to check on Rossen, but it was six hours before either one of them moved.

Jaclyn M. Hawkes

Chapter 2

The journey from under the anesthetic was a long one and Kit was in thick fog that was difficult to move through as she slowly came awake. She was so tired and her eyes were incredibly heavy. As she struggled to open them, she knew she was going to be sick, but she couldn't wake up enough to move. She was infinitely grateful when gentle hands turned her on her side and pulled her hair back. A quiet voice registered through the mist in her brain, and then she was mercifully oblivious once more.

Later, when the fog began to lift again, it was the same quiet voice and there was a gentle touch on her hand. When her heavy eyes finally opened, it was to see a middle-aged woman with a kind face hovering above her. She fought to voice a question, but her fuzzy brain couldn't make her mouth work. The kind woman seemed to read her mind as she said, "I'm Naomi. I'm just here because one of God's precious daughters needs a little extra care." Kit felt the touch on her hands again as she drifted back to sleep, wondering who the daughter of God was.

Finally, Kit felt herself wake up with less of the

mist drifting through her head. She looked up to find an extraordinarily good looking stranger with tired, deep blue eyes sitting beside her bed. She was instinctively afraid and tried to curl up and turn away, pulling the blanket tightly to her. She was too out of it to move much and felt the need to be sick before she could react. Her body began to wretch and she was too sick to shrink from him, as the tall, blonde stranger stood up to hold a bag in front of her and pull her hair back away from her face. He spoke to her softly, gently rubbing her shoulder and somehow she knew, even through the fog, that she'd be okay. She leaned her head back and closed her eyes again.

Sometime later, she was having strange dreams of a scary, dark street and a gang, and her foster father. Her fear was overpowering, but then there was a kind man and an angel with silvery, gold hair, then a dark haired woman talking about God. There was a baby and a muddle of pain, and fear and flashing lights. The images were disjointed and warped, and through it all was a horrible, queasy nausea. The strange images smoothed away to be replaced by a sweet unfamiliar sense of security. Even as she forced herself to wake because she knew she was going to be sick again, she still had this peaceful feeling that all was well.

She fought to open her eyes and realized there was someone there beside her supporting her back and smoothing her hair as she was sick into the blue bag he held for her. He gently wiped her face and helped her settle back against the pillows, then went to the restroom to dampen a cloth. Her mind was still zoned, and she couldn't quite remember who he was, or why he was sitting here beside her hospital bed being so kind to her. She couldn't even remember how she came to be here.

Her eyes sought his in a silent quest to understand. He met her gaze openly and honestly as he gently placed the cloth on her brow and said, "I'm not sure why it works, but it seems to. Try putting your hand here on this ice pack too. The nurse said it sometimes helps the nausea."

There was none of the horrible, suggestive leering she had come to expect from her foster father's eyes, or the cruelty she had seen in her foster mother's, or even the impatience she was used to from the case workers. There was only kindness and a sense of infinite patience.

She tentatively put her hand out to touch the indicated ice pack, still wondering what he wanted from her. She'd learned a long time ago that nobody did anything for her without a reason. She pulled the sheet up around her neck in a gesture of self protection, before returning her hand to the ice pack.

He reached out toward the I.V. line attached to the back of her hand and she flinched sharply. His eyes narrowed, questioning, but his voice was kind when he said, "I'm not going to hurt you. I was just unkinking the tubing. Dr. Sundquist wants to get as much fluids into you as possible." He slowly reached for the line and smoothed the bend, watching her eyes as he did.

He really didn't frighten her. The flinch had been instinctive. Years of being struck had made it reflexive.

Realizing she wasn't afraid of him filled her half drugged head with wonder. She believed him. He wasn't going to hurt her and she closed her eyes again, content to rest while he kept watch.

When she awoke horribly ill once more, he was still there, gently helping her and though she still wondered why, she knew she was safe and accepted his help gratefully.

An older, dark haired woman came in, followed by the nurse. The woman put her arm around him, took Kit's hand gently in hers, and asked, "Look who's awake! Still feeling lousy?" Her blue eyes were bright and warm.

Kit nodded wordlessly, her eyes going from one to the other. The nurse was doing something that squeezed her arm, and put an instrument in her ear again, then pulled out a keyboard to type something. She smiled at Kit. "Ready for some Jell-O or apple juice?"

Just the thought made Kit's stomach heave and the man barely made it to her with the blue bag from where it hung on the wall. Regretfully, he said, "I wondered if that was going to happen." He gently wiped her face once again. "I have no idea how you can throw up. You've eaten nothing for at least two days."

As the nurse went out the door, she said over her shoulder, "It's the I.V. fluids."

"Mom," He turned to the dark haired woman, "Can't they give her anything for the nausea? Isabel was this same way with her concussion."

His mother came closer to Kit's bed. "Kit, I know it sounds kind of backward, but food may actually really help. Is there anything that sounds good at all?" She took Kit's hand again. "I'm Naomi, by the way. I'm Rossen's mom. I've been here, but you've been pretty out of it."

Kit sighed. "Anything sounds wonderful. I'm starving. I just can't keep it down." She looked down at her hands. It wasn't a concussion that was causing this. She'd been this way for three and a half months, but she couldn't tell them that.

Naomi turned to the man. "Rossen, go ask at the nurse's station for some soda crackers and warm 7-Up, then go down to the cafeteria for a large cheeseburger and bring it back hot. Make it a double."

"It'll never work." He was shaking his head. She just nudged him toward the door.

"We'll at least try. Even if it only stays down for a moment, she'll get something from it."

As he went out the door, Naomi moved close again. "Kit, I don't mean to intrude, but Dr. Sundquist told me yesterday that you're expecting a baby. I've had six babies and I'm inclined to think this is probably more morning sickness than brain concussion. Is that a possibility?"

Kit raised her eyes to Naomi, completely ashamed to admit the truth to her, but then again almost comforted to be able to finally speak about her troubles to this woman who had been kind, even after finding out about the baby. She nodded and said, "I haven't kept much down in three and a half months."

Naomi put a hand on her bony shoulder and smiled. "You haven't had Naomi there to help you. With one of mine, I could only eat a tiny bit to keep it down, but with the other five I had to eat like a Sumo wrestler twenty-four seven to feel half-way decent. I'm just assuming you haven't had a lot because you're so thin." Kit shook her head no and Naomi went on, "Can we try to give you a lot. If it doesn't work we'll try the warm 7-Up and crackers. Somehow, you and this baby need a lot more nutrition to be healthy."

Kit started to cry. "I know. I know I'm not doing a very good job at having this baby, but I'm doing the best I can. I didn't want to get pregnant, but I did, and when my foster father found out, he was going to force me to have an abortion." She put her hand over her belly. "I didn't plan for this baby, but I don't want him to kill it. That's why I ran. He was going to make me." Tears escaped her eyes and ran down her cheeks.

Naomi's voice was gentle as she asked, "Kit. How old are you?"

Kit tried to control her sobs. "Seventeen."

"Who is the father?"

She wouldn't look up and Naomi came to her and leaned over, pulling her to her in a hug as she cried. Finally, in the smallest of voices, Kit said, "My foster father."

They were both in tears and didn't see Rossen when he came back in with the food. He looked from one to the other, then silently slipped back out the door unnoticed.

A few minutes later, whistling loudly, he came through the doorway again. This time, although it was still evident that they'd been emotional, the tears were gone and Naomi looked up as she was helping Kit brush her hair and said, "Ah, good. There you are. This girl needs some food. I know a cheeseburger isn't usually the first thing to try, but maybe it'll go down easy." Naomi smiled at her and squeezed Kit's hand.

"It smells wonderful." Kit took the burger and began to eat it. Rossen watched skeptically as he moistened a cloth. After just a couple bites she was sick again, but Naomi encouraged her to keep eating and miraculously she made it through the rest of the burger and kept it down beautifully.

Rossen was amazed and said, "Mom, you are a miracle. Do you know how sick this girl has been? That is so backward. I would have thought a tiny bit of bland food would be better. How did you know?"

Naomi just winked at Kit. "Moms know everything, honey. You know that by now, don't you?" She wrapped her arm around her son's waist.

"I should." He grinned. "You caught me every single time I did something wrong!"

Kit was still tired. Her head ached and her elbow throbbed. When she hadn't been able to keep pain pills down, they'd brought her a morphine pump. It kept the pain under control, but made her sleepy, and finally well fed, she went back to sleep almost instantly.

When she next woke, Naomi was gone, but

Rossen was still there asleep in the chair beside her bed. It was strange. Somehow as he had been helping her, she had come to trust him. There was something so innately safe about him that she'd been able to push aside the fear she'd come to have for literally every male she encountered.

She studied him in the dim quiet. He was tall with bleached blonde hair and long legs stretched out in front of his chair, crossed at the ankles. Faded jeans and cowboy boots exactly fit his casual strength. He was incredibly handsome, even with his eyes closed and she already knew that with his eyes open he was devastatingly so. His eyes were deep blue and although he always seemed to be smiling, they had a quiet depth that went on forever. Even in his sleep he had a hint of a smile in the tiny lines around them. She wondered how old he was. He obviously wasn't a teenager anymore.

She still wasn't exactly sure how she came to be here at the hospital with him and his sweet mom. She'd never been around anyone like them. Their love and affection was so obvious and comfortable it was remarkable. And the way they treated her was unbelievable. They treated her like she actually deserved to be cared for and watched over, even though they didn't know her. They had never even met her before when? She still hadn't gotten to the bottom of that.

The last thing she remembered was walking down the street in the dark, knowing she'd made a huge mistake assuming she could survive. The thought made her start worrying again. She hadn't seen her guitar or backpack and she wasn't sure, but for some reason she thought the guitar was gone. Just the idea made her sad. How would she ever support herself and her baby without it? It was the only thing she knew how to do.

She would have to find a way. She knew she would never give up and let them abort this baby. She sub-consciously lifted her chin as she put her hand protectively on her belly.

"What's wrong?" When he asked her the question in his deep voice, she jumped. She hadn't even realized he was awake. "Are you sick again?" She shook her head, amazed that she wasn't. It was the first time in weeks that she could say that.

"Why the frown?" She wondered how long he had been watching her without her knowing it.

She decided to be honest. "I was just trying to figure out how I got here, who you are and why you're here. And how I'm going to pay for all this, and where I'm going to go when they release me."

He smiled as he leaned forward in his seat. "I brought you here. Well, two of my friends and I. We basically stole you from a gang. I'm Rossen Rockland, rodeo cowboy slash petroleum engineer. I manage the oil wells on my parent's ranch about sixty miles north of here. I'm here because you need someone with you. We haven't gotten to the payment question yet, although the doctor donated his services and the hospital is considering it. And what was the fourth question? Oh yeah, when they release you, I'm sure you'll come home to my parents' ranch, unless there's somewhere else you would rather go."

He made it all sound so simple. She shook her head slowly and asked, "I'm sorry. I don't remember a gang. What happened?" She wasn't sure she truly wanted to know.

With a lazy smile, he said, "If you don't remember, I'm not going to tell you. It's better left forgotten."

She accepted his wisdom, but asked, "Where did you come along? The last thing I remember was walking late at night." She dropped her eyes.

"We were gassing up at a station there in Vegas when you obviously needed some help. So we helped. I wish we'd been about ten seconds earlier." At this last, his voice sounded sad.

Confused, she asked, "There? What do you mean, there in Vegas? Are we not still in Vegas?" There were more holes than she thought.

He gave her a brilliant smile. "Not even close. You're in Evanston, Wyoming. It's a long story, but in order to get that arm fixed, we had to come home to a doctor who knew us. Sorry, we couldn't really ask you if that was okay."

She looked unseeing out the window. "It doesn't really matter either way." Her voice was wistful. "And my guitar?"

He shook his head sadly. "It was pretty toasted. We left the pieces in the street." Somehow she'd known that and she tried to swallow the tears that threatened.

She brushed at them embarrassed.

"What about my backpack and my clothes?" There wasn't much in them that mattered, but without them she possessed exactly nothing. She'd discovered she wasn't even wearing underwear and her last four bucks had been in the back pocket of her cut offs.

He got up to open the small closet. It was empty and he said, "To be honest, I don't know what happened to them. It's been kind of crazy at both hospitals. They're somewhere. We'll ask the nurse when she comes in. The denim jacket they actually cut off because of your arm. How's it feeling?"

It hurt, but she'd been trying not to think about it. It was all but useless in the cast. It was another reminder that she was without money to live on. And if she couldn't play with it, she'd have no way to make any. Even if she had her guitar, she seriously doubted she could play well and she wondered if she would even be able to sculpt with it. Creating with clay was her one true passion in life and if she couldn't do it, she'd miss it immensely.

She hoped he couldn't see her despair as she answered. "It's fine."

After watching her for a long moment, he said, "You're a terrible liar. You actually shattered the joint. There are three pins under that cast. It's not the least bit fine. I've sat here helping you throw up, so we're buddies by now. You can at least be honest with me." He smiled as he finished.

She shook her head and smiled shyly back.

"Trust me. You don't want honest."

"You'd be surprised. I'm tougher than I look." He continued to joke while he asked a hard question. "While we're being honest, is there anyone we need to contact to let them know you're safe?"

She inhaled a big breath and shook her head. "Not a soul." She tried to be flippant, but the reality was devastating. She was alone and she knew it. It scared her.

He knew it, too. He had to. Much as she tried to shrug off his questions, the fact that she was alone had to be obvious.

He rose to stand by her hospital bed and slowly and carefully took her good hand and looked into her face. "God knew where you were, Kit, and the troubles you have. He sent Slade and me and Isabel to rescue you. He's got it all under control. He's got a secret weapon, you know. It's Naomi." He grinned and squeezed her bony shoulder. She looked up into his deep blue eyes and was confused and comforted at the same time. He was talking crazy, but in the last day or so she'd come to trust him completely.

He continued, "Speaking of Naomi, isn't it about time you ate again?"

As if on cue, the nurse walked in the door, set her dinner tray on the rolling table top and began checking her temperature and blood pressure again. Kit started to eat, slowly and carefully with her one hand. It took her nearly a full half hour, and Rossen had to help her open cartons or spread things occasionally, but she kept it all down and felt better afterward.

It wouldn't have mattered if she'd realized sooner that keeping food in her stomach all the time helped the nausea. With the minimal amount of food she had been receiving back home, she could never have succeeded. She couldn't remember a time that she hadn't been hungry.

He just sat and watched her eat, and dozed in his chair. He'd said he was here because she needed someone with her. She wasn't sure that was so. She would have survived, but she was indeed grateful that she wasn't alone like this. He'd been wonderful and just being watched over so carefully was an incredible boost to her self esteem. No one but her art teacher, Mrs. Webber, had ever treated her like she was important.

He spoke of God so matter-of-factly, like he knew Him well or something. Mrs. Webber had been like that. Kit had never really known what to think about God. She wanted to believe there was this Higher Being out there who was in control, but if there was, why did He let some of the terrible things that happened go on? She was still trying to figure out what she believed. Sometimes she didn't even have the energy to wonder. She was too busy trying to survive.

She finished eating and was soon back to sleep, strangely, more at peace than she would have thought possible, just from knowing he sat quietly beside her bed.

Wednesday morning she felt markedly better. Eating regularly and well was helping the nausea immensely and not using the morphine pump left her feeling much more with it, in spite of the painful arm. She found with consistent Tylenol she could get by and it was nice to feel good.

Naomi came in the morning and when Rossen left the room she put a shopping bag on Kit's bed and said, "I'm going to assume they took all your clothes and lost them like they do mine when I'm in the hospital. I've learned to have Rob take everything home as soon as they insist I take it off. You'd think they could work on your heel without removing your underwear, but they can't." Naomi's eyes twinkled. "Just in case they did, I brought you some things. I'm not sure they'll fit, but we can get some more later at any rate."

She unloaded underclothing, a sweat shirt, and a warm up suit that had zippers up both the legs and arms. "I thought it might be easier to get the sleeve over your cast with them." She'd also brought socks and snow boots and a winter coat. "These were Joey's. She's my daughter. They're probably way big, but they'll keep you warm 'til we get you home."

The nurse taped a plastic bag over Kit's cast and helped her into the shower. Then Naomi helped her to dress. They had to split the cuff of the sweat shirt to get it over her cast but when she was finally dressed she felt like a new person. The pretty, new clothing was a treat she wasn't used to and the underwear felt wonderful. She'd felt so undressed without any the last three days.

When Rossen came back in, Naomi was carefully pulling her hair into a pony tail and he knelt at her feet to help her on with the socks and boots. Kit wasn't at all sure how to deal with all the attention. She'd never had help like this in her life and it actually made her uncomfortable. She didn't feel like she deserved it, but she had come to understand that Rossen and Naomi were absolutely sincere in their kindness. She was unbelievably grateful to them.

Later, when Dr. Sundquist made his rounds he released her to go home with strict instructions to continue her eating regimen. Then he told Rossen to bring her back into his office in several days to have her stitches out and splint removed. Kit was at a loss as to what to do and where to go.

As soon as the doctor left the room, Naomi stood at her bedside and asked, "Would it be okay if we took you home to our house for a little while so we can help you get back on your feet?" Rossen smiled and nodded his head at her in encouragement.

Kit didn't understand why they were helping someone they didn't even know, but she was absolutely thankful. She had no idea how she would have survived without their help, at least for a while, and said gratefully, "I would love to. Thank you."

The nurses insisted she let Rossen wheel her down to the car in a wheelchair. Kit felt silly, but if she were honest, she was still too light headed and dizzy to walk. He gently helped her into Naomi's SUV and placed pillows to cushion her arm. As they drove through miles of rolling, treeless, sage-covered hills dusted with snow, she somehow felt like she was just starting out. For the first time she could remember she felt safe and secure and valued and she let the motion of the vehicle lull her to sleep.

Some time later when she woke up, they'd left the sage hills behind and were on a snowy road that wound through a pristine valley surrounded by pine-clad mountains. She'd never seen anything like it except in pictures. Even as she admired the beauty, she worried about what she would wear to stay warm.

Eventually they drove over a small rise and into a farmstead that was like a small city. Houses and barns and outbuildings clustered around and between corrals and pastures, and all of it was encircled by a fenced road. Horses and cows, looking like wooly beasts of the Arctic, watched placidly from areas cleared of deep snow. Rossen pushed a remote and pulled into the garage of the central and largest home.

When he helped her from the SUV to the house, she was shocked to be greeted by no less than four brothers and a father who so closely resembled Rossen that it was uncanny. When three young women appeared and another darker haired man, Kit was hopelessly lost as far as names, but she certainly felt welcomed into this large and boisterous family. They settled her into a chair in a big room near a huge rock fireplace, and she watched in quiet amazement as they all joked and teased and laughed while putting lunch on a massive table.

Chapter 3

Slowly, over the next couple of days, Kit began to feel more and more comfortable with the Rockland family. She came to understand that the tall, dark Slade Marsh and his blonde fiancée, Isabel, had been the ones who rescued her with Rossen. Slade, who was sort of unofficially adopted, and Rossen were obviously the closest of friends, and Slade and Isabel were engaged to be married shortly. Until then, Isabel was living with the Rockland's. Slade lived somewhere up the road. These three had just been leaving a rodeo in Las Vegas when they'd picked her up.

Rossen was the oldest sibling, but his next younger brother, Ruger, was married to the petite, dark Marti who was the local veterinarian. They lived in one of the other houses nearby as well. Joey, the tall and beautiful "little" sister, and the three younger brothers, Sean, Treyne and Cooper were all college students, home for the Christmas holidays.

Naomi was the only Rockland who wasn't blonde except Marti. Naomi was still quiet and reserved, but Kit found the rest of them spent their days laughing and teasing uproariously. She'd had no idea while Rossen sat patiently beside her hospital bed that he was the ringleader of the family's clowning around. She found herself laughing several times a day, something she couldn't ever remember doing. They all went out night and morning, bundled like snowmen, to feed the stock, but a lot of the rest of the time was spent just flat out playing.

The hidden treasure of the Rockland family for Kit turned out to be Joey. Although she was two years older, and a sophomore in college, she seemed to understand just what Kit needed and helped her fit in. Joey was great to help know how to handle all of the new things she was introduced to. She was tall—over five foot ten, and beautiful in a natural, almost wild way. Kit could see her as a sexy beach beauty or a strong frontier woman. Either way, she could have pulled it off with grace.

She helped Kit find clothes and shoes, and although most of Joey's stuff was a couple of inches too long, for the most part they were surprisingly alike in size.

Joey also subtly encouraged her to get some counseling to deal with what had been happening in her foster home and even though Kit knew she couldn't pay to go to a counselor, she followed Joey's recommendation to at least do some research about healing on-line. At first, Kit had been skeptical, but it didn't take long to find it was amazingly helpful.

Joey also helped Kit to be able to figure out how to fit into the family situation that was so new to her.

She'd never been around a real, happy, functioning family at all—especially one with so many handsome, teasing young men. Whenever Kit was unsure of how to take something someone said or did, or when she didn't know how to act, Joey was there to smooth the way for her. Sometimes Joey just coolly put her brothers into place with a wicked smile. Kit marveled at how this tall beauty could handle all these men with such comfort.

Still definitely recuperating, when Kit wasn't watching them tease each other, she slept a lot. She'd been wearing a series of sweat pants and shirts donated by various members of the family and an old cardigan Naomi had cut the sleeve on to fit over her cast, and was still fighting the nausea by eating nonstop. Naomi would help her tape off her cast to shower and help her dress, and when Rossen wasn't working, he would come and help her pull her hair back into a pony tail.

On Sunday, a week from the day they'd picked her up, they asked her if she wanted to go to church with them. The bruising around her eyes was still slightly colorful and she still had the nose splint, so she self-consciously opted out, but she was grateful they asked. She was surprised when every single person in the family piled in and left. Even the farm hands could be seen leaving their homes in their Sunday best. She'd never been around church-going people. It was striking that they were all so devout, but it was certainly a good thing. She'd learned they were kind, clean living, hardworking and honest people and she definitely wanted to know more about their brand of belief.

On the eighth day, Rossen loaded her up and took her back to the doctor in Evanston. Dr. Sundquist was pleased that her black eyes were so far healed and the whites were no longer bloodshot. He took the stitches out of her head, and when he removed the splint from her nose, she felt human again.

He was checking her chart and said, "You've gained nine pounds in seven days! That's excellent!" He turned to her smiling and gave her a high five.

Kit smiled back shyly. "It's because Rossen and Naomi feed me nonstop. I'll probably weigh two hundred pounds by next month."

He looked at her over his glasses. "A month might be pushing it, but for as tall as you are, and in your condition, 170 or 180 might be a realistic goal. Just try to eat as nutritiously as you can and keep up some moderate exercise. Swimming once the cast is off would be great." He scribbled on a prescription pad and ripped it off. "These are vitamins. If you can't keep them down, take them before bed."

After pausing for a moment, he glanced at Rossen and then looked back at Kit with a kindly face and gently asked, "How are you doing emotionally? Are you able to really talk to Naomi, or should I refer you to a counselor?"

Kit hesitantly looked over at Rossen, but answered, "I think I'm doing okay. Joey recommended I do some counseling research on-line and I think it's helping."

Dr. Sundquist met her eyes for a moment and

then nodded and said, "Some things take time. Hang in there. You're in good hands now. Try to put the past behind you."

He started to wash his hands. "All right, young lady, keep doing what you're doing, and I'll see you in three weeks. We'll change that cast, and re-evaluate. You can try squeezing a Nerf ball or playing with a set of magnets with that hand when you feel like it." He turned to Rossen. "Tropical fruit will continue to help the last of that bruising. Keep feeding her. She needs it."

As he walked out the door, he reached into a drawer and shuffled some papers. He pulled out a business card and handed it to Kit. "If you haven't already got one, she's very good. Make an appointment like yesterday." He shook their hands and left the room.

Kit stared at the business card in her hand. It was for an OB-GYN. She wasn't exactly sure what that was, but she assumed Dr. Sundquist wanted her to have prenatal care. She didn't have any way to pay for it and she didn't know how to tell Rossen she was pregnant, but she knew she needed to. She dreaded seeing the disappointment in his eyes and hated the fact that he would now think of her differently.

She couldn't look at him at first. Hesitantly, she said, "Uhm, Rossen, remember that day in the hospital when you said you wanted me to be honest with you?" She fidgeted with the edge of her cast with her good hand. "There's something you should know." She finally looked up into his eyes. "I'm expecting a baby."

She waited to see how disgusted he was.

His dark blue eyes calmly met her cobalt ones. "I know. I pretty much figured that out the night we picked you up." He held her coat to help her on with it.

Turning to slip into the coat he held, she frowned, questioning, "You knew the whole time? I've been worrying for a week about how to tell you, and you knew the whole time?" She rolled her eyes, almost a little mad. "Why didn't you tell me you knew?"

He started to help her fasten the snaps and she pushed his hands away as he asked, "Does it matter? What I know, or when, or how?"

She struggled to fasten the snaps one handed. "Of course it matters! How could being pregnant not matter?" He gently pushed her hand away and snapped her coat, then took her hand to pull her out the door.

Leaning near, he asked softly, "Could we finish this conversation in the truck where there's a bit more privacy?" He indicated the office staff as they made her next appointment.

On the icy walk to the truck, he kept hold of her good arm until he opened the door to help her in. With her cast propped on a pillow, he shut her door and went around to the driver's side and got in. Starting the truck to get the heater going, he turned toward her and took up where they'd left off. "Of course being pregnant matters, Kit. It's a huge deal. My knowing is what doesn't matter. Does it?"

His comment felt like a slap and she looked up, wondering why he was being so harsh when he'd always been so gentle with her. She searched his eyes and then looked down at her hands and mumbled, "I guess I just thought you would care, is all."

He reached across the truck to turn her chin up so he could look at her. His voice was infinitely gentle when he said, "I care more than you could ever imagine, Kit. That's not what I meant. Even if I hadn't gotten to know and care for you a great deal, I would still care."

He went on, "This is obviously not the ideal situation. You're too young. You're single. You're not really settled to have a child right now, and it apparently doesn't have an involved father, but it is what it is. We can't change it. It's not like you can say never mind and put it back. It's unfortunate that you're in this situation now, but the only thing to do is to handle it as well as possible. It's more than you now. We have to take care of you and the baby, so that her life isn't messed up because of something she had no say in." He was watching her eyes as he talked.

She looked down and was quiet for a moment and then asked, "Can I tell you something else?"

"Absolutely."

She looked up and his kind face was comforting enough that it wasn't as hard as she had thought it would be to say, "I had no say in this either." She took a deep breath. "My foster father did this to me. The reason I ran is because he was going to make me have an abortion." She put an arm protectively around herself.

The muscles in his jaw clenched, but his words were kind when he put his hand softly over hers on her belly and assured her, "You made the right decision. You absolutely did. In spite of the circumstances, this baby has the right to live and she'll be a great blessing."

She couldn't help the tears that filled her eyes. "How did you find out?"

He took his hand off hers to gently wipe her tears. "I held you on my lap for the seven hour drive from Vegas to here. Between trying to stop the bleeding, cushion your arm, and keep it and your face iced, the fact that you were young and underfed and pregnant was pretty obvious." He reached into the glove box for a napkin. "How old are you, Kit?"

"Seventeen." A sigh escaped as she leaned her head back against the headrest.

"Kit?" She looked at him. "I'm sorry you've had to grow up so fast. For what you've been through. I can't change the past. But I can do a lot with the future. Will you let me help you?"

She used the same word he did. "Absolutely."

He smiled down at her. "Good, because the two of you need it." He ruffled her hair, and put the truck in reverse. "Now, Christmas is day after tomorrow and I've been given strict instructions to take your pretty, straight, new nose to the beauty shop and buy you some clothes of your own. And I want to help you get some things for my family because they'll have some for you and I don't want you to feel self-conscious about it."

She started to protest. "I've never been to the beauty shop in my life and I don't think now is a good time to start."

He wouldn't take her no. "Mom told me I had to. She said if I didn't, the past week of black eyes, nose splint, and sweats would scar you for life." She laughed. "So while you have your hair done, I'm going to run errands and then we'll shop." He looked at her closely. "Actually, you look tired. On second thought, you relax in the chair and I'll shop, then we'll go home and put you to bed. Give me a ball park size and tell me what you like, and we'll try again next week."

****

Rossen left Kit at the salon, and although shopping was definitely not his thing, he did his best. When he came back to pick her up, he had three pairs of long, but slender jeans that would adjust around her tummy, several bright sweatshirts, a couple of pretty stretch T-shirts and dresses she could get on easily over her cast that he'd purchased at a maternity shop, and a prescription for prenatal vitamins.

As he walked back into the salon and caught sight of her, he could hardly comprehend what he was seeing. The abused waif they had literally picked up off the pavement just over a week ago with black eyes and a broken nose had ceased to exist. The beautiful woman who walked toward him rocked him to his toes.

Gone were the choppy locks, replaced by shining, almost black hair cut into a flowing mane around her face and down her back. The stylist had applied light makeup to cover the bruises and to highlight her eyes and lips, and the cheeks that had been too thin had filled out just enough to look as sculpted as a fashion model.

Her nose, now free of the splint, was tiny and straight and dainty above a perfect mouth, just now smiling shyly. Even in her borrowed sweats she was exquisite.

Without realizing it, Rossen had stopped and was staring wordlessly as she approached him. "What do you think?" She turned in a circle to show him.

When he didn't answer right away, she looked at him again. "Rossen? Is something wrong?" He was still too surprised to speak, and at his silence, her face fell. "Don't you like it?"

He struggled to focus on what she was saying and finally said, "Like it? I love it! It's beautiful. You're beautiful!" He turned to her again. "Wow. I think we'd better go back to Dr. Sundquist's and have him put the nose thing back on. My brothers are gonna come unglued when I bring you home looking like this. Cooper will be permanently impaired." His eyes twinkled as he pulled out his phone. "I'll call Dr. Sundquist's office."

She laughed and hugged him with her one good arm. "Then it's okay?"

He snapped his phone closed and put his hands on her shoulders. "You look like a princess. It's exactly you! Come on. Put some of your new clothes on, too. They won't even recognize you when we get home! I'll pay. Go dig through the bags in the truck for something you might like and you can change here."

****

Rossen had been accurate about his brothers. She

knew she looked good, when for once, the rowdy Rockland clan was speechless as she walked in. She'd put on an indigo blue dress that brought out the color of her eyes and made her hair look darker than ever. She walked past Treyne, Sean and Cooper without them saying a word. They just stared, until almost in unison, Naomi and Rob exclaimed, and Naomi gave her a hug.

"Look at you!" Naomi laughed right out loud. "We had no idea you were so pretty under that old splint. And that dress exactly suits you. Lovely and feminine, just like you."

Rob pitched in with a wink. "Absolutely bewitching. I don't believe I've ever seen these boys speechless, have you, Mother?" Even with the ribbing, the three of them just smiled and continued to stare.

Kit loved the attention, but Rossen was right, it had been a long day and she was tired. Her arm was throbbing, so after dinner, she took some Tylenol and excused herself to bed. Turning out the light, she stood in her borrowed night gown and looked through the window into the enchanting dark snowscape outside, remembering the way Rossen had looked at her as she walked toward him in the salon that afternoon.

He was always kind and respectful toward her, and although he was physically affectionate, he never did or said anything that could be construed as inappropriate or even flirting. That almost troubled her, because from the first time she'd awoken after her surgery to find him watching over her with those deep blue eyes, she had been drawn to him.

At first, sick and somewhat out of it, she'd just been humbly grateful for his steady, calm, gentle care, but as the days progressed, she had come to lean on his quiet strength in an almost physical sense. His confidence and maturity, tempered by his unquenchable sense of humor left her with a peace and security she'd never felt in the whole of her life. She knew he was years older, but instead of intimidating her, it simply reassured her.

When she'd realized after just a few days that she was attracted to him, it worried her. She knew it would be next to impossible to ever have a relationship with someone willing to overlook her history and the fact that she now effectively had a child. Still, she was quickly becoming attached to Rossen and was certainly wise enough to know a one-sided attraction would be very troubling. He considered her young, even though he knew she'd been forced into a maturity beyond her years by her circumstances. And though he never talked down to her, she had the distinct feeling he wanted to help her, but in a fatherly sort of way.

Even in her short life, her experience had taught her not to expect much. She'd learned to take that in stride, but her ever tenacious personality had always helped her to hold out hope that eventually, she would have a happier life.

All of these things had begun to trouble her heart through her days of wondering how she was going to survive on her own, and repay them for all their care and help. For years she'd known her background was less than desirable, and now for months she'd been realistic enough to admit that this baby would probably preclude the happy marriage she'd always dreamed of. Then she thought back to today.

Deep in Rossen's eyes, she'd seen something that gave her back the hope of someday finding the love she'd craved all her life. She wasn't even sure what she'd seen as she'd walked toward him, but it was an emotion so real and so honest, that the doubts and worries that she would never be desirable to a good honorable man fled in that instant.

She still knew it probably wouldn't be him, but she'd seen something that told her that someday, sometime, someone would look at her like that and claim her for his own. That one glimpse into Rossen Rockland's soul had returned a sense of hope for the future she'd given up on. That one little peek had been enough to strengthen her for whatever she would have to face.

Knowing it was all going to be okay, she walked back over to her bed and knelt beside it. She'd never prayed much before coming here. She'd never been taught to and had never even known for sure if there was a God out there. Somehow in the last week, she'd also gained a sure knowledge that her Father in Heaven truly was there and was watching over her as a loving parent. As she poured out her gratitude and love and hopes and troubles, her heart was full and she lay down happy and at peace.

****

Jaclyn M. Hawkes

.That night Rossen and Slade were at Slade's home, five minutes further up the road, watching the last few minutes of a movie in the theater room. Isabel had long since fallen asleep against Slade's shoulder, and he and Rossen sat in companionable silence as the credits began to roll.

Finally Slade spoke, "Kit was beautiful tonight."

Rossen didn't move as he answered, "Hmm. Yeah, she was." A few minutes later he continued, "She looked so good it almost scared me when I picked her up at the salon."

There was a long pause again before Slade asked, "Do you remember that time right after Isabel came with us, and you were teasing me about not being able to breathe when she was around?"

"Yeah, why? You're still that way around her sometimes." Rossen grinned.

Slade smiled back in agreement. "I know, but it's great. Now that I know things are working out, it's a nice feeling. At first it just scared me to death."

After still another few minutes of quiet, Slade continued, "Sometimes you look like you can't breathe when Kit's around."

Rossen leaned his head back against the top of the couch with a sigh. "She's seventeen, Marsh. I'm twenty six."

Slade played with a strand of Isabel's long silvery, gold hair. "Sometimes it's not the years, it's the miles. That girl has been through a lot in seventeen years. Isabel told me she's been in foster care since she

48

was nine and her real parents ran a meth lab."

Rossen replied, "It gets worse. The baby's father is her foster father. She ran so he couldn't abort it."

When Slade finally spoke, his voice was sad, "See what I mean about the miles?"

They each sat lost in thought. At length, Rossen asked, "Do you still have your dad's old guitar in the attic?"

"I'm sure I do."

"Wanna sell it?"

"I'll give it to you. Maybe it could be from Isabel and me, too." He was still smoothing her hair as he added gently, "You're happy when you're with her."

Rossen gave a sad smile. "She thinks I'm a white knight." He paused again. "It's been incredible to be able to help so much when she's needed it."

"You just don't want to help forever?"

Rossen shook his head. "No. I'd love to help forever. At least from what she's been like so far." He sighed again. "But she's seventeen."

Jaclyn M. Hawkes

Chapter 4

Christmas Eve day dawned clear and cold with a brilliant sun striking millions of diamonds in the snow. The Rocklands fed the stock in the morning and then they all hung out in the great room by the fire, wrapping gifts and playing games and baking. Later that afternoon, Kit, sporting her own new jeans and a sweatshirt, was helping Naomi cook as best she could with her cast. They talked back and forth as they worked.

The doctor had said she could start using her left hand and she was trying to grip a potato as she peeled with the other. The hand was stronger than she thought it would be after nine days of no use. She wondered if she would be able to play a guitar with the cast if she could find a way to buy one.

As she peeled, she was thinking of money and being more independent than she felt right now. She was so grateful for Rossen and his family's help, especially knowing that had they not been there, she and her baby would have been in desperate straits. But her nature was far too independent and she was too honest to want to take advantage of their charity. She knew she needed to figure out a way to earn a living before they grew tired of having her. The one night alone in Vegas was enough for her to realize that making money in that town would not be fast enough in coming for her to survive the wait, but as it was the only skill she had that she thought was marketable, she had to try.

She knew Rossen would stake her financially for a while if she asked him, but she knew he'd raise a ruckus if she said she was going back to Vegas, and honestly she didn't want to. She never wanted to go back there again. She sighed unconsciously and Naomi looked up from her pie making.

Seeing Kit's struggle to hold the potato, she suggested a trade. "Here, you crimp and I'll peel."

Kit accepted the pie shells hesitantly. "I've never made a pie in my life, but it's fascinating to watch you. Is there anything you don't know how to do, Naomi?" Once Kit got her hands on the pie crust she was comfortable instantly. The dough felt familiar in her hands. It reminded her of her clay and she made short work of crimping perfect edges.

Naomi came over to pick up the pie shells. "I thought you said you'd never made a pie! These are like a work of art!"

"Thanks." Kit smiled shyly. "I've never cooked much of anything. I haven't spent much time in the kitchen except doing the clean-up part. I'm afraid I have a lot to learn."

Naomi patted her hand. "You keep saying that, but whatever we're doing, you pick right up on. You must be a fast learner."

It was true. Kit could usually figure out most anything quickly. She had a good memory and had found that catching on fast helped ease the tension sometimes in the different homes she'd lived in.

Naomi continued, "I'll bet you're good in school."

Kit nodded. "I am. Or I was. School was a good way to not be home. I even got a job working there after hours for a while. It was wonderful. I could leave on the bus early in the morning, and not have to come home until evening. It was much easier to get along in my last home that way. My, uh, foster mother didn't like me very much. The only nice thing she ever did for me was give me bus money to run away." Her voice was matter-of-fact. "But school was great! I could excel without worrying. And in high school I had this killer art teacher who made me believe I could do anything! I swear she changed my whole outlook on life."

She didn't realize it, but her cobalt eyes sparkled as she talked. "She was the one who helped me get my job. She was the nicest person I've ever known until you guys. I think she really loved me." Sadly, she continued, "She tried to go to the DFS to get my foster father to leave me alone, but the only thing that happened was that I was forbidden to be around her and lost my job. She got officially reprimanded." Kit became wistful. "For a while I actually thought I was going to make it to college."

Naomi smiled and patted her again. "Oh, you'll make it to college. Don't worry. I can see it in Rossen's eyes. But you haven't even finished high school, have you?"

Kit shook her head. "I'm like four credits short, but I had to leave, and I can't go after my records or they'll make me go back." She continued adamantly, "I'm never going back there!"

Naomi tried to reassure her, "You don't have to go back, but I'm sure when the DFS does find out about your foster father, he'll be criminally charged."

Kit shook her head sadly. "He is the DFS there. There's no way to stop him."

Naomi got an angry look on her face, but then blinked and shook her head. At length, she asked, "When will you turn eighteen?

"March second. Why?"

Naomi was thoughtful. "The school superintendent here is a good friend of ours. Rob is on the board with him. I'll bet we could arrange for you to take E High online without your documentation up front. Then when you're eighteen and safe from your foster father, we'll go get your records and get your diploma, and you can get into college this fall."

Kit shook her head again and hugged Naomi. "You're a good woman, but you're forgetting one rather important thing. I'm due to have a baby in May. I know I should give it up for adoption, and at first I planned to, but I'm really not sure I can do it anymore. I'm afraid college is out of the question for a while. Maybe when this child is older."

She went on, "The funny thing is. I really wanted

to go to college, but I'm not sure why. There's not any certain field I'm dead set on. It's like I wanted to go to college to go to college. And now that I realize I won't be, I'm okay with that, too. Mostly, I just need to find a way to be able to make a living and take care of the baby, too. It's a little intimidating."

They were back to peeling potatoes, Naomi, fast as her mind seemed to be clicking away, and Kit, more slowly, struggling to hold one still.

Naomi questioned, "What do you *like* to do?"

Kit gave a short laugh. "Not very lucrative things. Sculpting, music, eating, flowers, the outdoors. More than anything I like clay. Dirty, slippery clay. No big gold mine there. Just things that cost money, not make it."

She sobered and spoke half to herself, "Maybe I could work at a daycare and keep the baby with me." They considered this in silence.

Eventually Naomi asked, "Have you discussed any of this with Rossen?"

Kit shook her head. "Not really. I get the impression he thinks I can just stay here with you guys indefinitely and finish growing up like some normal teenager. That somehow it will all just work out in the end, all hunky dory. It's almost like this baby, no money, and my less than stellar upbringing don't matter to him. He honestly thinks it's just going to work itself out." She sputtered. "He acts like I'm part of your family or something." The potato in her hand slipped and slid across the counter.

Naomi retrieved it and handed it back, but before she released it she asked, "Kit, what if Joey had somehow gotten into the same situation you're in? What do you think Rob and I would have wished for her?"

Kit took the potato and went back to peeling. "I'm sorry. I don't know what you mean."

Naomi looked into her eyes. "If Joey were in this situation, Rob and I would hope and pray that someone, somehow would step up and give her the help she needed to make the best of a much less than ideal situation. And Kit, if someone would offer to help, do you think Rob and I would want her to accept the help or turn it down in some twisted 'I don't deserve this' mindset?"

Kit's hands stilled as she pondered what she was hearing as Naomi went on, "Kit, sometimes this life is unfair and unfortunate and all manner of negative things, but there is a purpose here. Our Father in Heaven does have a plan for us. All of us. And part of that plan is to reach our absolute greatest potential while in this life, with whatever set of gifts and troubles we're given.

"He didn't take away your foster father's agency when he abused you because this life is a test for him too, but God *is* watching over you, and sad that someone has harmed one of His precious daughters. He's watching and hoping someone with a good heart will step in and help, just as Rob and I would be. If you can't accept our and Rossen's help for yourself, then do it for this baby. We're offering and want to help, and someday when you're able, you can help someone else and pass it on. Does that make sense?"

Kit nodded wordlessly, her eyes bright with tears. Naomi hugged her. "Good! And you're right. Rossen doesn't see a broke, pregnant girl with a quote less than stellar upbringing. He sees a beautiful, talented, sweet daughter of God. And as far as we're all concerned, you are a part of our family and have been for what, ten days now?" She smiled. "So lighten up and enjoy it! It's Christmas Eve!"

****

Rossen sat in a leather recliner across the great room amidst the rest of the family, watching his mother and Kit work side by side in the kitchen, occasionally laughing together and then settling into an obviously serious conversation. Somehow he knew whatever they were so earnestly discussing was important and he prayed silently in his head for the two of them. He knew his mother's heart and he was coming to know Kit's, and he prayed that they would recognize and accept whatever God intended for them. He ended his prayer realizing that in ten short days, Kit's well being had come to matter immensely to him.

He remembered his prayers in the truck on the way from Vegas. He'd committed to help her before even knowing anything about her and honestly, had expected a hard-headed problem youth with, at the least, a drug habit. Now that he'd gotten to know her better, he'd come to respect and admire her for her spirit, and goodness, and willingness to do whatever it took with the best attitude possible. She was an incredible young woman and he was grateful she'd come into his life for however long it lasted.

He was so drawn to her. But she was so young and had so much of her life ahead, and he had to respect that, no matter how attracted to her he was. It was a strange mix of caring so much that he would push her away in her best interest, and in some ways his heart was breaking over it. He just kept coming back to a belief that his Father in Heaven was watching over him and would help him get past this and find happiness. In the meantime, he would do all he could to help Kit pick up the pieces of her life and find happiness of her own.

A few minutes later, when Kit came in to sit on the floor beside him, leaning comfortably back against his chair, he reached down to squeeze her shoulder. She reached her hand up to return the squeeze, and the silence was comfortable as they watched the rest of the group laugh and interact. Rossen knew from her easy manner, that she'd won the battle over whatever she'd been wrestling with for days now.

They joined in a cut-throat game of Monopoly that lasted two and a half hours. He was amazed and proud when she won, sweetly beating out a relentless Cooper, who'd become known as the Monopoly King.

Afterward, she got up and excused herself to go to her room for a rest before dinner. Rossen followed her up and went to the garage for the guitar he and Slade had retrieved that afternoon. He'd dusted it off, wrapped a big red bow around the case, and now took it to her room door and knocked. She opened the door barefoot and yawning. When she saw the case her eyes flew to his, questioning.

Holding out the case, he said, "I don't know how soon you'll be able to play it with your cast, but I figured your guitar was pretty important to you, since it's about the only thing you brought with you when you ran away. It was Slade's dad's. It's from Slade and Isabel, too."

She took the case, set it on the bed and opened it reverently. Tears started to stream down her face as she stroked the shiny wood. She couldn't even speak as she turned back to him at the door and hid her face against his chest. He just held her as she cried until his shirt was soaked through, his quiet strength absorbing the overwhelming emotion.

At length, her tears spent, he left her there and went into his office down the hall. Staring out the window at the winter twilight, his thoughts tumbled about in his head as he tried to compartmentalize his feelings. Holding her, even with her little rounded belly between them, had been heaven, and trying to push those feelings into a manageable place was harder than anything he'd ever done. Knowing he had to do it for her own good made it doable, but only barely.

He locked the door and knelt beside his desk chair, then sat there silently, not even sure what his prayer should be, just knowing he needed divine guidance now more than ever. He finally settled for a simple plea for strength and selfless wisdom. When he was through, he got up and unlocked the door. But then, instead of leaving, he returned to the window to go back to staring unseeing out into the snow.

****

Naomi had been looking for Rossen and found him there, legs braced apart with his arms folded across his chest, silently watching night fall from the sky and settle into the surrounding hills. She put her arm around his waist and leaned her head against his shoulder and they watched the shadows deepen together.

Finally, she broke the silence. "How are you?"

"A mess." The simple two word answer, so quietly stated, spoke volumes. She patted his chest with her other hand and felt the dampness there.

"What happened to you?" She leaned around to look into his face.

He gave her a tired smile. "I gave Kit the guitar. She's a little emotional right now."

She leaned back against his shoulder. "She's an extraordinary young woman."

He didn't answer for awhile and then admitted, "I wish she were older." His wistful words broke her heart. She'd dreamed of the day when he would settle down with the perfect girl, and honestly, some of Kit's circumstances hadn't been in those dreams, but even at that she would have welcomed her as a daughter-in-law with open arms except that she agreed with Rossen. Kit was too young to settle down, even in the situation she was in. She had no answers for him and so they continued to stand there, wordless, in the dark, the depth of their love and friendship strengthening them together.

A few minutes later Slade came in. Quietly, and without turning on the light or saying a word, he walked past them to the window and silently pushed it open. At first, they thought he'd lost his mind on this frigid Christmas Eve, until they heard what he'd heard, drifting in the open window from Kit's darkened balcony outside.

On the clear, cold air came the voice of an angel singing Silent Night to the evocative accompaniment of an acoustic guitar.

Slowly, as they listened, one by one, the rest of the family slipped into the darkened office to huddle together and listen. It was the ultimate carol to the Christ child from a young mother who had known what it was like to find no room at the inn. Her voice in the dark was pure and sweet as she sang her hymn to the Son of God, born that first Christmas night so long ago. The spirit it brought, as she sang through the verses and then played through again with just the guitar, truly was heavenly peace, and they were all let down as her music came to an end.

At last, the clear notes drifted away into the winter's night. No one moved or said a word. There had never been a more sacred lullaby.

At length, Naomi whispered, "You'd better go

bring her in before she freezes." She nudged Rossen toward the door.

He paused at the door to Kit's balcony, hesitant to intrude. Only the bitter cold pushed him over the threshold. He rested his hands on her shoulders. "Apparently, the cast isn't a problem." His voice was low and soft to preserve the sweet peace. "None of us had any idea you could play and sing like that."

She was shivering under his fingers and he took her guitar and helped her to her feet. "We would all love it if you played inside, you know." They went in and closed the door behind them.

Looking down, Kit said, "My foster parents would never let me play inside, so I guess it got to be a habit. And I wasn't sure if I could manage it or what the guitar was like and was afraid I'd embarrass myself in front of my new family."

His eyes searched hers in the dim light and what he saw warmed his heart. He hugged her tight to him, his chin against her forehead as she added, "Naomi adopted me tonight, figuratively speaking." There were more tears shining in her eyes.

He smiled and moved away from her. "She adopted you ten days ago. You just didn't let yourself believe it until tonight."

****

The family gathered at the huge table for dinner and afterward, near the fire, to read the Christmas story from the Bible, followed by family prayer. Everyone said goodnight and went their separate ways until it was just Rossen and Kit, and Slade and Isabel, with only the flickering light of the fire.

Isabel asked her if she'd sing again and Kit began, softly and reverently. There in the firelight she sang carols to the Savior of the world who she was just coming to know through this strong family of true and honorable Christians. Once again the family crept back in, one by one, to sit in the dark and listen to an angel proclaim Christ's birth.

As Kit drifted off to sleep that night, comfortable in a warm, safe bed, surrounded by love and respect, she pondered on this Christmas compared to every other one she'd experienced in her seventeen years. She honestly hadn't known life could be like this. Her heart was so full, and she had a hope for the future she almost hadn't dared to voice as she knelt to thank her Heavenly Father for her precious gifts of this Christmas season. It was a feeling she wished she could catch in a bottle and keep with her always.

****

Christmas day was crazy! Kit had never seen so many presents and she'd definitely never seen so much food! She couldn't help feed the stock because of her arm and the baby, so often it was her and Naomi in the kitchen and they'd grown close. Naomi was teaching her to cook and basically how to be a good mom. Sometimes as they worked, Kit would also ask her questions about how she knew so much about God. Naomi had smiled as she'd admitted that before Rob she hadn't understood about God at all. They often ended up in incredibly thought provoking discussions before whatever they were making was prepared.

This Christmas morning had turned out that way as they were making piles of bacon and pancakes and fruit. Kit asked, "Naomi, how do you always just know what's the right thing to do or say like you do?"

Naomi chuckled. "Oh honey, if you only knew the great faux pas in my past, you would never ask a question like that." She laughed again. "I've made world class errors in knowing what to say or do at times. It's just a good thing my husband and kids are pretty durable and could handle my screw ups."

Kit smiled at her candor, but persisted, "You know what I mean, though. There has to be a secret to get it right like you do." She was turning bacon on a huge griddle.

"You're right. There is a secret, but it's not my secret. And it's not just to know what to say. We can know what God would have us do in every situation, if we listen closely enough. Sometimes His answers take time or extra effort, but He *is* all knowing and will lead us if we try to let Him. Everyone has the right to have personal inspiration. We're blessed with divine insight if we ask for it, and are worthy of it, and listen to it, and heed it, when we receive it." Naomi was at her side making hot cakes on an identical griddle.

Kit repeated this softly to herself, "If we ask, are worthy, listen and heed it. Okay, how do you ask?"

"The way man has communicated with God from the days of Adam and Eve. Pray. Everyday, several times a day, for all the things we're grateful for, or need, or are concerned about, or are happy and excited about. He's a loving parent who wants to bless us, but we have to ask." Naomi poured another round of batter out.

"And how do we be worthy of it?"

Naomi set the pitcher of batter aside to consider this question. "I guess the answer to that is to do our best, as imperfect mortals, to try to do what we know is right. The more we're in tune with deity; the clearer the lines of communication are going to be. It's sort of like tuning in a radio, in a way, I guess. If we're trying, and are doing good things in the right places, there's going to be less static and it's easier to hear. When we make poor choices, or are in places we shouldn't be, we chase the Spirit away and God can't communicate. The more we do our best, the easier and clearer it becomes. Does that make sense?"

"What did you mean by 'if we heed it'?"

"Well, think about it. If you were a parent and gave your child wise counsel over and over, if they didn't listen and obey, wouldn't you soon stop giving it to them?"

Kit nodded as she considered this. The more she learned about all this, the more it just made sense.

They had mountains of food when the others came in, but it didn't take long to make it disappear. After this long, Kit was still amazed at how much food this family put away. It's a good thing they had oil wells. It probably took the proceeds from one just to buy groceries.

They ate and opened gifts and even Slade's ranch help, Hank and his wife Ruby, who were family friends, showed up to be welcomed in. There was every gift imaginable, and some of the gag gifts were hilarious. Joey had given three of her brothers, Rossen, Sean and Treyne, girl watching glasses. They were huge neon colored plastic sunglasses to help them find wives. And she'd given Cooper fake dynamite to help him learn to fish better. Rob received a real "Fragile" leg lamp like in *The Christmas Story*, and even Isabel got into the spirit of the thing and gave the brothers Slade's collection of women's unsolicited phone numbers from a friendly competition he and Rossen had had on the rodeo circuit. There was a shoebox crammed full and Kit wondered if Rossen had collected one just like it.

Rossen had purchased board games for the family from her and many of them had given her clothing to build up her wardrobe. By day's end she had more clothes than she'd ever owned at one time in her life. Isabel gave her cosmetics and then helped her put them on and Naomi gave her her own Book of Mormon. Rob gave her a new ski parka and matching hat and gloves. It was slightly big, but she knew she would need the extra room soon.

Everyone pitched in to make a huge Christmas dinner with all the trimmings, and then helped to clean it all up when it was over. Afterward, they went to Slade's house to watch *A Christmas Story* in his theater room. The movie was funny, but Kit couldn't keep her eyes open and when Isabel noticed, she suggested Kit go into the bedroom next door to rest on a real bed.

As she led her in, Isabel mentioned, "This is actually Rossen's room. He lives here with Slade, but I'm sure he won't mind letting you rest for a few." Kit glanced around in interest. Rossen always seemed to be around his parent's house, but then so did Isabel and Slade, and she knew his office was there. Kit had had no idea he didn't live there. Looking around, she got a whole new sense of who Rossen was. On the wall were his Petroleum Engineering degree and a plaque about serving a mission to Peru. There was a photo of him whitewater rafting with his family and Slade, and another of him posing beside a massive, dead bear with a bow.

When she saw the huge gold belt buckle on the dresser that held the title World Champion Team Roper she couldn't even believe it! She picked it up to finger the intricate design and was surprised by its weight. She knew they'd been on the way home from a big rodeo the night they'd rescued her. Everyone had been talking about it a lot, but world champion? He'd never even mentioned it.

She wondered if she'd somehow taken some of the importance of it away by showing up in his life that night. She knew he'd spent the next three days beside her in the hospital. He hadn't had any chance to celebrate. She was feeling decidedly guilty about it all when he knocked.

She stood there holding the buckle in her hand as he looked in. "You're a world champion and I didn't even know." Her voice was low and miserable as she looked up at him with sad eyes. "It was the night you found me, wasn't it?" He nodded and she went on, "I'm so sorry. You were sitting in a hospital room when you should have been celebrating the accomplishment of your life." She looked down and her shoulders drooped. She felt like she'd messed up something priceless.

He touched her arm and she looked up at him. "It's okay. All we were doing was coming home. It sounds ungrateful, I know, but we were tired and just wanted to come back to the mountains. The only plans I had were to eat, shop and watch football."

She looked down again. "And you never even got to do that."

He lifted her chin. "I did something much more satisfying than any of those things. It's been nice to be needed. Helping you was important to me. Don't begrudge me that." She still felt terrible about it all.

He changed the subject. "I brought you something. I didn't want to give it to you in front of everyone because it's kind of personal. I hope you can understand and take it in the spirit it's given." Now he had her worried.

He pulled a small package and card out to give to her. "I hope you're not offended, but I wanted to make sure you knew . . . " He hesitated. "I wanted to make sure you remembered that even though your foster father uh abused you, it wasn't your fault. You're still the same sweet virtuous girl you would have been, had you been raised under better circumstances."

She looked up in surprise and her eyes were wide as they searched his. Could he really believe this? How could it be true after what she had been through? Her foster father had made her feel filthy and worthless and used up.

He must have been able to see her thoughts in her eyes, because he said, "Our Father in Heaven knows your heart, Kit. He doesn't blame you for the wrongs others have done you. Neither should anyone else. In His eyes you're still clean and pure and chaste, and I want to make sure you see yourself that way too." He pushed the card and tiny box into her hand. "I know that kind of abuse sometimes messes people up. And I'm sure I have no idea what you're dealing with. But, in just this short ten days I've come to know you're a good person. I have no doubt that you are indeed a virtuous woman."

Her eyes filled with wonder as she watched him. She could see that he really believed that. It was a completely foreign concept to her. For so long she had felt used and dirty. She could hardly even wrap her brain around this. She still looked at him as she opened the card.

It read, "Who can find a virtuous woman, for her price is far above rubies. King David, Proverbs 31:10"

Slowly she opened the small box, trying to see through the tears that welled in her eyes. A small gold ring containing a single brilliant ruby lay on a bed of black velvet. She looked up at him as the tears overflowed and trailed down her cheeks.

He was flustered. "Don't cry again. This is a happy gift!" He looked around as if for something to wipe her tears and finding nothing, gently wiped her face with his fingers. He folded her into a gentle hug and spoke against her hair, "I have no idea what to do when you do this."

That wasn't true. He knew to hug her which was exactly what she needed although she hadn't known that until she came here and had done the counseling research. She struggled to control her emotions. "I'm sorry." She spoke against his chest, "I don't usually cry this much. At home I never cried. Ever. Naomi says it's the baby. It might be the on-line counseling stuff. I don't know. It's just that I thought this whole virtuous thing was hopelessly gone forever." She raised her head. "Are you sure God still thinks I'm okay, even pregnant?"

He smiled and hugged her tighter. "Yes. I'm sure."

At length, he pulled away. "I want you to wear it and when you look at it, always remember that you are worth far above rubies. And someday, when some jerk insinuates otherwise, you'll always know what God and Rossen know—that Kit is a virtuous woman, of infinite worth. Deal?" He put his fist out to meet hers like a high five.

"Deal."

"Good." He ruffled her hair again. "Take your nap." He turned and left the room, and she lay down on top of the covers to contemplate her ruby ring. She drifted off in wonder. Could it really be true? She knew she could trust Rossen, so it must be.

****

Kit opened her eyes and for a second she wasn't sure where she was. Then she remembered Rossen's room and the ruby ring. She lay there for a moment wondering why the house was now dark and silent and she noticed that his bedroom smelled faintly like him. It was a combination of aftershave and leather and something uniquely Rossen. Somehow it was comforting. She climbed off the bed, slipped on her shoes and went to see where everyone was.

She found Rossen alone in the theater room working on his lap top. At first he didn't know she was there and she watched him work, his long brown fingers flying over the keyboard, his concentration intense. She wondered what he was working on. He'd told her he was a petroleum engineer slash cowboy. Then, she'd thought he was teasing, but she'd come to know he'd been serious. She didn't know the first thing about either subject and wished she knew more about his life.

She must have made a sound because he looked up and smiled. Finishing what he was doing, he shut down his computer. "Ready to go?"

Trying to comb out her hair with her fingers she asked, "Where is everyone?" The house felt deserted.

"They went back to my parents after the movie, but I didn't want to wake you. Did you rest okay? We were being kind of rowdy in the second movie. They were watching Remember the Titans, and kept singing along."

"Second movie? What time is it? How long did I sleep?" She yawned and stretched.

"You must have been tired. It's seven forty five. You've been asleep for almost four hours. Everyone else left about an hour ago."

She smiled guiltily. "I didn't use to need so much sleep. I feel almost lazy. I think the baby must make me tired."

He headed up the stairs grinning. "Sure. Blame it on the baby. What are you going to name her?"

Right behind him on the stairs, she questioned, "Her? What makes you think it's a her?"

He waited for her at the top. "I don't know. I just always picture a girl, with pretty dark hair like her mother. Where did you get the dark hair? Were your biological parents Hispanic?"

She shook her head. "My father was half Papago Indian. My real name is Kitawna Star. Kitawna is a native word meaning valuable."

"It's a pretty name. It fits you." He helped her on with her coat. "What do *you* think the baby is?"

They went through to the garage. "I don't know. Sometimes I don't even dare wonder." She hesitated. "It sounds awful, but sometimes I worry it will remind me of my foster father. Is that terrible?"

"No, it's not terrible." He helped her up into his truck. "You feel how you feel. I can see how you wouldn't want a reminder, but you should try to think positive. If you don't think you want to put her up for adoption, then try to be excited for her. Picture yourself thrilled with her. I'm sure the rest of us will be."

She mused almost to herself, "Sometimes when I think about it, it's hard to even believe this is all real. A year ago I still felt like a child. Now I'm going to have one." She picked at the edge of her cast. "If I think too much it scares me to death. How will I take care of a baby? How will I even know how to mother it?"

She could hear the worry in her own voice and he reached over to squeeze her hand. "You're gonna do just fine. You're kind and smart, and you've learned what you don't want. There'll be lots of people to help, and I believe our Father in Heaven gives moms special inspiration all their own to know what their children need. I think what some people call mother's intuition is actually specific inspiration for their families. I'm sure He'll send it to you if you ask." What he was telling her sounded just like what Naomi had been trying to explain to her as they cooked that morning.

He continued, "I worry more about it being physically healthy, as thin as you are. Did you ever make your prenatal appointment?"

She was slow to answer and finally said, "I have no money for it and how would I get there?" She looked up at him, feeling troubled.

He glanced at her and back to the snowy driveway. "I thought we already talked about this, and you agreed to let me help you." Pulling into his parent's garage, he shut off the truck. When she didn't answer him immediately, he quietly prompted her, "Talk to me Kit. What's going on in that head of yours?" She looked up, but still didn't answer. He went on gently, "Didn't you already agree to let me and my family help you until you could get your feet under you?"

She nodded and said the faintest, "Yes."

He put a finger under her chin and looked into her eyes. "So what's bothering you then?"

With a stronger voice, she said, "It's just hard. Sometimes I don't feel like I should use your money and live here, and act like I belong when I'm not even in your family. Naomi talked to me yesterday about this and I know I need to accept your help. It's just hard for me to feel like such a burden."

"I know you feel that way, Kit, but what are the options? You can't go back."

He went on, "My family would rather die than have you go on welfare, but even if that's what you wanted, it would still take documentation you haven't got. Even a job would need ID and stuff, and I don't think you should go anywhere near your foster father, at least until you're eighteen and he would have no control over you."

Shaking his head, he continued, "Even if you did get a job, it would mean a long commute or an apartment somewhere, and you'd be alone. It would still be hard to make ends meet, especially with a cast and getting further along with your baby. We'd all worry sick about you. My mother would never forgive herself."

His voice softened, and he was almost pleading, "Wouldn't it be better to stay with us? Let us help you. We'll find a way to get your high school diploma. Once the baby's here and your cast is off and you're eighteen, we'll help you get to college and make a living." His tone changed, "What if we found something for you to do here to help so you didn't feel like a burden at all? Or could you accept help now and help someone else in turn, once you're established?"

She turned toward him. "You make it all sound so logical, but I'm still a little uncomfortable."

He leaned back against the door thinking, and finally said, "Then do it for your baby."

Only considering it for a second or two, she answered, "Okay."

He undid their seatbelts. "Good! It's the right thing to do. Good moms have prenatal care. It's your first thing to do in raising her right."

He came around to help her out. "How much have you driven in snow?"

Taking her hand, he tucked it around his arm to help her up the steps into the house as she answered, "I'm sorry, I've never driven, in snow or otherwise. I've never had a chance to." She was embarrassed, but admitted, "Driver's Ed was extra money and they wanted me home to work in the motel anyway. I'm definitely planning to learn though."

The muscles in his jaw tightened, but his voice was kind as he said, "We'll teach you, although snowy mountain roads are probably not the best start. For the time being, one of us will take you to the doctor. Go ahead and make your appointment. It's important."

As they walked into the house, she faced him. "You're right, but can I take you up on finding ways to help so I don't feel like so much bother?"

"Absolutely."

Chapter 5

That holiday week flew by in a flurry of family activities and outings. They had board game all-nighters and movie marathons. They went into a nearby town and rented ice skates and skated in the dark on the town pond while Kit watched from a bench to the side near a huge bonfire.

Sometimes they took snowmobiles out to check stock and then they'd play on them in the fields and hill climb. Kit had never been on a snow machine and at first had no idea how to lean to make them turn better. She rode behind Rossen and Joey and began to get the hang of it. Finally Rossen took her to an open meadow of deep powder and played so hard that she almost fell off behind him and he knew it. She could only really hold on with her right hand and as he made a hard turn she slid. Only his sudden grab saved her from toppling into the snow and her heart raced as she clung to him until he had her securely back behind him. Had she not been pregnant she would have reveled on riding wild, but she worried about the tiny person growing inside her and asked to be taken back home.

When they got there and Cooper mentioned what

happened, Naomi put her hands on her hips and laid into Rossen, "Rossen Robert Rockland! Don't you dare be so rough with her! She has to be extremely careful right now. Think how you would feel if something happened to her baby." His face was so penitent that it made Kit laugh and it helped to ease the tension.

That night as Kit was heading to bed, he caught up with her in the hall and said, "Kit, I'm sorry again for being too out of control today. Are you sure you're okay?"

"I'm fine. We're fine." She smiled shyly. "Actually, it was really fun. I just sometimes forget I'm somebody's mother now and it brings a whole new set of rules. I'm sorry Naomi got upset with you."

He put his hand on her shoulder. "She was right, and I deserved it. I'm just glad you're both okay. I'll do better. I promise."

****

The next day was Sunday and this time Kit went with the family to church. Joey helped her decide what to wear and styled her hair, then she just loaded in with them all and they headed out. She'd never been inside a church in her life and had no idea what to expect, but she'd come to love and respect the Rocklands. She'd already decided that whatever it was they believed that made them the happy, honorable, good people they were, was great with her.

She wanted the values they lived in her life and her child's life, and she knew much of what she appreciated about them stemmed from their religious beliefs. The stark difference between the lifestyle she was living here with them and the world she'd known before, was to her a no-brainer. What they had was so much better than the rest of society, that she was thrilled to have the opportunity to be included.

Although Kit had often been timid in the past around others, her self esteem had blossomed so much here in Wyoming because of Rossen's family, that she walked into church that morning with confidence and curiosity, rather than trepidation. And even though everything was completely new to her, she knew she was a quick study and that it would all come together for her eventually. In the meantime, she intended to soak it all up like a sponge.

They were on their way back out of the church headed for the car, when she asked Rossen, "So what do I have to do to become a member of your church?" Slade and Isabel were walking with them and when Rossen stopped in his tracks and was all but speechless, Slade elbowed him and laughed.

Slade turned to Kit and said, "Isabel and I got just about the same reaction when we asked him that, too!"

Rossen was still staring at Kit. "How do you know you want to become a member? This is your first day. You just told me you've never been inside a church. How can you even make a decision yet?" He was looking at her like she'd lost her mind.

Kit calmly asked him, "Is there a problem with me becoming a member?"

"No. Of course not, but Kit, this is a big decision.

It can't be taken lightly. You have to know what you're getting into before you decide. You have to base your decision on something."

"I have based my decision on something. Fruit. This is a fruit thing. You know. By their fruits ye shall know them thing. I don't have to dissect the tree to tell if it has good fruit. This church has good fruit and I want to be a part. As soon as I can, so my baby can enjoy the fruit too."

Rossen still hadn't even closed his mouth by the time they reached his truck. Slade and Isabel were silently watching, both of them smiling from ear to ear. Rossen didn't say a thing as he tossed his keys to Slade and began to help Kit up into the rear seat. He climbed up in beside her and helped her buckle her seat belt. Then in turn, buckled his own. He opened his mouth to say something, then closed it again three times before he finally just left it closed.

Fully five minutes into the drive he asked, "How do you even know the whole 'by their fruits ye shall know them' thing. Where did you even hear that?"

Kit answered, "It's in both the Bible and in the Book of Mormon in several places each, but it's a relatively simple concept. It just makes sense." Rossen's eyes narrowed, questioning, before he turned to look out the window in silence for a minute.

Finally, Slade spoke from the front seat, "You never answered her question about becoming a member." His eyes met Rossen's in the rear view mirror.

"You're right, I guess I didn't." He turned to Kit. "I don't even know what to tell you. Usually you either have been raised in the church or have been meeting with the missionaries when you decide to be baptized. I don't have a clue what the bishop will say about someone being baptized because of fruit." At that, he smiled at Kit, shaking his head in disbelief. "I'm going to guess he's still going to want you to take the missionary lessons first, but I'm not sure. We'll have to call and ask. At the very least, maybe you should study a little about the basics so you'll know what you're in for."

Kit replied, "I've read the *Book of Mormon,* the *Doctrine and Covenants*, the *Pearl of Great Price, Our Search For Happiness,* and several other pamphlets your mom has lent me, and I'm almost finished with *Jesus The Christ*. And I'm slowly picking at the Bible. It's a bit intimidating. What else should I be studying?"

This time all three of them turned to stare. Even Slade didn't look back at the road until he hit the rumble strip.

Rossen looked shell shocked. He finally answered, "It sounds like my mom has it all under control. Maybe you'd better ask her what she has in mind next." After a second he asked Kit, "You've been here what, fifteen days, three of which you spent mostly asleep in the hospital, and you've read all that, including most of *Jesus the Christ?*" She nodded. "Holy cow! I couldn't do that in three months! That's unreal!" He was looking at her like he'd never really seen her before.

After a pause he asked, "Why?"

She shrugged. "I wanted to find out what you guys knew that the rest of us didn't, that makes you so good. I know it has to be something about the church, so I've been trying to figure it out."

"And did you find the secret?" Rossen finally broke into his usual smile.

"More like lots and lots of little pieces of the secret." Kit smiled back. "Mostly I just understand the simple stuff like fruit."

"Simple stuff. You read *Jesus the Christ* like it's nothing and you just understand the simple stuff?" He was shaking his head again chuckling to himself. "Simple stuff."

****

The next week she went into town with Naomi to shop and run errands. They went to the school district offices to talk with the superintendent, who was very cooperative. He agreed to help her get started on her last credits before they had her records and sent her straight to the high school. They signed her up for the two credits of math she was short and the one of English. Other than that, Kit believed she only needed one more credit of an elective to have enough to graduate.

The counselor cautioned her, "If it turns out that you need something other than that, we'll have to deal with it then. You can take this math and English on-line. What did you have in mind for the elective?"

Kit answered, "I have no idea. What are my

options?"

"You can probably take anything we offer that you could get into halfway through the year, but let's find you something you can work on at the ranch and not have to come in all the time. Usually students pick stuff they like for electives. What do you enjoy?"

Kit's eyes lit up. "I love art, especially sculpture. Is there any way to do something along those lines?"

"As a matter of fact we have an exceptional art department. Our teacher, Mr. Perkins, is actually a local artist who has been willing to teach part time. He's here now and I think his class is in an assembly. Let me see if I can find him. Just a moment." She got on the phone and confirmed that the teacher was in his room and sent them straight down.

As they walked in the door, Kit breathed in the smells and smiled. She could smell all the familiar scents of the art room from before, that she had loved, oil paints, thinner, and gesso, and the earthy smell of her beloved clay. She liked Mr. Perkins immediately. His quiet straightforwardness was instantly reassuring.

"Yes. I'm sure we can work something out where you can work at home and bring your pieces in to be graded and fired. Maybe you can do some research online into different techniques and styles, too. One credit actually only needs to be approximately one hundred hours of work and if you're passionate about your work like most artists, you'll have that done in no time. Let me load you up with clay today and when you're ready to come in, just call and make an appointment. You can even bring them into the studio in my home if you want. It's probably about twenty minutes closer to your place."

He helped them carry three large bags of clay to Naomi's SUV and stow them in the back. "Remember not to put much of this down her sinks." He indicated Naomi with his head. "You'll clog the drain lines sure as shootin'. Wipe off with something first before you rinse. Go to it! I can't wait to see your work!" He smiled at Kit, shut the door and sent them on their way.

Kit floated on the way back to the ranch. She truly hadn't dared hope when Naomi told her she thought she could work on finishing high school, and she certainly never dreamed she'd have the opportunity to work with clay as part of the process. Getting credit for doing something she enjoyed so much, and especially being able to work on her own ideas was far more than a dream come true. She was so excited to get started she almost felt a little silly.

Naomi interrupted her thoughts from the driver's seat. "I've never had any experience with clay. What else do you need to begin? Are there tools or materials we need to gather up?"

Kit's voice was animated. "Actually that's the beauty of clay. You can work it with anything or just your hands. About the only thing I need is a place to work, and some hand lotion." She qualified this. "The clay sucks the moisture out of your hands, and then when you rinse the residue off, it removes the oils even more. They can get trashed pretty quickly. Sometimes I even used just plain salad oil to help them."

Naomi smiled at her obvious enthusiasm. "I take it you enjoy this."

Kit smiled back shyly. "It's funny he talked about artists being passionate about their work. That's exactly how I feel. Sculpture is my passion!"

"Well then, we'd better find you a place to get started right away. Have you been up to the craft room back of the stairs?"

Kit shook her head. "I haven't."

"It's a large open room with a big work table in the middle. There's a sink and the whole west wall is windows, so the light is good. Maybe you could set up in there. Cooper and his friends never go in there, so hopefully nothing will be destroyed before you can get it in to be graded. I'm assuming things will be fragile."

"Until the clay is fired the first time it's very easily broken, and after firing it's similar to a piece of stoneware. I seldom do things that are terribly delicate, but I never know what I'm creating until I start, so who knows."

Naomi asked, "Is this like pottery kind of stuff you do, or is it sculpture or bronzes, or what's your work like?"

Kit stared out the window unseeing for a moment. "I have no idea what you'd call what I do. It's just what I do. Images and shapes just flow when I get the clay in my hands. I can't even explain it. It's like…." She hesitated. "I don't know what it's like. When I first started to use clay, all the frustration and hurt and discouragement I had stored up over the years poured out through my hands and it has been my outlet, my catharsis, when I had nowhere else to turn." She was slightly embarrassed.

Naomi commented as she drove into the grocery store parking lot. "You don't talk like a seventeen year old, Kit. You look it, but you don't act it or sound it. You're much better educated than I would have thought for your age and background."

Kit shrugged. "You're the only one I'll admit this to, but I'm pretty smart. I remember everything I read or hear, and for some reason I catch on quickly. Sometimes I've had to try to hide it. It can get on peoples nerves or make the other kids uncomfortable. Sometimes in school I would purposely miss stuff so I seemed more regular or something. I especially had to be careful around the boys. I think I intimidated them." She gave a self-deprecating smile. "Even Sunday when I told Rossen and Slade and Isabel what I had been reading, you know the books you've been lending me about the church? I think I kind of freaked Rossen out a little."

She smiled, but in a way, it made her sad as well. "It's actually been good. I've had to spend a lot of time alone and books and learning have been my friends. They're constant, even when I was being moved around from home to home a lot or ended up with a family that wasn't necessarily interested." She tried not to let her voice become wistful as she ended and looked out the window at the passing shoppers.

Naomi reached across to touch her hand. "I didn't mean to squelch your mood. Don't be sad. The foster homes are all behind you. And even if Rossen was a shade shell shocked at your amazing abilities, he still admires and respects your mind a great deal. We all do."

She went on, "I'll admit something to you, too. When they brought you home and we decided to help you, honestly we expected a troubled teen with an attitude and a drug habit. And we would have dealt with that as well as we could." She smiled warmly at Kit. "But look what a pleasant surprise you've been! Not only are you not a hassle, but you're beautiful and talented and brilliant! We just wish we'd have found you years ago!" She opened the car door. "And you help me with things like grocery shopping, which can be quite a project when we're all home. You've been a great help!"

They ended up with two huge carts full. Kit could hardly push hers around one armed, so they checked out once and came back for more. The whole cargo area of Naomi's Jeep Cherokee was filled up around the bags of clay. Kit was glad to see the whole family automatically file into the garage to help unload it after they drove in. They put all the bags on the huge dining table and then Naomi sorted it and asked various people to put it all where it belonged. Kit helped Rossen load frozen food into the deep freezers in the garage and on the way back in, asked him to help her unload her clay up to the craft room.

At first he had no idea what she was asking him to unload out of the car. When he went to lift them he exclaimed at how heavy they were. He pulled one out to carefully place it in her good arm, and then pulled the other two out and asked, "What in the world is it?" His look made her laugh.

"It's clay. For my elective credit they're going to let me do some stuff from here and take it in to the art teacher in town."

He looked skeptical. "I'm glad it's you, not me. I had no idea this was what clay was like." As they headed up the stairs he asked, "Are you sure you should be carrying something that heavy? Especially one handed?"

She smiled, grateful for his concern. She still wasn't used to people being this nice to her, and it was so sweet to be cared about. "I'm fine, thanks. It's really not too bad."

When they reached the craft room, she looked around, thrilled. This room would be perfect. She wished she could open one of the bags right then.

****

Rossen watched her touch the unopened bags almost lovingly before they went back down the stairs. The look in her eyes was the same he'd seen as she stroked the guitar that first time she saw it. It was a look that fascinated him. How would it be, to be that special to her? It was an intriguing thought.

Chapter 6

A week into the New Year, Sean, Treyne, Joey, and Cooper all went back to college and the house felt half abandoned. With their departure, the holiday atmosphere dampened down and everyone seemed to settle into a workaday pace. Ruger and Marti were getting ready for foaling season and came over less, and Rossen started spending longer hours in his office to catch up on a backlog from being gone to rodeos. Slade was busy on his own ranch and Isabel was planning their imminent wedding. She was living at Naomi and Rob's and even though she was around making arrangements, the house seemed much less busy and active than it had. For a few days, Kit really missed all the commotion.

Kit got into a schedule of doing her school work right after breakfast in Rob and Naomi's office that was right next door to Rossen's. She would usually work until lunch and then see what she could help Naomi with. When that was done she would go up into the craft room, and work with her clay. She tried not to spend too much time there, because she wanted to help as much as could so she didn't feel like a burden, but the time she spent sculpting was almost therapeutic.

At first she just worked on abstract pieces, letting the shapes flow from the images in her mind. Her work always reflected her mood and her attitude. She was intrigued to find that the spirit of her art had drastically changed since she'd come to Wyoming. The lines were smoother, the transitions more streamlined and the overall images more gentle and softer. She sometimes felt her work was like driftwood, with the roughness smoothed away by the peace of the mountains. The cool, slick clay almost seemed to shape itself under her slim brown hands. The feelings she could never express verbally, flowed easily into the clay.

Rossen worked most mornings in his office next door to Rob and Naomi's. Kit could often hear him on the phone as she worked on her English and math. Her classes were pretty elementary and she was able to finish her daily assignments quickly. Sometimes afterward she would stay on-line to research other things.

She knew next to nothing about rodeo and she was able to find information about the sport and even about Rossen and his standings relatively easily. Reading about it was interesting, but she still felt like she didn't have much of a grasp on it, even after studying. It was definitely an action sport and she realized it would have to be seen in action to begin to understand it.

She also pulled up Wyoming and the southwest area in particular to find more about the place she was so happily living. She hadn't paid particular attention in school because it hadn't been of much interest to her, but now she needed to know more.

She Googled petroleum engineering one day, too. It was probably foolish, but she wanted to know everything she could about what Rossen did professionally. Even though she tried not to let herself dwell on him or what he did, she was still so drawn to him and wished she understood his world better.

Sometimes he left the ranch to work and one time he even had a helicopter out there flying him and Rob around looking at the snow covered countryside. Kit was more intrigued than ever.

Even after several hours of research, she understood somewhat, but was sure she still hadn't a clue what it was he did. A few days later she had a chance to find out more.

She was doing her school work and could hear him working next door, but for the first time he didn't sound very happy. He was on and off the phone and she could hear his computer keyboard, and papers rustling. Finally she heard him swear.

She was so surprised that she got up from her chair and went next door. Hesitating at the threshold, she stood there and watched as he talked on the phone, then hung up to run his fingers through his already mussed hair. When he saw her standing there, he turned and asked, "What? You're not ticked off at me too, are you?" His obvious frustration, compared to his usual easy going charm, for some reason made her laugh out loud. Once she got started she was having a hard time keeping a straight face and when she thought about him swearing, she laughed again. He was a hoot when he was aggravated!

At first, he just looked at her in disgust, but the worse he fussed, the more hilarious he was to her. Finally, he cracked a sheepish smile and chuckled with her. "It's not really funny, you know!" She cracked up again. "I'm in a government bureaucracy quagmire and all you can do is laugh." He tried to make his tone severe. "Just for that, you can get in here and help me. Can you keyboard in your cast?" She nodded, trying not to laugh again. "Good. I need you. Have you got time to work for me for a while?"

She finally realized he was serious. "Sure. All I was going to do was go fold laundry. Tell me what to do."

He sat her at his computer to fill out an official report. He explained what figures went where and said, "If there's something you don't understand just ask me."

She went to work and he began pulling stacks of computer printouts, correlating them to several large maps spread out on the big central drafting table. As he worked he scribbled notes. Occasionally she asked him questions. As she worked through the report, eventually he sat beside her with a monstrous calculator. It had buttons she'd never dreamed of understanding and she'd never seen anything like it. He calculated and penciled in figures for her to input and she entered it all.

They worked that way side by side for a couple of hours. Eventually Naomi came in carrying a box of crackers and said to Kit, "I wondered where you'd gone off to." She glanced at her son and laughed which sent Kit into the giggles again.

He looked at his mom. "Not you too! Kit has already filled the 'laugh at Rossen' quota for the day. She thinks this is funny!" Naomi laughed again as she tried to smooth down his hair.

She sweetly asked, "Apparently you have government business today? What report is it this time? Or are we applying for some kind of permit?" He began to grumble under his breath and both women went off into peals of laughter again.

After a few more minutes of pestering him, Naomi left saying she'd hold lunch until they had time to eat. Kit was grateful for the crackers. It had been too long since breakfast and the nausea was threatening again.

It was after three o'clock when they finally finished the report and went to eat. Walking down the hall beside him on the way to the kitchen, she realized she was going to be sick and told him to go on without her. She tried to wait until he was into the kitchen, but she had to hurry. She could tell by the look on his face when she finally made it in, that he knew she'd thrown up.

He came up to her and rubbed her shoulder and said, "I'm so sorry." He pulled her chair out to seat her. "I completely forgot that you had to eat sooner. You were such a great help to me and I made you sick." He pushed her soup over to her. "Come on. We'll feed you quick and you'll feel better."

It didn't exactly work that way. She was ill the rest of the day and several times in the night and Naomi brought food to her right in bed to try and get a handle on it from the start of the day.

Rossen came in looking seriously penitent with a jar full of M&Ms to give her. He looked down at her as she sat at the breakfast table still feeling slightly green. "I've brought you a 'please forgive me' gift of chocolate. Maybe this will work."

Naomi put pancakes and sausage in front of him and said, "Technically, M&Ms aren't terribly nutritious food, but I guess they can be considered the fifth food group in a pinch." She winked at Kit.

Whether it was the M&Ms or not, something helped and she felt much better that day.

After that, Kit helped Rossen in his office more days than not. He was doing the engineering and paperwork to drill another well on the ranch and it was a lengthy and in-depth process. Kit didn't always understand what she was working on, but she felt much more useful.

At the end of two weeks when he came to her with a sizeable wad of cash, she thought he was nuts and said, "I'm living with you, and your family is paying all my bills. This would be too much even if I wasn't. Don't be silly."

Rossen replied, "No Kit. It's not too much. We'd have to pay someone this much anyway and you've caught on in record time and never make mistakes. Not only that, we know we can trust you to work here in our home and that's something that can't be bought at any price. Take the money. It's important that you have some of your own to get things you need or want, without having to ask for it every time." He pushed it into her hands. "You've earned it Kit. It wouldn't be right not to pay you. I'm sorry we can't get you a bank account without some ID. If you aren't sure you can manage it well, take it to Slade. He's a financial wizard and handles money for several of us."

Again, she was floored by the goodness and honesty of this family. Back home, her foster parents had demanded she hand over the meager amount she'd earned at her job at the school, and made her work as a maid at their hotel without ever even mentioning pay.

****

Her first prenatal appointment was that week and she was nervous about it. She had no idea what it would entail and secretly worried she'd somehow injured the child inside her with her previous malnutrition. Naomi took her into town and as they were sitting in the waiting room she patted Kit's fidgety hands with her calm ones.

"There's no need to be nervous. She'll probably just talk to you and measure your tummy. Maybe some blood tests, but nothing too scary. You'll be fine."

Kit was still glad when it was over and they could go home. They'd determined she was about twenty weeks along and was due around the end of May. They made another appointment for a couple of weeks out for an ultrasound, then sent her home saying everything looked good.

On the way out of town Naomi stopped and bought her some books about pregnancy. One was a kind of reference book about what to expect and the other was a book of the most amazing photographs. It was actual photos of developing fetuses in different stages of gestation, Kit was overjoyed with it. Somehow the appointment and books helped her to understand much better what was happening and she began to look forward in anticipation instead of worrying about how she would manage.

She was in the great room on the couch looking through them that night when Rossen came through. "What are you reading?" He leaned to look over her shoulder. "What is it?"

She answered, "That is a newly conceived fetus. Look at this one!" She turned over several pages. "This one is about the same far along as I am. Check this out!" They stuck their heads together to study the tiny human being in the photo. "It's even got finger nails already! And hair! It's only about ten and a half inches long, but is that cool or what?"

****

Naomi watched them pore over the book together as she made spaghetti and garlic bread. A few minutes later when Slade and Isabel came in, all four of them studied the book in rapt amazement. Naomi smiled as she bustled around her kitchen. It was going to be really fun to be a Grandma and watch all of this unfold.

Isabel came into the kitchen to make a salad. As she chopped she commented, "Those pictures are incredible! I had no idea it was like that!"

Naomi just smiled, thinking to herself. "You'll get an idea what it's like soon enough."

****

Slade and Isabel's wedding was just another ten days away. Kit had nothing dressy enough to wear and they didn't want to brave the snowy roads all the way to Salt Lake City, so Isabel and Kit got on-line to shop. She ended up with a sapphire blue dress that was almost floor length. It was a princess cut that was flattering, but would hide her tummy somewhat. She could no longer conceal her obvious pregnancy even under her big sweatshirts.

It was that evening she first felt her baby move inside her. She'd been sitting cross legged on the couch in the dark, quietly playing her guitar and singing when she felt it. At first it almost felt like her stomach growling, but then became unmistakably different. When she realized what was happening, her guitar fell silent and her mind raced. The fact of a small human being inside of her had never been so plainly manifest. She sat deep in thought with her hand over her belly.

Over the past month she'd gone from constant worry about how she would survive with an unplanned pregnancy and all that it entailed, to looking forward to a precious new life with anticipation, and with sweet feelings of peace. Rossen's encouragement to picture joy and in some deep sense, coming to terms with the reality of a child, combined to fill her heart with a mother's love and need to nurture and protect.

The next day, sitting in Rossen's office at his computer, she felt it again. She forgot what she was entering and put her hand to her tummy, hoping to feel more, this time thrilled with the life that was growing inside her own body. It was an incredible thing!

****

He heard the abrupt end to her keyboarding and glanced over at her, as she slipped a slender brown hand over her rounded stomach, wonder on her face. He understood she was feeling the baby inside and his own emotions somersaulted in reaction. He tried to look away and focus on his work, but the mother and child across from him owned his concentration.

He'd been doing better. He'd thought he had. They'd been working side by side most days comfortably, and she'd been a huge help to him through this project. What he'd thought was a lessening attraction, he now realized was just the fact that he wasn't frustrated about her when she was right there with him. Their friendship was so easy and comfortable he'd almost decided the overpowering interest would wane in time.

What he was feeling now, watching her with her baby, was in no way a waning emotion. He'd never imagined in his life this urge to take care of another person or persons. His need to care for them was a primal instinct that left him completely at a loss as to how to deal with it. And that frustration wasn't even dealing with the fact that when she was close or when he watched her, she truly did make it hard to breathe. He sat at his drafting table almost groaning to himself as he tried to tell himself over and over and over that she was only seventeen. Finally, unable to even start to get his emotions under control, he set his work aside, quietly got up and went to his truck and drove home.

****

Slade heard Rossen's truck pull into the garage and he was surprised. Rossen had left early that morning planning to be gone all day and possibly into the evening to try to finish some sticky government project he and Kit were working on. It was only late morning and Slade wondered what was up. He wandered through the house after a few minutes and saw Rossen through the glass windows in the pool house, furiously slamming away at the speed bag. He heard him out there for most of an hour, his speed intense at first, then eventually slowly winding down to an exhausted stop. He went down into his room and Slade heard the shower start up. Rossen never emerged from behind his closed door before Slade had to leave for an appointment.

****

Rossen had been working steadily beside her all morning, then somehow he was gone and Kit hadn't even heard him leave. Granted she had been a little preoccupied with the baby this morning, but he'd never just walked out without saying anything before. It wasn't like him.

She saved her work and wandered into the kitchen. Naomi and Rob were there with lunch prepared and Kit asked, "Did Rossen come this way?"

Naomi shook her head. "I thought he was in his office with you. Have you lost him?"

Kit smiled. "I have. One minute he was there working and the next he was gone without a word."

Naomi looked puzzled. "Really? That's weird. That doesn't sound like Rossen." She placed chicken pot pies on the table, and Rob walked back into the hall and up and down the stairwell calling for him. Finally, Naomi called his cell phone but there was no answer. She came back in and sat next to Kit as Rob asked a blessing on the food.

His empty place at the table worried Kit through the whole meal. Had she somehow offended him this morning while they worked?

Nobody saw Rossen for the rest of the day. Kit didn't think he'd even shown up to help feed that afternoon and she went to bed with a troubled heart.

Late in the night she was awakened and it took her a few minutes to realize that what she was hearing was the sound of the printer in Rossen's office printing page after page. This was stranger than ever. She'd never known him to work at night. She got up and slipped a robe over her night gown and went in, wondering what was wrong.

****

She was standing quietly at the door when he

noticed her. She was wearing a white nightgown with a matching robe over it, belted neatly over her tummy in front. Small brown feet peeped out below. She somehow seemed taller in the floor length gown. She was still obviously sleepy and her dark hair was tousled around her wide blue eyes as she watched him in silence.

Neither of them spoke for a few seconds after he saw her. Their eyes locked and held momentarily. When he broke the gaze to look back at his papers, she asked him in a soft voice, "Are you okay?"

He was slow to reply and his voice almost sounded sad when he answered, "Yeah, I'm okay. I just have to get this whole thing finished and postmarked by tomorrow. I'm sorry I woke you."

She didn't move, just continued to watch him from the doorway. At length she asked, "Did I make a mistake on something yesterday?"

He looked up at her questioning, "No, of course not. Your work has been perfect. Your mind is like a machine. Why do you ask?" She just shrugged and continued to watch quietly.

Eventually she questioned again. "Did I do something to offend you, then?"

He got up from his desk and came to her at the door, his voice gentle as he spoke, "You didn't do anything to offend me yesterday." He ran a strong, brown hand through his hair with a sigh. "I just have a lot on my mind." He brushed her dark hair back from her shoulder. "You're tired. Take the two of you back to bed and get some rest. I'll try to be quieter. I'm about through printing." He squeezed her shoulder and nudged her toward the door as their eyes locked again. Turning to go, she raised her right hand to gently touch his cheek for an instant. "Good night."

****

She didn't go back to bed immediately. He could hear her in the darkened great room playing her guitar so softly it almost seemed like his imagination. The music, sweet and mellow, was soothing to his troubled mind. At last, she switched over to some old James Taylor songs and sang along, the lyrics adding to the web of calm she was weaving in his heart. When the guitar finally fell silent and he knew she was gone, he was able to return to his task with a clear head, knowing somehow he'd get through this. He had no idea how it would work out, but her music left him at peace as he worked through the night.

****

The next morning, Naomi found him asleep on the sofa in the great room, one arm draped over the edge to rest on Kit's guitar on the floor below. She gently covered him with a throw and decided they'd eat cold cereal this morning so she didn't wake him cooking.

When Kit came in a few minutes later, she had great dark circles under her eyes and Naomi encouraged her to go back to bed after she ate. She gratefully accepted and stopped next to the couch to look down at him sleeping on the way out. She asked Naomi, "Did you ever find out what's going on with him?"

Naomi shook her head. "No, I haven't talked to him." But as Kit walked away, Naomi knew it had to have something to do with the tall, dark haired, seventeen year old beauty who returned to bed. She sighed as she went about her morning. His obvious inner turmoil hurt her heart. She wished she knew how to help him get through whatever was up, but she still was unsure of what to do or say. She decided to see if Rob would take her to the temple when the stock was fed. Maybe she'd find some answers there.

****

Kit had been working with her clay almost everyday and she'd come to the end of the three bags within less than two weeks. Her next prenatal appointment was two days away and she had set up an appointment with Mr. Perkins for the same day. She stood in the craft room looking at the ten or twelve small figurines she'd crafted over the last days, wishing she'd brought four bags instead of just three. Finally, she decided to rework clay from a few of the pieces she liked the least and went in search of a five gallon bucket. She found one in an equipment shed and brought it back to the craft room, which she now thought of as her studio, and filled it partially full of water. She was just starting to put the few pieces down into the water when Isabel walked in.

"Kit. Your dress just came." Isabel looked around the room at the free form sculptures sitting on various countertops. "Wow! These are really good! Did you do all these?"

She turned toward Kit and realized she was breaking one of the pieces and dropping the fragments into the bucket of water, and nearly shouted, "Kit! What are you doing?" Her voice held a note of almost panic. "Why are you destroying them? They're magnificent!"

Rossen and Naomi showed up at the door to see what was going on, as Kit answered, "I'm out of clay and was just going to break a few down to rework the clay. I'll make more once it's rehydrated again.

Rossen and Naomi began to walk around the room in wonder, with Isabel right behind them. They looked in silence until finally Naomi whispered, "Oh my." Kit was almost a bit nervous at their reaction until Naomi turned to her with tears in her eyes and said, "You have an incredible gift."

Rossen went over to look down into the bucket with the three works that had already started to dissolve in the water. He looked up with something unfathomable in his eyes.

Isabel broke in, "Don't destroy any more. We'll get you some more clay."

Kit was openly surprised at their reaction. "I can't just keep everything. I'd soon be buried. Reworking the clay let's me stay occupied without ten gazillion pieces piling up."

Isabel looked her in the face and answered, "Kit. I don't think you understand. This is more than a high school art class. Your work is deeply moving. These pieces are evocative and profound. They're not something that should be recycled for the sake of space or clay. They need to be finished and placed in a gallery so others can enjoy them and take them home to feel the same deep emotion we've felt here this afternoon. It's almost a responsibility. When you have a gift like this, you can't not share it. Do you understand what I'm trying to say?"

Kit started to nod, but it came across as a noncommittal nod, slash shake.

Isabel tried again, "Do you ever do anything larger? These would be incredible slightly larger. And how do you complete them? I can't wait to see them finished! I have a dear friend in California who is an art connoisseur. I can't wait until he sees your work! He's going to love it!"

Naomi and Rossen slipped back out the door while they talked. He still hadn't said a word and Kit glanced at his back as he disappeared, wondering what he was thinking. It mattered a great deal to her. She valued his opinion more than anyone's. It was probably foolish, but it was a fact.

Jaclyn M. Hawkes

Chapter 7

Two days later Naomi got a phone call in the morning as she and Kit were getting ready to go in to her prenatal appointment. One of their neighbors was having a minor emergency and wondered if Naomi could help her out for awhile. Naomi immediately asked Isabel if she could take Kit in, but she had an appointment that morning with the caterer for her wedding.

It was Rossen who ended up taking her in and he decided not to stress about being with her for this one day and was thoroughly enjoying her company. He could tell she was nervous again as they drove and she fidgeted nonstop.

He finally asked her, "Was your last appointment that bad? You look like you're heading to the principal's office." He grinned across the truck at her.

She smiled back self-consciously. "No. It wasn't bad at all actually, but today she scheduled an ultrasound. That's what I'm afraid of. I wish I knew what it would be like." She continued to pick at her cast. "I have no idea how painful or dangerous it will be."

He pulled the truck off the gravel road onto the paved highway and turned south. "The only ultrasound

I've seen was on Slade's liver last summer, but it didn't seem too bad to me. The girl put some gel on his skin and then pushed what looked like a smooth microphone around on it. I don't think he felt a thing."

She turned to him. "You mean this isn't the long needle into my stomach thing?" She shuddered as she asked.

Sheesh. No wonder she was nervous. "No. I don't think there are any needles involved. You don't need to worry at all." He tried to reassure her, but she still seemed uptight all the way to the waiting room. When they called her name, she almost jumped and he decided he'd go with her if they'd let him.

He stood and offered her a hand to help her to her feet and asked, "Can I go back with you?"

She nodded almost woodenly and said, "Yes, please." Her hand was like ice and he kept hold of it, trying to reassure her as they followed the tech.

She showed Kit to a changing room and gave her a hospital gown to change into. She came back out momentarily and they went into a darkened room where she instructed Kit to lie on her back on the table. As she placed pillows under Kit's knees to support her back, Rossen felt compelled to explain. "I'm not her husband. Just a friend, but she's a little nervous. Can I stay with her?"

"Sure. Why not? Are you the father?"

Rossen could feel himself blush and was grateful for the dim lighting. "No, just a friend friend. More like the baby's uncle, sort of."

The tech smiled as he stammered and said, "In that case, I'll be careful to be discreet." He breathed a sigh of relief.

He stood beside Kit's head and she gripped his hand tightly in hers. Now he was nervous too.

The tech discreetly put a folded blanket under Kit's gown and over her from the waist down, then pushed the gown up to expose her stomach. She pushed the blanket down slightly to reveal the smooth round bulge of the baby and Rossen swallowed hard. She proceeded to squeeze a bottle of gel over Kit's brown skin. He felt torn about whether he should look away or watch the procedure. Telling himself she was covered more than a bathing suit, he watched in fascination.

The tech turned on her computer, put the rounded transmitter into the gel and slid it over and around Kit's tummy trying to figure out where the baby was and in what position. Rossen alternated between watching what she was doing to Kit's belly and watching the monitor.

****

Kit alternated between watching the monitor and watching Rossen. She was surprised that he'd come in with her, but very grateful. Holding his hand helped her to push her fears back so she could focus on what was going on. It didn't hurt after all.

They were all three watching the monitor when the scrambled image cleared to distinctly become the form of a baby. Kit heard Rossen gasp above her, but was too fascinated to look away.

They could see its moving arms and legs and it turned its head slightly. They could even see its face. The tiny features showed up clearly. The tech was pushing buttons and sliding the transmitter and its miniature heart appeared in the image, its beat clear and rhythmic.

Kit laughed and Rossen was awestruck as the tiny fetus wiggled and floated completely upside down and then distinctly put its tiny thumb in its mouth. Rossen barely breathed, "No way!"

The tech smiled as she printed a still photo of the baby sucking it's thumb. "The more advanced our equipment gets, the more obvious it is that they have a personality even this early." She took a few more measurements and asked, "Do you want to find out if it's a boy or a girl this morning?"

Kit and Rossen turned to look at each other. She said, "No." at the same instant he said, "Yes."

The tech smiled again and leaned into Rossen to whisper something in his ear. He couldn't help the huge smile that spread across his face.

When she was finished with her exam, the tech sent them on their way. "Everything looks good. I'll get this report sent to your doctor. You look like you're on track for twenty three weeks along."

On the way out to the truck, he took her hand again on the icy walk and squeezed. "That was awesome! I'm so glad my mom and Isabel couldn't come! Those images were unreal! It was such a little person!"

His voice was happy and filled with enthusiasm and Kit was relieved. She'd seen his face when the ultrasound technician uncovered her tummy and what she saw there made her pulse jump at the same time she began to worry. Every time she saw that he felt something for her, she knew soon thereafter he'd pull away from her hard. She couldn't exactly name the emotion she'd seen on his face, but she knew without a doubt that he cared deeply for her, so she was glad that for once he wasn't trying to push her away.

She smiled shyly. "You are never going to be able to keep its gender a secret. I'll bet I know within the week.

He laughed and pulled her into a hug as he opened her truck door. "Never!"

Their next stop was Dr. Sundquist's to have her arm checked and her cast redone. When he finished cutting it off, she was somewhat taken aback to see the three pins sticking out of her elbow. It was almost gruesome, but it felt fine. He declared everything looking perfect and put another one on and they set off for the art teacher's.

Mr. Perkins was thrilled with her work. He thought they were every bit as good as Isabel had said and seconded her recommendation not to destroy any more.

They talked finishes and glazes, and she asked him about a special treatment she'd read about on the internet, "Are you familiar with a process called Raku?"

"Absolutely." He motioned them to follow him into another room. "That would actually be ideal for you to use on your work, because it doesn't require a commercial kiln, so you could finish the final glaze right at the ranch. It can be fired in metal garbage cans filled with straw and an accelerant. You'd still have to bring in the green ware for the initial firing, but the rest you could do on site."

He showed them a collection of pieces. "These are some samples of Raku finishes." They were varied in colors and even sometimes in texture. The colors ran from cream to black with the vast majority being blues and purples. Most of it was a mottled metallic that at times looked crackled and sometimes even iridescent. It was striking and was exactly what she had in mind. She loved it!

"It's perfect!" Her blue eyes were intense as she turned to her teacher. "How can I learn to do it?"

"I'll take these in with me tomorrow and load them in the kiln. Could you come in to the school, say in a week, and I'll show you and my school classes how it's done at the same time?"

They finalized arrangements and Kit and Rossen loaded up on clay and headed home. She felt almost tired from the emotions she'd gone through this day. She glanced at Rossen, wondering what he was thinking so quietly on his side of the truck.

He looked over at her and gave a tired smile, and Kit thought to herself, *There he goes.* She could almost feel him distance himself from her.

Chapter 8

After Rossen's initial reaction when Kit had asked about being baptized, she'd backed off and hadn't said anything more, but she continued to go to church every week with the family. And privately, known only to Naomi, she had continued to study on her own. One day the bishop asked her about having the missionaries come and teach her, but she declined, thinking it would somehow strain her and Rossen's relationship again.

She almost quit going to church altogether when she overheard two women in the restroom there talking about her. One was saying something about what Rossen had been doing while he was away rodeoing and then gave a nasty laugh about bringing home a pregnant girl. Kit was horrified! Only the other woman's retort kept her from leaving the building in tears.

The other woman replied, "Gladys, don't you dare insinuate what you are! We've known Rossen all his life and a more honorable man never lived. Don't stand there and insult him to me. I won't have it!" Kit heard the women leave the room, but it took several minutes for her to gain enough composure to walk out into the hall.

She struggled through the rest of the meetings woodenly and when they got home, only the threat of nausea forced her to eat lunch before going to her room. She lay on her bed all afternoon, alternately crying and worrying, and when she came out for dinner she had almost nothing to add to the conversation over the meal. She kept telling herself she'd been through a lot worse than this and that it was no big deal. She would just have to be sure to be discreet when she was in public. But she was much quieter over the next few days, and on Friday evening, the night of Slade and Isabel's wedding, she didn't really feel up to going at all. She had to drag herself into her room to dress in the exquisite sapphire dress with the princess cut. They'd brought in a stylist and she went from Isabel, to Joey, to Naomi and then to Kit, creating hairstyles for this momentous occasion.

Kit had never attended a wedding and had no idea how to behave or what was expected of her, but she did understand that at the reception that evening there would be a huge number of people who were the Rocklands', Slade's and Isabel's friends. After the woman's comments at church Sunday, Kit didn't want to be seen anywhere that she could tarnish this great family's reputation.

Even the look on Rossen's face, as she descended the stairs in her dress and an up-do of cascading curls studded with sparkling blue stone pins, couldn't quell the ache in her heart.

She loved Slade and Isabel, and she was happy

for them, but her smile hid a deep sadness as she discreetly slipped out the door of the reception room when it was time for the family photos. Outside, she found herself in a darkened hall and stood near a glass door to look out at the glittering cold stars above. She remained away most of the evening, aware that less tongues would wag concerning her and the Rocklands if she was out of sight.

At length, she found her way up a back stair to the landing Isabel had descended from to approach her groom and the others. Kit seated herself near the top step where the lights had been dimmed over the spiral staircase, and she watched the celebration from there. The whole family was wearing finery for the occasion and Rossen was more handsome than ever in a black tuxedo with a sapphire tie and cummerbund. She'd never actually been where there were tuxes and evening gowns and it would have been fun if she hadn't been worried about protecting this family from gossip.

Eventually the evening wore down and they cut the wedding cake and threw a sacrificial bouquet. After the newlyweds slipped out to leave on their honeymoon, the guests began to leave. The family started to pack gifts out to the vehicles and gather up odds and ends that had to be taken care of. Kit slipped in beside Cooper to help carry packages with a smile pasted on to pretend like she had been a happy party goer the whole night. An hour later, riding home in the truck with Rossen, Cooper, Joey and Sean, she felt she'd pulled it off. She finally let her guard down some in the darkened cab and unconsciously released a deep, soft sigh.

****

Riding beside her, Rossen knew there was something terribly wrong, and had been for days, but he sure didn't know what. Several times since she had come out for dinner Sunday evening with deep, sad eyes, he'd tried to encourage her to talk, but so far she hadn't opened up even a crack. She hadn't even said anything to Naomi, which worried Rossen all the more.

At home he helped her out of the truck and into the house, all the while trying to catch her eye, but she never once looked up before slipping into her room to quietly close the door.

After several minutes she came out in search of Naomi or Joey, but they'd both gone to Slade's to unload gifts, so she hesitantly asked Rossen, "Would you mind helping me with my zipper? I've tried and tried and can't manage it."

He followed her back to her door in silence, but before starting to unzip her, he tipped up her chin to look into her eyes. "I'm a good listener. Are you ever going to tell me your troubles?" His blue eyes searched hers for a long moment, watching them wash with tears, but she only gave a miniscule negative nod and turned her back to him.

He unzipped her dress and watched her step away and close her door, feeling lonelier than he ever could have imagined. He climbed back into his truck and drove up the road to Slade's, passing two truckloads of his family, before he pulled into a house now dark and quiet and empty. It was just the way his heart felt tonight. He'd been careful to keep his distance for weeks, sometimes consciously pushing away from her and apparently it had worked well. He couldn't have felt more distant from her if she'd been in China.

He stepped into the house, pulling off his tie to toss it over a chair, as he walked through the lonely, dark silence. He went to stand before the wall of windows and stare out at the frozen river bottom below. The myriad of stars glittering white in the night sky reminded him of the way her hair had glittered and sparkled as she'd come down the stairs tonight. Her eyes had glittered like that too, with tears, just before she'd turned her back on him and stepped away.

He felt like he should pray, but for what? What he really wanted, he knew wasn't right to ask, so he ended up just standing there not praying at all, feeling a deep, slow anger that was easier to deal with than a trampled heart.

He stood there like that until he finally backed up to sit in a recliner. Over the next several hours he took stock of his life, where he'd been, and where he was headed. Looking back, he didn't know what he'd have done differently, and looking ahead simply made him tired. He knew he needed to get out of his home office to meet some girls and date, but to be honest; he only wanted to be with Kit. That led him around in the same dismal circle to the reality of her youth and his heart felt like it was in a trash compactor.

Eventually his exhaustion won out to ease his body into oblivion for a few peaceful hours.

He woke up stiff and irritable and stayed and ate cold cereal alone, rather than drive up home and have an undoubtedly good breakfast with the rest of his family.

He was still in his wrinkled tux, hunched over a bowl of Wheaties when his mom came in the door.

She poured herself a bowl and sat beside him. They ate in silence for awhile, the only sound the crunch of the cereal and the clink of their spoons against the dishes.

Finally, he asked, "Is Kit any better this morning?"

She finished chewing her bite and swallowed. "She's okay, I think. Unless you look into her eyes."

After another bite or two she glanced over at him. "She looks better than you. She's at least trying to fake happy. You just look ticked. If you don't mind my saying so." She smiled sweetly.

"I am ticked. That's exactly what I am. My whole life I've tried to do what I've been asked and be a good example. I followed the plan to the letter. Group date, single date, mission, college—the whole bit. Where has it gotten me?" He toyed with his spoon. "I had a shoe box full of women's numbers just like Slade's that Isabel gave the guys at Christmas. I've turned down a gob of trashy women over the last three years rodeoing." He pushed his bowl aside roughly. "Listen to me. I sound like a pouty baby.

"Do you know what I spent half of last night doing? Trying to talk myself into wanting to go meet girls." His voice was deeply bitter. "I've tried, Mom. I've honestly tried to do what I thought I should. Now I feel like I've been cheated for being a good Samaritan. Cursed by a sweet, beautiful, smart, cruel joke. I never thought I'd be mad at God, but I think I am. He's in control. He could've helped me. You're right. I am ticked. Royally ticked!"

He smiled ruefully and finished humbly, "So now I feel ticked, and guilty for feeling ticked."

Naomi still had no answers and she placed her hand over his in silence.

Rossen's voice softened, "She could have used a friend these last few days, but I've spent so much time trying to keep her at arms' length that she won't even talk to me. She seems more alone now than when we first picked her up. And I can't blame her. I feel like Jekyll and Hyde. I catch myself enjoying her company, or noticing how she looks, or how smart she is, then I feel instant remorse, and fall all over myself trying to keep my distance. It's killing me, and it's not working anyway. I love her more than ever. I can't even imagine what my moods are doing to her."

He stood to walk to the window again. Finally he turned. "Well?"

"Well, what?"

"Come on, Mom. You're the parent. Where's the wise counsel? The 'mother knows everything' solution? I could really use one about now."

Naomi was slow to reply, "I don't know how to make you not love her, Rossen. She's very loveable. And I have no idea how to make you want to go out and date. I'm sorry to let you down. But I can tell you not to give up on God. It's not that He's not helping you right now. It's just that we don't understand His plan at the moment. I think He understands your anger. What He won't understand, is if you don't trust Him through it. He's never failed you. He's not going to start now, even though it feels like it.

"I wouldn't have thought you'd need a refiner's fire, but what do I know? Maybe it's as simple as choosing you because you're the only man strong enough to be selfless and resist her for her own good. That's my theory. No other man could be around her and realize how beautiful, and smart, and talented she is, and still allow her to finish growing up. God knew she needed your goodness, and self control, and strength to give her the time and freedom she needs to reach her full potential."

A shadow of Rossen's true smile showed up. "Now you're really making me feel like a shmuck."

She laughed. "That's what you get when you ask for mothers to know everything."

She walked over and embraced him. "Now that we've got the answers to the universe figured out, help me figure out what happened to Kit at church. I've been thinking about it, and I'm sure that's when this all started."

He considered this at length and decided she was

right. It had been at church. "Great! Leave it to us Christians to thrash her before she even has a chance to figure the gospel out."

Naomi mused, "Yes and no. Somebody has done something to hurt her, but you're deluding yourself if you think she hasn't got it figured out. She's done an unbelievable amount of research you have no idea about, and she's got a photographic memory. I daresay if it's something you can pick up from a book, or a website, she understands it. She just doesn't feel like she can let on, because it kind of freaks you out. Those are her words, by the way."

Rossen turned to stare at his mother. He mentally started to squirm when he remembered hassling Kit about fruit those weeks before. She hadn't said a word to him about the church since, and he'd assumed he'd been right about her jumping the gun knowing what she was getting into. It took him a minute or two of sorting through various conversations, before his mom's reference to a photographic memory clicked in. She must have seen the lights come on in his head, as he thought back over the past weeks of working beside Kit in his office.

"Holy cow!" His voice held a note of reverence.

Naomi cautioned, "And don't you make her feel self-conscious about it. She already feels she needs to hide it to fit into society. Don't make her think she can't be herself around you. Her self-esteem doesn't need any more trashing."

"Mother, it's a gift, not a flaw. Give me a little

credit."

She put her bowl and spoon in the dishwasher and picked up her car keys. "I give you more credit than you'll ever know. Now change out of that smelly tux and come home and help Kit. She needs you." She hugged him and walked out the door.

As the latch clicked behind her, he repeated, "Smelly tux . . . What's she . . . " He raised his arm. "Smelly tux."

Rossen showered, put on a turtleneck and ski sweater and by the time he was ready to go, he was also ready to hit his knees and pray. A part of his prayer was a big thank you for his wonderful mother who was willing to leave the ninety and nine so to speak and go in search of him, her lost sheep, and smooth out all his wrinkles. He smiled remembering her sitting beside him eating Wheaties. She hated Wheaties.

The balance of his prayer was devoted to asking forgiveness for his discouragement and asking for wisdom and peace in his relationship with Kit.

He got off his knees not knowing what he should do, but having faith that the Spirit would guide him. One thing he felt for sure was that he should be more emotionally honest. At least with himself, if not her. He needed to remember that his goal was not to not fall in love with her, but to not do things that would keep her from spreading her wings. He was already in love with her, so that was a moot point.

On his way to the truck he took a load of his stuff, wishing he'd finished building the house he'd designed, and had had drawn up and engineered. He'd bought the ground from his dad to build it on years ago, but had felt like having all three of him, Slade and Sean live in their own houses by themselves, was overkill, and had put off building. Slade and Isabel had both encouraged him to stay with them, but he intended to be completely moved out by the time they returned next week anyway. They needed to have their home to themselves. He could go stay with Sean in his house, but opted instead for his old room in the basement of his parents', telling himself it made more sense to be near his office.

He came into the house out of the garage, his arms full, just in time to tell the departing college bunch goodbye. They joked and teased and slammed out the door and as he began to load his things into his old room, he felt like he'd walked through a brisk wind.

He set his stuff down and went straight upstairs to his dad's office to find Kit. She wasn't there, so he went up to look in her studio.

He found her there so engrossed in her clay she didn't even hear him come in. He leaned against a counter and folded his arms, fascinated at watching her work. She'd pulled her hair up into a haphazard knot on top of her head and was wearing an old button down he recognized from college over her clothes. It was huge on her and even though she'd rolled the sleeves up several times, it still hung past her elbows.

She'd covered her cast with a rubber glove she'd cut the fingers out of. He wondered why she didn't just work in full gloves, but as he watched, he realized what she was doing was all tactile. Her small brown hands were covered in the slick clay and she pushed and smoothed with an almost sensual touch. Her dark head would bend over her work and then rise to move around to another angle. Strands of loose hair slipped across her lips and this time when he thought about her mouth, he just let the thought be, instead of shying away like a frightened colt. Immediately, he was more comfortable with her and knew his idea to be emotionally honest was right.

He heard himself take a deep breath and she abruptly turned to look in his direction, her blue eyes wide.

"Oh, Rossen! You scared me!" She went to put her hand to her chest, but then looked at them and thought better of it. "What are you doing here?"

At that moment he decided to be forthright and see how it went. "I've made up my mind to haunt you until you talk to me about whatever it was that happened to you in church."

Her eyes flew to his, and for just a split second, he thought she was going to tell him, but then the sadness shuttered her eyes and she turned back to her clay.

She didn't look up as she asked, "Oh you have? What makes you think something happened to me at church?"

"Hmm. An educated guess maybe." He could have said the fact that she hadn't smiled in a week, but he didn't.

He actually got a break much sooner than he thought he would, when he suggested they get out of the house and go have some lunch in town somewhere. He was hoping simply to have enough privacy to be able to really talk, but he began to get the picture when she looked squarely at him for a moment as if trying to read his mind, and then commented, "I don't know if that's such a good idea." She glanced up at him again. "Being seen with me in public might not be very good for your reputation."

She went back to focusing on the clay under her hands, while the wheels in his head began to turn. Someone at church had insinuated, or possibly worse, something about her that could involve his reputation. Her line of thinking was pretty transparent and a face popped into his head as he tried to picture what might have occurred.

"How about if you let me worry about my reputation?"

"Fine, but I'll help." They were both silent for several minutes while she smoothed the clay. Then she abruptly smashed the figure she was working on. She pushed the clay back into a ball and began kneading it under her palms like bread dough, adding drops of water occasionally from a nearby sponge.

He asked, "Are you turning me down flat?"

She slapped the clay against the table. "Yup." She sounded okay, but she brushed at a tear with the back of a clay covered hand and a second later another one dropped and splashed across the now smooth round lump of clay on the table.

He took two long steps over to her and almost pushed himself between her and the table. "Why?" He took her chin gently in his fingers to raise her face to look at him. He repeated his question. "Why?"

She pulled away and stepped around him to pick up the clay. "It's probably just not the best idea. That's all." She carefully wrapped the clay in a couple of layers of plastic and set it aside with the other bags. Then she pulled several wet wipes out of a nearby carton and proceeded to painstakingly clean the table top and her hands.

When she finally quit scrubbing, she went to a bottle of hand lotion and began to rub a generous amount into her hands. He pulled another wipe from the carton, tipped her chin up again and began to gently remove the clay smudge from where she had wiped at a tear with the back of her hand.

"So, then what are you going to do now?" He leaned against the counter again.

She hesitated before she asked, "Why?"

He smiled a lazy smile as he folded his arms across his chest. "Well, if you won't go to lunch with me, I was just wondering where I need to go next to continue to haunt you."

She took his big shirt off and folded it nervously. "I'm not sure, actually. I should be doing my English, but I wasn't much in the mood for it earlier. What I'd like to do is go outside, but I get so cold here. I guess I'll just go see what your mom needs help with this morning. We were going to take Isabel's stuff over to Slade's for her before they get back."

"We have more than a week, but I can help you. Where did you not get so cold? Where did you come from?" He'd wondered that for six weeks now.

She looked down as she answered, "Arizona. Just west of Tucson, near the Tohono O'odham Nation. But actually I got cold there too, sometimes at night. I think it's hard to stay warm when you're too skinny."

He smiled at her. "But you're not too skinny now. You look just right!"

She looked somewhat self-conscious. "I've gained thirty-five pounds since I've been here."

He laughed. "Really? But you needed it. And you'll probably do it again, before it gets here." He nodded at her tummy. "I've gotten really good at calling it an it. Have you noticed?"

She gave him a hint of a smile and he felt like he'd won a prize. "I have noticed. When you smiled at the doctor's office, I figured it must be the girl you pictured, but now I'm beginning to wonder."

"I'm not letting the cat out of the bag. You'll see. He'll be two weeks old before you'll hear anything out of my mouth!"

Changing the subject he asked, "Do you like to ride horses? I have an idea."

"I don't know. I've never tried."

"Well, it's time you tried. We'll go bareback. It's much warmer that way in winter. And I'll put you on our sweetest old plug and ride behind you. You'll love it! It's the best way to enjoy the outdoors in the winter."

Naomi was skeptical when he announced his intentions and said, "Rossen, she's five months along. And she has no snow pants."

He hugged his mother and reassured her. "We'll take Tessie and walk and stay on the plowed. And I'll find something to bundle her up with. She'll be fine. We'll be careful. I promise."

They dug through the winter gear until they found a pair of Rob's ski pants that would fit over her tummy. They had to roll them up, but they'd keep her warm. He insisted she wear a turtleneck and fleece and hat and neck gator under her parka, and even Naomi commented, "I imagine she'll be warm all right."

She cautioned again as they went out the door, "You be careful with her." Turning to Kit she said, "If you're uncomfortable at all, make him bring you straight in."

Twenty minutes later Kit was far from uncomfortable. He'd helped her up onto a mountain of a horse and then gotten on behind her. He was right. The body heat of the horse seeped through their clothes and with him against her back, she was fine. He had both arms around her holding the reins and she'd pretty much decided that riding horses was her new favorite pastime.

She didn't have to look at him, and the close physical contact was comfortable and the conversation flowed.

****

She didn't know it, but that's exactly the reason he'd chosen to come. He'd been hoping she would open up to him, and she had. Just not about what had gone on at church.

She fit perfectly in his arms in front of him and he could smell her hair as it brushed against his chin. He realized this wasn't going to help his heart later, but he didn't even care. He was enjoying this ride immensely and he'd worry later.

The weather was perfect. The winter sun was finally moving north again and the wooly livestock were basking in it everywhere they went. He took her on a gentle circuit up the valley on the route they kept plowed for the animals, and from the top of a ridge they could see down into Slade's valley that the river wound through.

They rode for an hour, during which he felt they'd gone far in renewing their friendship, but she still hadn't opened up about how she'd been offended, so on the way back he asked her right out.

"Kit, what did someone say to you at church that made you worry about my reputation?" He didn't think she could sidestep the question, but he assumed she'd try and he was right.

After a second she asked mildly, "What do you mean?"

He chuckled in her ear. "Nice try. You know exactly what I mean. Answer the question."

"Why does it matter?"

He breathed in against her hair. "Well, since you

haven't cracked a smile since then, I'd say it really matters." She didn't answer right away, and he continued, "And if I ventured to guess, I'd say that come Sunday morning, you're going to try to stay home in some valiant attempt to defend my honor. Am I right?"

She still didn't answer and he felt her sigh as she leaned against him. It was a gesture of sadness and defeat, and it tore at his heart.

Finally, she asked, "Do you remember when you were talking to me about this baby and you said 'it is what it is'?"

"Yeah. Why?"

"Well, you were right. It is what it is. And I am what I am. An unwed, very pregnant girl you brought home from the rodeo circuit. Unfortunately, human beings, being the humans they are, some of them aren't going to concern themselves with anything more than those couple of facts.

"You're a good man, Rossen. Too good to let a minor thing like the church attendance of a non-member throw your moral integrity into question. It's not some valiant attempt to defend your honor. It's the right thing to do."

They rode in silence for several minutes.

Finally Rossen asked, "What about taking the sacrament? What about meeting together often, and regular attendance so you can be baptized, and eventually get a temple recommend? What about her." He placed his hand on Kit's belly for just a moment. "And, what about Kit?"

She sighed before she answered, "Kit's tough." He could hear some deep emotion in her voice that made him sad as she added, "Someday I'll deal with all those things, when it won't hurt the people who have been so good to me."

They rode the rest of the way quietly. Rossen felt like he'd won the battle and lost the war. His heart was heavy, but he had to admire her character.

The horse took a misstep in the crusty snow and his arm tightened around her waist above the baby, and he just left it there.

Back at the barns, as he slid from the horse's back, then helped her to the ground, he was more at a loss as to how to handle this girl than ever.

She stood between him and the big horse and looked up at him. "Thank you for taking me. You're right. That is the best way to enjoy the out-of-doors in winter. I loved it. Maybe we could go again sometime." She hesitated for a second. "And thanks for trying to change the world, Rossen. You can't do it, but thanks for trying."

****

When Sunday rolled around, Kit had actually come down with a cold and it was obvious she wasn't faking. Naomi offered to stay with her, but she declined and they left without her. Rossen's blue eyes held hers for what seemed like days before he shut the door into the garage.

She drank some orange juice, wishing she knew if a cold pill would harm her baby, and then armed with a box of tissue, went back to bed.

An hour and a half later there was a quiet knock on her door and Rossen poked his head in. "Are you up to some company? There's someone here to see you."

She dragged herself out of bed, slipped on a robe and followed him out, wondering what was going on.

Seated on the couch in the great room was a woman Kit remembered seeing at church. Rossen made introductions. "Kit, this is Gladys Maggleby from our ward. Gladys, this is Kit Star. She's an official member of our family now. I'll leave you two to talk. Excuse me." Kit's bleary eyes followed his back out, feeling like she'd been left with the executioner.

The two women fidgeted a moment in silence, then Gladys looked up at Kit with troubled eyes and started, "I guess I should tell you why I'm here. It's a bit of a long story, so please forgive me.

"Today in gospel doctrine class, the bishop talked for a few minutes before the class got started. He said he had a problem he needed some help with. He told us a little bit about you and even some personal stuff like where they found you and who the father of your baby was. I hope it's okay I tell you that." She hesitated, then continued, "Then he told us how you've been studying and were about ready to be baptized, but had decided to quit coming to church because you didn't want to give Rossen a bad name. Rossen had told him someone at church had insinuated something about Rossen being the father."

She looked down and back up with tears in her

eyes. "I'm so sorry. I'm such a terrible person. The bishop asked if whoever had done that would please apologize and make it right, so you'd come back. He reminded us all that this was the gospel of Jesus Christ, and I've never felt worse in my life."

She dug in her purse and pulled out a wadded tissue, then went on, "I'm so terrible. My husband knew it had to be me and turned and looked right at me." Gladys began to blubber in earnest. Kit would have smiled at the poor woman, but she didn't feel good enough to.

The older woman sniffled and blew her nose loudly. "Please forgive me. Maybe this can be a big lesson for me and I'll quit gossiping forever. Anyway, please know that our ward welcomes you. They're such good people. They'll love you no matter who the father is. That's what the bishop was saying to us. That Jesus loves us all no matter what the circumstances, and that we shouldn't be judgmental. He's right, and I was wrong, and I'll just die if you don't get baptized because of me. So please come back. I'll understand if you can't like me, but come back to the others in the ward. They're all much better Christians than me, obviously."

Kit sneezed violently and Gladys jumped. She stood up. "I can see you're sick. I'd better let you get back to bed. Thank you for listening to a silly old woman, and once again, I'm sorry. Please come back."

She got up and took her purse and wadded tissue, and saw herself out, while Kit sat on the couch wondering what had just happened.

Rossen came in with a bowl of cold cereal and a silly grin. He sat beside her on the couch and crunched away happily. Kit smiled even as she sniffled. "You're pretty pleased with yourself, aren't you?"

He nodded his head as he chewed. "Yes I am. Your personal salvation is a rather big deal to me. You should know that by now." He continued to eat with gusto.

She shook her head and laughed. "She said her husband turned and looked right at her. Poor woman."

Rossen chuckled. "Oh, I think she's had it coming for years now. I knew who'd done it. I just didn't know what she'd said."

"Did you really tell your whole ward I'm ready to be baptized?"

"Yes. Aren't you?" He was looking into her eyes.

"Well, yeah. But you didn't know that."

He gave her a wicked grin. "How do you know what I know?"

She laughed and waved a tissue at him. "Oh, you're easy! I can read you like a book."

"Really?" It was a serious question.

She laughed again at his apprehension. "Yeah, really."

He considered this for a moment, watching her. He was probably wondering if she meant it. She did. He was actually a pretty easy read, all in all. She smiled at his look and he commented on it, "You haven't smiled for days, you know."

She dropped her eyes. "Yeah, well. Beginning to

know God and being part of a real family are rather extremely gargantuan blessings in my life. The thought of turning away was pretty bleak."

"Then you're not mad?"

She shook her head. "No one on earth could be mad at you, Rossen Rockland. You're too dang nice a guy."

"Oh, good. I was kind of worried."

"But you did tell me it was a girl over this whole deal."

"I did? No way! When?"

"The other day on our ride."

His face fell. "I did? Aw, I'm sorry. If I tried to tell you it was a boy again, could I mix you up?"

She smiled quietly and shook her head, thinking of how she'd felt when he put his hand on her stomach. "It'd never work."

Jaclyn M. Hawkes

Chapter 9

February came and went in what felt like seconds. Rossen took her in to have her cast redone again, and they sedated her and took the pins out. She finished her math and started on her second English credit and Rossen took her in to watch how the Raku process was done. He agreed it would be easy to set up at home and committed to start helping her do it the very next day. On the way home, he put her behind the wheel once they were off the paved highway and began to teach her to drive. She continued to gain weight and was beginning to feel truly big and ungraceful. At times it was a struggle to get out of a chair.

The winter sun had begun to take its toll on the south faces and by the time March blew in, there were new colts in Ruger and Marti's barn and slushy holes melted into the snow pack on the gravel roads.

The herds of cattle began to calve in earnest and the family and the hands were kept busy twenty four seven. Every few days there would be a calf that either the mother would abandon or the cow wouldn't make it, so there ended up being a pen full of calves that had to be bottle fed. It was a chore Kit could handle, and she finally felt like she was contributing to the ranch.

With calving, Rossen cut back drastically on the hours they spent in his office doing engineering work. They were just waiting for the permits to be approved to begin test drilling for the new well.

Naomi had flown to Tucson to see about getting Kit's records and birth certificate and social security card. The day Kit turned eighteen, Naomi gave them to her like an award. All the college kids came home and they had a big birthday cake and ate ice cream and Kit cried. She'd never had a birthday party.

One morning the next week, Rossen took her into Evanston to get her cast removed for good. Even though the muscles in her left arm were much smaller than her right and she had a long pink scar where they had pinned it back together, she was overjoyed to finally be free of it and jumped off the exam table to hug the doctor and Rossen and even the nurse! She turned a circle in the waiting room and Rossen laughed at her as they went out the door.

That afternoon, she picked up her guitar and played rock and roll as loud as she dared. Later, Rossen took her to Ruger's barn to see the foals and Kit was in love. She'd never seen anything as intriguing as those sleek babies and she laughed right out loud when they all went to bucking and playing when they were turned out.

That evening in her studio, she began to work on some models of the young horses in clay. Her studio felt rather empty because Isabel had shipped several of the finished pieces to California and Jackson Hole to art dealers and galleries.

Rossen finally baptized her on the first Saturday in March. They'd been waiting for her to turn eighteen and her cast to be removed and they scheduled it the very next day. The whole family came home from college again to be there with her. As all the brothers and Rob and Slade and their bishop placed their hands on her head when she was confirmed, it was the most amazing feeling. Better even, she thought, than the baptism itself.

All her life she'd dreamed of being adopted into a real family. She'd fantasized during the long, lonely times at different foster homes, of a family that really loved her and wanted her and was good to her, too. In her heart she hadn't really thought it was possible, but it was nice to pretend. The weight of these men's hands felt like that family of her dreams.

She went to bed that night with a heart so full, she couldn't think of one thing to ask for, except for God to continue watching over those she loved.

****

A week after he baptized her Rossen took her for another prenatal checkup, and an appointment with her teacher.

Her doctor declared that everything looked good and inquired about whether she was pre-registered at the hospital and had signed up for a childbirth class. Rossen knew from the look on her face that these were another couple of mental hurdles she would need encouraged through.

They got through the preregistration hurdle relatively easily. He just punched in the number on his phone and handed it to her as he drove, and she had to face it head on.

She was frankly floored when she realized it was going to cost somewhere between five and ten thousand dollars to deliver this baby, and he decided to deal with this land mine before she tackled the classes.

He had her drive all the way home once they reached the gravel road, and he pep talked her the entire time about what was best for the baby. By the time they reached the Rocklands, she was excited to be driving and seemed slightly less devastated about what a financial burden she was.

That week he started talking to her about the childbirth classes, but the idea took some getting used to. Two weeks later she finally called and registered for the class. At the end of the call, the woman on the other end of the line mentioned that Kit and her "coach" would be in a class with eight other couples and Kit changed her mind and unregistered immediately—only Rossen didn't realize it.

It was two more weeks before he figured out she had no intention of taking the class and they got into it on the way home from the doctor's office again. With more frustration in his voice than he usually had, he said, "Kit, you're due in less than eight weeks. You're running out of time! You need to do this now! What's the problem? The class is free, for Pete's sake!"

Her reply was calm, "Women have been having

babies for thousands of years without childbirth classes. One more won't hurt."

He pulled the truck over to the side of the road to stare at her. "You're kidding me! You're planning to go have a baby without being as prepared as possible? I'd think it would be plenty exciting, without wondering what the heck was going on! Kit, this is childbirth! Childbirth!" He repeated these last two words slowly as if she were having a hard time understanding.

She calmly faced him. "Don't be demeaning. Not having the class couldn't be any worse than sitting in a room full of blissfully wedded couples talking about labor and breathing! You've read the book, too. I've seen you. You know this isn't going to be geography 101!"

He was quiet, thinking. Something was going on here. This wasn't like Kit to be intimidated by any subject, even one as unglamorous as labor. That was it! It was the blissfully wedded couples she couldn't face! That made more sense. He started the truck and pulled away, wondering if he really had the guts to go with her. He grasped at options, only to discard them one by one. Taking his mom wouldn't help the couples thing. Joey could be the dear friend coach, except she was still at school in Logan. Kit was pretty adamant. He doubted she could be nagged into going alone.

Realizing he was out of options, he had a mental tug of war with himself all the rest of the way. She couldn't face the class alone. He wasn't sure he could face the class at all, but she had to go.

As he turned off the truck in the garage, he squared his shoulders and turned to her. "I'll go with you."

She raised her eyebrows. "Uh huh. Really." She obviously didn't believe him.

"But you owe me! Big time! You're gonna have to balance my checkbook for a year! And prepare my financials for the CPA at tax time next march. And I'll think of some other stuff, too!"

She laughed. "Now you're scaring me! Are you serious?"

"Just make the call, Kit. I don't care what women have been doing for thousands of years." She finally registered.

When Rossen told Naomi he was going to go with, she raised her eyebrows at him, too. "Oh my!" That's all she had to say to make him blush. "Are you sure you're up to this?"

Rossen shook his head. "Of course not! It's just the only way she'd agree to face it at all. She can face labor, just not married couples. I can face married couples, just not labor."

Kit's bedroom was directly above his and lately at night, he could hear her get up and walk around at all hours. One night when he went up to check on her, she was pacing the hallway, her eyes tired, her face exhausted.

He whispered to her from the stairwell so he didn't frighten her in the dark, "Kit, what are you doing?"

She made a sound of disgust as she whispered back, "Just trying to survive this night."

He came all the way into the room. "What's wrong?"

She whispered fiercely, "Nothing's wrong. Apparently it's supposed to be this way. I just can't breathe, I have raging heartburn, my hips ache and when I lay down, I fear becoming beached like a great blue whale. Not that I'd ever whine or anything. What are you doing?"

He grinned. "Smiling at you. You're a very entertaining pregnant lady, you know?" She gave him the look as she continued to pace.

He extended his hand. "Come on. Let's go for a walk, before the whole house thinks you're cute when you have heartburn. It'll take your mind off of it." He got in the coat closet and held her parka for her.

She whispered, "You're crazy! I'm in my slippers!"

"You're right, but I'm not boring. And I'm in my slippers too." He held the coat and she put it on.

They quietly went out the French doors to the deck, and he took her arm as they went down the stairs to the lawn. They walked past Ruger's broodmare barn to the path beyond and slowly wended their way up the hill behind and Rossen asked, "Would it help to remind you that you're soon going to have a beautiful little daughter out of all this?"

She stopped to rest. "Actually, that's exactly

what I needed to hear right now. The heartburn is gone. Now I'm just out of breath."

After a minute they walked on until they came to a group of boulders beside the trail, and he pulled her down for another break. They faced the east where the sky was starting to lighten, the blue gray clouds showing barely a hint of purple in the dusky pre-dawn. She leaned against him to watch the sunrise and said, "I thought you were nuts, but taking a walk at this hour is glorious. You were right, again. I feel much better." She sighed and leaned against him in the first light of day. "Wyoming is a beautiful place."

****

He knew she'd fallen asleep against his shoulder, and he wasn't sure what to do about it. Should he wake her up to go back where it was warm and comfortable? Or should he let her sleep while she could? He leaned his back against another rock and pulled her against his chest and held her as she rested.

****

Later that morning in Sacrament meeting, he was sitting on the back row between her and his dad, trying to focus on the speaker. It was High Council week and he was struggling to find the point in the lengthy dissertation, feeling thoroughly tempted to fall asleep. Beside him, Kit abruptly sat more upright. He glanced down at her just as the side of her tummy began to bump and he felt the baby kick him in the back of his forearm. It was all he could do not to jump like he'd been shot. His eyes grew wide as he tried not to stare down at her belly and she smiled up into his eyes at his expression. The baby had kicked him! He could still see a small arm or leg bumping around inside her. How he wanted to put his hand there and feel what was happening! If they hadn't been sitting in church he probably would have.

The same thing happened the next night as they drove home from watching a movie at Slade and Isabel's with Ruger and Marti and his parents. This time in the dark of the truck she took his hand and laid it against her tummy, so he could really feel the baby move. It was the most incredible thing he'd ever felt.

****

The first night of their childbirth class arrived and both of them were complete wrecks. He kept having to remind himself he was there to make her less nervous and he still didn't think he could pull it off. He knew she really could read him like a book when just before they walked in the door, she turned to him and smiled her heart stopping smile, and said, "Calm down, you're gonna be fine." He grabbed her hand and held on for dear life as they walked in.

In some ways it wasn't so bad and in some, it was worse than they'd thought. Once they got past the fact that some of the couples were enjoying the most graphic stuff and one of the couples was naming their baby girl Bruce, they did all right.

When the instructor asked what they were naming their baby and Rossen answered Rocky Star, Kit laughed and he finally decided they were going to be okay. There was actually more good information than he had expected and they learned a lot. When there was something that made them uncomfortable, they either ignored it, or blushed, and they got through that first night.

After class, the instructor recommended they all tour the labor and delivery wing sometime before their next week's class. Rossen and Kit decided to go up right then while they were already in town. It was actually very cool. The rooms were almost like hotel rooms and going past the nursery window Rossen could hardly pull himself away. Looking at these tiny babies and trying to equate them with the kicks he felt this last week was incredibly intriguing. Each little finger and toe fascinated him. Even the baby that was screaming its little lungs out as its diaper was being changed was its own miniature miracle.

Kit finally dragged him away, saying, "C'mon, I wasn't able to force much down at dinner because of nerves and now I need to go home and eat something."

Still looking back at the babies, he said, "I'm starving too. Let's stop at a café on the way home."

As they sat across the table from each other while they waited for their food, he asked, "Well, what did you think?"

She colored slightly. "I ran the full gamut from cool, to gross, to oh brother, to this weird feeling that any minute they are going to say, 'Just kidding! That's not really how you get these things out. That's not actually possible, but we had ya going for a minute there didn't we?'"

Rossen laughed so hard at her that he choked on his water and she looked embarrassed. When he could finally breathe, she asked, "And you?" She was looking at him like she truly wanted to hear his answer.

"Honestly, I have more respect for women than ever before. I'm grateful you're willing to go through all this to get these little people here for us. I'm afraid if it were up to men, the species would die out." He gave a sheepish smile and continued, "Seriously, it's just like that ultrasound. I was worried and nervous at first, but now I'm so glad I came. There's a lot more that goes on with your body than is obvious, and it's probably good for us clueless wonders to know and understand, so we can at least sympathize, if not help out."

As he continued, she stirred her water with her straw. "Mostly, I just wish I could make it all easier for you. I would if I could." He reached across to squeeze her hand as it lay on the table.

She said, "You're here. And I know you didn't want to be. That helps more than you'll ever know. Thanks."

"You're welcome." He fingered her ruby ring before letting go.

****

He heard her up that night walking, and he wondered if he should get up and be with her again. He decided against it. Sometimes he got so mixed up about what their roles were in this relationship. He heard her open the door to the deck and told himself he should go back to sleep. He got up and looked out to see her sitting in a chair out there. At least she wasn't walking alone. Maybe he shouldn't have taken her outside the other night.

Chapter 10

April came in with a vengeance and an early heat wave made the river rise fast. The National Weather Service kept a close flood watch as the Rockland herds dropped their last calves.

Kit had never seen such a marked change in the seasons. The deep cold and snows of winter melted into a hesitant spring and frost appeared at night long after the snow was gone. And then, almost overnight, the world turned a deep, rich emerald from horizon to horizon. Only the thickest pines broke the brilliant spring green.

The days warmed up and Rob tilled Naomi's garden. She and Kit planted peas and lettuce and beets. There were so many things here that Kit had never experienced. She'd always loved flowers, but this was her first experience with growing anything and she found she loved it. There was something about dirt that was so basic and wholesome. She knew she'd found a new hobby for life.

The guys loaded the snowplows, snow cat and snow machines into the back of an equipment shed and Kit helped Naomi pack what seemed like truckloads of snow gear into storage.

Kit had been experimenting more and more with the lifelike sculptures of the horses and calves, and even Slade and Rossen roping. She was pleased with the way some of them were turning out and decided to ask Mr. Perkins about learning to cast bronze.

She did a figurine of Slade and Isabel walking near the pond. It took her several days to finish the raw clay and she decided she liked this kind of work even better than her free form stuff. The realism was more challenging and the satisfaction as she was done was intense.

She started a series of foals in several poses bucking and playing. They were larger and more lifelike than anything she'd ever done and she threw herself into it with such a passion that she found her back aching at times from working too many hours at a stretch.

She started swimming at Slade and Isabel's pool more often, as it seemed to soothe the aches and pains and muscle spasms that became more bothersome the larger she got. Several times since her and Rossen's initial night walk, she'd gotten up to go outside, rather than try to pace off her heartburn inside and chance waking someone.

Without her knowing, Rossen always checked on her to make sure she was safe and never went far. He just watched from a distance and let her go, her white nightgown and robe easily seen in the dark.

One early morning when she was feeling particularly miserable, she couldn't seem to walk out the spasms in her back and wished she dared sneak into Slade's pool house at this time of night. She walked the entire perimeter of the pond several times, but nothing was helping. She'd waded the pond a few times lately in the daytime where they'd piped a hot mineral spring into it, and although so far she'd only dipped her feet, she walked that way wondering if the hot spring would bring relief.

She kicked off her slippers, left her robe on the bank and tentatively put a foot into the water to check the temperature in the wee hour chill. The mineral water felt like warm silk and she didn't hesitate to wade all the way in. She swam to where the water spilled in from the pipe and turned to float under it letting the weight of the miniature falls pound her back where it ached. It helped almost immediately and she was so grateful for the relief. The warm water, the night air and the mystique of the dark were powerful medicine, and she basked in its spell. Her body felt so much less awkward and big in the relative weightlessness of the water.

Finally relaxed, she was still loathe to go, but went because she knew her body needed rest. She came out of the water wishing she'd brought a towel and hoping she hadn't ruined her white cotton gown. She stepped into her slippers and wrung out her hair, and carrying her robe to keep it dry, she fairly floated back up the path to the house. Her gown was actually somewhat dry as she slipped back onto the darkened deck feeling immeasurably better.

****

Rossen heard her get up and let herself out and checked on her several times. She'd never walked this long before and he was just wondering if he should go out to see if she was okay, when she disappeared.

He waited a few more minutes, then threw a hoody on over his sweat pants and went to find her. When he got to the pond, he realized she was, in fact, in it. Just for a split second he thought she'd drowned and his gut wrenched. Then she turned over to lay her head back in the water and he understood she was just floating under the piped spring. He climbed up the hill a way to let her have her privacy and so he wouldn't scare her here in the dark. He watched over her until she climbed out of the warm water and headed back to the house, her white gown clinging to her skin and occasionally blowing in the night wind.

He followed her at a distance until he'd made sure she was back safe, then he sat on the deck in the dark letting the same night wind cool his head. Several minutes later, he let himself in.

Her night swims became quite common, but after busting her in her almost transparent gown, he only checked to make sure she made it safely in.

****

One day she came in from a walk around the ranch in the daytime and changed her clothes to go work in her studio. When she walked in the craft room door, Rossen, Slade, Isabel, Naomi and Rob were all five standing inside, staring at the foal sculptures in silence.

She instantly wondered if there was a problem. "What's going on? Is something wrong?"

Naomi answered, "No honey, there's nothing wrong. It's just none of us had been in here for several days, and we hadn't seen the change in the style of your work. When Isabel came up and found these, she wanted all of us to come up and see."

Kit looked from one face to the next, trying to read their expressions. "Well?" She wasn't sure she could take it, if they disliked her latest stuff.

Slade and Isabel looked at each other and finally Isabel asked, "Do you do commissions?"

Kit was still hesitant. "Commissions like what?"

"Could Slade and I hire you to do a series of these horses, but in larger than life size for our farm in California? We want to have them bronzed."

Kit was stunned. "Are you serious?" She looked back and forth at them.

Slade nodded. "Yeah, we're serious. They're incredible!"

Kit was somewhat hesitant. "I can try. I've never done anything like that before, but it would be way cool."

Rossen and Naomi grinned at each other at her terminology and Naomi said, "World class talent and she calls it way cool!"

Kit went over and tossed a towel over the bust of Slade and Isabel as she turned to them and said, "Don't see this one. It's a surprise gift for you, but it's not done so pretend you don't know about it, 'kay?"

"Know about what?" Slade smiled at her. "Find out how to do the bronzes. We'll bankroll the whole project and pay your commission. Just let us know what you need."

They all left except Rossen, who stood looking for the longest time in silence. Finally, he said, "When I first met you, I thought God had dealt you way more than your fair share of trials. I had no idea then about your gifts. I've never known anyone like you in my whole life, Just Kit. About every other day, you amaze me."

****

As April drew to a close, Kit finished all of her high school work and she and Rossen went in to take the last childbirth class. They'd made it through four weeks, and Kit felt they should have been given a diploma or at least an "I survived" T-shirt.

They'd been reading her pregnancy books and between the books and the class, they'd had some rather interesting talks in the truck on the way to and from.

That Friday, Sean was graduating from college and the whole family drove the two and a half hours to Logan to attend the commencement. The Rocklands had bought a house there that they'd turned into three apartments for their kids and their roommates to live in. Everyone had moved home except the family, so they all stayed there for the night.

The next morning, Naomi and Joey took Kit on a mini tour of campus. They stopped at the bookstore and Naomi bought a current student catalog. Kit wondered what she wanted it for and she was floored when Naomi gave it to her on the way home saying, "Just look through it. You never know, you might end up there sometime. They have one of the best art schools in the country."

Naomi and Rossen were always talking about when she went to college. Kit thought they were nuts. New mothers didn't go to college.

Kit really had reached one hundred and eighty pounds over the last weeks and even though her doctor said she was perfect, she still felt as big as a house.

Playing her guitar had become awkward and she could only work at Rossen's computer for a half hour or so at a time, before she had to get up and move around. Sleeping through the night had become a fairytale and she could only eat a few bites without the fear of heart burn. She'd pretty much decided this pregnancy stuff could get old fast and she wondered how in the world she was going to make it through four more weeks.

Her prenatal appointments were scheduled just a week apart now and they did another ultrasound. Rossen didn't go in this time and she was relieved. She wasn't sure she wanted him to see her huge tummy. She got another great photo, though. This time they could even see the baby's hair. On the way home she and Naomi stopped at Shopko and bought things like diapers and a car seat and some tiny clothes and blankets.

The first week in May, Rob asked Rossen to take a bull to Alpine to a rancher friend of his there. Joey was good friends with his daughter and wanted to ride along, so Naomi suggested Kit go with, saying, "The scenery is marvelous if you think you can stand to sit for sixty miles. You can take the suburban. It rides smoother."

Anything was better than sitting just hanging out waiting, so she went, and Naomi was right. It was a breathtaking drive. They left at six in the morning and drove up through Star Valley and after dropping the bull and visiting, they headed back down on the Salt River road on the east side of the drainage. It was about the same distance, but a whole new country for her to see.

About halfway back, Kit decided this trip had been a mistake. Everything she owned began to have charley horses and her back began to cramp miserably. On top of that, they were stopped by a flagman who reported a wildfire up ahead that was uncontained and threatening the highway. He let them pass with a warning that the road could be closed at any time and they may have to turn and backtrack to Alpine and come down the other way. Kit groaned inwardly. She didn't say anything, but she felt awful.

She kicked off her shoes and began trying to stretch and relax as best she could. When they safely passed the place where the fire came closest to the road, she breathed a sigh of relief. The smoke was blowing straight toward the highway and she knew it would only be a matter of minutes before this route would indeed be blocked. As it was, the visibility was terrible and she was grateful Rossen was the one driving the Suburban and trailer.

Several miles past the smoke, the road narrowed and began to wind with a large river on one side and a steep ridge of mountains on the other. At this point Kit started to get carsick on top of her other miseries.

Traffic slowed behind several big rigs in a row and Kit began to pray, realizing that if she had to be sick, there was nowhere to pull off out of the way.

She was watching the line of trucks ahead when everything seemed to go into slow motion. The double tanker three vehicles ahead of them lost control on a turn and began to fishtail back and forth, then skidded as its rear tanker slid toward the river. The trucker finally got stopped, but not before the back wheels of the rear tanker went over the edge to dangle in space above the bank. In a chain reaction, the next two trucks careened as everyone tried to stop before they hit the vehicle in front. Rossen hit his brakes and the suburban skidded hard to the right as he, Kit and Joey were all three thrown forward.

Neither airbag deployed, so Kit assumed they were all okay, until she felt a frightening pull, low in her stomach, and an even more frightening warm gush of liquid begin to soak her sundress and run off the leather seat and down her legs.

She was horrified and looked up at Rossen with panic in her eyes.

****

Rossen instantly realized Kit's water had broken

and several different anxious emotions washed over him, as he looked backward and then forward, trying to decide what to do. The trailer directly in front of them had jackknifed across the road. The trailer they were pulling had jackknifed too, as well as the big rig directly behind them. Beyond that he couldn't see, but both he and Kit knew there was a dangling tanker in front of them and a wildfire closing in behind. Reality settled in fast.

Joey leaned forward from the backseat and asked, "Kit, are you okay?"

Kit's voice wavered as she answered, "I think so."

Rossen immediately tried to get on his cell phone, only to find they had no service. Tensely, he said, "Joey. Dig around and see what Dad has in here that'll mop up water. I'm going to climb up one of these hills and see if I can get cell service. I'll be right back." He gave Kit an intense look as he squeezed her hand and jumped out of the truck, to scramble up the steep ridge.

He had to climb ridiculously high, but he was finally able to call out and report what had happened. His voice was slightly unsteady as he reported on Kit. From his vantage point he could see there were a total of seven vehicles affected. Two in front, his and four behind, and he realized with a sick heart it would be hours before the road was clear. The wrecks were clear across both lanes and even a helicopter couldn't land in this!

He ran and slid back down to the road, reminding himself to be calm in front of Kit. Coming around to her side of the truck, he opened her door. As he did so, water ran off the floor mat and over the edge of the door opening, to drip down onto the pavement below. He looked at her and smiled. "Kit, honey. Aren't ya glad you took those classes?"

He expected her to go right into labor, but other than saying she didn't feel very good, nothing that radical happened. She got out to walk around and stretch and except for her soaking clothes, she looked great. He remembered first babies should take awhile and tried to comfort them all by saying they'd be home and to the hospital long before the baby arrived.

Joey was perplexed at his anxiousness and said, "So, her water broke. That's no reason to panic. She's still almost a month early. Chill out."

Rossen looked at her like she was brain dead. "Joey, once her water breaks, the baby has to be born. Today. Or at the latest in the morning. There are no other options."

Joey's eyes grew wide. "Oh." She looked at Kit again with a new urgency. "All righty then."

An hour after they'd been sitting there, they heard sirens. It was in front of them and stopped a long way away. It was another thirty five minutes before a highway patrolman and an EMT walked through the maze of trucks to check on Kit.

She'd been intermittently walking and sitting in a lawn chair they'd found in the back of the truck and put in the meager shade. The EMT knelt beside Kit to ask her some questions and the cop told Rossen that although there were multiple wreckers on the way, it was going to be awhile. The patrolman continued to walk down the road and Rossen went back to Kit, wondering how long it would be before she went into labor.

The EMT had one hand on her belly and the other held up so he could see his watch. Rossen almost started to tell him she wasn't even in labor yet, then he saw the man's face. The mild mannered EMT of two minutes ago had switched into work mode, big time.

Rossen went to Kit and really looked at her, and suddenly came to a rude awakening. She was indeed in full blown labor and was just trying to downplay it. He took her hand to look into her face. "You turkey. I didn't even realize you were in this much pain. Why didn't you say something?"

Now he could see the beads of moisture on her forehead and upper lip. He dug in her purse for a clip and pulled her hair up and twisted it into a rough knot on top of her head and secured it.

The EMT asked, "What have you got in your vehicle? Any towels or anything?"

Joey answered skeptically, "Two car blankets, one of which is scratchy wool, a travel pillow, some insulated coveralls, an emergency kit, several napkins from McDonalds and an old horse halter. That's as good as it gets. Sorry."

The EMT, whose name turned out to be Seth, instructed Joey to lay the rear seats of the suburban down and open all the windows to cool it off.

He turned to Rossen. "Can we unhook the trailer and pull ahead enough to be able to get those back doors free?"

Rossen rushed to do as he asked, while Seth went back to Kit. He got her up to walk again while he talked to someone on his radio. With the trailer unhooked, Rossen went back to her side and put an arm around her waist to support her as she paced. Almost immediately he could feel her have a contraction under his hand. Either it was milder than it felt or she had amazing self control.

After a few minutes she went to stand near the back of the suburban and as he stood next to her and brushed her hair back with a gentle hand, she leaned into him hard and put her head against his chest. He could feel her tense and she groaned almost silently.

He sat inside the back of the truck and gathered her onto his lap and began to rub the small of her back firmly with the heel of his hand. He leaned his head against hers and said, "Talk to me Kit. This is no time to shut me out and try to go it alone." He continued to rub and massage her shoulders. "Tell me what you need. What would help?"

She pulled back enough to look into his eyes. "Just hold me, and we'll get through this. Rubbing my lower back helps." She leaned back toward him and tensed hard as he pushed against the strain in the small of her back. When she finally relaxed, he felt her release a deep sigh and he tried to relax as well.

They went on like this, over and over, and he

continued to marvel that she didn't say a negative word. She hardly said a word at all.

He didn't think this was supposed to happen quite this fast. At least their instructor had said it wasn't. He looked around them to see that virtually nothing had moved in the last three hours and tried to make himself loosen up. It was going to be a long day.

Watching her struggle over these hours, he thought back to their conversation over dinner the first night of their class. He wished there was some way to trade places with her. He'd do it in a heartbeat. He continued to hold her like she'd asked, talking and encouraging as well as he knew how. How one young body could handle this much pain for this long he didn't know.

By the end of another two hours he respected her strength more than ever. Seth was timing her contractions and Rossen could tell by the look on his face that this baby wasn't going to wait for a nice, cozy hospital. He prayed the baby would be okay, even though she was coming a few weeks early.

Rossen turned to Seth. "You aren't by any chance LDS, are you?"

Seth smiled. "I was just thinking a blessing would be a good thing. I have oil." The two of them moved close to her and proceeded to give her blessing as her body tensed into another long contraction. As they said amen, Rossen gathered her close again and continued to rub as he talked to her.

Talking seemed to help. He could feel her relax

and breathe as he spoke and he began to ask her questions to help her focus away from the pain. Between the next contractions, as she lay back against him, he turned to his sister, glad she wasn't one of those emotional, ditsy types and said, "Joey, go see if any of these truckers have a blanket or sheets or towels or anything like that. We're going to need something better than a wool blanket for this baby."

Kit didn't even look up and he realized she already knew she was going to give birth in a beautiful wooded canyon in the back of his dad's Suburban.

Seth had his case open and was sorting through, pulling a few things out to set them aside.

Her contractions were coming one on top of the other and surprisingly, Rossen could feel himself grow singularly calm. They'd do what they had to do as well as possible. It was as simple as that, if you figured in constant prayer.

He held her to him and asked what she was going to name her. She'd just started to answer when another contraction hit. She almost arched with this one and groaned right out loud.

Joey came back with an armful of folded linens. "We're in luck. One of those guys had just done his wash this morning."

Seth took a deep breath. "Can you help me stretch her out a little up into the back? I think I'd better check her. Here, Joey will you help me?"

Rossen pivoted with her and pulled her legs up into the truck and back toward the driver's seat. He was talking her through another contraction as Joey covered her with a sheet and Seth snapped on a pair of exam gloves. Rossen raised a knee to let her lean against so she could recline, but he could still hold her close. He kept his head tight to hers, talking to her and pushing hard against her back. He could hear Joey and Seth talking back and forth, but his focus was on trying to ease Kit's pain. He prayed over and over in his mind as he held her.

He felt himself panic just slightly when Kit cried right out and gripped his shirt in a near strangle hold. Seth spoke to her, "Kit, you're doing fine. She's coming along. You're almost done. Hang in there. It won't be a whole lot longer." Rossen felt himself calm down again as he struggled to release Kit's hands from his shirt. For a second there, she had it so tight at his throat that he couldn't breathe. He continued to talk to her, his voice low and steady, not even sure what he was saying as she relaxed into the brief lull.

She tensed again and tried to turn over, gasping from the pain. Rossen let her turn, but she came right back and buried her face against his shirt, clutching him. He heard his shirt start to tear before she finally let go again.

The next contraction hit with a vengeance. This time she had his hands in a grip that actually hurt him. When she let go she was panting and Joey handed him a small towel to wipe her face. As he gently smoothed away the perspiration, she started to cry and hid her face against him. He held her and stroked her and the tears seemed to help. She didn't tense so on the next one.

Seth began to talk to her again, "Okay, Kit. This is it. You're doing great, but it's time to push this baby all the way out. When the next one hits, push for all you're worth."

Almost instantly her body almost convulsed, the contraction was so strong. For someone so fine boned and gentle, this strain was intense enough that it was scary. She had hold of his shirt again, but he was so focused, he didn't know. He was talking to her and Seth was talking to her, but she was completely into the pain and didn't hear either one. Rossen couldn't get her attention and felt like he'd completely let her down, as he heard Seth say something urgent to Joey.

He heard the baby gasp and cry as Kit relaxed in his arms. She began to cry again and he was suddenly a nervous wreck. He glanced back at Joey and Seth for the first time to see them working with the tiny, purple, dark haired baby.

The sight of that baby rocked him to his toes and he felt like he couldn't get a breath. The magnitude of it all became overwhelming and he pulled Kit against him tightly, words of comfort forgotten, as he worked in vain for some semblance of composure. He tried repeatedly to swallow and wondered for a second if he could get a breath and then if he was going to hyperventilate. Kit whimpered in his arms and brought his focus back instantly.

He'd been holding her too tight and he released her to carefully help her sit up and see her baby. She looked up and gave him a beautiful, tired smile, then relaxed back in his arms and closed her eyes. He brushed her hair back again and gently kissed her forehead and whispered, "You were incredible." She opened her eyes for one long moment to look into his, then closed them again and turned her head against his chest and sighed.

He studied her face for a moment, trying to sort through his jumbled feelings, then decided it was impossible and looked back at the baby. This was too precious a moment to try to think through. He felt how he felt. Right now it was all okay.

Joey and Seth worked together like they'd done this a thousand times. They were cleaning and drying the baby with the towels and some sort of wipes, and then worked on the cord and Seth put some drops in her eyes.

She was pretty ticked about the whole deal and screamed at the top of her lungs, her tiny arms and legs pumping furiously. Rossen laughed softly as he watched. Even mad she was exquisite.

Finally, they wrapped her in the other clean sheet until the only thing that showed was her miniature pink face. She calmed right down and immediately her small blue black eyes began to look around. They handed her up to him, as they began to straighten up the aftermath of this amazing happening in the back of the vehicle. He held her close to him for a moment, marveling at this new human being in his hands.

He gently touched Kit's shoulder. "Hey, sleepy

head. I have a present for you." She opened her eyes again, their cobalt depths tired.

She reached out a slim brown hand to touch the baby reverently with one finger. "Is she all okay?"

Rossen glanced back at Seth who said, "As far as I can tell, she's perfect."

Rossen repeated to Kit, "She's perfect." His voice was husky.

Kit looked up at him with wonder. "She is, isn't she?" She gave one more tired smile and closed her eyes again.

Rossen held the baby and watched her watch him, her eyes alert and shiny. Kit slept against him and Joey and Seth talked quietly in the back. The sudden tranquility in the truck was almost eerie after the tension before.

Rossen was almost angry when within minutes of the baby's birth, they could hear the low growl of a big truck's motor not far ahead. Within the next hour the road was open and passable. Seth had been watching both Kit and the baby and seemed to think that even somewhat early, the baby was fine. Rossen sat quietly in the back of the suburban with Kit and the baby sleeping against him, while the others pulled the truck around to hook back onto the trailer. Joey went in search of the trucker who had loaned the linens and they gave him fifty bucks and a delivery report.

Saying goodbye to Seth was almost painful. After their time together he almost felt like another brother, and Rossen was glad he left a card so they could talk to him again if they had questions on the way back.

At the end of their prenatal class, Rossen had thought he had a handle on all of this, but now, as Joey finally pulled away from where they'd been stranded, he realized he had no clue how to handle it at all. He'd stayed where he was to let Kit rest and he cradled the baby, wishing they had a car seat with them to buckle her safely into.

A half hour from home, Kit woke up and tried to sit up and look around. She looked at the baby again without trying to take her from him and he wondered if she was afraid to hold it. He hoped it was just that it was new and strange, and not that her fears of it reminding her of her foster father had come true. But then as he watched the wonder in her eyes, he knew she loved it and placed the baby gently in her arms.

Kit looked scared and Rossen encouraged her, "You did a great job, both in carrying her and delivering her. You were a trooper and I'm proud of you. You finally got your sweet baby girl and she's as beautiful as you."

The baby woke up and started to fuss and they weren't sure what to do. Kit started to bounce her and when she didn't respond, she sang to her. The baby still wasn't happy and began whimpering with her little lips pressed together almost making an "mmm" sound. Rossen took her and unwrapped her until he found a tiny hand and put it up near her face. She began to suck on it immediately. Kit smiled as the baby mellowed right out and asked, "Hey, how did you know to do that?"

He laughed. "I just remember that first ultrasound."

He'd been thinking about what they needed to do and asked Kit, "Is it okay if we drop Joey by home before we continue on to the hospital?"

Kit looked at him in surprise. "Why do we have to go to the hospital *now*? I already had her."

"Don't you want to go in and be checked and make sure everything is all right? She'll have to have some tests anyway. They can watch her and help you in case we don't know what to do."

Kit looked as tired as he knew she was and said, "Seth thinks she's okay. Don't you think it would be okay to just go home and ask your mom if we have questions? Tomorrow or sometime we can go to the doctor. Right now I just want to go home." She handed the baby back to Rossen and while he considered, she lay back again to close her eyes.

Rossen looked down at the tiny, little human and gave a small smile. "Home it is. If we think there's a problem, we'll take you in then."

****

At seven o'clock that evening Joey stopped the truck in front of the house and helped all three of them out of the back of the suburban. They hadn't had cell service until they were almost home so they decided to just show up instead of call.

Rossen opened the door to the house and helped Kit in, wishing she would have let him carry her. Joey brought up the rear with the baby. As soon as Naomi saw them she rushed over, talking up a storm about how worried she'd been. When she saw Kit looking positively haggard with Rossen basically supporting her, she broke off mid-sentence, and when Joey came past and handed her the baby and followed Rossen and Kit back to Kit's room, Naomi came unglued.

"Oh, my stars!" She was almost yelling and Rob rushed in from his office just as the baby began to scream. Naomi hurriedly said, "Oh, I'm sorry. Shhh. There, there. Don't cry." She began to frantically try to quiet the baby, who only got more upset because she was.

Rob walked over and took the tiny infant and held her close, and she settled right down. He turned to his wife. "What in the world are you doing, Naomi? Whose baby is this? And why are you bawling?" Naomi had commenced to cry and she went to him. He put his free arm around her, asking gently, "What's wrong?" She sobbed all the harder and the baby began to cry again.

Cooper, Treyne, and Sean came in the kitchen door at the same time that Slade, Isabel, Ruger and Marti came in from the garage. Slade said, "I see they're finally home. Is everything okay?" He saw Naomi crying and instantly asked, "What's wrong? Were they in that accident then?" Naomi still had her head buried against Rob's chest and none of them could tell what was going on. Finally, Isabel asked about the baby and it was as if a light clicked on. The whole family made a bee line for Kit's room, except Naomi, who still stood and cried.

A minute later Rossen came back in and wrapped her in a bear hug. "Don't cry, Mom. We didn't mean to scare you." He patted her back. "She's okay, they're both okay, we're all okay." He pulled back from her. "You're okay." She gave him a watery smile and went back to sobbing again.

When he finally got her settled down, he took her hand and led her toward Kit's room. "I'm glad you're okay 'cause Kit really needs your help. When we finally got out of that canyon, she just wanted to come home instead of going to the hospital. She's hoping you'll know what she should do with that hungry, small human in there. And do you know what happened to the diapers and stuff you bought the other day? We could really use them." Naomi smiled and was back to her usual calm competence as she went through the door.

She walked up to the bed to smile down at Kit, who new held her daughter and say, "Apparently, you got more than scenery."

Kit gave her a tired smile. "Way more."

****

At ten o'clock that night, Rossen felt like this day had lasted through four. The baby and Kit were both finally resting. It had taken hours to get the baby fed. At least that's what it had seemed like. He'd actually felt left out. While Kit and his mom were doing that, he and his dad had gone into the attic and brought down the antique cradle his mom had used with all of them. They dusted it and scrubbed everything with antibacterial detergent and put new clean linens on it. When they'd finally let them back in the room, he'd put it beside Kit's bed and laid the tiny bundle in it.

They'd found the diapers and things they'd bought, and though the baby seemed to be perfectly well clothed, Naomi had still sent Joey into town to buy some things she didn't think they could live without overnight.

Rossen was sitting in the great room wondering if he should go to bed or sleep in here so he could help Kit if she needed it. He finally opted for his own room and hauled himself up. He stopped at Kit's door for one last look before he went down. He watched the two of them sleep for a minute. How was he ever going to get this day out of his mind? There was not a chance he ever would.

Several times in the night he heard the baby fuss just for a moment and wondered if she needed any help. Finally, after four he heard the baby fuss for longer and went upstairs to check on them. The baby was in her cradle, but Kit was still dead asleep and he knew she was exhausted from her labor and restless night. He picked the baby up, thinking he could keep her entertained for awhile and let Kit sleep just a little longer.

He wrapped her back up in her blankets that had come loose and as soon as he did, she settled right down and began to look around again. He took her with him to the great room, settled into one of the recliners that rocked and began to slowly rock her back to sleep.

****

Kit found them there in the morning. For just a moment, when she'd woken up and realized her baby wasn't there, she'd panicked, but it had only taken her a minute to know that Rossen had probably come and taken the baby so she could sleep. She dragged her tired and sore body in search of them and found them in the rocker, snuggled up together, both of them dead to the world. She took a picture of them with her phone and then went and got in the shower.

She was stiff and tender and the shower felt good. When she shut it off, she could hear the baby through the closed door and hurried as fast as she could make her thrashed body move to rescue Rossen and apologize, "I'm sorry. She was sleeping soundly when I got in." She took her into her room to nurse her and once she'd fed her, took her back out.

He got up to take the baby again. "Let me hold her while you rest." He took her from Kit and brought her right up to his face. "She smells amazing. I had no idea babies smelled this good." He turned to Kit. "By the way, what's her name? I don't know what to call her."

Kit looked slightly bashful. "I was thinking of Tawna. Do you think your mom would be offended if I used Naomi for a middle name?"

"I think she'd be honored."

Kit went back to her room, saying over her

shoulder as she left, "Pat her on her back if she gets fussy."

Rossen played with the baby, letting her grab onto his fingers with her teeny hands. He unwrapped her and took off her socks so he could see her toes, too. He hadn't been around a baby since his nineteen year old brother, Cooper, was born. He had no idea they were this fascinating.

Sean came through the kitchen door and tried to take her from him. When he didn't give her up, Sean complained to their mother when she came in next, "Mom, Rossen's hogging the baby! He won't even give me a short turn."

Naomi swatted Rossen as she went past. "Share, you big, fat hog!" To Sean she said, "Wash your hands first."

Rossen regretfully handed the baby over. She instantly started to fuss and he said, "See? She doesn't want you. It's me she likes. 'Cause I'm the one who bout had his clothes shredded helping get her here. Kit said to pat her back if she seems unhappy."

Naomi asked, "Is that really what happened to your shirt yesterday? I saw it was all ripped, but didn't suspect it was Kit."

Rossen gave her a self-conscious smile. "The rips are nothing. At one point she had it gripped so tight at my throat I couldn't breathe and I couldn't get her to let go. She's stronger than she looks."

"I hope it gave you a whole new appreciation for women and babies."

Rossen began to unload the dishwasher. "That's a no-brainer. Even after that danged class I never dreamed it would be that hard on her. It was awful to watch."

Sean had been patting the baby and she gave a very unladylike burp just as Cooper walked into the kitchen. He thought it was great. "Yeah! Now that's my kind of baby!" He tried to take her away from Sean. "Mom, Sean's hogging the baby! Tell him to give me a turn." Both Rossen and Sean cracked up and Naomi turned to look at them with her hands on her hips.

"Do you want me to put that baby in time out?"

Just then, Treyne and Ruger came into the kitchen. "Wow, she's already in time out and she's only one day old? What'd she do?"

Both Rossen and Sean cracked up again as they said in unison. "Burped."

By the time Slade and Isabel came in five minutes later, they were all in stitches and Naomi had no clue how to corral them. Isabel went straight to the baby and took her from Treyne without even asking. She unwrapped her blanket and held her up to look at her in wonder. "Holy Moly, she's a miracle." She snuggled her up to her neck. "And she smells like heaven."

She handed her to Slade who looked like he was afraid she'd break if he moved wrong. Rob came in and tried to take her from Slade and whined, "Naomi, Slade's hogging the baby. Tell him to share." Every one of the brothers went into fits.

****

When Kit dragged back in she looked confused and didn't understand why Naomi handed her the baby and told her not to let anyone else near her. That breakfast was the silliest meal she had attended yet and that was saying something.

Seth called that day to find out who Kit's doctor was so he could help her get a birth certificate. Joey had been the one to answer the phone and they ended up talking for half an hour. He asked her out for the next night. She got off the phone with the most unusual smile. Rossen didn't think he'd ever seen her like that.

That afternoon Kit came into the great room to sit down next to Rossen on the couch. She was moving slow and he could tell she was sore. As soon as she got settled, the baby began to cry from her room and she unconsciously let out a small sigh. Before she could start to get up, he stood. "I'll get her and bring her to you."

She grabbed his hand to stop him. "No. It's okay. I'll have to take her back in there to nurse her anyway."

Naomi piped in from the kitchen, "No you don't, Kit. I always felt like I had to go to the dungeon to feed my babies. I vowed that would never be the case in my own house. Just keep a blanket over you. These guys will need to get used to it sometime. They'll all have wives and babies. If you're not comfortable that's fine, but don't feel like you have to go."

Kit smiled shyly at Rossen as she slowly got up. "It's not them that have to get used to it. It's Tawna and me. You'd think humans could figure this out better than farm animals, but that's not necessarily the case."

He carefully nudged her back down. "You stay. I'll go out for a while after I bring her to you."

****

Over the next couple of days, Kit felt like she was beginning to figure this motherhood thing out. She and Tawna got used to each other and nursing got easier, until the morning of the fourth day. Kit woke up and was amazed when she looked in the mirror. Her milk had come in and she had become markedly voluptuous overnight. It was extremely painful and she was miserable. She didn't have a clue what to do about it and hurriedly dressed to go in search of Naomi.

She stepped into the hallway just as Cooper walked past and his eyes grew wide. He turned back around in the hall and went toward his parent's room yelling, "Mom! Mom! Come quick! Kit's gonna blow!"

Naomi and Rob reached her at the same time Rossen came around the corner. They all stopped dead still and stared at her for a second. Rossen punched Cooper in the shoulder. "Have some respect, dude. Knock it off."

"What do you mean? I could never have anything but respect for a figure like that!" Cooper winked at Kit as Rob intervened.

"That's enough, Coop. You owe her an apology."

Cooper tried to look penitent as he said, "I'm sorry, Kit. I'm sorry I said you have an especially nice figure this morning. Will you forgive me?"

Kit smiled shyly. "Cooper, you're terrible. Just remember I owe you." He was the perfect little brother and she thought he was adorable even when he embarrassed her.

Naomi put an arm around her shoulder in concern and said, "Oh, honey." She took Kit back into her bedroom to help her as Rossen shook his head at Cooper.

****

Rossen couldn't even be mad. Cooper was right.

****

After a few days the household got used to having a new baby. The boys quit fighting over her, mainly because if they did Naomi would put her in time out and then no one got to hold her except Kit.

She'd become comfortable enough with nursing to throw a blanket over her shoulder to feed Tawna without having to leave the room, and she grew accustomed to the fact that Rossen would come and take the baby to burp her after. He started calling her Mimi because of the way she made this little "mm" sound when she was sad and it stuck. The whole family called her Mimi Star and the world pretty much revolved around her.

One day as they were clearing breakfast, Rossen walked over as Kit finished nursing and she automatically handed him the baby to burp. He patted her back until she belched and then played with her shamelessly until she started to fuss. He took her back over to Kit and handed her back, saying, "Here, Momma. Time for her second course."

Kit took her and fed her on the other side and then he automatically took her and burped her again and began to play with her. A few minutes later she got whiny and Rossen handed her back and went outdoors while Kit went to lay her down.

****

Rob leaned against the counter and watched this whole thing as Naomi finished loading the dishwasher and started it. He turned to Naomi with a puzzled expression and asked, "Did they get married and I just missed it? I swear they can read each others minds."

Naomi smiled her mellow smile. "They're very good friends. They've been through a few things together. They're close enough that I almost worry sometimes. Rossen thinks he's sending her off to college here in a couple months, only he hasn't told her that. She's not going to just mind him like he thinks she is, and if she does, it will kill him. I have no idea what to do about the two of them. Just pray. I guess that's all anybody needs though."

She put her arms around him. "You don't have to be married to read each others' minds. We were like that before we got married."

"Yes, but we were planning to get married. He thinks she's too young."

"She is."

"Naomi, would you have wanted to be single in her situation? I think it would be hard to be a nice girl

179

who was also an unwed mother in a largely religious community. How does he expect her to act like an incoming freshman and date and attend a singles ward and the whole nine yards with Mimi? I mean, it can be done. And it certainly would weed out the wishy-washy men. But I can't see her being a good mom and doing all of that on a long term basis. If I were her, I'd hate it. I'd just want to settle down and get on with my life."

Naomi nodded in agreement, but then said, "But there's the flip side. What if she settles down at seventeen, never having gone to school or traveled or even attended a prom? Later, won't she regret that bitterly? Won't she feel like she missed something her whole life."

He kissed her. "I suppose you're right. You always have been the ultimate wise woman." He kissed her again. "But just to be on the safe side, we'd better keep praying for them."

She smiled at him. "I wasn't planning on stopping anytime soon."

Chapter 11

They blessed Mimi when she was just two weeks old. Kit asked if they could do it at home because she was still somewhat worried about gossip. Rossen did the actual blessing with all the other men standing in the circle. It was the fruit she'd been talking about that she wanted in her daughter's life. It was a good day.

Mimi fit right in to the Rockland Ranch lifestyle. Kit would put her on a blanket on Rossen's office floor when she was working for him or near her in her studio. Sometimes others would take her off to play while Kit was doing something, and they all adored her completely. Kit was so grateful for them. Her baby didn't have a full-time father, but she didn't lack for care from any of them.

One day when Mimi was not quite three weeks old, Kit looked out the window of her studio to realize Rossen had her with him in the arena on a horse. Kit wasn't worried, but when Naomi caught him, she was hot. Kit could hear her, "Rossen Robert Rockland" clear inside.

That night Mimi was hopelessly fussy and finally, at two thirty, Kit put her in her tummy pack and slipped out the French doors to take her outside, so she didn't wake up the entire house. Not three minutes later she heard Rossen calling her name as he hurried to catch up to her.

She waited for him and asked, "What's wrong?" She wondered why he had come out.

"Nothing. I just wanted to make sure you didn't go climb in that pond this soon after you had a baby. It isn't clean enough."

She turned to stare at him even in the dark. "How do you know I sometimes swim in the pond?"

He put up a hand defensively. "No, I haven't been spying on you in the pond. But I do always make sure you come in safely." He must have felt he needed to clarify. "Actually, the first time you went swimming I was worried and went to check on you, but after that I only waited for you to come in."

She was still looking at him and she was glad it was dark as he asked, "Are you mad?"

She shook her head. "No. I told you before, it's impossible to be mad at you." She wasn't mad. She loved being watched over. She'd never had that kind of care her whole life.

Nodding at the baby, Rossen asked, "How come she's so fussy?"

Kit couldn't hide the smile in her voice. "Maybe she wants to go horseback riding."

"I guess you heard my mom bust me. I don't know why she was mad. She knows I take good care of her."

Kit laughed. "I think it's a hoot when your mom gets after you. That's the only time she ever uses your middle name. She's so cute when she's all motherly."

****

One day, toward the end of May, Naomi came in to sit down next to Kit as she nursed the baby and asked, "Kit, have you got a minute?"

Kit laughed softly. "Naomi, you know as well as I do, how many hours today I'll sit and feed this baby. I think I spend about a third of my time doing just this."

Naomi smiled. "Doesn't it just make you proud to look at her and know you've done this marvelous work? I sometimes still feel that way when I look at my kids."

Kit mused, "I guess I've never thought of it that way. Without you, I shudder to think how I'd have ever managed Mimi at all. Thank you for all you've done for me. I know I don't thank you enough, but please know that I'm eternally grateful."

"I think we should be thanking you for how much we all enjoy her." Naomi played with a tiny stocking that poked out from under the baby blanket and went on, "Speaking of her, there's something I'd like to talk to you about. I kept her little umbilical chord and sent it in to be paternity tested. I want to go after your foster father so he can't abuse any more young women. What would you think about that?"

"I've thought about it a lot actually. When I first came here I didn't think he could be stopped, but I've grown so much here and I can't help but think there should be someone who can bring him to justice. Honestly, the thought of ever seeing him again scares me, but the thought of him doing what he did to me to someone else is worse. If you can figure out how to go after him, I'll put everything I've earned working for Rossen into the pot to help pay for an attorney, and I'll support you all the way, even if I have to testify against him."

Naomi was thoughtful. "I'm wondering if with such concrete evidence as an umbilical cord of a baby conceived by a seventeen year old girl, if you'd have to testify at all. I'll have affidavits from people like your doctors with it. And as far as attorney fees, I'll handle this myself. I've kept my license up to practice in Arizona. I'll probably have to fly out there a few times, but I can do it all."

Kit turned to stare at her. "What are you saying, Naomi?"

"What do you mean, sweetie?"

"What is it that you're saying you're licensed to do?"

"Practice law, Kit. What do you think I'm saying?"

Kit was stunned! "You're an attorney?"

Naomi nodded. "Of course, I'm an attorney. Didn't you know that?"

"I've lived with you for five months and haven't had any inkling you practiced law!"

Naomi laughed, "That's a good thing, isn't it? Attorneys typically don't have very nice reputations.

It's probably better not to act like one." She patted Kit's hand. "Now that that's settled, let's talk about college. We have your high school diploma and we should see about having you take the ACT. With your intelligence it's really just a hoop to jump through, but you might be able to get a lot of scholarships. Who knows? And then you can decide where you want to go and we'll start to make arrangements for all the loose ends from there. What do you think?"

Kit just looked at her like she'd lost her mind. "Naomi, I know you mean well, but can you just picture me doing what I'm doing right now at a college apartment? It's not going to happen. It's not fair or right that I won't be going to college, but to take a phrase from Rossen, it is what it is. How can I go to college and take a baby?"

"Oh, come now, Kit. There are mothers all over the world in college. Parenthood doesn't preclude higher education. It just makes it less convenient. But there isn't one thing in the world that children don't make less convenient."

She must have been able to see that Kit wasn't buying in, because she added, "Okay, but can I just ask you one thing? Would you promise to at least take this idea out and examine it? Give it an honest analysis. Whether you get a college degree doesn't matter a hill of beans to me, but being able to feel like you didn't miss any important steps in your life later on means a great deal. I don't want you to look back in ten or twenty years and say I wish I'd tried to go to college. Deal?"

"You sound just like Rossen."

"I'll take that as a compliment."

Kit smiled at her. "It is. I'll think about it. I promise."

****

Naomi filed charges for several different crimes against Kit's foster father, only a few of which Kit would have even thought of. When Naomi had been doing the research for the case, she'd found that because Kit was part Indian, she was actually under a number of jurisdictions.

Kit had thought her real father was half Papago Indian, but Naomi had dug and found he was actually one quarter Papago, although they disliked that name and called themselves another, and one quarter Apache. So Naomi was attempting to have the different Indian nations and their law enforcement departments work with the local law enforcement and the state of Arizona's Department of Family Services.

She'd gone after him for his sexual abuse and also child abuse and neglect. She also tried to have him charged with fraud in his use of the foster system money. Then she filed several civil suits in Kit's behalf. She asked for financial remuneration for what Kit had been forced to go through during her abuse and because of it, with the assault in Vegas and the baby. She also filed civilly for any Indian moneys he'd been given for Kit, for wages from her job and the labor she'd done at their hotel and never been paid for, and even for foster care money that had never been spent on her and child support for the baby he'd wanted aborted.

She filed charges with both Indian nations, because they actually sometimes function as sovereign nations, and with the state. Then she asked that his wife be charged as an accomplice to all of it. She knew she wouldn't get all of it, but she wanted to put this guy out of action with foster kids forever!

****

When Mimi was two months old, Kit's doctor told her she could go ahead and ride a horse and even go in the pond if she wanted. Kit had loved riding behind Rossen in the winter and she wanted to learn to ride on her own. Rossen set her up with a sweet old horse and the tack she would need, then took her to the arena to learn to saddle up and all the basics. He even took her and bought her a pair of cowboy boots, saying they were safer and easier to ride with. After awhile, she felt like she could handle the horse well enough to ride in the hills with him.

At first Naomi insisted they leave the baby with her, but as she got bigger and stronger, they took her with them. Rossen would put her in the tummy pack and keep her with him, so Kit could focus on riding.

Kit loved it all. She loved the horses and the country and the fact that this man adored her daughter so. She would have added this man to the list, but she knew that was against an unspoken rule. It was a stupid rule, but for now she would go with it.

Who did he think he was kidding? She could see it in his eyes. But then again, he was such a white knight kind of a guy he might never give in to his feelings. For now she was content to be with him and follow the stupid rule and hope one day either he'd change his mind about her being too young, or she'd finally grow old enough. As she rode beside him, she wondered how old, old enough was. It was an intriguing question. She'd have to ask him one day.

Although she knew Rossen had rodeoed with Slade full time the last three years, this year they'd decided to retire from full time and it was the Fourth of July weekend before she finally got to go to a rodeo. They had someone come and watch the ranch, and for about a week Kit got to see what the rodeo life was like. Rossen and Slade roped together, and so did Rob and Sean. Even Ruger and Treyne went a couple of times. Rossen and Slade let her and Mimi and Isabel stay right in their trailer with them. The rest of the family stayed in Rob and Naomi's.

Kit had never seen anything like it. She was fascinated by the actual rodeo, but honestly, other than the team roping, which Rossen and Slade invariably won, she enjoyed the behind the scenes stuff even better. She loved watching the guys warm up their horses, wearing their competition shirts with all the sponsor patches. She loved it when even the cowboys in the warm-up arena all took off their hats at the same time to show respect to the flag. She loved watching them saddle up and get themselves and their horses mentally ready to compete. She loved watching the barrel racers before they actually came into the arena. Their horses were so keyed up that sometimes they had to come in backwards or have somebody lead the horse to the gate.

It was an exciting lifestyle and she was almost envious of Isabel's opportunity to travel with them the last year. That's how she and Slade had met, when they hired her to help them.

Watching Rossen and Slade rope together was incredible. She'd loved watching them at home, but in competition there was a whole new level of focus that was awesome to see. The men and their horses were in perfect harmony, and it was like watching a finely tuned outdoor ballet. The attention the announcers always gave them because of their ranking as reigning world champions thrilled her to hear it every time.

After being with them for the better part of a week and watching how much they enjoyed this, she had to wonder why they stopped. One day she asked Rossen and his face clouded for a second. It was as if he didn't know for sure or perhaps just didn't know how to voice it. He finally settled for, "It was time. We just wanted to come home."

Kit noticed that even with Mimi and Isabel's wedding ring, when she and Joey and Isabel went places, they attracted a lot of attention. Somehow it was very good for her ego. Of course, all the Rockland men attracted their own brand of chaos, and that was a little hard on her heart. Still, after it all, what she saw in Rossen's face when he saw them coming, made everything okay.

Finally, much too soon, they all went back home

and to business as usual.

Kit was getting closer to having her sculptures bronzed. She'd begun building the actual larger than life models in an empty shed and was pleased with how they were coming along.

The Rocklands had hired some extra men to help with the farming and cows. There was one who made Kit markedly uncomfortable when he was around. She tried to stay clear away from him, but he was always showing up when she didn't expect it and she was coming to be afraid of him. When he found where she was working on her sculptures, she went to Rossen and asked him to tell him to stay away from her. After that things got better for a while, and then he went back to practically stalking her again.

One day, as she was saddling her horse at the hitch rack in front of the indoor arena, she felt a hand on her shoulder and instinctively she knew it was him. She could feel herself try to shrink into the dark, safe place where she'd tried to go whenever her foster father came near her like this, and she couldn't seem to remember any of the counseling tips she'd studied so carefully. The despair she suddenly felt was worse than ever, because of the many months of safety and respect she'd lived with here. It made her feel absolutely defeated.

When he addressed her, she felt compelled to face him. "Hey, Kit." He looked her over with a grin that made her want to throw up. "Baby, you're looking better everyday since you had that kid. What say you and me go work on another one sometime?" She was immediately sick to her stomach and looked down at her hands.

What she saw there changed her whole heart in an instant. She looked at the small gold ring with its brilliant ruby catching the sun and she remembered the words Rossen had said to her the day he gave it to her. "And someday when some jerk insinuates otherwise, you'll always know what God and Rossen know. That you are a virtuous woman of infinite worth."

Suddenly she was mad. Fire in the belly mad. Deep, white hot, searing mad and as she looked at that ring, she doubled up her fist and turned and hit him with it like she'd never dreamed of striking another human being. She put everything she had into it and he wasn't expecting it when it came. She hit him square in the eye as hard as she could swing and knocked him flat on his butt. Then she climbed on her horse, turned it toward the hills and took off as fast as she dared run this close to the house.

As she went over the hill and out of sight, she turned in the saddle to look back and saw him still laying there with a couple of the guys looking on. Rossen was right. And man, was she grateful he'd given her that ring.

****

When Kit took off, Sean walked out of the arena and Rossen appeared from the shed beside it. Sean went to tear into the guy, but Rossen stopped him. "Easy, she's looking back. She needs to know she can handle stuff like this." Sean looked at him like he was crazy.

Rossen calmly spoke to the man who was slowly getting to his feet. "I don't know what you said to her, but you musta had it coming. Come up to the house and draw your time."

Sean broke in, "I know what he said to her, and I don't care who's watching. I'm gonna beat his face in."

"No, you're not." Rossen was watching her horse go over the hill. "'Cause I am." He tore into the hand with a fury he'd never unleashed before and Sean was the one who tried to pull him off. Rossen finally backed off when Ruger came over to help Sean.

Rob and Slade showed up and escorted the man off the ranch and outside the security gates. When he turned to walk away down the gravel road, Slade said, "That black eye belongs to Kit and you ought to 'fess up to it when people ask, or the Rocklands might find you and finish the job."

An hour later when Kit came back to the house, she picked up the baby and took her to the couch to feed her. Naomi came in and asked, "Are you okay? Rob said there was a problem with one of the hands today."

Kit looked up at her, unsure of what to say. "It was the strangest thing. When he put his hand on me, it was like back with my foster father all over again and I almost thought for a minute that I had to take it. Then when I looked down and saw my ring, I knew I didn't have to take anything. I think I hit that guy with all the pent-up anger from the first eighteen years of my life. I almost feel bad. I hit him right in the eye as hard as I could."

"Rob said you laid him out on his fanny. Are you okay?"

Kit rubbed her knuckles. "Hand's sore. But my infinite worth is intact."

Jaclyn M. Hawkes

Chapter 11

That week, Naomi got word from the authorities in Arizona that Kit's foster father had been arrested and released on bail. Three separate dates had been set to try him for the charges she'd filed. Naomi and Rossen were also pleased to learn that when the police had gone to serve the warrants on him, they'd suspected a problem. They had subsequently searched his home and motel and found a fully functioning meth lab in a back room. Those charges had been added to the original charges, and his wife had also been arrested and released on bail.

The same day Naomi got this information, the security people at the locked gates outside the Rockland Ranch signed for some paperwork from another attorney in Arizona. It was the service of a countersuit brought by Kit's foster father for custody of the baby he'd tried to force Kit to abort.

Naomi read the legalese in disgusted silence, and Rossen reacted with a deep seated, slow burning anger. What kind of monster was this guy?

Naomi figured there had to be a reason for the man's interest in the baby and she started to dig. What she found was that there had been some one-time Indian moneys from a record year's earning at the reservation casinos set aside for members of the Apache Nation and the baby was eligible for a portion of it. This man had already taken possession of the money awarded to Kit, and now he wanted the baby's share. Naomi was furious. Apparently this guy really did think he was untouchable.

Rossen was angry, but he watched over Mimi and Kit with a whole new level of diligence. The thought of Kit and little Mimi Star in this guy's custody was sickening and he was horrified all over again at the thoughts of what Kit's life had been like then.

When he broke the news to Kit, his respect for her grew as she resolutely took the information without undue fuss. Rossen did notice when she held Mimi that she didn't ever want to let go.

****

Cooper got his mission call to Paraguay. He was due to leave the last week in August and the whole family was helping get him ready. It was a strange combination of emotions. They would have all been so disappointed if he'd chosen not to go, but the thought of living without his particular brand of sparkle was devastating. Kit knew she would miss him desperately. She'd come to adore him, even when he teased her mercilessly.

One night when it was just them, she tried to tell him what life without the gospel was like. She didn't know if she'd made him understand, but at least he knew she felt incredibly grateful for the gift the gospel had been to her.

Kit was as good as her word when she told Naomi she would think about college. She spent weeks stewing over it, but nothing made it feel possible. She knew she was smart and was immensely grateful for that. Her intelligence had been the one bright spot in her life as a foster child. She could bury herself in school or books and experience things she felt she would never have the opportunity to do in real life by reading about them. It was the only thing she'd felt like she could compete in with the other "normal" kids from regular homes.

And in that area of Arizona, largely populated with Native Americans and their cultural norms, books and the internet had opened her eyes to whole facets of the world and society that she never would have known about had she only dealt with the people and ideas right there.

Maybe that's why the thought of college had been such a big burn for her. She knew there was so much more out there, but then again, maybe that's why she was content to accept her life as a new mother and let the dream of a higher education go. She knew that wherever she was, she would always be able to search and learn on her own as long as there were books and a computer. In the last months she'd truly come to understand that love, security, and respect were of vastly greater importance than anything or anyplace else.

She'd promised Naomi she would seriously think

about college, and she had. But Mimi and money, and if she were honest, the thought of leaving Rossen behind all made her come to a decision that if she ever attended college it would be far in the future when her daughter went as well. And her decision wasn't all based on her own wants and needs. The way Rossen had come to love Mimi made Kit realize that separating the two of them was out of the question. It would be detrimental to both of them to an extent that she would never consider college worth the cost. Sometimes she wondered if Rossen didn't love Mimi more than she did. She loved her dearly, but he openly adored her daughter in a manner that she could hardly comprehend. And the baby girl was as happy and content to be held and cuddled by him as could possibly be.

All these thoughts filled her head as she went about her days and finally she'd made up her mind. She took her decision to her Father in Heaven to know for sure that not going was indeed the right course for her to take. Over her time here she'd gained a sure knowledge that God was watching over her and that if she asked like Rossen and Naomi had counseled He would answer her questions.

She prayed about not attending college and pondered it while she lay trying to go to sleep, but for some reason she was unable to relax and rest. Knowing she would be up again nursing the baby, she was frustrated at her restlessness, but the more she stressed over it, the more wakeful she became.

This wasn't like her. New motherhood had been

a tiring experience. She'd been breastfeeding Mimi almost exclusively because the things she had read and been told by both of their doctors indicated that it was much better for Mimi in the long run. Kit didn't mind nursing, but it meant no one could fill in for her when she needed a break, and sometimes she had to literally drag herself awake in the night to calm her hungry child. They'd given Mimi a bottle a few times just to make sure she'd take one in a pinch and she did fine, but Kit's role as chief food supply sometimes wore her out, so she tried harder than ever to get to sleep.

It wasn't working. Her mind just kept going over the idea of going to college and the pros and cons of both sides, and when she finally did drift off, she wrestled with higher education in her dreams.

When she woke up to realize the sun was starting to rise and she hadn't fed Mimi, she felt both guilty and dead tired. She went to the cradle with bleary eyes and for just a moment was terrified when she found it empty. Then she thought of Rossen and went in search of them, knowing he had again rescued them both in the night.

He was asleep in the recliner with a very happy, small girl snuggled under a blanket on his shoulder and a mostly empty bottle of infant formula resting on the table nearby. Kit took another picture, kissed them both on the forehead without waking either up, and went back to bed.

A few hours later when he knocked on her door with a baby that was hungry again, Kit wasn't nearly so tired, but she was still troubled about the question of college. He came into the room and handed her the baby, asking, "Are you okay? You didn't even hear her cry in the night and you never sleep this late."

She self-consciously ran a hand through her wild hair and answered, "Your mom made me promise I'd seriously consider college and I stressed over it all night. I'm sorry she woke you up, but thanks for feeding her. Actually sleeping through a whole night would have been luxurious."

When she mentioned college he perked right up and reached for the baby again. She automatically handed her over, as he suggested, "Get dressed and come feed her out here, and talk to me while she eats." He went back out the bedroom door without her saying anything and Kit got up to close the door and dress, knowing he was going to start up where Naomi had left off.

Admitting to herself that she didn't usually oppose Rossen's good intentions very well, she dressed, wishing she had a power suit that would bring both wisdom and confidence. This college talk had been a long time coming. She settled for the jeans and shirt she felt prettiest in and wended her way to the great room. They were there cuddling and when Rossen watched her walk toward them with open appreciation in his gaze, she was encouraged enough to feel like she could manage this discussion.

Everyone else had already eaten and left and Kit knew it was just the three of them as she tossed a blanket over herself and began to feed her hungry infant. Rossen was quietly watching her and his silence gave her butterflies. Maybe she couldn't handle this conversation. She still hadn't even gotten the answer to her last night's prayer. He didn't say anything and she met his gaze openly, wondering why he didn't just get to the point. The only sound in the room was the baby nursing hungrily and she had begun to feel self-conscious by the time he asked, "Are you going?"

She hadn't expected a question. She'd assumed he would try to reason with her, and try to convince her, and get that "come on, you can do this" tone in his voice the way he usually did. The question threw her and for the first time, she wondered if the reason she hadn't felt that sense of calm after her prayer was because God was trying to tell her she should go. It was a disconcerting thought.

She tried to buy some time to gather her thoughts. "Go where?"

Even to herself she sounded unsure, and he smiled. "Nice try, but I know you way too well. Why couldn't you sleep?" He obviously did know her well to make her face her own question. She could tell from the look on his face that he knew she was unsure of this whole issue, which was a turnabout from her usual 'there's no way I can go to college' mindset.

She leaned her head back against the top of the couch knowing she should just be dead honest with him from the start. He was wise, and she knew he had her best interest at heart, so why should she feel like she had to oppose this? The same chaotic mix of issues filled her head and she was more confused than ever.

She finally looked up and answered his question, "All this time, since I found out I was expecting her, I've felt like college had become out of the question. But I promised your mom, so I really did give it some thought. I came to the same conclusion, that there's no way I can be a single mom and a college student too, so I took it to God in my prayers last night—the way you guys have taught—the whole 'make a decision based on your best judgment and information and ask Him if this is the right thing to do', kind of prayer." She sighed, "And I haven't had much peace of mind since."

Rossen didn't say anything, just kept looking at her in that calm, steady way he had and she felt like squirming at the obvious answer to her prayer. Finally she said, "Okay, so I realize I need to go, but I still can't see how I possibly can. I have no money, and letting you help me survive is a whole different issue than letting you pay for school. I have a baby, and I'm not sure I could just hand her off to a stranger to watch while I went to class or to the library or somewhere. I haven't taken an ACT or even applied. I'd have to get accepted, find the money, make arrangements for an apartment, find childcare, the whole nine yards in slightly over two months. Now, I'm not questioning God, but maybe we're just reading this wrong. Maybe I'm supposed to go next semester or next year or something."

He still didn't pitch in and she said, "Remember

when I said no one could be mad at you? Well, sometimes I'd like to be! Why are you just sitting there watching me? Can't you at least tell me what you're thinking behind those blue eyes? What is this? Death by let's make her decide for herself?"

He began to laugh and sincerely apologized, and then she really did want to be mad at him, but it was still impossible. The baby started to stir, and she covered herself and handed her over, then got up from the couch and went to get herself a glass of milk.

The baby burped and she watched him begin to talk to her and cuddle her and let her play with his fingers. She softly asked, "And how can I take her away from you? Won't it kill you?"

He looked up at her and she felt like she could see into his soul when he answered honestly, "Both of you leaving will kill me, but you need to do this."

She knew he was right because of her prayer, but she still didn't understand. "Okay, but can you please at least tell me why? What would be wrong with just settling down and being a mom and a secretary slash sculptor? Isabel has already found that I can make a decent living with my art. Your dad has said that he'd let me either buy or lease some land here near your family and Sean said he'd help me build a little house. What would be the problem with that?"

His voice was sad when he asked, "Kit, how many states have you traveled to?"

"Four, why?"

"And how many real dates have you gone on?

Or proms?" She looked down at her hands, embarrassed to admit she'd only dated a few times and had never been to a prom, but he went on, "I'm not being rude. I'm sure there were tons of guys in your high school who dreamed of going out with you, but my point is, you can't skip a whole season of your life. I know you have a beautiful little girl, and some things have happened along the way that make it seem like this is out of the question. But if you don't spread your wings now, the opportunity will be gone and you'll be settled down without ever being able to enjoy being a young adult. There's supposed to be a space in between childhood and settled down that's fun and exciting and you learn and grow at an incredible rate right now." He paused and handed the baby back to her to feed again.

"I'm not sure why you need to go do this, but I truly feel you should. At least try. God wouldn't have made you feel like you should without providing a way to do it. Move ahead like it's going to work out and deal with the issues as they come up. Yeah, having a baby is going to make for some awkward conversations on a few dates, but good honorable men will be able to know your heart and the ones who bail aren't worth the bother anyway. Who knows, maybe she'll turn out to be the short cut to sorting through the chaff."

He smiled, but it didn't come anywhere close to reaching his eyes. She almost came right out and asked him why he would send her away when she knew he was in love with her, but she didn't have the guts. And she probably knew the answer anyway. He was doing this for her. Thinking it was in her best interest and she knew he thought she would go off and find a boyfriend who was in the dating stage of his life like she should be. It was a great theory—who knew, maybe it would even work. In her heart she didn't think so.

If he would do this for her, she would do it for him. She knew even as she made the decision that it wasn't going to be a long term thing, but he didn't have to know that. Perhaps if she went and made an honest effort at living this season of her life, then she could come home and someday he'd consider her grown up enough. If not, then she'd come home anyway and raise her daughter here where she was loved.

He was watching her closely and she knew he saw when she made the decision.

With a sad smile, he said, "Go learn and grow and have fun. Eat pizza at two in the morning and date and break a few hearts. Go to prom looking as beautiful as you did the night of Slade and Isabel's wedding, and take a karate class and statistics."

He gave her another sweet, sad smile. "You probably won't struggle with that one like I did, but everyone should have an experience with stats. Find out what it's like to have roommates. Some will be friends the rest of your life and some you'll want to murder, but you'll learn how to deal with them. Have your own phone that all the guys are gonna want you to keep their numbers in and find out who and what you love and don't love. If you hate it, you can quit and come home and cuss me."

When she said, "Okay," he gave her a high five, but he looked sad as he did it.

He said, "I don't think you'll ever regret it."

She already did, but he needed her to do this.

They went ahead like they'd talked about, acting like it would all work out and for the most part it did. Kit decided to go to Utah State University. It had a reciprocity program because they lived so close, so with her grades, she could have in-state tuition, and she could live with Joey and Treyne, and also because USU had great programs in both the fine arts of sculpture and music. She went right to the university to take her ACT to expedite it and with her scores in hand, went back with Rossen to the student financial aid office to determine what might still be available for scholarships and grants. Her grades and ACT scores were high enough that she got an Honors-at-Entrance general scholarship. And because of her Native American ethnicity there were a number of scholarships set aside that were available too.

By the time she, Rossen, and Mimi left to go home to Wyoming that afternoon, she had enough financial backing for her entire four year degree, tuition, books, and living expenses included. As they drove they were quiet except for the radio playing softly. She cried quietly because her dream of college was actually going to come true and she no longer wanted it. Knowing now that she would really be going, she couldn't even begin to face the idea of living away from Rossen in just a few weeks time. He'd become the best friend she'd ever had and even if she hadn't been in love with him, she'd have been sad. As it was, she didn't think they could do it and wondered why she'd felt God wanted this.

****

He thought she was crying because she was finally on her way and he was sadder than he'd ever felt. He had some questions for God too, wondering why He had ever let him fall in love with someone he couldn't have.

****

When they got home, she put the baby down for a nap and went to saddle her horse. Slade found her in the main barn, sobbing her heart out against her horse's neck. He asked her what was wrong and she tried to tell him. She didn't think he could understand, but he actually appeared to understand a lot more than she thought he would. He was far enough removed and he knew Rossen well enough to know what was going on, and he seemed sad for them both. He tried to comfort her and he was actually the one to suggest she leave Mimi at home with Rossen when she left.

At first she was horrified at the idea. How could she even dream of driving away from her little daughter for what right now seemed an eternity? Slade reminded her that USU was only two and a half hours away and that she could come home when she needed to. She thought out loud, "But I don't have a car and the others won't want to come home that often."

Slade shrugged. "Why don't you just buy one of your own?" She'd never even conceived of the idea and he laughed at her and said, "You have the money for it in your account. I mean you can't buy a Ferrari, but there's enough for a safe, nice car."

She climbed on her horse and rode off with her mind going a million miles an hour. Leave the baby and buy a car. The more she thought about it the better it sounded. It would solve the childcare issue. Rossen would probably agree to watch over Mimi if Kit could arrange someone to provide back-up help sometimes. Kit thought of Slade's ranch hand Hank and his wife Ruby. They were only five minutes away and Ruby adored Mimi. Then too, she'd have an excuse to come home when she needed to without it being that she was coming to see Rossen. She rode back to the house to find him.

****

At first, Rossen shook his head. He didn't think she'd be able to leave her baby when it came right down to it, but she looked okay with it and he knew he'd like it better. This way he wouldn't have to lose both of them and she would come home a lot more often. He didn't analyze that thought too closely for fear he would see the incongruity of it, in light of him sending her away to meet other guys, while he hoped she would hurry home.

****

When she registered, she signed up for a sculpture class, a guitar class and a Spanish class. At the last minute she and Joey added a karate class together.

She only had one Spanish class on Wednesdays. She was going to leave it as open as possible so she could go home midweek if she was dying without Mimi and the others. As she said that to herself she laughed right out loud. She did love all the Rocklands, but who was she trying to kid?

Jaclyn M. Hawkes

Chapter 12

The day finally came. Joey and Treyne had already gone back to Logan the day before and Kit knew she needed to be on her way or she'd be driving in a canyon in the dark. She'd become a good driver, and her new car was safe, but she didn't really want to make her first long road trip alone late, so she was trying to find the courage to say goodbye. She told Naomi and the others, and Rossen walked her to her car carrying Mimi. Kit was so upset she couldn't even look up and Rossen tried to talk to her, "Kit, I know this is hard, but you need to calm down or you aren't going to be able to drive safely."

He was so wise and kind. She hugged them both collectively until she thought her heart was going to break. Finally, she looked up, trying to smile through her tears. "This was the dumbest idea we've ever come up with. How about if you two just come to live in Logan, too?"

Rossen smiled sadly. "We might just do that."

She leaned into him to kiss the sleeping baby and then reached up to kiss him gently on the cheek. "I love the two of you, you know. Don't let her forget me." She

211

wanted to say *or you either*, but she knew that was one of those stupid unspoken rule things. Their eyes met and held for a long moment. Finally, she pulled away and got into the car.

She stopped when she was out of sight of the guard shack, knowing she had to get enough control of her tears to be able to see. When she'd agreed to this, she'd had no idea it would be this hard.

****

He'd have been okay; at least he thought he would have, if she hadn't told him she loved him too when she left. He was more mixed up than ever and he put Mimi in her little pack and left to walk through the hills of the ranch. He walked as fast as he dared go with her for almost two hours, and then stopped to give her a bottle and head back. He'd given himself a pep talk enough to have his head back on straight just in time to go home and receive her phone call saying she'd made it there safe.

That night he moved the new crib he'd bought Kit into his room. He shut the door to her room and tried to not even notice it was there. He fed Mimi and put her to bed, honestly wondering if he could do this, and he prayed for Kit, hoping it wasn't this rough of a go where she was.

Naomi and Rob watched, their hearts almost as hammered as his.

****

Kit threw herself into college with a vengeance. She had to get through the next fifteen weeks and she had to make them count. She went to her classes that first Monday with more confidence than she knew she possessed. She already knew she was only going to stay for one semester. She'd do that much for him, but she couldn't face living apart longer than that.

Her art class was heavenly. She learned things the first day, but she also realized she was in a world apart from the rest of her fellow students and her professor figured that out within a few minutes, too. He asked her to go back to the registrar and change to a 300 hundred level class taught in the afternoons instead of mornings. She was thrilled—not so much to be considered a superior artist, but he just made it so she could stay home in Wyoming over Sunday nights and drive back to school on Monday mornings. After giving her the form she'd need with his signature, they talked for almost half an hour and he suggested he help her get some college credits for her bronzes when they were complete.

As Kit hurried to her Spanish class, she was formulating a plan. She'd ask her academic advisor about taking some tests to get as many credits passed as fast as she could. It would appease Rossen that much more when she announced she was coming home for good.

Her Spanish class was a bit intimidating at first. There were a hundred and fifty students enrolled and it met in a large auditorium. She had never encountered anything like it before. She must have looked somewhat unsure of herself because one of the guys next to her asked, "No Spanish in high school for you either, huh?"

She shook her head with a hesitant smile. "I'm afraid this is my first experience with any foreign language." She didn't even understand the natives back in Arizona usually. Languages held no interest for her. She was only taking it because Rossen spoke it fluently and it accumulated credit.

The guy nudged her arm. "Come sit by me and we'll muddle through it together." Kit was pleasantly surprised. For some reason she'd expected this to be like high school where the guys were 'cool', but not necessarily friendly. She'd mentally made a checklist of all the things Rossen wanted her to experience in what he'd called this season of her life. She didn't even consciously realize she was doing it, but she was planning to check off as many of them as she could in the next three and a half months. One of them was dating, so when her Spanish buddy, whose name she found out was Ethan, asked her out after class she accepted with a smile.

Her and Joey's Karate class was at eleven o'clock and they met at the door with a hug. Kit was surprised at how much having Joey there brightened up the day. She'd been having a good day, but Joey was family. Kit adored her and was glad she was there.

Kit was normally a gentle soul who would never show aggression. The time she'd belted the ranch hand was the only time she could ever remember wanting to strike someone, so the whole idea of Karate took a minute to catch on. Not so with Joey. In fact, she volunteered to be the guinea pig that first day and took their instructor by surprise when she really did try to kick him when he asked her to. Joey loved it from the first and Kit didn't have to stretch her imagination far to know what was going to happen in their apartment.

Matt, their instructor, was not much older than them and was good looking and funny. When he offered to hold an extra lab in the evenings sometimes, Kit and Joey put their names and numbers on his list.

Kit's last class of the day, guitar, was the one that had her most worried. She could play, but she'd never read a note of music in her life. She knew she would have to in this class and she was prepared to do whatever it took, but she walked in feeling the most nervous she had all day.

There were eighteen other students in the class and she took a seat near the back, put her guitar down and took out a notepad to take notes. The students in the class were an interesting mix. Some were just your basic student she'd seen all day around campus, obviously taking an elective to rack up a few more credits. The rest were undoubtedly musicians, but it was like there was a line drawn down the middle. Two were into classical acoustic guitar and the others were blatantly rockers.

She'd never seen this variety of dress and hair colors and styles in her life. There were tattoos and piercings and dog collars and stuff she had no idea even what to call it. Some of them were loud and obnoxious, but some of the most outlandish looking people were, by far, the most focused students.

The professor was a middle aged man who dressed conservatively, but obviously enjoyed working with the students and the kids liked him. The class turned out to be interesting and fun.

First he gave them some basic information about grading and the books they would need, then passed out some single sheets of music and they got right into playing. Kit couldn't read along so she let everyone play it through one time while she pretended to tune up and then the next time she played it through with them from memory. She figured out right away that not everyone played it correctly so she listened closely to the instructor to follow him.

The next song she did the same, and on the third one she realized the instructor was playing the harmony after she played along with him for a few moments and what she was doing was different from those around her. She hadn't noticed the first time through because she was focused on the professor. She listened to a talented player next to her and the next time around got it right.

After class as everyone packed up to leave, the professor pulled her aside. For a minute she thought she was in trouble, but he didn't appear mad as he said, "Excuse me." He glanced at the class roster in a clip board in his hand. "Kit. Is that right?" She nodded.

He waited until the last student left the room and then looked right at her and asked, "How much music can you read?"

She looked down for just a second, then raised her head and answered, "None, Dr. Mitchell, this is my first music lesson in my life. But I promise I'm a fast learner. If you'll let me stay, I won't hold your class up." She waited for his answer without breathing.

He smiled at her reassuringly. "I have no intention of kicking anyone out of this class, Kit. I just know that what you were playing just now, you played from memory having only heard it once, because I wrote it and I've never given it out before. Would you mind if I asked you some questions? Have you got a few minutes?"

Kit was a touch wary as she nodded her head and he continued, "Good. Get your guitar back out. No, better yet, just grab that electric there beside you." Kit nervously picked up the guitar. She'd never touched an electric in her life and though she'd always wanted to play one, she didn't really want to try it the first time in this situation.

He interrupted her nervous thoughts to ask, "Can you play my part of that third song again? You play it. I'll play the other. On three, one and two and three." Kit didn't even have time to prepare; she just had to start right in playing. She missed a couple of notes at the first as her hands tried to get accustomed to the different instrument, but then she played beside him without a hitch. He sped up a couple of times and slowed down once and then switched to the part she was playing and told her to switch back to the student part. They played it through three times before he finally stopped her. He was looking at her, thinking, and she wasn't sure what to do.

Next he said, "Listen to what I play and then play it back for me." For a minute or two he played an incredibly intricate set that was fast and had an irregular rhythm. Kit worried she'd mess it up, but she played it back exactly. After that he asked her to play something she'd come up with herself, so she chose a lullaby she'd written for Mimi and she sang along under her breath. Next he asked her to play a rock song off the radio and she played Adrenaline by Nick Sartori.

She'd never actually played it on the instrument it was written for and she loved it even better than on her own guitar. She finished playing it, but without the long drawn out buzzing whine at the end. She'd never figured out how to make that sound on her acoustic and she didn't know how to make this guitar do it either. She finished and Dr. Mitchell took the guitar away from her to make the last long whine. He showed her how to do it and handed it back asking, "How much have you played an electric?"

She shook her head again with a wry smile. "Never."

"Really?"

"Really."

He was shaking his head and mumbling to himself. Finally he said, "Well Kit, what do you want to be when you grow up?"

"A mom. And a sculptor. Why?"

He smiled and shook his head some more.

"Guitar isn't your burning passion?"

She had no idea what was going on. "Well, I love to play, and even sing, but I wouldn't call it a passion."

At that, he asked, "How are you paying for school? Do you mind if I ask?"

"I got some scholarships. Why are you asking me all this?"

He acted like he wasn't sure what to say to her. "I guess I'm asking because I'm curious. You know every couple of years I get a student through here who's really good. A natural. A prodigy if you will, but I've never seen anything like you." He was shaking his head again. "Well, you're taking my class; I assume you want to learn to read music, right?"

"Yes, very much."

"I guess I don't have to ask if you're a quick study. Let me show you something." He went to a marker board and talked to her for a minute about the base and treble clefs and timing and different notes. Then he walked into his office and came out with a book. "This is the guitar basics book my level one class will be using. The first section is devoted to reading music and how notes correspond to the guitar. I'll give you this one in the interest of time because the book store is already closed for the day. You can pay me later. Are you driving or did you walk or ride the bus?"

He'd seemed normal through most of the class, but now she was beginning to wonder. "I drove. My car is in the student lot out back."

"Perfect, because I want you to take this electric

guitar and amp home with you tonight. Bring it back to class with you tomorrow; you can pull right up to this back door tonight and again tomorrow to unload it. If you get a ticket, I'll take care of it. Take it home, fiddle around with it and we'll talk again tomorrow. You can tell me what you think. Oh, here, you'd better take these." He handed her a set of head phones. "They'll keep the early birds happy. You plug them into the amp. Just leave your guitar in my office and I'll lock it up. It's a beautiful guitar by the way, one of the top makes. Where did you get it?"

"It was a gift."

He smiled down at her kindly. "The guitar is nice, but your talent is the gift. It's a shame it isn't your passion."

She pulled her car around and he helped her load in and she went to their apartment. She was tired, but she felt like her first day of college had gone well overall.

Joey and Treyne met her at the door as she struggled in with her pack and the new guitar. Treyne asked, "What in the world are you doing, girl? What's with the new guitar?" He took it in and immediately plugged it in and began to mess around with it.

Joey told him to quit. "You're hurting my brain and today's the first day. I can't spare any."

Kit got out the headphones and handed them to him and said, "Don't break anything," as she wandered to the kitchen in search of food.

She was starting to eat an apple when Joey

grabbed it. "No! We're going to a ward Family Home Evening dinner in ten minutes. Didn't you read the flyer on the door?"

Kit had no idea what a ward Family Home Evening group was and she wasn't sure she was up to it, anyway. She was tired and she missed Mimi terribly. Just thinking of her made her milk start to let down and Joey grabbed a dish towel with an "Oh my," that sounded identical to Naomi. Kit went to change her shirt, telling herself it would get easier with time.

Their Family Home Evening group was fun and several of them came home with them. As soon as Kit came in, she went into her and Joey's room with her books and the new guitar and shut the door. She put on the head phones and plugged the guitar in to experiment with it like she'd been told. It was actually a blast and within a half hour or so she'd figured out how to make a lot of the sounds she heard on the radio. The wailing guitar in her ears helped to keep her mind off of home for a while, but eventually she wasn't in the mood and sat at her desk to see if studying would occupy her head. She had the Spanish down and was working on reading her music when there was a knock on her door.

It was one of the guys from their group. "Hey, Kit. We're just heading out. I was wondering if you have plans for Friday night. There's a pep rally and hello dance and I was hoping you'd come with me."

She smiled up at him. "I would love to, Nate, if I were going to be here, but I'm planning to go home after my last afternoon class that day. But ask me again, okay?"

He gave her a disappointed, "Sure," and left and she went back in and got ready for bed.

When Joey came in an hour later, Kit was asleep, but there were still tears on her eyelashes and every once in awhile, she breathed with a little sob.

Day two was a lot like day one except it seemed to drag along because she was so focused on being able to leave to go home after her last class. She and Ethan sat together again in Spanish and in Karate she got up the nerve to yell when she attempted to kick Joey. By the end of class she'd begun to wonder if she and Joey weren't getting the lion's share of Matt's attention. It was turning out to be a fun class. Art was interesting. The professor had them listen to a short lecture before letting them get started on an animal of their choice. Kit chose a dragon and was satisfied that she was finished and set it to dry in less than an hour.

She was in her guitar classroom forty-five minutes early and was quietly studying when Dr. Mitchell came in and asked her how she'd done with the new guitar. She picked it up to show him the licks she'd figured out and he nodded his approval. "How about understanding reading music?"

Kit shrugged. "I understand the concepts, but I'm sure it takes a while to be able to see the music and have your brain tell your fingers at the same time. I can hardly imagine playing as fast as you played yesterday from a sheet of music."

He answered, "It'll all come in time." He

changed the subject. "How many credits are you carrying this semester?"

"Twenty one, why?"

His answer was animated, "Unlike you, guitar is my passion!" His eyes lit up. "I like to play it, I like to teach it, and more than anything I like to play with others to whom it's a passion too. Once or twice a month I fly out to LA to sit in as a studio musician. The planes and the city are a hassle, but the music and the money are great! I get to play with some of the most talented musicians in the country and they pay me seventeen hundred bucks a day."

Kit's eyes grew wide. "No way!"

"I was hoping you'd perk up when I said that. You see, they need me about three times more than I want to go. I have my family here, and although it's fun and exciting, it's too much with my work at the university too. Now, rarely would I ever recommend a student. In fact, you're the first I've ever even approached, but with your ability to pick things up so fast, you would be very good at this. They need someone who can pick up music quickly so they can record as fast as possible. They record just regular albums of their own and sit in on others', and also do things like movie scores and commercials and stuff like that."

She was puzzled. "But I don't even read music."

"That's true. And eventually you'll have to learn. But I have no doubt you'll have it down in no time. In the interim, if you think you could make it out there, either I'll play it through quickly for you or I'll find someone else to. Sometimes they'll even email the scores out so we can get a look at them beforehand. That way, even if you had to take your time learning it, you would have it memorized when we got there."

It was a wild idea. For just a moment or two she wondered if her professor was interested in more than guitar music, but then he continued, "Think about it. The next time I'll be going is over Labor Day weekend. My wife almost always comes with me. She's a pianist and backup singer. We'll fly out that Thursday and be back Monday night in time to teach Tuesday. Think about it. If you're nervous about it, bring a friend to check it out. At the least you could say no, but it might be a really fun, part time way to make some good college money. I was telling one of the main guys I work for about you last night and he's willing to bring you in and give you a try."

The fact that his wife would be there was reassuring to her. The thought of time away from her family, she was forcing herself to think of them as that, rather than Mimi and Rossen, would be a struggle. But if she only did it a couple of times a month and it would help her support herself even after she stopped her guitar class, it might be a good thing. Maybe they could even come with sometimes.

"Can I think about it for a day or two, or do you need to know right now?"

He waved a hand at her. "Take your time to think about it. I can let them know any time before I leave."

Her mind was buzzing during the whole class and when she got back to the apartment she was disappointed that Joey wasn't there. She'd decided she'd go home and talk to Rossen and if he thought it was okay, she'd see if Joey would go with her to check it out. She threw a few things into her car, left a note and headed out. She sang along to the radio as she drove, wishing that home wasn't so far away.

Jaclyn M. Hawkes

Chapter 13

When she pulled in, she couldn't believe how good it felt to come home. She knew she'd only been gone two days, but it felt much longer. She went inside and looked around for everybody. She didn't see Naomi or Rob or Sean, but she found Rossen working in his office with Mimi laying on a blanket at his feet, happily playing with the toys hanging from a mobile he'd set up over her.

She walked in and hugged him without even hesitating, then picked up the baby at his feet. Her milk immediately began to stream and she was embarrassed, but she hardly even cared. She knew he'd understand. She took Mimi into the other room, hoping she'd be hungry when they got there. She was settled with her nursing, when he came in a moment later, a tentative smile on his face.

"To what do we owe this surprise visit? I thought you wouldn't be home until Saturday." He leaned against the nearby counter as he spoke.

She wasn't sure how much to tell him. She didn't think she should come right out and say that she planned to come home every Tuesday night if she could.

She just smiled and answered, "It's been a little harder to quit nursing cold turkey than I thought. I should have listened to your mom and stopped as soon as I knew I was going to be leaving her here. And I only have one Spanish class on Wednesday. I was hoping you could help me brush up on my els and ellas while I'm here."

They talked for an hour, still sitting there. Mimi was long since fed and burped and fed and had fallen asleep against Kit's shoulder. She felt like heaven there. Kit told him all about her classes and being moved up in art and about the proposal to go to LA. She asked him what he thought and he said go for it, and that taking Joey was probably a great idea and she'd love it. She didn't want to hurt feelings, but she wanted him to know she was honestly trying so she told him about Ethan in her class who she was going out with the next day, and how Nate had asked her except she'd already be on her way home.

Rossen put out his hand to interrupt her. "Whoa, right there. You're planning to come home the first Friday of the year, even when you've been asked out? Kit, this first week or two of the year is when they do all kinds of fun stuff to help everybody get to know each other. You need to be there to enjoy it."

She looked at him, floored. "No way, buddy! You think I can just leave and stay away? I would never have agreed to that, and you know it. The deal was I could come home when I needed to. I accepted one date and took a rain check on the second one. What more do you want me to do?"

"I want you to stay there Friday night and go to the pep rally and the dance, and come home early Saturday morning. That way you can do both."

She was disgusted. "You're changing the deal mid-game. And why do I have to date regularly, when you aren't even trying to get out? If I have to, you have to."

Rossen looked at her in surprise. He should have stopped when he was ahead. She was right and she knew it, much as she hated to encourage he see other girls. He probably ought to be moving on as well. He sighed. "Okay, okay. Fair's fair. I'll go out."

She looked him in the eye "Thursday *and* Friday?" She was feeling pretty seriously defiant.

"Kit!"

She shook her head. "Nope! Fair's fair."

Naomi and Rob were just coming in from the garage during this last exchange. They stopped dead still listening and when Kit demanded that Rossen date too, they gave each other a silent high five and Rob whispered, "Serves him right, big bully." They pretended to come in again and made a lot of noise, so Rossen and Kit wouldn't know they'd been overheard.

This time when Kit left, it wasn't quite as bad as the first time. She was concerned about being on time to class so she had to just leave and she didn't want to look like she'd been crying for two hours, so she tried not to.

She called Joey to see if she knew Nate's phone number so she could attempt to fix her Friday night plans. He hadn't asked someone else yet and she was glad she called. If he'd seen her there he would have thought she'd lied.

When she talked to Joey, she asked about going to LA and Joey was stoked, so they arranged to miss that week's Thursday's classes and made plane reservations. Dr. Mitchell was thrilled and insisted they stay at the same hotel as he and his wife and even said he'd get his musician friends to pay for it.

Saturday morning Kit, Joey, and Treyne, all three, came home for Cooper's talk in church the next day and they had a mob of family and friends over to the house to eat Sunday afternoon. Kit was still concerned about gossip and she put Mimi in her pack and took her for a walk around the ranch. They ended up at the pond where Kit let her play in a few inches of water at the pond's edge and Mimi thought it was great. She'd splash and then startle when the water hit her in the face and it made Kit laugh.

****

Rossen found them there, late in the afternoon. He watched them for a few minutes as he skipped rocks. He knew why she was out here and it frustrated him to death. It wasn't fair for her to feel like she had to fade into the woodwork around their neighbors and friends, but she felt like she should. And the sad truth of the matter was that there probably were those out there who did talk, even though Kit and the baby, and even he were not at fault. Slade and Isabel came around the pond holding hands and even that frustrated him. What would he have given to be able to take Kit's hand, instead of having to watch from a distance and be only a friend?

At length, she came over to him and said, "So, I told you how my dates went. How were yours?"

That's probably why he was so irritable. He'd been miserable both nights. And to make matters worse, both of the girls he'd taken had texted him several times. At least they'd had a good time.

To Kit he said, "They were fine." She laughed at him and he knew she was reading him like a book again.

Kit had to leave on Sunday evening with the others this time. They'd all come in the same car and Treyne had an early Monday morning class, so she had no choice. When she kissed Mimi Star goodbye in his arms again, he knew it was far too hard. When Treyne turned on the radio as they got in, Rossen knew Kit turned her head to the window to cry.

****

On Wednesday morning the college bunch drove to Salt Lake where they met the rest of the family and drove to Provo to take Cooper to the MTC. When they returned and split up again, Kit had never felt so lonely in her life. Cooper gone for two years, on top of being away from her baby and home, seemed like more than she could stand. When they pulled into their house in Logan, Treyne asked, "Kit, are you gonna be okay?" She nodded and he added, "Maybe you should just do this for one semester. You don't seem very happy."

She hugged him as she went past him up the steps. "I have to do this, Treyne. Otherwise Rossen will feel like I missed a whole season of my life and he'll never forgive himself. It doesn't make a whole lot of sense in a way, but it's something I have to do. But you're right. I'm a one semester flash in the pan. Just don't tell him that. I don't want to argue about it until I have to." She gave him a watery smile and went in and picked up her guitar.

Later that night when Matt came by and asked if she wanted to go workout, she went with him gladly. She worked until her breath was coming in gasps and Matt finally took her hand and led her outside. He walked beside her for more than half an hour before he finally asked, "You ever gonna tell me what's wrong, or am I just going to have to keep trying to come up with ideas on my own?"

She started to cry and he turned and pulled her into a hug. She finally admitted that she was homesick and told him part of the story. She told him about Cooper leaving and how much she'd come to love him as a younger brother. She told him about Mimi and the Rocklands and that she didn't really feel strongly about college, but felt she needed to be here for a while to put the missing this season thing to rest.

He took her hand and started walking again. Eventually, he asked, "Does he know you love him?"

She turned to look at him in the dark. "Who?"

"Whoever it is who has your heart in Wyoming. Have you ever told him?"

Kit sniffled. "I'm sure he knows. It's just something we can't talk about because I'm only eighteen."

They walked for a while longer and when he took her back to her door, he hugged her again and whispered into her hair, "It's all going to be okay, Kit. You're a strong woman and you can do whatever it takes. I know that about you." He kissed the top of her head. "See you in the morning."

****

When she and Joey walked in the next morning a few minutes before class time, he came over to her and looked at her and then asked Joey, "Is she doing any better today than she was last night?"

Kit smiled self-consciously and Joey laughed and said, "Yes, she is."

He smiled. "Good, 'cause she's a wimpy martial artist when she bawls!" At that Kit came at him and actually kicked him pretty good before he rounded on her and threw her to the matt. Then he collapsed next to her to look her in the eye. "You look better. You okay?"

"Yes, thanks to you. Thanks for walking with me. It really helped."

He stood up and pulled her to her feet. "You're welcome. Anytime."

The Karate class was turning out to be awesome and both Kit and Joey loved it. Matt had arranged to hold an extra class every weekday morning at eight and they both went almost every day. When Kit began working out on Monday and Thursday afternoons with him too, Joey started to tease her. Kit only smiled and said, "Rossen wants me to date, and I want to learn

Karate. It's a two birds with one stone thing. Plus, Matt's really fun." Kit was getting good fast and Joey had to work to keep up with her.

Her academic advisor had arranged for her to take a series of CLEP tests to effectively test out of classes. They staggered them so Kit wouldn't be overwhelmed, and she started with a basic English class the next week out. Kit was surprised that it seemed simple to her. She'd expected it to be much more difficult.

That Thursday morning, she left the Rocklands' knowing she wouldn't see them again for six days. Even though she was getting tougher about her goodbyes, that seemed like a long, long time.

Chapter 14

She and Joey boarded the plane with mixed emotions. It was the first time flying for Kit and Joey knew she was a little nervous about the whole thing, so she was trying to look out for her. At the same time, they were both excited to be on an adventure. When they arrived, Dr. Mitchell and his wife ushered them into a waiting limo and Joey laughed as Kit swallowed a huge lump in her throat. She was suddenly beginning to wonder just what she'd gotten them into.

They stopped at their hotel and dropped their bags, then got back in the limo and went to meet whomever it was that they would be working with, for lunch. The car stopped in front of a trendy restaurant and the door was opened and they were led inside. Dr. Mitchell leaned over and apologized for the marked attention they received as they climbed out of the long limousine. "Try not to let it bother you. You'll soon get used to it and it's nice to always be picked up and dropped off."

By the time they were seated, Kit had decided she either had to quit worrying that she was going to do something socially incorrect, or she couldn't even consider doing this again. She knew she wanted to try to play here, so she let the worry go and tried to remember that she was the same person here as at home.

They were in a relatively private dining area and Dr. Mitchell took a phone call and then reported, "Nick's going to be late, so let's go ahead and eat. If he doesn't make it here, we'll meet him at the studio."

They ordered and were served and it was a good thing Kit wasn't terribly hungry. The portions were miniscule and even though they were colorful and unique, they weren't very tempting. She forced herself to eat, wishing for Naomi's home cooking. She was losing weight fast at school and didn't have a whole lot to spare.

They were just finishing when Kit heard Joey say, "Holy Moly," under her breath. Kit looked at her to see what was up and followed her eyes to see three men walking toward their table. The one in the lead was rock star Nick Sartori. Kit had played his song for Dr. Mitchell just a couple of weeks before. Kit didn't recognize the next two, but they stopped as they walked by a table to talk to someone else who looked familiar. Nick spoke to him and gave him a handshake of sorts as they walked by. She was grateful she'd brought Joey as she thought to herself, *He told me some of the biggest music stars in the business.*

Nick continued on to their table. As he looked from the Mitchells to Joey and Kit, he raised his eyebrows appreciatively. "Which one is the guitarist?" Dr. Mitchell indicated Kit, and Nick took her hand in both of his to shake it. "You said she was good. You didn't say she was gorgeous." He smiled at Kit as he released her hand and turned to Joey.

"Please tell me you're a musician, too."

Joey laughed as she deftly removed her hand from his. "The closest I come to being a musician is singing in the church choir when they're truly desperate."

He didn't look like he believed her and said, "You're her agent then?"

"Actually, I'm a mechanic. Kit is my sister."

Nick looked Joey up and down, and then looked from her fair hair to Kit's all but black hair. He chuckled. "A mechanic and her sister. Right." He acted like she was making a joke and they both let it go, but neither of them smiled. He looked at them again. "You're serious?"

At that, they both laughed and Joey said, "I'm serious. Kit is sort of adopted."

"I see." He looked somewhat skeptical as he pulled out a chair and sat down. He waved the waitress away and turned to Dr. Mitchell, surprisingly all business. "We're too late to eat. And we really need to get going. We'll send out for something later."

On the way back out of the restaurant, he stopped at the table of the other man again, and Kit remembered where she'd seen him. He was Bryan Cole, a country music singer who had recently received an award for his music. Kit remembered Joey had been disappointed at the time because she thought his lyrics were crude and demeaning to women and marriage. She'd turned him off in disgust. Kit turned to look at Joey, who was watching it all with a bland look on her face, and wondered what she was thinking under that innocent façade.

Nick was telling Bryan that they'd be recording for the next few days and concluded with, "We'll be ready for you on Saturday. Be there about eight."

Bryan nodded, watching the girls as he did and said, "I'll see you then."

Back in the limo on the way to the studio, Nick and Dr. Mitchell had an in-depth conversation about what they would be doing. As they drove, Kit quietly watched Nick. He was not what she would have expected from a rock star who specialized in loud, rowdy, hard rock. He was obviously a serious musician who appeared to be an astute businessman, too. Kit understood they were going to be working on songs he was recording personally, as well as a movie score and several commercials this week end.

She studied Nick as they talked. He was dark and very good looking. Flashily dressed, he wore chains at his neck and a huge diamond stud in one ear. His hair was a tousled mess that must have taken hours to achieve with the help of a lot of hair product. Probably just over six feet, he had a distinctive air about him. He was confident almost to the point of cockiness, but not obnoxious. Kit was frankly floored by his level of diplomacy. The two other men were apparently members of his band and he handled everyone with an air of respect that she hadn't anticipated. The tabloids and press had painted a spoiled and selfish image of most stars and Nick was a pleasant surprise.

As she checked out this mega rock star, she couldn't help but mentally compare him to the long legged, jean clad man back home who quietly did his engineering with her baby at his feet. Her mind was seven hundred miles away in Wyoming when she realized Nick was studying her as well. At first she wished she'd worn something fancier than her jeans and heeled boots with a cropped jean jacket, but then decided she'd worn just what she felt like that day and it was a good idea to be who she was, regardless of where she was. Nick must have thought so, too. His gaze held open appreciation.

He took a phone call as they rode and it soon became apparent that whoever was calling had seen him with Kit and Joey and had called to ask him about them. He grinned at the girls as he talked openly about them to the person on the other end of the line. Whoever it was wanted to know about Joey, especially.

Ending the call, he smiled at them and said, "You've already turned heads in LA. We'll have to guard you from the paparazzi! I'm getting calls about you and you've only been here an hour. He'll die if he ever finds out you were sitting right here." He laughed out loud and it was an infectious sound.

At the studio, Kit was surprised at the level of security they had to go through to get into the building. There was a cluster of people outside the main doors waiting to get a glimpse of whomever would be recording that day, and Kit and Joey were almost overwhelmed by the jostling they received when their group tried to walk through. Nick smiled at the fans as they pushed through with the help of two security guards, but the smile never quite reached his eyes. Cameras popping in her face left her nearly blind momentarily and Nick took her elbow and put up a protective arm as one of the others helped Joey get through the crush. When they were finally safely inside, they were greeted by yet another set of locked doors guarded by armed men. This time they were escorted through without the physical mobbing.

As they emerged into the safety of the interior of the building, Nick apologized, "Sorry about that. We usually just drive into the underground parking, and no one can bother us inside the car, but they're doing some kind of maintenance on the concrete and we're stuck going in the front doors for awhile. The press is having a good time with it."

Nick was still jovial, but it was obvious that the hassle had been frustrating and once inside, he wanted to get right to business. Dr. Mitchell settled Joey in a booth with a man named Ian who wore a headset and sat in front of ten thousand lighted buttons. Then he took Kit into the actual studio and fitted her with her own headset and electric guitar. They were off to one side and he quickly went through the music they were going to be playing that morning. Kit tried to just focus on the music and ignore her nerves.

Shortly, the other musicians and a backup singer came in and got set up. There was Nick on the guitar, as well as Kit and Dr. Mitchell, and Mrs. Mitchell on keyboards. One of the two men who had come in with Nick was his drummer, Shane, and the other was a singer named Joss who played a number of instruments. Before the day was out he played six different things ranging from the mandolin to the alto sax. Shane was about half kooky, with a perpetual smile and enough energy for ten people. Kit liked him instantly and enjoyed his nutty enthusiasm as he mixed a passion for music with a screwball sense of humor. As they worked, it became apparent that he both tempered the work atmosphere and kept up the intensity at the same time.

Joss was so mellow she almost wondered if he was on something, except there was no way he could have been drugged and so utterly with it musically, at the same time. Kit didn't hear him make a mistake the whole day. He was a machine, just a very low key one.

As they began Kit was sickeningly uptight, but within just a few minutes, as she became confident she could do everything they needed, she loosened up. She decided being a part of a band was much more fun than just playing alone. There was something about working together to create the music. The complexity and depth were immensely satisfying. The all-encompassing sound and the rhythm and passion of the musicians fed an emotion that was almost a physical high. She soon found herself immersed in the music and was dancing and playing along with Nick as they worked.

She knew he'd been watching her. She would have expected nothing less from any boss. And when he came and stood beside her, she looked to him for suggestions and instruction just like the others did. Once in a while, if he got too close, she would back away from him, and a time or two she saw something in his eyes she wasn't completely comfortable with. When that happened, she dropped her own eyes to focus on her instrument for a moment.

They played consistently through three different songs, working until they were near perfect enough for Ian, the sound guy in the booth with Joey. It took a few times through, but Kit was surprised that they could polish a song in such an amazingly short time. Her respect for the musicians around her grew as the hours passed.

They began to have trouble on the fourth song, but it was with the back-up singer, not the instrumentalists. Kit could sense that Nick and the others were frustrated with the woman, who became more and more put out as they asked her over and over to sing it the way they wanted. Kit couldn't even read music, but she understood what they were asking long before the finicky vocalist. Finally, Nick raked his hand through his messy do and asked Kit quietly, "You don't by any chance sing do you?"

Kit glanced at the woman who was now glaring at her as she replied, "A little."

"Do you understand what we're after here?" Kit

wordlessly nodded her head. "Okay. Let's try it with Kit singing and see if we can get past this. From the top. One, two, three, four."

Kit began to sing the part, her clear voice a perfect blend with Nick's and Joss's, and the piece came together on the very first run. Nick gave Joss a silent glance that held some meaning Kit didn't understand, and spoke over his headset to Ian. The pouty backup singer snarled something unintelligible, glared at Kit and left, leaving Kit as slightly unsure of herself as she had been at first. Nick gave her a reassuring smile, struck a chord and they continued on as before. Kit didn't figure out until that night when she and Joey had a chance to talk, that the singer had been sacked and sent home. And, it was a day or more later, before she understood that they intended to keep her singing if she would.

They played until six-thirty California time, when they decided to call it a night. As they pushed through the crowd at the doors and climbed into the limo for the ride back to the hotel, Kit suddenly realized she was tired to the bone. The intensity of the work, coupled with her initial nerves, had worn her out and as she settled into the plush seat of the luxury car, she felt her weariness kick in.

Nick and the guys asked them all if they wanted to go to dinner together, and then out to a club after. The four of them said yes to dinner, but declined the night on the town later. Kit was tired enough as they pushed through another bunch of cameras and fans to get into the restaurant, where they were rescued discreetly by the staff and led to an out of the way table, that she wished she would have declined dinner and gone back to the hotel hungry.

Nick and Joey realized she was tired and kept the conversation going on around her at dinner without a lull, content to let her eat and watch in relative silence. She still had little appetite and struggled to eat even a minimal meal.

Walking back out to the limo with both a superstar and his entourage of fans, Kit marveled at how far away this morning in Wyoming felt, and even how normal the crush of onlookers had become. This time as she was seated next to Nick in the limousine, the brush of his shoulder and thigh against hers didn't even seem out of place. She'd come a long way in one day.

Nick helped them out of the car himself at the hotel with a tired smile. "See you at eight." His and Kit's eyes held for a brief moment and then she turned to walk away into the revolving door. She made it to their room, showered, prayed, and talked to Joey for a few minutes before nodding off with thoughts of Rossen and Mimi in her head.

****

A good night's rest did wonders and the next day she was excited to get started when they arrived unscathed in the sound room of the studio. She soon understood they were going to work on the soundtrack of a movie for the day. She wasn't even unduly concerned that Dr. Mitchell and his wife would be working in another part of the building, except for worrying about when she'd have to admit to Nick that she didn't read music fast enough yet.

She quietly got her headset on and made sure her guitar was tuned. When Nick came to her and discreetly went over what she would be playing that day, she realized Dr. Mitchell had talked to him about her needing to play the music through once. She looked into Nick's eyes as he helped her and didn't see impatience or frustration, so she grew to trust him even more. He was not what she would have expected of Nick Sartori at all.

They got started playing right away and Kit was stunned to realize that although today's music did include some rather intense rock music, the bulk of it was, in fact, beautiful, almost wistful instrumentals for the love scenes in the movie. Kit was just beginning to understand what was involved in studio music, and the fact that this group of rockers were also talented classical musicians, wasn't all that surprising after all.

As they played, Nick would come and talk to her, helping her to understand what they were working toward. He ended up standing behind her left shoulder for most of the morning. They each slipped one ear of their headsets off, and as often as not, it was Nick's low voice she heard in her ear instead of Ian's, helping her to blend smoothly into the mix. She'd come to know Ian called a lot of the shots, but Nick didn't hesitate to overrule him if he thought differently about what sound he was after.

Sometimes when Nick watched her, there was an almost tender look in his eyes that made her glad she had her back to him most of the time. It was something of the same thing she saw in Rossen's eyes at times, and it could be disconcerting. When she noticed it more toward lunch, she passed it off as the talented body language of a man used to millions of women being attracted to him. She was sure a guy in his position had a girl in every port, so to speak, and she figured his interest was simply a matter of habit and didn't really give it another moment's thought.

As they played and sang from one song to the next, Kit wondered if they were progressing faster or slower than usual with her help. She was encouraged that they all seemed to be pleased with the headway they were making.

When noon rolled around, they ordered in lunch and sat around the lobby eating and laughing with Joey blending in like just another one of the guys. They really didn't believe she was a mechanic until mid-afternoon when one of their complicated machines went on the fritz. The technicians had no idea what was going on and had resorted to calling in a repair man, which was completely throwing off the schedules of both humans and the studio.

Joey began to pick the technicians' brains as to which machine and what it was supposed to be doing, then looked into its innards. The three techs watched her with half skepticism and half nerves. Twenty minutes later, when she found that it was simply a matter of a cooling fan malfunction, and had the entire studio up and running again, they finally decided she and Kit might be serious. Apparently LA had never seen a stunning five foot ten blonde woman mechanic before.

They went back to work and the next song they worked on was actually the love theme for the movie. It was a romantic ballad that Nick and Kit sang and also played and she had to work at focusing more than she'd had to up to this point. They ended up playing across from each other as they sang and it was a great time. When they finished, Kit took a deep breath at having gotten through without messing up either the words or the music and they went on to work on one more song for the day.

Their last song was classic rock and roll with a strong backbeat and awesome guitar licks. Kit and Nick and Shane got into it and Kit was having a ball with the ripping part she was playing. She felt like she finally had a handle on the volume the mixer wanted from her, and was playing and singing much louder than she'd dared to before. They played like they were in front of ten thousand fans, and when they finally finished, they collapsed into the chairs in the lobby amidst applause and catcalls from all of the people working with them.

It was the first time Kit ever wondered if she might like performing in front of a crowd. It was strangely easy for her to loosen up and perform with her guitar, while sometimes she was almost shy in front of others without it. When Ian called it a wrap, she drew another deep breath and decided that even though she was tired, she couldn't believe they paid people to have this much fun.

The guys all offered dinner and a night out again and they agreed again to dinner, but no clubbing. Kit hadn't even dared tell them she was too young to get into a club legally, even if she'd wanted to, for fear they would think she was too young to play with them. They went to dinner and waded through the cameras and fans again to do so. Kit wondered why they were taking her and Joey's photos when they weren't even famous.

Back at the hotel after dinner, they got a call from Dante, Isabel's brother, who lived not far from where they were. Isabel had told him they were there and he and his fiancé offered to come by and get them to take them to a movie, or show them around town. They knew he would entertain them without asking them to go anywhere or do anything they weren't comfortable with, so they accepted and had a good time. He had them back to their hotel by ten thirty and although that was eleven thirty Wyoming time, they were still rested the next morning to go to work.

That wasn't necessarily true for the rest of the crew. Nick and Shane were late and looked tired when they got there, carrying mugs of coffee as they pushed through the front doors. While they were waiting for them, Bryan Cole showed up. Kit had heard Nick talking to him that first morning about working together on Saturday, but Joey was surprised, and didn't appear too enthusiastic, when he came over to introduce himself while they hung out.

He walked over to them and put out a hand. "Bryan Cole. And you are?" Kit thought he was good looking and funny, but Joey didn't have much patience with him. She still hadn't warmed up to him as she went into the booth and they went inside and began to play. They were working on another movie score that had a more subtle country feel, and Kit spent the morning playing and singing beside Bryan.

He made her laugh when he teased her with his eyes as they sang the love theme. Nick laughed too, as he complained, "Bryan, I swear you can't be serious for your life. You're supposed to make them think you're romantic in the love song, not funny. Knock it off. We're trying to work here!"

Bryan laughed. "Hey, it was her fault. She was winking at me." Nick glanced at Kit for just a split second, until he understood that Bryan was still teasing her.

Nick rolled his eyes. "Let's take lunch. Maybe Bryan can get into a more romantic mood by the time we get back."

They went out to another trendy restaurant and Bryan scored some points with Joey on the way to the car, when he got a bit testy with a camera man who practically hit her in the face with his lens as she walked by. He helped her into the limo and sat next to her to ask her if she was okay. Kit had been somewhat shaken up too and thought to herself, for the first time, that her new Karate skills might come in handy in this town.

Inside the car, Kit and Nick looked at each other with a grin, when a few minutes later, they heard Joey say to Bryan, "No, I'm sorry. I'm not terribly familiar with your music. I always turn it off when I've heard enough of your lyrics to realize it's just another crude or demeaning Bryan Cole song." Leave it to Joey to tell it like it is. The others in the car just laughed at Bryan and teased him about his romantic prowess with the girls today.

Bryan smiled good naturedly as he took their ribbing, then turned back to Joey. "You're ruining my reputation here, you know."

She had the grace to look apologetic. "Sorry. I have my own reputation for being more forthright than is polite sometimes. Please forgive me."

Smoothly, Bryan said, "Maybe I need someone to be forthright with me once in a while."

****

Later at lunch, when only she could hear him, he asked Joey, "Crude and demeaning, huh?" He was smiling, but he looked her in the eye as he spoke, "What exactly did you mean by that?"

She looked down at her food for a moment and then thought to herself, *He's honestly asking.* She looked directly at him and asked, "Well, how long has it been since you did a song that didn't include infidelity, promiscuity, or inappropriate descriptions of the female anatomy?"

He took another bite and chewed it, before he smiled at her and said, "You did say you were forthright."

She gave him a rueful smile. "That word usually comes up just before I have to apologize again. I'm sorry, I was rude. Please forgive me one more time."

He shook his head. "No, you're right. The problem is, that kind of stuff sells, and this is my business."

Joey turned back to her plate and murmured, "I guess at that point, you have to decide how much your personal integrity is worth." He turned to look at her without an answer and she honestly met his gaze.

****

Two chairs down, Nick asked Kit if she was ever going to go out clubbing with him after work. She gave him an apologetic smile. "Nope."

"I'd kind of gotten that impression. Can I ask why?"

Candidly, she replied, "Honestly, I've had enough cigarette smoke and dealt with enough drunk people to last me the rest of my life. But thank you anyway." She didn't explain, and he didn't delve.

"If partying is out, how about a quiet beach?"

She searched his eyes and then said, "It sounds heavenly."

"If I promise not to crowd you, can I at least hold your hand?" He gave her a hesitant grin.

She laughed as she leaned her head against his shoulder. "Sure."

He leaned around her to Bryan. "Hey, Cole. If I take Kit to a quiet beach tonight and hold her hand, can you entertain Joey?"

Bryan gave Joey a crooked smile. "I'm not sure. She thinks my lyrics are crude."

Nick replied, "They are. So just don't sing to her and you should be fine." Kit laughed again.

Bryan looked questioningly at Joey. "What about it? I can just about bet you don't want to go out drinking. What about dinner and a movie? I'll let you pick."

Joey smiled at him reassuringly. "Dinner sounds great, but no movie. There are too many people and cameras and women. How about the other end of their quiet beach? Or even better, take me to dinner and then drop me off at the hotel. Then come back and get me at sunrise to go beachcombing."

Nick and Bryan looked at each other and Bryan said, "I don't dare even ask if I can hold her hand." This time Joey laughed.

****

After working through the afternoon, they took the girls back to the hotel to change, then came back to pick them up. As they'd let the girls out, Kit glanced around at the people watching them get out of the limo. She asked Nick if she could just come out to meet him at his car later, so she wouldn't have to deal with the public quite as much. It was refreshingly the opposite of what most women wanted, and made him laugh as they pulled away. He wasn't sure it was completely complimentary, but she had a way of being completely, comfortably unfettered by status and he loved it.

An hour later, when he got there in a plain black Mercedes that he assumed she'd be more comfortable in, he called from the parking lot. As she stepped out of the revolving doors in a simple white cotton dress that showed off her coloring to perfection, he pulled the sleek car up and got out to open her door. Both of them ignored the people looking at them.

He fed her New York style pizza, smiling at their casual conversation as she wrestled with the cheese, then drove around and through a set of locked gates and into a private beach. The sun was just starting to set and the ocean was as beautiful as he'd hoped, when he'd offered this.

When they got close to the water, she ran and kicked off her sandals and played in the waves and the foam. He watched her, captivated, wondering why he'd never met anyone like her before. She was completely different from other women. She seemed as pure and unspoiled as the ocean breeze that blew her dress against her legs. There was nothing artificial about this girl. She didn't fuss with her hair or makeup like most women and she'd never done any of the suggestive flirting he inevitably encountered.

As she played, he commented, "You act like you've never seen the ocean before or something."

She laughed as she kicked water toward him. "I haven't."

He stayed beside her for a half hour or more, while she waded and found shells and driftwood, watching the way her hair shone in the last rays of the sun and the muscles of her calves glistened with sea water. Her dress showed off her figure and her tan and he could have been content to stay right there for hours, but she finally came back to him and shyly offered her hand. By then it was all but dark and they walked hand in hand, in and out of the surf, each carrying their shoes and quiet with their own thoughts.

They reached an outcrop of boulders and sat down to watch the moon come up. When it was fully in the sky above the horizon, he asked, "Where did Dr. Mitchell find you?"

She leaned back against his shoulder to look up at the stars. "In a guitar class at Utah State. I couldn't read music and I thought he was going to throw me out of the class."

Nick smiled in the dark. "I guess not, huh? Did you grow up in Utah?"

"I grew up in Arizona and moved to Wyoming last December. Utah State is just the closest university." She glanced up at his profile. "Where did you grow up?"

"New York City, born and raised. We lived on the seventeenth floor of a high rise apartment. When I decided to be a musician full time, I came out here and I've been here ever since. Unless I'm on the road. It's going on twelve years now."

"You're very good. I guess that should be a no-brainer when you're this big of a star, but honestly, I wouldn't have pegged you as I've found you to be these three days."

Chuckling, he asked, "You expected all drugs and women and no brains, right?" She looked up at him in the dark and laughed her musical laugh and he went on to admit, "Actually, for a while that was accurate, and I still have my moments."

She leaned against his shoulder again. "At least you're honest."

He considered that for a moment as he stroked the back of her hand with his thumb. "I guess you're right, although I haven't really thought of it that way. Things like honesty aren't necessarily priorities in this business."

She looked up at his profile, then looked back at the night sky and said, "I think you're wrong and just don't realize it. Look at the people around you. You would never have the trust and respect of your associates like you do if they didn't think you were honest. Even in just three days, I've learned to believe in you. And I'm sure Dr. Mitchell would never have brought me with if he thought you were less than honorable."

He smiled and leaned toward her to murmur, "You make me feel like one of the good guys and guilty at the same time. What you don't realize is that he brought you knowing you could handle anything you had to. It had nothing to do with my character, thank goodness, because heaven knows I'm no saint. Dr. Mitchell just recognized that you were as strong as they come."

They were silent as she thought about this, the

only sound the surf on the sand. At length she asked, "Is that good or bad?"

He laughed as he stood up from the boulder to take her hand and walk again. "I've never known anyone like you, Kit Star. It's good."

After a while she had him take her back to the hotel. When he offered to walk her up, she declined. "We're both too tired to face your fame right now. I'll just go up blissfully anonymous. But thank you anyway. And thank you for dinner and taking me to the ocean. I've wanted to do that my whole life." He went to kiss her and she smoothly turned away. He gently kissed her cheek and she got out and walked in without looking back.

****

Kit was just opening her room door when the hotel phone rang. It was Nick. "Hey, I just got a call from Ian. He said he's been going through the tracks and things look good enough that we won't need to record on Monday after all. I just thought I'd let you know." She thanked him and told him again that she'd had a nice night and hung up. Her mind was already planning ahead. She wondered if she could talk Joey into taking an early flight. Just the thought of going home to Wyoming for a couple of days before going back to school Tuesday energized her, and she was happily checking into flights when Joey walked in fifteen minutes later.

Kit got off the phone and asked, "Well, how'd it go?"

Joey laughed at her tone. "Fine. It was actually fun. I don't think he's used to girls trying to keep him at arms length. He wasn't entirely sure what to do with me." Joey smiled her widest. "I was almost tempted to tease him. How did your date go?"

Kit felt her eyes light up. "The ocean was great! I'd never been to a beach before and I loved it!"

Joey chuckled. "And the gorgeous and wealthy superstar?"

For some reason, Kit felt self-conscious as she said, "Nick is very nice. You know that. It was fun." She changed the subject. "I don't have to record Monday after all. Could we go home?"

They found a five thirty a.m. flight, and were back in Wyoming in time to drive straight to church.

When they walked in just a few minutes late and sat with the family, the look on Rossen's face and Mimi's smile as she reached for her, were worth all the rush and lack of sleep. Over Sunday dinner, they told all of their stories, and then Kit fell asleep on a lounger on the deck with Mimi cuddled close and Rossen in the chair beside them.

Jaclyn M. Hawkes

Chapter 15

Nick woke up Sunday feeling better than he'd felt on a Sunday morning in a long, long time. It was early and he realized he hadn't been home by midnight on a Saturday night since he could remember. And his head was completely clear. He'd had nothing to drink at dinner or at the beach last night with Kit. It felt good.

Thinking about her, he laid there and smiled. He'd never been around anyone like this girl in his life. She was the absolute antithesis of the average rock band groupie. She hadn't wanted to be seen with him and didn't even act like she wanted him physically. She got spooky and shied away if he stood too close or even looked at her with a little too much interest.

There were people who would have given anything if they could be on stage with him, but she didn't even seem to realize she had world class talent. And her mind was amazing. He'd never known anyone in his life who could think and remember and understand the way she could. Dr. Mitchell had tried to tell him, but he hadn't believed him. It had seemed too implausible. She had her music memorized after hearing it played one time through and she seemed to understand what he was trying to do with a song by only looking at him. It was like she was reading his mind. He shook his head when he realized he was actually thinking about a beautiful woman's mind for a change.

Playing beside her through the hours had been an uncanny experience. The music had flowed in perfect rhythm and their voices melded like magic. He couldn't have found another player and singer like her if he spent the next twenty years of his life looking. Dr. Mitchell had indeed dropped the ultimate gift into his lap when he'd shown up with her.

He smiled again, thinking about her last night at the ocean. She'd laughed out loud when the waves flowed over her bare feet and she'd played in the foamy surf like a small child. But she definitely didn't look like a small child. She was the most physically exquisite creature on the planet. Watching her in her white sundress in the sea breeze had been incredible, and when she'd turned to him with that glossy mane of hair and those brilliant blue eyes, she'd made him feel eighteen again.

Even when they'd been working together and he'd been trying to be professional, he'd sometimes had trouble focusing on the music and not how attractive she was. And she had known it. Every time she'd subtly pulled away from him.

That was intriguing as well. It had been years since a woman had turned him down for anything. Kit was never overt about it, but she never gave him an inch of encouragement. Taking his hand last night was the closest she'd come to flirting, and if he were honest, she had probably only done it because he'd asked. She had coolly avoided his kiss last night and never looked back. That had *never* happened.

He shook his head with a rueful half smile as he got up to shower. The one who wasn't offering was more intriguing than any girl he'd ever met.

Ten minutes later when he called her hotel room to ask her to do something with him that afternoon, he was stunned to learn she was gone. Just gone! Both she and Joey had checked out at four o'clock that morning. He knew they'd planned to stay until Monday evening and he wondered what had happened. He called Dr. Mitchell to see if he knew what had come up, and was told that when Kit had found out she wouldn't be needed Monday, she'd decided to go home early.

Nick put down the phone with mixed emotions, foremost being disappointment. He'd really wanted to see her today. He shook his head again with a self-deprecating smile. Apparently the feeling wasn't mutual.

He puttered around through the morning and early afternoon and finally decided to call her. Maybe there had been an emergency at home. He'd never even told her how pleased he'd been with her work at the studio and had made no plans for her return. There was no doubt in his mind that he wanted her to come back. He needed her professionally, but much more so than that, he couldn't wait to see her again. He called Dr.

Mitchell and got her cell phone number.

****

Rossen was sitting on the porch enjoying the view of Kit and Mimi Star sleeping in the chair beside him, when the phone in the pocket of her dress rang. She'd only had it since she'd gone off to school and he'd never heard it ring before. He didn't think she usually even carried it when she was here. The sound of it now was troubling to him somehow, and when she answered it and then said, "Nick. Hey." with a sleepy smile, something in his heart landed with a sickening thud.

Mimi started to wake and reached for him with a dah sound and he stood to pick her up and walked back into the house. As he fixed her a bottle and gave it to her, he waged a battle in his head and heart. He'd encouraged Kit to go to school, and to LA. And he knew somehow it was the best thing for her, but he also knew who the Nick on the other end of that call was and his heart was sick.

She'd come home tired, but happy, and both she and Joey had told the whole family what they'd been up to and who they'd been with. He'd wanted her to spread her wings. At the time he'd recommended college, he'd had no idea she'd spread them this far, this fast. This wasn't exactly what he'd bargained for. In a way, he was thrilled for her. What an opportunity to use her gifts. But in a way, it was killing him too.

He tried to bury his feelings and focus on the sweet baby in his arms. Somehow, the fact that Kit had spent half the night getting home as soon as she could helped a lot, but he wasn't even sure he should be happy about that, or encourage her to stay away next time. He finally decided he was only human and that being grateful she'd come home wasn't a bad thing. By the time he took Mimi back out twenty minutes later, Kit was not only off the phone, but already back to sleep.

****

Back at school, Kit continued to strive to make this semester count. She took two more CLEP tests and went out with Nate again and two other guys from their college ward. She was still working out with Matt and not only had she already earned her green belt, but he'd become her best friend outside of the Rockland family. He'd given up on any romantic notions with Kit and their friendship had become Kit's favorite thing about college. She still loved her sculpture, and Matt appreciated it too. He would sometimes bring something to do and come and sit in the clay lab with her while she worked. He'd figured out several ways to cheer her up when she was homesick, and Kit knew he would brighten her spirits when she needed it most. She'd almost worried that he still liked her, until he started hitting on Joey when they were there.

Her art class was going well. She was learning new techniques and ideas she'd use her whole life. She was going to be able to get internship credits for her horse bronzes and the pieces she had in private galleries. Spanish was the only class she had to work at and it was only because her heart wasn't in it. She had no real interest. It was just a class to her and even her friendship with Ethan didn't perk it up. He kept trying to hold her hand and she had resorted to showing up late and hoping there were no seats available near him.

In guitar she was enjoying the music more than ever. Dr. Mitchell had arranged to get her some credits for her work in LA and she could now read music, slowly, but well. Nick had asked her to come back the fourth weekend in September and she was trying to cram everything in so she could take that Thursday, Friday and Saturday in LA, as well as spend some time at home Sunday and Monday. Joey was going back with her again and she was trying to tie up all her loose ends, too.

When Kit went home to Wyoming, she tried to leave school and homework behind in Logan. Except for talking to Rossen about some of what she was doing there, so he would know she wasn't missing out, she came home to bask in being home. She had all but quit nursing Mimi Star, a fact she truly regretted, but didn't see any way around. She'd begun to fix her a bottle just like Rossen did and it made her sad every time she did it. Mimi Star was four and a half months old and she could wiggle faster than they could keep track and Rossen had put a play pen in his office filled with every toy possible.

They still took her on rides with them and Kit tried to ride at least once every time she came home. Her friendship with Rossen was her greatest treasure, but there were times when the pressure to keep it platonic was so at odds with what she was really feeling, that it was almost hard to be with him. Man, she hated the stupid rules.

The Wednesday before she was to go back to California, she was tired to the bone. She'd gotten everything done and was spending the afternoon enjoying Rossen and Mimi as she worked beside him in his office. They could do this without pressure to stay away from each other and his engineering work had almost become a haven for their relationship. For some reason, Rossen didn't feel like working together was against the stupid rule, so Kit tended to spend a lot of time in his office.

****

After dinner, Rossen turned on the TV to watch a ball game. He loved having Kit home, but it was hard sometimes, too. This life they were leading was definitely not what he'd have chosen, if he could choose. Kit sat on the couch beside him and fell asleep within seconds with Mimi asleep on her lap. Her head fell against his shoulder and her hand relaxed onto his thigh. He'd known she was tired, but holy cow, that was fast! And she was so gone! He hadn't seen her this tired since right after Mimi was born. What was she doing at school to wear her out this much? He'd have to ask Joey how it was all going again.

Twice Kit's head slid off his shoulder. The third time he eased off the couch, picked up Mimi Star and gently laid Kit down full length. He put a pillow under her head, covered her with a throw and pulled a Love Sak over beside her to finish watching the game.

Eventually he leaned his head back against the couch and closed his eyes too, content to rest beside her with her little daughter. When Kit turned on her side and draped her arm over his shoulder, none of them woke up, but they all three rested easier than they had in a whole month.

Naomi found them there at midnight. She turned off the TV, turned out the lights, and went to bed, wishing she was wiser and knew how to solve everything for them.

When Kit woke up sometime in the night and realized he was there under her arm, she rolled over close to his head and wrapped her arm around his neck, deciding that all stupid rules were off when he was asleep.

When he woke up toward morning with her arm around his neck and her head close to his, he just basked in the feel of her near him as she slept. He could smell her shampoo and reveled in the feel of her arm on his skin. He wasn't going to worry about keeping his distance from her in her sleep.

Naomi came back in at five thirty to start breakfast before the girls had to catch their plane. She found the three of them still there and scooped up the waking baby before she disturbed them. She knew Kit's bags were packed and waiting by the garage door. Joey had told her some of what Kit had been doing at school and Naomi knew she had to be exhausted. She let them sleep, fed Joey and Mimi, and packed a breakfast Kit could take with her, before waking her at the last possible moment.

Kit smiled at Naomi and raised her head to look around. When she saw Rossen was still asleep leaning on the couch beside her, she leaned over to gently kiss the top of his head, then gave Naomi an impish grin and whispered, "Don't tell him,"

Jaclyn M. Hawkes

Chapter 16

Nick himself was in the limo that met them at the airport at ten thirty California time. Kit was finally awake. She'd touched up her makeup and hair and had eaten the breakfast Naomi had sent, and felt ready and excited to face the next three days. When Nick climbed out of the car at the curb to help them with their bags, looking just like the star he was, she was honestly glad to see him.

They headed straight to the studio and as they drove, Bryan Cole called Nick's phone. He answered and handed it to Joey. Nick and Kit smiled at each other as they listened to her side of the conversation. Bryan was apparently cajoling Joey into spending the day with him instead of just waiting at the studio with Kit. She was giving him flack, but they both knew she'd eventually give in.

She did, and Kit was glad. She knew Joey had been bored last time, but they didn't really want her hanging out in the city alone.

Nick was watching Kit and she knew it, but she wouldn't meet his eyes. She knew he was interested in her, but she truly felt it was no more than the interest he had in a hundred other girls in this town. Still, she was actually a little glad when they unloaded and had to face the cameras and fans at the studio.

Bryan was already there, waiting in a sleek Porsche with tinted windows. Joey ran from one car to the other as Nick put his arm around Kit to shield her as they pushed through. Dr. and Mrs. Mitchell brought up the rear with relatively little trouble.

Once inside, they got geared up and then Nick began talking Kit through the lineup while they waited for Shane and Joss. He took her to a quiet corner and began to play and sing her parts to her. He was so close she could feel his breath on her skin and smell his aftershave and she unconsciously backed away from him.

They would be working on Nick's own music all day. One of the songs was a his and hers duet about finally coming home, that he told her he'd written on that Sunday morning when she'd left without saying good bye. It was the perfect combination of ballad and classic rock and roll, and Kit loved it, although she still worried a bit about something tender she saw at the back of his eyes.

Shane and Joss showed up and they worked the rest of the morning straight through, the seven of them focused and intense. Just before one o'clock, they started on *Coming Home*, and the song came together almost effortlessly. Nick and Kit's voices were as if they were made for each other and the harmonies flowed between the rocking back beat and hot guitars. Kit was having a great time dancing and singing with Nick beside her as she played. They sang to each other time and again and she knew without a doubt it would be a new big hit for him. Her guitar was a living thing in her hands.

Kit was into the music and singing her heart out when she glanced up and into Nick's soul. The look in his eyes as he watched her rock out shocked her to her toes. She hit two wrong notes in a row as she dropped her eyes to dance away. Nick groaned, and his guitar screeched into silence as he let it fall to hang from the strap over his shoulder and ran a hand through his hair. The others stopped playing in bewilderment, looking at each other and wondering what the heck had just happened. Kit never hit wrong notes, and Nick was not a temperamental musician and nobody else had a clue.

Nick started to slip the shoulder strap over his head. "Let's break for lunch and try it again after. Somebody . . . Shane, call and order us some lunch, would you?" He set his guitar down and stalked out the door. Kit set hers down and followed him. Behind them, the other four and Ian in the control room all remained silent, until finally Shane said, "Okay. So . . . What sounds good for lunch?"

Kit followed Nick up the stairs to the second floor, where he stood looking out some big windows into a garden courtyard behind the building. He ran a hand through his hair again as she came to stand beside him. She leaned against his shoulder as she quietly said, "I'm sorry."

He gave a self-deprecating laugh as he wrapped her in a hug to rest his cheek against her hair. "What are you sorry for?"

She shrugged in his arms. "I'm not entirely sure. I just know you're upset with me and I'm sorry."

He pulled back far enough to look into her eyes and then turned away to stare out the window again. His voice was gentle and almost sad when he said, "I'm not upset with you, Kit." Finally, he turned to her again and asked, "How old are you?"

At first she didn't even want to answer him and when she did, it was her voice that was sad, "Eighteen."

She stood beside him looking out the window in silence, unsure of how to comfort him and wondering how they even got to be here in their friendship at this point in time. They'd been together a total of three and a half days, really with a three week span between. It was the fifth time in two weeks she'd found herself apologizing for that look in a man's eyes and she honestly didn't think she'd led any one of them on.

Nick was by far the most troubling. He wasn't some punk college kid and she'd grown to have a great deal of respect for him. She finally decided to try to downplay things and be as cheerful as possible.

She took his hand and said, "Come on. Let's go eat, I'm starving! We'll play this afternoon and be fine. Maybe we can try that song again in the morning when we're fresh and not tired."

They ate and played and got through the afternoon, and when he asked her to have dinner with him, she was surprised. She agreed to, even though she was unsure it was wise. He rode with them in the limo to drop them at the hotel and left her to change, saying he'd be back to pick her up in an hour.

Joey came in as she was dressing and mentioned, "This gorgeous rock star just drove up in an awesome Maserati downstairs and is about being mobbed by fans. You might need to rescue him."

Joey was having dinner with Bryan, so Kit didn't worry about leaving her as she went to rescue Nick.

She came through the revolving doors in a slim fitting black dress that just brushed the top of her knees and two and a half inch black heels that put her height at five eleven. Her hair was almost the color of her dress and she felt pretty as she walked toward him with a smile on her face. Cameras flashed over and over in her eyes as he disentangled himself from the crowd to take her elbow and help her into the waiting sports car. He smiled over at her as he pulled away from the curb and said sincerely, "You look like a million bucks."

She smiled back shyly. "Thank you. It's probably a good thing. It would be a shame not to look pretty in this car." Tonight he looked like a rock star and had an almost animal grace behind the sleek wheel.

He drove far into the foothills, the car purring over the winding, hilly road. He finally pulled into a small elegant restaurant. A valet took the car and they were shown discreetly to a quiet table overlooking the entire city with the ocean behind it in the setting sun. She'd never been anywhere even remotely close to this kind of elegance, and she sat and stared out at the lights below, wondering what the man across from her was thinking. She looked up into his brown eyes, trying to read his thoughts, but their chocolate depths remained a secret.

This afternoon, when she'd told him she was eighteen, she had fully expected him to walk away and even wondered if he would ever have her come back again to play. Then he'd asked her out with totally unfathomable eyes, and now she was wondering what was up with him more than ever.

She was glad she'd worn the dress and was trying to figure out why he had decided to reveal this more luxurious lifestyle with the car and the opulent restaurant. Even braving the crowds at the hotel to pick her up was more of a publicity move than he'd indulged in much with her before.

When the server came, they ordered and Nick chose a glass of wine with his meal, but didn't even ask if she wanted one, and didn't seem to notice when she ordered only water again with hers. While they waited, he talked to her about growing up in New York City and how California was different. Occasionally, he asked her a question about her own life, but she usually gave him one word answers and coaxed him back into telling more about himself with another question.

When the meal ended, he sat for a moment looking into her eyes in the candlelight, but when she looked away to study the city lights spread out below, he stood up and helped her out of her chair. Taking her hand, he walked to the car in silence. She almost felt like he was trying to decide something in his head as he went.

****

He was trying to decide something. He'd never felt this way about a woman in his life and didn't know whether to flat out run from these feelings, or try to get close to this girl. She was only eighteen. And although she was exquisitely beautiful and graceful, and unbelievably talented and smart, she was also unabashedly sweet and innocent, and obviously clean living and wholesome. He honestly questioned whether he even had any right to be with her after the life he'd led.

He wasn't necessarily a bad guy, and now he was considerably more respectable than he'd been at times in the past, but he'd had his moments. No one could describe his lifestyle as clean living, no matter how much of a stretch they tried. Although she was the first girl he'd ever been truly fascinated by, she was still one of a long line of hundreds of girls and he knew it and he was sure she did too. He also knew she'd seen how he felt about her today before lunch. And where most every other woman he had known would have been thrilled, Kit hadn't hesitated to shy away.

For whatever reasons, she wasn't just another groupie, happy to be included in his life for however much time he gave her. It both intrigued him and challenged him. At the same time, he hesitated to even consider being with her for fear of ruining something so pristine and unspoiled. As all these thoughts went through his head, the one that finally won out was the simple truth that she was absolutely worth trying to obtain for his own and that was what he really wanted.

Never in his life had he even considered settling down with one woman, but he'd known for three weeks now that he'd do it in a heartbeat with Kit if she'd have him. The only problem was she hadn't shown even once that she wanted him. She was friendly and polite, and even openly appreciative of his talent. And she danced and laughed with him as they played and sang, but she would have been that way with her brother, too.

She treated him with respect, but she'd never once given him so much as a come on with her eyes, and he honestly wasn't even sure why she accepted his invitations. Sometimes he wondered if she wasn't actually trying to want to be with him. It was a bit hard on his ego, but it was the truth.

Back in the car, he turned onto a road that wound along the base of the mountains where the view was incredible and turned the radio on low as they drove. He started asking questions about school and that was somewhat easier to talk about as she actually opened up. He asked what she was majoring in and was surprised when she said Fine Art Visual.

"Not music?"

She laughed her magical laugh and answered, "That's exactly what Dr. Mitchell asked me. He said it was a shame guitar wasn't my passion."

Nick looked back at the road. "It is a shame.

Your talent is an incredible gift. So, what's your passion?"

"Sculpture."

He was surprised, but he considered this for a long moment and then said, "It's funny. With your mind you could be the most gifted physician or scientist, and yet you've chosen the arts. And I'm sure you're as talented a sculptor as you are musician." He reached across the car and took her hand. "I've never known anyone like you, Kit Star."

She was hesitant when she asked, "Is that good or bad?"

He chuckled and shook his head. "That's good. You're good. You're good enough that I question whether I should even be around you. You're a much better person than I am. I'm just selfish and I want to enjoy you, even if I don't deserve to." He stroked her index finger with his thumb. "See, I'm being honest about having a questionable character. I'm not sure how that all works."

Kit looked at him in the dim light of the car. "You're not very complimentary about yourself sometimes. You put yourself down, but never once that I've been around you have you behaved questionably. I've learned to respect you a great deal after having come to know you." She gently squeezed his hand.

"Maybe you just haven't seen the real me." The thought made him somewhat sad.

She shook her head and said gently, "Maybe the man I know is the real you." She turned toward him in the car. "You know, Nick, everybody has their moments. We all have regrets and mistakes. If there's stuff that bothers you, then make it right. That's what we all do. That's what Christ gave his very life for. But I think you're a better person than you give yourself credit for. It's only when you honestly know better and still choose to make poor choices that mistakes are a problem."

He looked over at her earnest face in the peacefulness of the car and admitted, "I guess my only excuse is that, until you, I thought everyone lived the way I have. I've never been around people like you and Joey. I had no idea there was even anyone like you around."

At that, she shifted in her seat and seemed uncomfortable, and finally asked, "What exactly are we talking about here, Nick? What do you mean, people like me and Joey?"

He down shifted to go up a long hill. "That's a good question. And I honestly don't know the answer. I just know it didn't take any of us long to figure out that you weren't going to go out drinking and carousing and sleeping around." He smiled at her. "Shane doesn't even swear around you. I've never seen anything like it!"

She laughed. "And I've never seen anything like Shane. He should charge admission just to be with him!" She became more serious and continued, "If you've honestly never been around people who don't drink and carouse and sleep around, maybe you should find some new friends. That could get old fast. And it can't be a very satisfying lifestyle."

He thought about that for a minute. She was right. It had gotten old and had never, ever been satisfying. He looked back over at her with a smile. "How did you become so wise? I thought you said you were only eighteen."

He glanced at her and saw her face cloud up for just an instant and she said, "I guess I've just seen the difference between the two lifestyles. One is much happier than the other."

They drove in silence until he finally asked, "Are you telling me you used to party and sleep around?"

"No! No, of course not! But before Joey's family, the only people I was around much lived that way. Now, after having seen both, there's really no comparison. The Rocklands are immeasurably happier, healthier, more productive, and much nicer to be around. It's almost like the people I knew before had no understanding that there was a purpose in life. They acted like honesty or fidelity, or even just kindness never crossed their minds. Now that I understand better, I feel so sorry for them."

Nick drove feeling slightly bewildered. He wondered if he was included in the group she felt sorry for. What did she mean about the purpose of life? And there was something wrong with the way she was talking about the people before the Rocklands. He couldn't quite figure what, but that sounded like a strange way to talk about her family. And she was only eighteen. How did she have so much better an understanding about things he'd only begun to question at nearly thirty?

He looked over at her in wonder and found her watching him intently. She asked, "I'm sorry, did I offend you somehow?"

"No, but I'm a little lost. Am I one of the ones you feel sorry for?"

"No, not the way I do them." She smiled an impish smile at him. "You know a lot about the good qualities in life, a lot more than you admit. Probably a lot more than you even understand. You even know that drinking and carousing and sleeping around are wrong and you shouldn't do them, but you don't really want to admit that." Now she was laughing up at him.

He shook his head, laughing with her. "You're probably right. What do you mean 'not the way I do them'? So, you do feel sorry for me?"

She seemed hesitant to answer him at first. Finally, she asked, "Nick, if being physically intimate is no big deal, then how can you ever someday expect your wife to be faithful to you? Because it probably becomes no big deal to her either. So, if fidelity isn't an issue, then why do people care if their spouse is faithful? The way society seems to think, it shouldn't matter. But people do care. People care a lot when it comes right down to it. But you can't have it both ways. The sad part is that most people in our society either don't figure it out before it's too late, or they never figure it out. Most people don't realize that absolute fidelity is essential to a happy, healthy marriage. Some people never even figure out that being happily married is an important part of a happy life. If you really do think sleeping around is what everybody you know does, then yeah, in a way I do feel sorry for you."

It was a full two minutes before he looked up at her. "You make me want to believe there really are marriages out there that are happy and healthy and that last. I'm not sure I believe you. I've never seen one. My grandparents were married for like sixty years, but I don't think he was faithful to her. At least, he didn't treat her very well. She was always just his old lady."

"I know what you mean. I hadn't ever seen one either until about nine months ago, but since then I've been around a lot of happily married couples. You should meet Joey's parents. Their friendship is the coolest thing I've ever seen! Coming to live with them has changed my life more than you could even comprehend."

He was mixed up again about her life before Joey, but didn't press. Instead, he asked, "And you think being faithful is the key?"

She sounded absolutely confident when she said, "Maybe not the only key, but I don't believe you can have a strong marriage without it. I think there must be a lot of keys. I'm sure I don't have a clue about what it really takes, but I've seen a few things I know don't work."

Thinking about some of his friends and associates, he knew what she meant. He mulled all this over in his mind for a while and then lightened the conversation up slightly. "Maybe you should switch to a philosophy major. With a mind like yours, we could have all the answers to the universe in no time."

She laughed. "Now you're making fun of me."

"No. I just can't delve all that deeply without knowing I'm hopelessly toasted at judgment day. So I handle it like any red blooded American male. I put that thought away in its little compartment and don't go there. Knowing I can't ever undo some of the things I've done is too hard to face." He gave her a sad smile and they drove on through the foothills for a while.

At length she softly said, "You forgot about the atonement."

He looked over at her. "Come again?"

"You forgot about the atonement. It's kind of a biggie. Not something you want to forget."

He gave her a blank look. "You lost me."

"You said you were hopelessly toasted at judgment day and that you could never undo some of the things you've done. You've been suckered into what Naomi, Joey's mother, calls the Big Lie. If Satan and the world can get you to truly believe that trying is hopeless, then you're right, it is, and you'll give up and he's got you. But that's exactly opposite of what our Father in Heaven and Jesus teach. It's never hopeless. They'll always take us back no matter what kind of mistakes we've made, if we just ask."

This time he looked at her for so long that he must have made her afraid he was going to drive off the road. "Um, Nick." She pointed out the windshield. "You better drive. At least until you've finished all that repenting." She smiled at him again. "It'd be a shame to crash this gorgeous car while you're still hopelessly toasted."

Focused on driving again, he asked, "You really believe that? That bit about always being welcomed back?"

She squeezed his hand. "I didn't believe it either at first, so I've been kind of studying up on it. Now I know it to be true from the bottom of my heart."

Shaking his head, he said, "Yeah, but I told you before, you don't know what kind of guy I am."

"God does. And He loves us all anyway."

A few minutes later he pulled the car off the road onto a scenic overlook and got out to come around and open her door. He took her hand to walk over near the guardrail and gaze out over the cities and the ocean. "You'd never been to the beach, but you know the answers to the meaning of life. It's gonna take me a while to figure you out, girl." The breeze up the canyon was cold and she backed up to him to lean against his chest and he put his arms around her.

"I have a jacket in the trunk, should I get it?"

"No, I'm fine if you hug me. We'll have to go back soon anyway or I'll turn into a pumpkin. We take an early flight to get here in time to work and I'm always dead by this time of night the first day."

He hugged her tighter. "You definitely don't feel dead to me." He felt her laugh. "How come you don't just fly out the night before?"

She turned around to face him. "I'm glad you asked that, because in light of our conversation tonight, there are some things about me you need to hear from me, not someone else." She looked down at her hands. "I don't come out the night before because of a lot of reasons, one of which is my four and a half month old daughter." She looked up into his eyes as he struggled to fit this new little earth shaking detail into his brain. His eyes narrowed, questioning and she put up a hand defensively. "It's not because I've been sleeping around. I promise." She looked down again and started to toy with the ring on her right ring finger.

"I um, I had this foster father who wasn't a very nice guy. He uh, he…" She hesitated as she struggled to voice what he grasped instantly. It made his heart sick. "He's the father." She left it at that and continued to twist the small ring. He put both arms around her and wrapped her in a tight hug. They stood there like that with her head tucked under his chin for several long moments. She didn't cry, but he could feel the deep sadness that seemed to radiate from her.

Finally, he asked, "Do you want to talk about it?" She shook her head without looking up. Eventually he lifted her chin to look up at him. "Can I just ask you one question?" She looked at him with those brilliant blue eyes. "Are you okay?"

She gave an almost undetectable shake of her head as she questioned back, "Do I have any choice?" He pulled her back into his arms. No wonder she always seemed so much older than eighteen.

When she began to shiver, he took her back to the car and they headed back to her hotel. They were quiet as they drove for the first several minutes. There were so many things he wanted to ask her, but he wasn't sure if he should. He'd imagined she was thought provoking before. Holy Toledo! First she rocks his world with the idea that God wanted him and then this!

When the silence became uncomfortable, he asked, "Do you think you'd want to talk about things tomorrow night? Could we have dinner again? Just the two of us?"

"I think I said a bit too much already, don't you? I shouldn't have told you about Mimi. I'm sorry, I just didn't want you to hear it from someone else and think I was a hypocrite after talking about fidelity."

He took her hand again. "I'm glad you told me, and no you haven't said too much. I didn't assume you'd been sleeping around either, by the way."

She sounded bitter when she admitted, "If you had, you wouldn't be the first."

He looked down at her. "Kit, anyone who knows you and still thought that would be brain dead. They wouldn't even be worth stressing over. It's not like you not to let it go."

"You're right. Hey, how do you know that?"

He shrugged and smiled. "You deal with stuff too well to be a grudge holder. You didn't say you would have dinner with me."

Looking across the car, she asked with a ghost of

a smile, "I'd love to, but do we have to talk about unwed mothers?"

He checked his blind spot and changed lanes. "No, but you might have to explain to me more about how God still loves wild rockers."

She held his hand with both of hers and said, "Nick, I'd be only too happy to tell you anything I've learned in the last year about God. He's been the greatest gift I could ever have from the Rocklands, but you know who could explain about that better than me? God. You should ask Him."

****

Alone in his darkened living room that night, listening to music, he almost got up the nerve to do it.

****

When Nick showed up the next morning to play, he didn't look like he'd slept all that well. He met Kit's eyes when he came to walk her through the day's music and she wasn't sure what she saw there. At least he hadn't sent her packing. They played through the morning and he was quiet during the lunch they ordered in. They never even tried to play *Coming Home* and by the time they left for dinner, Kit had no clue what to think.

He picked her up in the Maserati again, but this time they got takeout at a drive through and took it back to the beach. They walked back out to the boulders they'd sat on the last time and began to eat, side by side. Finally, she said, "Nick, even if you tell me to go to China, I need you to say something. What's in your head? What's going on?"

He finished his bite and shrugged. "I have no idea. How's that for honest?"

Leaning against his shoulder, she answered, "It's good for honest, bad for Kit understanding."

"What would you say if I told you I thought I was falling in love with you?" He turned to her and took off his sunglasses, and she saw an emotion she didn't know how to deal with.

She searched his eyes at length and said, "Nick, I know I'm young and unsophisticated, but don't tease me. You've become my friend and I'm trusting you." She looked down at her sandwich, and then wrapped it up and put it back in the bag. Talk of love ruined her appetite.

With a sigh he put his sandwich away too and ran a frustrated hand through his hair. "Baby, I wish I was teasing, 'cause I'm way out of my comfort zone here." She just looked at him, more confused than ever. Finally, she hopped off the rock and took his hand to pull him to his feet beside her.

They walked down the beach in silence for several minutes and then she asked, "Why would my telling you about my daughter make you think you were falling in love? Isn't that backwards?"

"Last night has nothing to do with my feelings, except that I'm sorry for what you've been through. It makes me wonder if she's as beautiful as you. And how in the world I'll figure out how to hold a baby, but this isn't about your daughter. I don't even know what this is about. I don't think I've ever experienced this before."

She stopped and looked at him again, trying to figure out if he really would tease her about this. She honestly didn't think this was possible, but he looked so serious. As she studied him, he shook his head and said, "Geez, girl. I'm bearing my soul to you and you don't even believe me."

"Nick, you have five million women after you and I'm just Kit. How do you expect me to believe you? How could this be possible?"

They started walking again and he mumbled under his breath, "Just Kit." He turned to her. "Do you have any idea how ridiculous that sounds to me? You're the most fascinating human being I've ever come in contact with, not to mention that you're exquisitely beautiful, unbelievably smart and completely refreshing! Just Kit." He turned back away and went to the edge of the water to skip rocks, almost angrily.

Walking up to him again, she gently touched him on the arm. When he looked down at her, she said, "I'm sorry."

He smiled at her and wrapped her in a hug again. "What are you sorry for this time, Just Kit?"

"For not taking you seriously, and for . . . " She was confused for a minute. "I'm not sure what else for. For screwing up somehow."

He laughed at her and turned with her to continue on down the beach. "Is that what you call this love thing? Screwing up?"

She turned her face up to his. "I guess so, because

I have to be honest with you, Nick. I like you, I respect you, and I think you're adorable, but I don't think I'm in love with you. I'm sorry."

He put his arm around her shoulders and turned to walk back down the beach toward the car. "I know, Kit. And it's okay. I'll keep trying, and if it never works, then at least I'll have had the chance to have loved a truly good woman."

Back at the door to her hotel room, he took her in his arms for a moment, then kissed her on the forehead, and said, "See you in the morning."

****

The next day went somewhat better. He still looked at her with those deep brown inscrutable eyes that she didn't know how to deal with, but she knew they were friends no matter what. And when they played *Coming Home*, she played and sang with him wholeheartedly, in spite of the fact that she wished they could go back in time.

When he asked if he could see her and Joey to the airport that evening, she accepted, even though this time she was sure it wasn't wise. She just had no idea what else to do. Kit insisted he let them out at the curb. She didn't think she could bear to face those eyes in front of a bunch of his fans. He helped them get their bags checked and then hugged her like he never wanted to let go, and kissed her on the forehead again. Somehow he must have known she would be too uncomfortable if he really tried to kiss her and she was incredibly grateful for that.

As she went to go, he reached out to pull her back. She turned to him and he looked deep into her eyes and asked, "Kit, would you think about something while you're home? Would you think about coming back to LA forever?" Her eyes flew to his in a panic, but what she saw there was real. She knew he was absolutely serious.

She had no idea what to do, but she knew his question deserved an honest response. "I'll think about it." She gave him one last long hug and he got back into his beautiful car and drove away.

Once he was gone and they walked inside, Joey looked at her long and hard, but she never said anything. Kit was glad. She had no clue how to handle any of this, let alone talk about it with someone else. All the way home she felt guilty, but she could never pin down exactly what for. By the time she walked into the house at eleven thirty to find Rossen waiting up for them, she was exhausted.

Chapter 17

When Rossen saw them come in, he knew right away that Kit was troubled about something. He stood up from the couch with Mimi sleeping on his shoulder and accepted hugs from both of them. Kit hugged him first, leaning in to kiss Mimi gently on the cheek and then asked him if she could take her to bed with her. He handed her over and watched her walk away. Once she was gone, Joey plopped down on the couch with a sigh and he sat back down next to her. "What's going on? Why does she look so hammered?"

Joey laughed. "Rossen, even hammered that girl looks better than ninety nine point nine percent of the women in this world, and you know it. She's just tired. She's dancing about three times faster than most women, trying to keep my bone headed brother happy. Cut her some slack. Plus, this time I think she's struggling to balance a lovesick rock star into the mix and he's depressed the heck out of her."

Rossen turned on the couch to look directly at her. "Whoa, whoa, whoa. Say that again. What's going on?"

Joey yawned. "I'm not sure, because you know

how Kit is. She keeps her troubles to herself. But if I had to make a guess, I'd say that Nick has fallen hard and fast for her and she's trying to figure out how to deal with it."

Rossen leaned back against the couch and put his head back to look at the ceiling. "What else were you saying? What's she doing to try and keep Treyne happy?"

Joey sat up to look at him like he was crazy. "What are you talking about?"

"You just said she was dancing trying to keep your boneheaded brother happy. What is it Treyne's unhappy about?"

Joey gave an exasperated sigh and stood up. "Rossen, I swear for an intelligent man, you're a dork sometimes!" She headed for her room saying over her shoulder as she left, "You're the boneheaded brother, not Treyne. He loves her no matter what she chooses to do. You're the one she has to try so hard to please."

He sat on the couch alone, utterly stunned. He had no idea what Joey was talking about. He sat and tried to figure it out, finally gave up and went to bed. He'd ask his mom what was going on tomorrow.

****

Kit made it through church without falling asleep and felt like she'd won a sizeable battle. After dinner she was back out on the deck again with the baby in the lounge chair. The leaves had started to change on all the hillsides around and even though the air was brisk, the scenery was incredible. She had Mimi wrapped snuggly in a blanket and was enjoying the feel of her little body cuddled close when Rossen came out to pull up a chair beside them. His hair was windblown and he was wearing a USU sweatshirt from college and a well faded pair of jeans that fit his body to perfection and she watched him come over and sit down with pleasure. He was a gorgeous man. Mimi reached for him saying, "Dah," and he picked her up.

He watched Kit watching him and she didn't even try to hide it, as he came and sat down and asked, "So, how was LA?"

She studied his eyes, wondering what she was hearing in his voice as she answered, "Good. Hectic, but fun. California is like a whole different planet sometimes."

"What do you mean?"

She shrugged. "I don't know how to explain it exactly. It's like life speeds up and becomes more superficial all at the same time. It's really fun to go for a couple of days, but I think living there would be exhausting."

"You've looked tired when you've come home these two times. Are you doing okay?"

"Actually, this time it was more my school stuff from before I left, than California. And then some of the people we work with there can be a little hard to figure out. But it's fun. Honestly, we took a Maserati through the drive-through at McDonalds yesterday. It was great!" Her eyes sparkled. "I mean, who gets to do that? Nick is talking about doing a benefit concert and I love being a part of a band, but it's heavenly to come home."

He was watching her intently and asked, "What's going on at school that's so hectic?"

Feeling slightly guilty that she had to work to shrug, she said, "I've just been trying to get everything done so I could go to LA and then come home here without falling hopelessly behind. Being a studio musician in another state, a full-time student, and still trying to be even a part-time mom is a stretch sometimes, but I think eventually I'll get a handle on it."

She wasn't mentioning coming home permanently in December because there was no point in arguing about it until she had to. She was still hoping all the extra credits from her CLEP tests and the internships would smooth him over somewhat. He was looking at her like he was skeptical and she wanted to squirm. Finally she decided she was too tired to feel guilty for trying to eventually please him and she closed her eyes. She still hadn't asked him how old she had to be, to be old enough to settle down.

****

The day and a half break before going back to school was smart, because she had tests, projects and big assignments due all that week and the next, then midterms rolled in. She only had to do a big test in Spanish and a major sculpture project, and pass off a song for guitar, but she was taking another CLEP test and Matt was encouraging her to try for her next belt. Add to that three dates a week and the drive time back and forth to Wyoming and her life felt crazy. But she hoped it would all be worth it.

The first Monday back, Nick called and then about every three days roses began to arrive. If there was any doubt that he was serious about making sure she knew he was thinking about her, they were dispelled when the mailman showed up with a glass jar full of sand and a shell with a tiny guitar carved into it, and a CD with a new song he'd written just for her.

He called her every couple of days and she always tried to steer the conversation away from herself. It worked because Nick usually asked her questions about God or life, and they had some great discussions about the principles of the gospel. The fact that Kit was a recent convert somehow made everything easier to grasp for him and she could sense that he had some deep questions that he'd only lately begun to have answered. She tried to help him understand how happy living the gospel made her.

He'd asked her to come back in the middle of October and this time Joey couldn't go. Kit would only be staying for two days, and she knew she would be fine, but she still wished Joey would be coming.

The day before she was scheduled to fly out, Mimi came down with her first bad cold. Kit held her as she fussed and rocked her several times in the night. Toward morning Rossen came to rescue them again. He held Mimi and rocked her, and when she was still fussy he gave her a priesthood blessing, and she was able to finally snuggle against his neck and rest. It was another morning when Kit woke up lying on the couch with the two of them on the floor beside her. It was the closest she'd felt to being a real little family of their own, and she left for the airport more determined than ever to move home soon. Leaving Mimi in Rossen's arms sick was hard, and she cried half way to the airport.

****

Nick met her at the airport in his Mercedes this time. The Mitchell's had been unable to come at the last minute, so it was just her and him, and the deep chocolate ache in his eyes that hadn't let up in the preceding weeks. She knew he wanted to kiss her and it scared her to death. For some reason she felt strongly that she didn't want to go there. Even after all the dates she'd accepted at school, she'd never let any one kiss her. It wasn't that she thought kissing was wrong. It was just that she didn't want any of the guys she'd gone out with that close to her. With Nick, it wasn't that he wasn't extremely attractive, but she didn't want to encourage the feelings he had for her that she couldn't return.

The two days actually went more smoothly than either of them expected. Without the Mitchells they had to scale back the work load. They ordered in meals and all in all, when Nick took her back to the airport, she felt like it had been a successful trip. She and Nick had found a sort of professional, slash dating, friendship that wasn't entirely what either of them wanted in the long run, but it was comfortable and when he hugged her at the curb and gave her a tender kiss on the head again, she smiled an honest smile at him and walked away.

He called her the next day and arranged for her to

come back two weeks later. They'd be doing their regular recording and there was also a masquerade ball being put on for a local charity, and he asked her to go with him. Then Nick passed his phone to Bryan and he asked Joey to accompany him as well.

Even Joey had never gone to anything like a real masquerade ball complete with the who's who of all of LA, and they planned their costumes on a professional scale. Bryan had told Joey he was going as a pirate, so she was going as a colonial lady with the hat, the parasol, the corset, the whole bit. Nick wanted to surprise Kit with his costume so she chose to be a mystical fairy in a filmy dress and wings that sparkled an iridescent blue to match the glittery do she would have, and her shimmering skin. The dress showed off her figure and brought out the color of her eyes, and she hoped it would give her the confidence she'd need to associate with the famous people she knew would be there and the women who would all be vying for Nick's time.

That week, Kit and Matt drove to the foundry near Salt Lake City, where her bronzes were being finished, to go over them for the final approval before they shipped out the next day for their new home. Isabel's and Slade's Thoroughbred arm in California was actually within an hour and a half's drive from the recording studio and she was going to try to break away to go check on them when they were finally placed. They were the crowning work of her artistic career and she was thrilled to see them nearing completion.

The grueling pace she'd been keeping trying to get everything done was starting to wear on her and one Tuesday night, as she pulled into the ranch house, Rossen met her at the door with a happy baby and a concerned face. He looked her up and down unabashedly as she reached for the smiling child in his arms. She wasn't sure what to think of the look he was giving her and she looked down at herself. Her clothes were clean, everything done up correctly, she was modest, she was stylish. She had no idea why he was looking at her that way. "Is something wrong? Why are you staring at me?"

He laughed as she kept checking her clothes, but then his face sobered and he asked, "How much do you weigh right now?"

She stopped kissing Mimi Star to look back at him. "I beg your pardon?"

"How much do you weigh?"

"I have no idea, why?" She looked down at herself again. "Why do you ask?"

He shook his head. "Just every time you come home, you've lost more weight. Are you eating okay? You're nearly as slender as when we found you. Dr. Sundquist would have a fit." He actually put a casual arm around her waist as he walked them into the great room, and although he didn't even seem to notice, Kit about came unglued. Her life had become the most insane ballet of dodging the guys at college and even Nick. They were always trying to hug her and hold her hand and she'd become adept at staying out of their reach. She had learned to love physical affection while here in the Rockland's home and she thoroughly enjoyed being hugged by the brothers and even Matt was great, but the guys who really liked her, she struggled to keep at arms length.

With Rossen it was just the opposite. She would have loved to have him near her anytime of the day or night, but he'd become a slave to the stupid rules and hardly ever got near her anymore. And then tonight he puts his arm around her and doesn't even realize. She could have clobbered him except she was too happy about it. His concern felt wonderful.

Kissing Mimi once more, she assured him, "I'm eating fine. I'm just busy. Give me about another six weeks and I'll be home and the pressure will be off and I'm sure I'll be back to my regular chunky self again."

His smile brightened her whole world up. "Yeah sure, you chunky. You weren't chunky the day before you had Mimi." He walked over to the fridge and started to dig through it. "Isabel made dinner tonight. It was great! We saved you some." He took a plate out and put it in the microwave to reheat. "Maybe you should cut back on things at school somewhat and add an extra meal or two." He leaned against the kitchen counter to watch her play with the baby.

"I can't cut back until the end of the semester. I have too many things to finish first. Then I'm going to cut back in a big way." She looked up and into his eyes. Their two sets of blue eyes locked and held and she almost wondered if he knew her thoughts, but then the microwave went off and saved her.

He put her plate in front of her and poured her a huge glass of milk and took Mimi back. The food was wonderful. Food at home always was and she was definitely hungry. He was silent for a minute while she ate and then asked, "This isn't another money thing is it? Do you have enough groceries?"

Kit laughed and almost choked on her food. She loved him all the more when he watched over her. "No, Rossen, I promise I'm not skimping on food. Actually the scholarships are paying for all of my college expenses and I've put all of the money you've been paying me, as well as the money from the bronzes and other pieces into my investment account with Slade. Slade found out they would've had to pay another sculptor almost forty thousand dollars for the bronzes and they paid me that much! I told them I wouldn't take it, but he put it in anyway. And I haven't even deposited the two checks from Nick yet. I'm not exactly sure how he's paying me, but he told me he's giving me the pay for both playing the guitar and singing, and my first check for those three days was almost eight thousand dollars."

She took another bite and chewed it. "I've never had money and I'm afraid I'll blow it if I start spending it, so other than some school clothes Joey helped me pick out, I haven't spent any of it at all."

"What about money for movies and stuff there in Logan? Don't you need some entertainment or eating out?"

She looked at him and was somewhat hesitant to answer. "Rossen, I've been going out at least three times per week religiously, sometimes it's more like six, in order to fill your 'enjoy this season of my life' requirement. There's nowhere else to fit in another movie or dinner out. I'm never the one doing the asking and they seldom let me pay. Between dates and LA, I have all the entertainment I can handle, thanks. What I'd really like is a little more time on a horse here at home and a peaceful walk by the pond."

He just looked at her quietly for a minute, his arms folded across his chest while Mimi pulled herself up against his pant legs, two slobbery fingers in her mouth. Finally, he said, "Finish your dinner. It's too dark and cold to ride with the baby, but we can take your walk."

Chapter 18

The day came for them to head back to California and although it had now been nine weeks of walking away from Rossen and Mimi, leaving had never gotten easier. This time she wouldn't be back home in Wyoming for eight days unless she missed the big student Stab in the Dark Halloween party and dance at the university, and she knew it would be a discussion with Rossen if she tried that.

Four different guys had asked her to go. She'd finally asked Matt if she could hang out with him for the night to avoid it all and had mentally begun to gear up to stay away from home that long. Now when she was actually walking away, she wished she'd just had it out with Rossen and planned to miss the student party. She stood beside them snuggling Mimi as Rossen held her until Joey started to honk. He finally put his arm around her and hugged her tightly as the tears ran down her face, then gently pushed her away. "You're gonna miss your plane."

As they drove to the airport, Joey eventually reached an arm across the car to gently pat her and say,

"Just a few more weeks, Kit. This will all be over in just a few more weeks. And then maybe if Rossen ever quits being such a bonehead, he and Mimi could start coming with, instead of me."

Kit managed to smile through her tears to say, "Bryan's gonna love that!" They laughed and it had helped, but her heart ached as she looked out the window of the plane to know the mountains of Wyoming were disappearing in the clouds behind her.

When Nick stepped out of the limo to take their bags, he looked at her hard and she knew he could tell she'd cried a good portion of the trip. After they got to the studio and he came to her to go over the agenda for the day, he stood looking at her in silence with a hand on her shoulder, until he finally asked, "Are you okay?" His gentle question started her tears again and he hugged her. "Rough morning?"

She shook her head without looking up as he held her. "It's just really hard to say goodbye at home sometimes."

With sheer will power, she pulled herself together enough to find a smile and play and sing. It was a little easier to focus with the amps up loud and a thumping back beat egging on their guitars. By lunch she felt markedly better, but that afternoon when Bryan showed up to sing another love theme to a movie with her, she struggled again. It was a mellow country ballad about a cowboy and his love, and Kit felt like a marshmallow by the end of the day.

She knew she was playing and singing okay. She

actually performed better in her quiet mood with the sweet, slow song, but even Bryan sang along beside her, looking into her eyes, obviously concerned about the deep sadness he saw there.

She pleaded a headache and went back to the hotel and ordered room service while the others went to dinner that night. She'd known Nick was watching her as she stepped out of the car and went through the revolving door to the lobby, but her spirit was too tired to do anything about it. She turned and gave him a tentative smile and told herself she'd snap out of this by morning. He deserved better than this. They all did. She ate and watched an old movie and then decided to call home.

Rossen answered on the second ring and she could tell from the tone of his voice that he knew she was struggling. They only talked for a few minutes, but his strong, gentle, deep voice telling her she was going to be okay, was all she needed to make her world right. She said goodbye, showered and prayed and he was right. By morning she was fine.

They made amazing progress that day as Kit tried to perform better than ever to make up for her dismal energy of the previous one. Shane was in rare form at lunch and had her in stitches as they went back in for the afternoon. She sang and danced happily with Nick and by about mid-afternoon, he'd quit watching her like he expected her to vaporize at any moment. He asked her to dinner with him that night. This time they drove out to the ocean again and ate at a tiny quaint cafe right on the water with marvelous seafood and the tang of the sea in the air. After they'd eaten, he pushed her to eat dessert. She had to smile when he asked her, "Are you eating okay?"

"I'm fine. Really. A little busy, and I guess food is not necessarily a priority enough. You're about the fourth person who has tried to get me to eat better this week. Buy me two desserts. I'll eat them both."

Nick laughed. "Good, because there are several things I want to talk you into and sweets just might be the ticket."

As they sat over their dessert, they talked for the next hour. He was getting ready to release a new album, and wanted to include several songs she'd worked on, one of which, she was the featured vocalist and he basically backed her up, instead of the other way around. He wanted to get the legal rights to produce it and, in fact, had written another song he wanted her to sing with him as well.

She agreed, but asked him if instead of paying her outright, he could let her have a small percentage of record sales instead. He nodded his head looking at her with obvious respect. "You're wise beyond your years, Kit. Most people your age would take the cash and run, but in the big picture you'll make far better money."

He continued, "I also wanted to see if you would be willing to come more often. I know you're busy with school and Mimi, but I could use you as often as you could come."

She sighed, "Actually, I'll be done with school in

just over five weeks, and I'm not going back next semester. Someday I might, but for now it's too much. I just want to go home and be a mom and sculptor and part-time musician. By about mid-December most of the pressure will be off and I can come more if you need me. I might have someone come with, so I can bring Mimi and not have to leave her, but more time here could be worked out."

"Cool. My business manager has been after me to get more time arranged and get contracts with you and the others. I'm excited about the contracts. That way, even if you dump me socially, I can still enjoy your incredible talent." He smiled as he said it. "I need you to be here professionally as well as personally. You've become an integral part of my studio work and we get a lot done with you here."

He'd been joking, but he looked at her steadily and said, "You're an incredible talent, in spite of being as sexy as all get out, and I've never once had to wait for you to recover from a hangover or bail you out of jail! Definitely a plus! You're like the guitarist of my dreams." He smiled and reached across the table to take her hand. After a moment, he added, "Seriously, you're a good person and I've grown to admire you a lot. The strength of your convictions has renewed my faith in the human race and especially God." He squeezed her hand. "Thanks.

After another short pause he continued, "I'm also going to do a concert here in LA on the fifteenth of December. I'm not on tour, so I'm not sure how I got into this, but it's for a good cause. It's a benefit concert for organ donation. Would you be willing to come and be in the band for it? Concerts are incredibly draining, but there's nothing like it in the world. You'll love it!"

The thought scared her to death. "Nick, I can't play in a concert with you. I've never played in front of anyone but you and the guys or my family in my life. How do you know I won't just freeze up and panic?"

He only shook his head. "Kit, Kit, Kit. I'm surprised that you even question your personal strength. I've only known you how long? And even I know you have whatever it takes. I can't imagine anything that would even fluster you. You're bulletproof. Don't you know that by now? You'll be fine and we really need you. My band will never be the same since you came."

Hesitantly, she said, "That's what I'm afraid of."

His voice softened as he said, "My last request is completely personal. That's all the business. I'm going to be the MC for a big show next month. It's going to be a big deal, with all the who's who of both the music and film industry. I want to be there with the most beautiful, talented, and smart woman I know. Will you go with me?"

She looked up at him and searched his eyes. This was the most he had intimated about his feelings the whole two days she'd been here. She'd almost been hoping he'd forgotten he thought he was in love with her. Looking now into their chocolate depths, she knew he'd forgotten nothing. What she saw there was stronger than ever and she inhaled as she asked, "Are we talking the whole red carpet, Entertainment Tonight, designer dress, Emmy kind of deal or is it just another performance for you?"

"If I tell you the whole big deal are you going to turn me down?" He was smiling, but his question was sincere.

"No." She shook her head. "Of course I'll go with you, Nick. I'd be honored, but you'll have to help me know what to do and what to wear. I'd never forgive myself if I embarrassed you in public." She grimaced. "I'm afraid I'm a clueless wonder in Hollywood society."

He smiled a huge, gorgeous smile. "Baby, I could never be embarrassed to be seen with you. Everyone there and those watching on TV will be absolutely jealous. The only problem will be that then everyone will want to steal you away from me and I already hate sharing you." They stood up to get ready to go. "As far as what to wear. I'll help you with whatever you want. We'll call one of those consultants who help people find clothes and they'll bring a whole bunch of things right to your hotel to let you choose what you want. Do whatever you like. Just tell my manager Joe, and I'll pay for it all. I think Bryan is going to ask Joey too, and you can shop together." He put his arm around her on the way out the door. "Thank you for saying yes. I think it will be a memorable night for you."

On the drive home he casually asked her if she had thought about coming to LA permanently. The way he'd worded his questions made her hope she could talk about this without discussing his feelings, but when she answered him by saying she needed to stay with her daughter, he said, "Kit, I wasn't asking you to leave your daughter. I wouldn't ask that. I want you and her to come." He pulled into the hotel and parked in the parking garage instead of driving up to the front door.

He switched off the car and turned to her. "Kit, I'm not sure what you think I'm asking, but I love you. I want you to come to California to marry me and I'll adopt your daughter. We'll get a nanny to take care of her while you're working."

She turned to look into his steady brown eyes, wondering how she ever got into this situation. She was going to school to appease Rossen, and in a way was even here to make sure he knew when she came home that she hadn't missed out on anything. She prayed in her mind to know what to say to the man in front of her, then wondered if Rossen had had any idea of the places she would find herself when he'd encouraged her to come.

When she answered Nick, she followed the thoughts that popped into her head, hoping her answer would be a no that was buffered enough to not weaken their friendship or belittle this strong man's feelings. She so didn't want to cheapen the fact that he'd asked her to be his wife and offered to adopt her fatherless child. "Nick, this is all too fast for me. How can you even know you love me in this short of time together? And you've never even met my daughter. How can we make plans this fast?"

He was quiet for a moment, watching her as he

considered what she said. Finally, he answered, "I'm twenty nine years old, Kit. I know what I feel for you is something I've never felt before. I've never been married before. Never even wanted to be, but for the first time, I want to spend the rest of my life with one person. I've thought about it and I actually do believe you're right; there are people who stay married forever and are devoted only to each other. You've helped me to understand that there's a point to all this life. For some reason, before you there wasn't much of one."

He sighed. "I know this is sudden and I understand that this is too fast for you and I'm sorry. I'll try not to pressure you, but please don't tell me no. At least leave the offer on the table and we'll continue to work together and see each other. Maybe someday you'll take me up on it. I'd be a good husband, even if I am a rocker dude." He ended on a teasing note with a smile.

She smiled back, although she was somewhat sad about all this. "You will be a great husband someday. Okay, I won't say no, but you have to understand that I can't marry you if I'm not in love with you. That wouldn't be fair to either one of us."

His smile was somewhat sad too, as he answered, "I understand. But you have to understand that I'm going to keep trying to make you fall in love with me."

The next evening was the masquerade ball. They stopped playing mid-afternoon so everyone could go and get ready. Joey and Kit had fun even before the party as they were trying to get each other into their costumes and get ready to go. Kit began to strap Joey into her corset and they both ended up on the bed in fits of giggles, when Joey said, "Now I know just how Miss Swan felt in *Pirates of the Caribbean,* when she said 'the women of Paris must have learned how not to breathe.'"

When they were dressed they went down to the hotel salon to have their hair done and got laughing again when they tried to fit Joey's hoop skirt into the styling chair.

Their two costumes were polar opposites, but when they went to meet their dates for the evening neither one of them doubted they could hold their own with the best of the California beauties. Neither of the men in the sports cars doubted it either.

Nick's eyes lit up to the bottom of their cocoa colored depths as he came around to open Kit's door. He was dressed as a cowboy, and other than the fact that he still had that pretty boy California glitz that she knew, from close personal experience with cowboys, would have embarrassed a real cowboy to death, he looked incredibly handsome.

Activity in front of the hotel pretty much came to a grinding halt when passers-by stopped to stare, as the famous pirate and his damsel in a full hoop gown stepped into the shiny Porsche, while beside them a wildly popular rockin' cowboy helped an exquisite fairy into his racy black Maserati.

Kit had almost gotten the giggles watching Joey

try to gracefully wrestle her dress into the small space, but she'd thought with that many people watching her, it wouldn't be prudent. She controlled herself until they got rolling, and then burst into laughter as Nick's car squealed past Bryan's.

The actual party was a blast. Kit decided before hand that she wasn't going to worry about being socially adept. She knew Nick cared for her and that he would help her to do what was expected of her. She laughed and smiled up into his eyes as they danced and mingled, without worrying about impressing any of these people she didn't know anyway. There were a couple of occurrences to dampen the atmosphere, but the girls handled them in stride and enjoyed themselves. Alcohol was the cause of the negatives. Many of those present had been imbibing and there were a few women who weren't very happy to find Nick with a new unknown. The more they drank, the cattier they became, and shortly Nick found himself apologizing for the rudeness of one in particular.

Joey actually handled that one. As she was standing next to the woman near a buffet table laden with drinks, she simply picked up a tall brilliant red frappe' of some sort and when the tipsy woman bumped into her roughly, Joey let the full drink tip all over the other woman's tight fitting, white Vegas Showgirl costume. Joey quickly stepped back to save her own dress and then graciously offered to help wipe off the red stain that had utterly destroyed the immodest costume. The obnoxious woman disappeared after that.

The other instance happened near the women's restroom. Kit had noticed several times during the evening that there was a man watching her. She finally even asked Nick if he knew who it was. Nick said he was the boyfriend of some movie starlet she wasn't familiar with, but at any rate, the guy made Kit's skin crawl.

She and Joey were just coming out of the ladies room around the corner from the ballroom when he staggered away from the wall, slurring as he addressed her, "There you are. I've been trying to catch your eye all night." Kit looked at Joey nervously as he walked toward them eyeing everything he could get his eyeballs on.

As he approached them, he actually put out his hand as if he was going to touch her chest. Kit's reaction was instantaneous and decisive and surprised even herself. He made his disgusting gesture and she whirled and kicked his hand in a lightning fast spin. He was knocked back against the wall where he slowly slumped to the floor, gripping his arm with a shocked look on his face. Kit and Joey continued walking as if nothing at all had happened and as they rounded the corner into the ball room, Joey whispered, "Dang! Matt would be proud!"

They continued on toward Nick and Bryan who led them out onto the dance floor for a slow dance. Kit and Nick had only been dancing for a minute when he pulled back marginally to look down into her face and ask, "Are you okay? You're heart is beating like crazy."

She just looked up at him and smiled. "Must be your animal attraction." He looked at her again in obvious skepticism and pulled her back in close to dance.

That evening as he walked her to her hotel room door he asked, "Am I ever going to feel like I dare kiss you good night?"

She looked up at him, wishing he hadn't asked that. She hated feeling like she was toying with him. He bent to place the gentlest of kisses on her mouth, watching her eyes as he did. "Goodnight, Just Kit. Call me when you make it home safe."

This time Bryan took them to the airport, by way of Isabel's horse farm to see the bronzes. They only had a few minutes to admire them, but Kit couldn't have been happier. They'd turned out just as she had envisioned them. Three spirited foals bucking and kicking at the gated entrance to the beautiful sprawling farm. They were magnificent!

Bryan hadn't understood why he was bringing them here and he asked, "Now why are we here looking at these statues?"

Joey grinned and gave Kit an exuberant high five. "Kit made these, Bryan! These are her latest pieces of work!"

Bryan looked from one to the other in amazement as they climbed back into his Porsche and said, "No way! Serious?"

Jaclyn M. Hawkes

Chapter 19

They made it back to school and the Stab in the Dark party was fun. Matt was always good for a laugh and Kit enjoyed him a lot. Every once in a while she still wondered if he didn't have a thing for her, but then she'd decide everything was fine. She took another CLEP test the next day and she and Joey finally went home. It felt like she'd been gone a month.

When they arrived, Naomi told her she'd gotten word that the trials in Arizona had been postponed due to some minor legal detail. Kit wasn't sure what to think about it, but Naomi was disgusted.

That afternoon when the girls had had a chance to nap, Rossen showed up with horses saddled and Mimi bundled into a heavy coat. The leaves were all gone and the weather had turned cold, but Kit didn't have to be asked twice.

They rode for almost two hours in the foothills around the ranch and although she hadn't seen much of the ranch in this late fall, she thought it was as beautiful as ever. The grasses and brush were all browns and tans and grays, and the trees were like stately black and white skeletons against the muted background. Behind it all was the deep green of the thick pines and then the flat sky, just now low and gray with the threat of the season's first snow. It was so different from the brilliant green of summer and the stark whites of the snow, but it had its own sense of waiting for the coming winter. Riding beside Rossen in the cool wind off the ridges made her feel vigorous and alive.

She loved to watch him ride. Even just walking his horse along the trails, he was so masculine and in control. His confidence was maddeningly attractive and she let her horse have its head to follow as she focused on watching him. All too soon Mimi began to fuss and they headed back. Rossen took the baby in to his mom and then came back out to help Kit unsaddle the horses and put them away.

He was pulling his horse's cinch when she sighed beside him, wondering about his family's ranch. He came over to where she was leaning against her horse's shoulder looking out over the neutral landscape and glanced to where she was looking across the ranch yard to the bench on the other side, as she asked him, "If you were going to build a house here, where would you put it?"

He nodded to right where she was looking. "Right up there on that bench, back from the edge some, but out from the trees. The view is incredible from there and it's protected from the storms that come in over the ridge. You'll be able to watch the sun rise or set from the same rocker on the front porch. I actually bought that piece from my dad and have already had a set of plans drawn up and engineered. I just haven't ever gotten around to building yet." His voice was wistful as he ended and picked up the saddle to take it into the tack room. He paused beside her. "Why do you ask?"

She was still looking out toward the bench. "I'm going to build a house here too. Next spring, as soon as the snow's gone. Sean's going to build it for me. Your dad said he'd sell me a place to put one. I just don't know where I'd like it to be."

He took his saddle in and put it away and came back out to pick up hers, as she gathered up the blankets and bridles to follow him inside. He was quiet and didn't say anything even when she came out to stand beside him as he continued to look out toward the bench. Untying their horses, she led them off to put them away. She'd give good money to know what he was thinking behind those blue eyes. When she came back around, he was standing over against the corral, leaning on the top rail looking across the valley at the bench he'd been talking about. She wanted to go to him and ask him what he was thinking, but she knew he probably couldn't tell her anyway. Another one of those stupid rule things. She went inside to take care of Mimi, but her thoughts and her heart remained outside with him.

****

Kit was so busy that the days began to run together. Her life became a blur of school and dating and driving. The only things that even stood out and seemed to matter were her meager time at home with

Rossen and Mimi, and the upcoming night as Nick's date for the Hollywood Awards show.

When she was at home she was more conscious than ever of the passage of time. The snows had come to the Wyoming mountains and the ranch was looking like the first time she'd seen, it almost a whole year ago. It was amazing how far she had come from that momentous night they'd picked her up.

Mimi was now six months old, had two tiny front teeth and could crawl and pull herself up to anything handy, usually Rossen's long, denim clad legs. She would reach up one little arm to him and say, "Dah." Her hair was getting long, and Kit laughed the first time she came home to find he'd pulled it up into a tiny whale spout on top of her head with a pink bow around it.

Mimi had become far more attached to him than she was to Kit and if Kit thought about it too much, it made her deeply sad. She tried instead to remember how grateful she was that her daughter was so well loved and cared for. Every once in a while she would imagine what her and Mimi's lives would have been like if he hadn't picked her up off that dark Las Vegas street that night. It made her love him all the more.

This time home, she and Naomi had a long talk while they cooked, something they hadn't done in a while. Mimi was napping and the rest of the family had gone to feed and it was just the two of them making lasagna together. Kit was layering the noodles in the pans while Naomi added the final seasonings to the meat sauce, when Naomi said, "I know Rossen has been after you to eat more, but you're still pretty thin. Are you still working yourself to death at school?"

Kit shook her head. "I'm not working myself to death. I'm just trying to fit enough into this semester to keep Rossen from hassling me to death when I come home to stay next month. It's been pretty hectic. I think half the stress is trying to date a lot without leading a bunch of guys on. I don't have much of an interest in any of them really."

Naomi smiled a sympathetic smile. "And the other half of the stress?"

Kit gave her a sad smile as she said, "Trying to figure out how to let my rich and famous boss down gently when he asks me to move to LA and marry him."

Naomi gave her signature, "Oh my!" with a shade more enthusiasm than usual. "Joey told me she thought he liked you, but I had no idea he was that serious! Is he one of those rich and famous people who have been married seven times, or is it just that he's figured out what a keeper you are this quick?"

Kit sighed. "That's part of the problem. I almost wish he was one of those disposable wife kinds. It would be easier to blow off his attention. Actually, he's never been married even though he's almost thirty. Even knowing about Mimi doesn't matter to him."

She layered pasta and sauce as she continued, "I felt like I had to go out with him at first because of Rossen. I figured he could never say I hadn't dated enough when I wanted to come home, if I'd dated one of the most famous guys in the country, but now Nick has become a good friend who I have a great deal of respect for. He's a really nice guy. And he made me agree to at least keep his offer on the table. That's a hard one."

Setting aside the cheese grater, Naomi said, "Well, playing the devil's advocate, have you thought about what you're turning down?"

"What do you mean?"

"Well, he *is* very wealthy, and famous, and you'd have a relatively easy in if you wanted to become a famous star yourself. He's good looking, and apparently treats you well. That's a lot to walk away from"

With another sigh Kit said, "It is, but what about being a worthy priesthood holder? He's actually pretty open to gospel ideas, but I'd be like number two hundred as far as women he's been with. What about raising my daughter in the church? Could she and I ever be happy in the city after living like this? And I guess most importantly, I'm not in love with Nick. If I were, a lot of these other things would be non issues, but I'm not. And honestly, I don't see myself ever falling in love with him. Anyway, can you imagine me trying to separate Rossen and Mimi? I couldn't do that to either of them."

Kit spread the grated cheese on top of the finished pans. "No. If it's still okay with you, I'll come home, build a house here next spring and raise Mimi where she's loved. It's going to be hard enough on her growing up an only child with an unmarried mom. Dragging her off to the big city would be too much. If

I'm still single when she's grown, I'll worry about getting married then."

Naomi was quiet, thinking for a moment. At length, she said, "I'm glad you've decided against marrying him. It is a lot to walk away from, but you're right. Raising Mimi Star in the church is more important than money or fame. And having the priesthood in your home, or at least next door, is important." She put her arm around Kit. "And I would miss you both terribly. But you need to do what you feel is the best decision for the both of you to be happy. Of course, it's still okay with us. You're one of us completely now. It will be nice to have you home and fatten you up again!"

Kit thought of that conversation again later that night when she watched Mimi climb all over Rossen as he lay on the floor in front of the TV. She pulled herself up against him and crawled right over the top of him. Even when she pulled herself up by grabbing a handful of his hair, all he did was turn her over on her back and make her laugh uncontrollably when he gave her zerbits on her little tummy. She continued to laugh and pull his hair as they played, until she finally wound down and crawled over onto him and went to sleep.

Kit lay on the couch above them watching. In some ways their love for each other made her heart full and in some ways she felt left out. Rossen openly adored the baby and there were no stupid rules. Kit closed her eyes to doze off, wondering if she was jealous of her own daughter.

Chapter 20

Finding fancy enough dresses in time for their red carpet Hollywood show was no easy trick; in fact they ended up flying back to California again just to find them. The consultant who helped them with their dresses helped them with shoes and arranged for jewelry to be basically rented from a local jeweler too. When Kit realized how much the jewelry was worth she would be wearing that night, she considered renting an armored guard as well.

Flying back out for the actual show, Kit was so uptight she almost wished she'd told Nick no. At least saying goodbye at home had been easier this time. She'd been too nervous worrying about falling off her heels in front of millions of people to be as sad as usual about leaving.

Naomi and Rob came with them. Bryan had been able to get them tickets, so Naomi was there to help the girls get dressed in all their finery after having had a stylist come right to their rooms to do their hair. Nick and Bryan called from the limo when they got to the hotel saying there were so many people out there waiting for celebrities to show, that they worried if they came up they'd never get back in the car in one piece in time.

The girls went down the grand staircase of the hotel in all their glory on the arm of Rob dressed to the nines in a tuxedo of his own. Naomi came right behind. The chauffer opened the door of the car and Nick and Bryan got out to help them all in. The girls thought they'd gotten used to the crush and flash of cameras by now, but they were wrong. Kit was nearly blind by the time they were safely seated next to their famous dates and the limo pulled away. She felt so harassed that she couldn't imagine anyone wanting to live this way.

When she could finally see again, she realized Nick was watching her every move with deep brown eyes and an appreciative, satisfied smile on his face. She was almost a bit shy when he didn't say anything, just kept checking her out. When she couldn't stand it any more she asked, "Do I look all right?"

He gave her his famous drop dead gorgeous smile and said, "Oh yeah! Way more than all right! It's a good thing they'll have tight security tonight, because otherwise someone would be tempted to steal you away!" He turned to Joey and told her with a touch less enthusiasm, "You look awesome too, Jo. Don't you think so, Bryan?"

He answered the same, but with his typical cheerful southern Alabama drawl, "Oh yeah!"

Nick must have been aware of Kit's case of nerves because he leaned over to whisper in her ear, "You look great and you're gonna be just fine!"

She gave him a small grimace. "Coach me through this, okay. I have no idea what I'm supposed to be doing. I should never have agreed to come."

He slid over close to her on the leather seat. "Sure, I'll coach you. But honestly, all you need to do is be the same Kit you always are and you'll be great—like you always are. If you get uncomfortable, just take my hand and smile and you'll be all right. This is Kit, the woman who can handle anything with style, remember? That same girl who knocked my socks off the instant I met her." He leaned into her and kissed her temple. "Relax; it's going to be fun!"

She looked up into his smiling face and decided he was right. And if Nick said she could do this, she could. She'd trust him and relax and enjoy her one shot at fame. As the long limousine pulled up beside the red carpet, she got out, smiling like a princess and fairly floated up the walk lined with photographers and fans.

Nick held her hand and smiled and actually posed in front of a couple of the cameras with her as they made their way along. Everywhere she looked there were famous faces and press, and even though for a while she lost sight of Joey in the crush, she hoped she was having a good time too, enjoying the insane glitz.

They eventually made their way inside and were ushered to what turned out to be the head table, right near the front of the huge venue. There were tables toward the front, then only chairs, and then further back, stadium seating. Kit was a bit intimidated until she remembered that Nick thought she could handle anything.   His belief in her helped her to have confidence in herself and she turned to him and smiled again.

The program began and Nick stood to address the audience with his usual dashing style, the diamond stud in his ear flashing lightning in the floodlights. Throughout the evening he went to the nearby podium between the different segments of the show to introduce the performers and speakers. At one point he stood and introduced Bryan, who also went to the microphone. Kit didn't know Bryan was part of the show, and she didn't think Joey did either.   When Bryan began to speak, Joey's eyes filled with tears.

He looked at Joey and said, "This is the first time I've sung this song in front of an audience. It will be on my new album. I want to dedicate it to a dear friend of mine, Joey Rockland. She encouraged me to stick to my convictions, no matter the cost, and she's helped me find something priceless that I'd lost somewhere along the way. So thanks, Joey. This song's for you."

With that, the lights went down. He began a song about all the things that made life great and how good it was to enjoy the everyday things that really matter. It was sweet and soulful, but with an engaging rhythm that fit his smooth voice and happy demeanor exactly and when he finished the crowd was on it's feet clapping and cheering wildly. When he left the stage to return to his seat, there were still tears slipping down Joey's cheeks. He stopped to bend down beside her chair and wipe gently at the tears, before sitting in his own seat.

Kit hardly had time to be emotional as Nick went back to his microphone and began to announce the next portion of the show. She nearly had a coronary when she understood what he was saying, "This next song is one I wrote for a friend, too. She's here with me tonight. I'd ask her to marry me in front of you all, except I think she'd turn me down in front of ten million people and my ego would never be the same. She is an incredible new talent in the music industry! I'd like to introduce to you tonight, musician extraordinaire, the beautiful Kit Star!" The crowd went off again as Kit realized he was strapping on a guitar, while a stage hand held one for her.

She walked up onto the stage too stunned to do anything but smile and take the instrument. She had to hear the introduction before she could even figure out what they were going to play. She looked up at him standing in the spotlight as the house lights dropped, wondering if she should kill him later or thank him for sparing her the knowledge and therefore the nerves. He winked, hit a plaintive guitar lick and she just had time to let her instincts kick in, before she began to sing *Coming Home*.

The guitar seemed slightly strange with the formal gown at first and she was glad it was a relatively mellow song. Then she was into the music, dancing smoothly alongside him as he sang in her ear like they'd done so many times in the studio. He was even more focused in front of this huge crowd, and his intense showmanship calmed her nerves so she could put her heart into the song. Their harmony was smoother and sweeter than ever, ringing over the speakers in the huge stadium and her first experience in front of a crowd became an incredible high.

She'd wondered how it would be to sing in a concert. Well now she knew! And he was right. She did love it! He could read all of this in her face as he sang to her in front of millions and she knew she needed to thank him later, not kill him, when he gave her his dazzling smile as they played the last notes.

She was just wondering what she needed to do next when the crowd came unglued. She'd never heard anything like it in her life. Standing on the stage in front of the audience gave a whole new meaning to applause. He took her hand and gave a nod to the roaring crowd as they both waved and smiled for the viewers and fans. It felt like an eternity of standing and acknowledging the appreciation. Finally, he walked her to the edge of the stage where an usher helped her back to her seat as he returned to the podium to introduce the final act of the night.

He walked back to their table with a wide smile on his face and he too bent beside her chair as the lights dimmed for the final singer. He just looked at her for a moment with open admiration in his eyes before he said huskily, "You were great up there." He touched her cheek with his hand and sat down in his chair.

Kit's heart had still not returned to its regular speed by the time they made it out of the crowded stadium and into the car. Even with hordes of security and walkways cordoned off, there were still incredible numbers of people to greet and be introduced to, or even just walk past, and Rob and Naomi chose to simply take a cab back to their hotel. When the limo door finally shut behind the rest of them, the evening had become almost surreal. Kit's brain had a hard time even acknowledging the fact that she was indeed here and not watching all this happen to someone else on TV.

Nick sighed, pulled the tie of his tuxedo loose and tossed it onto the seat beside him as Bryan followed suit. Joey leaned back into the seat and took off one dainty high heel to stretch out her foot. Nick opened the mini fridge to pull bottles of water and sparkling apple juice out and offer them around. "I had the fridge stocked especially in honor of you two ladies tonight! There's not a drop of booze to be found. Honestly, this is the first time I've ever finished one of these things without drinking, but I won't tell you that."

Kit laughed at his ludicrous honesty, which was exactly what he had in mind and he went on, "There are approximately six thousand four hundred and twenty-three fashionable parties we could attend tonight. Or we could go back to my place and listen to music and relax where we won't be bothered by any drunken Las Vegas show girls. What do you say, ladies? What's your preference?"

Kit had had enough crowds for the night and apparently Joey had too, when she opted for the quieter private celebration at Nick's home. Had Kit been honest about her preference, she would have called it a night right then, but she felt like she needed to let Nick continue to celebrate; after all, he had been the Master of Ceremonies.

When they arrived, Kit was surprised to find that Nick lived in a condo in the foothills in the twentieth floor penthouse. It was luxurious, but she couldn't even begin to imagine coming home to this everyday. You couldn't have come up with a more opposite setting to the wooded bench of the Rockland Ranch if you tried.

Nick showed them in, turned the sound system on low, and invited them all to come to the kitchen and find something to eat. He and Bryan hadn't eaten since they'd had a late lunch and they were both ravenous. They took king crab legs out of the freezer to steam and teamed it up with a loaf of French bread and several kinds of fresh fruit. Nick was inordinately pleased with himself when he went to his wine cooler and produced another bottle of sparkling cider. Kit and Joey shared some of their dinner and wandered around his beautiful condo.

Kit ended up on the balcony overlooking the city lights below. She wondered what Rossen was doing right now, however many miles away. It felt like ten million. The music drifted from an outdoor speaker behind her and far in the distance she could see the dark, flat horizon of the ocean. The lights surrounded her on every side for almost as far as the eye could see and that many people made her feel smothered, almost as if she couldn't breathe.

What she wished she were seeing was that snow

covered mountain valley with its towering, pine clad, guardian peaks surrounding it. She knew she could breathe freely there. She was struggling to comprehend this much humanity in one place when Nick came out to stand beside her. She began to shiver in the coolness of the November evening and he set down his champagne flute of cider to come up behind her and wrap her in his arms.

"Are you warm enough? Do you want my tux coat?"

She shook her head. "No. I'm fine if you hug me again. I was just admiring your view. You have a beautiful home."

His voice was close to her ear when he said, "It's beautiful with you here." He turned her in his arms and began to dance with her to the slow music.

She was honestly trying. The setting was perfect, the city lights and the stars and the opulent home. A good looking, wealthy and famous man. The gala evening, her first performance and then slow dancing here in the dark, but it was all she could do to hide her thoughts so she didn't ruin his big evening.

She pushed her dreams of the home on the bench from her mind as well as she could. She'd agreed to be Nick's date tonight and she felt like she needed to enjoy herself and help him have a good night just to be honorable. With this thought in mind, she came back to the present and concentrated on listening to the man whose arms she was in as he talked into her ear about the different things they'd seen that night. He was bright and funny and she wasn't miserable as she waited patiently for this night to come to an end, but if it were sooner than later she wouldn't mind at all. They went back inside after a couple of songs and when she knew that Joey was enjoying Bryan's company, she tried even harder to be a good sport. What was wrong with her?

Finally, Joey suggested it was time to take them back to the hotel. Kit didn't say anything, but she was tired and wanted to go to bed. The ride back in the limo was still enjoyable, but the energy had begun to run out on this glamorous night, and when they reached the hotel she was glad. The two stars offered to walk the girls up to their rooms, but the hotel still seemed pretty lively even at this late hour and they all knew they'd just be mobbed.

Saying goodnight was slightly awkward and finally Bryan opted to brave the gauntlet and walk Joey up to the room. Kit wasn't sure if being alone with Nick was more comfortable or not. She knew he wanted to kiss her goodnight, which wasn't that big of a deal, after all he was a very attractive man, but she hated to lead him on. If she wondered if he still had strong feelings for her, all she had to do was look into his eyes. He never even tried to hide his emotions anymore.

He slid closer to her on the seat and wrapped an arm around her. As she looked up expectantly at him, he studied her face at length. His voice was a little husky when he said, "Thanks for not being totally ticked off at me. I wanted you to sing with me tonight, but I was afraid you'd tell me no if I asked you beforehand. I knew you'd be a good sport and you did an awesome job! I knew you would, but you still never cease to surprise me. You're a one in a million, Kit Star. Are you still sure you can't marry me?"

She looked down, sad to disappoint him. "I'm sorry, Nick. I'm still not in love with you." She tried to inject a lighter note. "Maybe I will be tomorrow." She smiled up at him and then her face sobered. "I had a wonderful evening, one I'm sure I'll remember for the rest of my life." This time she was the one to raise her face to his. "Good night, Nick."

He met her lips with the lightest of kisses and then increased the pressure for just the shortest second. "Good night, Just Kit. Thanks for being there for me tonight."

Chapter 21

From the second she left, Rossen stressed about this trip to California. This was the only time she'd left since she'd gone off to school and left Mimi with him, that she hadn't broken down as she got in the car and drove away. He tried to chalk it up to nerves, until that night when he turned on the TV just in time to see her being filmed stepping out of a long limousine next to that hyper-famous rock star. In her designer dress and jewels, with the professional do, she looked perfectly at home on the red carpet and when she took his hand and they posed for the camera, Rossen felt a hole somewhere in the center of his chest.

He was watching the televised show when Sean came in and said, "Geez, Rossen. You're not just a bonehead to keep sending her away, you're a masochist too." He sat down to watch with him, and when Bryan Cole dedicated the song to Joey, they gave each other a high five. A few minutes later, when Kit was being brought on stage and Nick talked about asking her to marry him, Sean looked at him, but Rossen was too floored to even look up and meet his eye. This guy had only known her for two and a half months. What the heck did he think he was doing?

Then Rossen thought about what an extraordinary young woman she was and he understood exactly. He'd only known her about ten days when he'd fallen in love with her himself. He wanted to reach through the TV and tell this stupid superstar to leave her alone and let her have time to grow up, but when he looked at her with her guitar on stage, singing in her gown and heels, he knew there was nothing ungrownup about her. She was all woman and the crowd knew it too, when they went nuts at the end of her song. Their applause felt like the death knell to his secret hopes. How could he expect her to walk away from all that to come back to a lonely ranch in the wilds of Wyoming?

He watched the rest of the show and then the media highlights that felt like the Nick and Kit special. Every photographer had a fascination with who the new girl was with Nick Sartori that he so obviously adored. Nobody seemed to know much about her and that only made everyone more curious. There was shot after shot of them together in every situation that night and there were even a number of shots of them at other times.

Rossen couldn't even count the photos that flew across the screen of the two of them together, usually trying to avoid the cameras as they got into or out of a car somewhere. Some of the time it was in a limousine and there were several that had Joey and even Bryan in them too, but there were others of just the two of them getting into luxury cars and one, a racy, black Maserati.

There was even one taken from long range of the

two of them on a lonely beach, walking together hand in hand, her in a lovely white sundress with the breeze blowing her hair. When that one flashed across the screen, Rossen groaned out loud, and Sean got up to give him a look of pity and go back out the door.

Rossen took the now sleeping baby, and switching off the TV with a deep sigh, went down into the basement to take out his frustrations on the speed bag hanging in the game room. He put Mimi in her crib and was twenty minutes into a brutal attack on the bag when he slowed to a halt and dropped to his knees to pour out his frustration and loneliness to the only one he knew would understand.

He had so many questions he just didn't get. Why had all this happened to him and Kit? Why did he feel he was being punished for trying to help a young woman who had desperately needed him nearly a year ago? Why had God allowed him to feel the way he did but then also know he needed to send her away? At length, he got to his feet, feeling like the poster boy for a broken heart and a contrite spirit.

He tried to read, but gave that up and went to bed, only to admit defeat and give that up too, sometime in the wee hours of the morning. He went up and into Kit's room to stand in the dark, looking out the window into the snowy night, breathing in the subtle smell of her and almost wallowing in his trashed heart.

He remembered the first time they'd heard her sing. She had been sitting just outside this very window on a night not unlike tonight. So much had transpired in the last year. Both of them had changed so much. She'd blossomed like an exotic rose, while he had become quieter and more inside himself. His mother had been right about the refiner's fire. The months of trying to put the natural man aside to give her her freedom had made him stronger. Stronger, and sadder. Sometimes he wondered if the happy, teasing side of him was gone forever.

Knowing he'd never find the answers out in that beautiful, cold winter's night, he was about to take his exhausted, emotional self to bed again when his phone began to ring. He'd left it on an end table in the great room and the second he heard it go off, he knew who it was.

****

The hotel sheets were cool and crisp and Kit's body was absolutely weary, but sleep would not come. She kept thinking of Rossen and wondering what was going on in his life as she'd been in LA. She wished he could have seen her. She didn't think Kit, the rocker was necessarily the real her, but she knew she was good at what she did and he would have been proud of her.

She tossed and turned and finally got up to check her watch. It was after two thirty California time. That made it after three thirty in Wyoming and she wondered if he would be mad if she called. Frustrated with her feelings, she got up to take her phone into the bathroom and shut the door.

He picked up on the second ring and she could tell by his voice that he hadn't been sleeping either. His deep, tired hello was exactly what she needed to hear.

Now that she had him on the line, she wasn't sure what to say and settled for, "Hey, Rossen."

She could hear the concern and the smile in his voice. "Hey yourself, Kit. What's going on? Is something wrong?"

With a sigh, she replied, "Nothing's wrong and somehow everything is. I'm sorry to call so late. I just couldn't sleep. I'm incredibly homesick tonight. I wish I were there instead of here."

It was a long moment before he replied, "We wish you were too." He paused. "You shouldn't be homesick. You've had quite a night. We saw you on TV here. You never mentioned you were performing at that shindig. I wish you would've told me. I'd have recorded it for you." He sounded slightly sad on his end of the line.

"I would have told you if I'd known. Nick sprung that on me in front of all those people. He said he thought I would turn him down if he asked before hand. I probably would have. I'd have been a nervous wreck if I'd known I was going to be playing."

He laughed at the tone of her voice and said, "No way! You didn't even know that was coming and you got up and performed like that? I thought you were great! You looked incredible and I had no idea the two of you sounded that good together. It made me want to come with you sometime when you're recording. You have an amazing stage presence and I was proud of you." That was so good to hear. She valued his opinion more than anyone's. She knew he would always be honest with her.

There was a pause on the line before she said, "I don't know what I wanted to say. I just needed to hear your voice for some reason. How is Mimi Star?"

"She's good. She laughed when she saw you on T.V. I'm not sure she was impressed, but she certainly thought you were entertaining."

Kit wondered why he was up. "Did I wake you or were you already awake?"

He hesitated before he answered her, "I was awake. Honestly, I was worrying about Nick's little comment about asking you to marry him. Why would he say that about you turning him down in front of ten million people?"

Kit laughed somewhat stiffly. "Uh, because I have every other time."

She wondered if she should have been that forthright when he didn't say anything for the longest time. Finally he said, "Oh, well I guess that makes more sense. How many times has he asked you to marry him?"

She decided to be vague, "A few. Sometimes he just says things like 'Come to LA to be with me forever.' It's not really a proposal. But he's honestly asking."

"Is that something you'd seriously consider?"

"Would I be up, hopelessly homesick at three thirty in the morning after singing with him in front of half the country, if it was?"

He laughed at her for a second. "Maybe, if it was a serious question you were wrestling with."

"What I'm seriously wrestling with, is why I ever leave there at all."

There was a long pause, and then he sighed as he replied, "Good, because we'd all miss you desperately if you were living that far away." There was something in his voice she couldn't exactly figure out. She wished she could've seen his face when he said that.

She answered, "I'm afraid you're stuck with me. I'm not a twenty stories up, penthouse kind of a girl. This many people take up all the oxygen."

She could hear the smile again when he said, "Well, come on home then. We've still got plenty of oxygen."

"I'll be there on Wednesday for five whole days over Thanksgiving. It'll be heaven! Is there too much snow to go riding?"

"There's never too much snow to go riding. We can even take Mimi. Grandma bought her a great new snowsuit that turns her into an Eskimo baby."

Kit smiled. "I'll bet she loves it. She always loves to go outside."

"Actually, she's a tad unsure of all the cold, white stuff. She loves to stand and look out the window, but she doesn't want to touch it."

"Well, I'll come home and touch it for her, while I'm breathing the oxygen." There was another silence and then she said, "Thank you for not being mad at me for calling in the middle of the night. I think I can sleep now."

His deep voice was husky and warm when he

said, "You're welcome. Now that I'm not worrying about you moving to LA, I think I can too. Good night. Be careful coming home."

"I will. Kiss Mimi Star for me. Good bye." Kit didn't want to hang up and she just sat with the phone to her ear for a minute before she finally pushed end. There were so many things she would've liked to say to him, but she couldn't because of the stupid rules. Maybe someday she'd be able to just tell him she loved him as she hung up, like she dearly wanted to.

****

When he'd answered his phone to hear her troubled voice telling him how much she missed home, he finally felt some peace in his tortured heart. Maybe somehow this was all going to work out. When she spoke of needing oxygen, he knew just what she meant. Their conversation had been short, and neither one of them had been able to say what was honestly in each other's hearts, but his pain from wondering if he had lost her to the rock star, who was as opposite of himself as night and day, had been eased by that one short taste of her own loneliness in the middle of a dark California night. He hesitated to hang up the phone after they said goodbye, wishing he'd been able to tell her how much he loved her out loud. He took his exhausted body to bed to finally be able to rest.

Chapter 22

Nick woke up from a deep sleep, knowing instantly that someone was trying to break into his front door. He lived in a high security building and wondered how they'd gotten this far, even as he called that same security to have whoever it was apprehended. Hanging up his phone, he pulled his own pistol out of the drawer in the table beside his bed and threw a robe over his shoulders, prepared to defend himself if the intruder made it inside before help arrived. He heard the shouts and scuffle outside and when he heard the head of security call to him through the intercom, he opened the door to find out what was going on.

He'd had trouble like this before. Usually it was the jealous boyfriend of an ardent fan or a lovesick female stalker, but this time it was a slovenly, middle aged, heavy set man. Nick had no idea what to think, until the man asked him where Kit was.

It only took about ten more seconds until Nick understood this was the foster father who had been the cause of so much heartache and trouble for the sweet, innocent girl he loved and a deep, hot anger filled his heart instantly. He wasn't normally short tempered, but realizing that this foul, disgusting man, who had caused so much hurt already, was for some reason trying to find Kit again, made his blood boil. It was all he could do not to hit the guy as he stood on the elevator landing spewing vulgarity and profanity from his unkempt mouth.

When the police showed up to take him away, Nick told them to find everything they could dream up to pin on this guy and he would press charges to the fullest extent possible. He hoped they could put him away for years. Knowing sweet, pure Kit had been in this man's custody made him want to be sick.

Nick had calmed down somewhat by the time he made a phone call to Wyoming the next morning. He didn't want to call Kit directly and tell her what had happened, but he felt something had to be done to insure her safety, in case the guy got out on bail or wasn't working alone. Nick didn't know what this guy wanted, but there was no way he was going to let this scum get near her again, if he had anything to say about it.

He knew Joey's mother had been trying to have him put away down in Arizona, so he called Joey's home to try and reach either her mom or dad there. They weren't available, so he talked to the man who answered the phone who was Joey's older brother Rossen. Nick told him what had happened and knew from this man's reaction on the phone, that Kit would indeed be protected from their end and that the possible threat would be taken seriously.

After offering to pay for security, he was assured it would be handled and was told that when she was home, she was safe behind locked gates guarded twenty-four hours a day. Together the two of them talked about how to ensure her safety while at school, and by the time he ended the phone call, Nick trusted that Kit would be safe and had gained a respect for this brother of Joey's out in Wyoming. He was obviously sharp and his quiet, intelligent manner inspired Nick's confidence.

****

When Rossen got off the phone with Nick he was disgusted. The thought of Kit's foster father coming in contact with her again was horrific. The man Nick had described sickened him and made him want to take care of her with a whole new passion.

Rossen was also somewhat troubled to find that Nick was such a likeable guy. He was deeply and honestly concerned for Kit's well being and Rossen couldn't help but appreciate him, as they discussed how to keep her safe and happy on two fronts. Of course, he just had to be a nice guy. Rossen tried to put Nick out of his mind again as he began to formulate a plan to safeguard Kit for the next three days until she was safely home in Wyoming for Thanksgiving. He'd go, but decided to stay with the baby to keep her safe, too.

He called Joey and together they opted to see if Sean could go to Logan for a couple of days. They would try to have either Sean, or Treyne, or someone named Matt with Kit twenty-four-seven for the next couple of days.

Kit had talked to Rossen about Matt a couple of times. He'd never gotten the impression he was anything more to her than the other guys she went out with, but Joey sounded like Matt was a much better friend than the others and now Rossen began to wonder about him too. He'd sent Kit off to school hoping she would have a good college experience, but some parts of it had become pretty hard for Rossen to deal with. Not only was he hurt or even jealous about these other guys, but he also felt guilty for wishing they'd go away and leave his Kit alone. He had to get a handle on what exactly his and her relationship was. This roller coaster was killing him.

****

Kit walked in the door to their apartment and was surprised to see Sean there, hanging out with Treyne. Sean was an architect and now had a growing construction company of his own at home, and she knew he had been fairly overwhelmed with keeping up with his projects the last time she'd talked to him. To see him here, hanging out as if he had nothing better to do than visit, was quite a shift.

She was even more surprised and pleased when both of them asked if they could come with her to her class that afternoon to hear her play. As they walked across campus and the two of them made a big deal about checking out the girls, Kit laughed and decided that was the real reason for Sean's visit and their tagging along.

She never realized over the next three days that she was watched over religiously by the people around her who loved her. The only time she even wondered what was going on was when Matt insisted he help the two girls get packed and loaded for their trip home. Then he helped her into the car and told her goodbye with the most unusual look in his eyes. Kit wondered again if there was a chance that he thought of her as more than just a good friend.

Kit and Joey traveled home with Sean and Treyne in the truck in front of them until they reached Evanston, where the guys pulled on ahead, driving much faster in Sean's big truck than the girls wanted to in Kit's little car. Kit was so excited to get home, but she just wasn't as comfortable on the snowy roads as these guys.

Jaclyn M. Hawkes

Chapter 23

Knowing it was the day before Thanksgiving and the whole family would be home and he wouldn't get much engineering done in the next several days, Rossen was working in his office late, trying to tie up a few loose ends. He'd almost accomplished all he wanted to, when Mimi began to fuss in earnest, standing at the edge of her playpen and holding out her hands saying, "Dah." She finally said, "Dah-eeee!" in such a demanding tone that he walked over and picked her up to take her to the kitchen, feeling slightly guilty for letting her play by herself for so long this afternoon.

He fixed her a bowl of baby cereal and put her in her highchair to feed her with one of her little spoons. He'd figured out early on to give her one of the tiny rubber coated spoons in each hand and then carefully guard the bowl of cereal. By dodging the other spoons as he gave her each bite, he managed to keep her somewhat clean and the cereal in the bowl from landing upside down on the kitchen floor.

When she was through, he wiped off the odd smears of the porridge from her hands, face and hair and picked her back up. She laid her head on his shoulder and he was cuddling her, knowing she would soon be asleep, when his phone rang. It was another business call, and he grabbed a pen and was taking notes to himself, occasionally rubbing her back as he talked.

She hadn't been asleep long when the doorbell rang. It scared her and startled him. He hadn't heard that doorbell ring more than a handful of times in the last four years since they'd drilled the oil wells and installed the locked gates and guard house. Nobody but family could get in very easily, so no one rang the bell.

Mimi started to cry and he rubbed her back and patted her gently as he walked to the door with his phone still to his ear. He pulled open the door and tried not to stare as he motioned for the two men standing on the porch to come in as he said into the phone, "Hey, could I call you back on Monday and we'll finalize all the figures? Something just came up." He closed the front door, shut his phone and put it in his pocket so he could extend a hand to first one and then the other.

"Nick, Bryan. Come on in. Rossen Rockland."

****

Nick was taking it all in, eyeing the tall, blonde man and looking at the baby that was without a doubt Kit's. She had Kit's rich dark hair with the same tiny nose and arched brows over thick dark lashes just now lying against her little pink cheeks. Sporting tiny pink overalls, she rested on this large man's shoulder as he ended what had obviously been a business call. The two of them stared at each other for just a second like two posturing herd stallions, with Bryan looking on. Almost immediately Joey's dad and another man came in from a hallway, and a third appeared up a stairwell.

Nick and Bryan looked at each other. Joey's dad and the man with him and Rossen could all have been twins except for the differences in ages. The man who came up the stairwell was dark and certainly not related, but he acted like he lived here anyway. There was just a split second of awkward silence and then another door opened to admit a fourth and a fifth blonde twin. The younger of the two burst out with, "Hey, there's a Maserati out there in the ditch!" He looked around at the several men oblivious to the drama of the moment. "Wow! I know you! You're Nick Sartori. I've got all your CDs! And you're Bryan Cole! You were on TV just last week with Joey! What are you guys doing here?"

They didn't have a chance to answer to his exuberance before Rossen, still holding Kit's daughter, said to him, "Treyne, mind your manners. I'm sure they're here to see Kit and Joey." He turned back to them. "I'm sorry. The girls aren't quite here yet. They're still on their way home from school in Logan. They should be just a short while behind these two." He indicated the last two to enter.

Bryan replied, "They uh, don't actually know we're here. We thought we'd surprise them."

Nick added forthrightly, "Actually, we came to find out what Wyoming has that California doesn't."

Bryan glanced at the six men in front of them and he grinned as he remarked dryly, "It didn't take us long to figure that one out."

Nick looked around at these men. All of them stood inches over six feet with heavy shoulders and long legs. They all wore jeans and even just standing there in their own home; they looked like a whole troop of the Marleboro Man. If they hadn't all appeared friendly, he would have been extremely intimidated. Knowing Kit would arrive any second, he came right out and asked, "Which one of you is the one Kit's in love with?"

Simultaneously, five of them turned to look at the man with the baby, who looked around in surprise. He said, "Oh, come on! Be serious, you guys." At his outburst the baby startled and began to cry. He pulled her close under his chin and began to quietly talk to her and rub her tiny back to settle her down while his eyes watched Nick's.

Nick looked across at him and shook his head. "You don't even know?"

Rossen answered, "Of course Kit loves me. She loves us all. But she's not in love with me." To a man, all of the rest of them turned to look at him again without saying a word. Rossen looked around at them in disbelief as Nick shook his head again, and Bryan grinned. The baby started to cry in earnest and Rossen took her into the kitchen and began making her a bottle, talking softly to her all the while.

Joey's father turned to Nick and Bryan and extended his hand to both of them in turn, "You remember me. Rob Rockland, Joey's father. It's good to see you again. Welcome to Wyoming." He hesitated for a moment and then asked, "Do you mind my asking? How did you find us?"

Bryan grinned. "We asked in town how to get here."

Rob seemed incredulous. "Someone in our town told you, strangers, how to get here?"

Bryan laughed and looked slightly sheepish. "He was a fan of mine."

"How did you get past the guys in the guard house?"

This time it was Nick who grinned. "Uh, well, they were fans of mine."

Rossen was watching their exchange as Rob shook his head and laughed. "So much for homeland security. Come on in and sit down. Meet the family. After dinner we'll go out and pull your car out of the ditch." Nick and Bryan went in and sat down in the great room with Rob and Treyne, while one went back down the hall and another went back out the door. The dark one leaned against the counter next to Rossen to spectate.

It wasn't two minutes later that the garage door opened and Joey and Kit came in. Joey set her bags down and turned to close the door while Kit came straight into the kitchen to put her arm around Rossen's waist as he held the baby. She put her face close to his neck to give her daughter a gentle kiss.

Nick was watching all this from the couch and Rossen raised his head to see his eyes upon them as he said, "Uh, Kit. You and Joey have company." She looked up at him questioning, and he nodded toward the great room. She followed his nod and then looked back at Rossen. Their eyes met and held for a full second before she advanced into the room to greet them.

Rossen took the baby and walked down the hall to disappear around a bend and Nick looked up into Kit's eyes as he stood to greet her. He wasn't sure what he saw there, but he knew it wasn't the same look he'd just seen her give Rossen as she came in the door. The gentle touch she'd given as she leaned in to him to give her daughter a kiss had been subtle, but she'd never once touched Nick like that in all the time he'd known her.

What he'd suspected all along was blatantly obvious to him, even if it wasn't to Rossen, and it filleted his heart even as he realized he was glad it was someone who undoubtedly treated her the way she deserved to be treated. He hadn't missed the long look that hung between them. He didn't understand what was going on here, but he thought Rossen was a fool if he let her get away.

Nick's silent figuring was interrupted when Joey's mother, Naomi, and two young women came in the same door the others had all come through. One of the young women was blonde and beautiful, and one was small and dark and beautiful. He had to wonder how many more people belonged to this family as Naomi walked toward them with her hands out and a welcoming smile on her face.

Three hours later, his car was safely out of the

ditch, he'd hesitantly held Kit's baby, and they'd joined the family at the largest table he'd ever seen for an unbelievably delicious family dinner. Naomi had been flat out offended when they'd gone to leave and had insisted they stay and have Thanksgiving dinner with the family the next day.

Nick didn't think he'd ever been quite so sweetly mothered before, and he knew he'd never been around a family like this one. He could understand now what Kit had been trying to tell him that night when she said that coming to live with the Rocklands had changed her life. The happy spirit here was almost palpable and he'd never seen anything like the friendships that were obviously so tight within this family. Rob and Naomi had been unreal and he remembered Kit saying their relationship was the coolest thing she'd ever seen. Watching them, Nick knew that Kit had been right again. He honestly could picture these two being happy and faithful to each other forever.

One thing Nick was still somewhat confused about was the strange relationship Kit and Rossen were caught up in. They were extremely close. Anyone with half a brain could see that, but they weren't acting like a happy couple, at least not overtly.

Later that night, when he finally had the chance to talk to Kit alone, he asked her right out about him, "So what's up with you and Rossen? Why do you even go out with me when you come to LA, when you feel the way you do about him?"

Kit looked at him with a level gaze, not even

flustered at his question. "Rossen is my best friend, but we don't date, ever. So why should I not go out with a very attractive man who asks me?"

Nick returned her honest look, trying not to show how disappointed he was to know for sure that her heart was fully engaged with someone other than himself. "I didn't say you shouldn't accept dates. I asked why you do when you already know you're in love with someone else."

Kit sighed. "Who has all the answers to questions like that in this life, Nick? If I didn't go out, would that change anything except that I'd be lonely and discouraged? I've never tried to lead you on. I've always been honest with you, and I do enjoy being with you. I still hope we can go out again. I can't help the way I feel about Rossen anymore than I can change the fact that he thinks that at eighteen, I'm ridiculously young. I think deep down he feels the same way about me that I feel about him, but I can still imagine myself growing old alone, because in some twisted, chivalrous way, he feels like my settling down this young, or with someone that much older than me isn't right." She looked suddenly tired and he felt guilty for asking her such a tough question.

She got up and came over to him to hug him as he stood by the fireplace. "I'm sorry for not falling in love with you, Nick. It's just not something you consciously decide. Please forgive me. Maybe someday when I'm older and wiser, I'll have a better handle on all this. Right now, I'm a hopeless failure in the romance department." She yawned and said, "If you don't mind, I'm going to bed. It's been a bit of a hectic week. Do you have everything you need?"

He hugged her back, with his cheek against her hair. "You always apologize when it's me who should be sorry. I have everything I need. Go to bed and I'll see you in the morning." He kissed her gently on the forehead and pushed her away.

Ten minutes later, when Rossen came in and sat down in the recliner across from him, Nick was surprised that he honestly kind of liked this guy. He knew Rossen had Kit's heart, but he was just such a good guy he was hard to even be jealous of. They sat in relatively comfortable silence for a few minutes, until finally Nick said, "She's a lot of woman to keep pushing away."

Rossen leaned his head back and closed his eyes. His voice was tired when he answered, "She's an eighteen year old girl, Nick."

His quiet answer made Nick feel a bit like an old letch for just a moment, until he thought about Kit and how mature and strong and talented she was. "She is young, but she's not a child, Rossen. She's strong and smart and incredibly well grounded. She's all woman and no one has the right to make her life's big decisions for her, not even when we think we're meddling for her own good."

****

Nick got up and walked out of the room to leave Rossen behind him wrestling with the huge weight of

the bombshell that had been dropped in his lap. Was
that what he'd been doing? Taking away the agency of
a grown woman?

On his way to bed a few minutes later, Rossen
stopped at Kit's bedroom door. He'd brought Mimi's
crib up and put it in Kit's room for the long weekend
and he missed the baby as well as being completely
mixed up emotionally about Kit. The door was ajar and
he pushed it open silently, just wanting to check on the
two of them before he retired for the night, but Kit
wasn't in bed. She was standing in the dark in her
white robe looking out the window at the snowy
mountains. He walked into the room to stand beside
her.

Neither of them said a word, and after a second
or two, she took a half step to lean her head against his
shoulder. Maybe they didn't have all the answers, but
just for tonight, this was enough.

Nick and Bryan left on Friday afternoon. Nick
had sought Rossen out that morning to double check on
Kit's security, and had been absolutely forthright when
he told Rossen he wanted to marry her and adopt Mimi
and move them to LA to stay. He'd ended with, "You
need to understand that I'm going to do everything in
my power to make her want to be with me and forget
she's in love with you. I have to be honest."

Rossen hadn't known whether to smile or hit him
as he replied, "I can understand that." They shook hands
and Nick walked away. You had to admire the guy.

He was in his office when they loaded their bags out to the little black sports car, and was looking out the window when Kit walked Nick out and gave him a hug. Slade came in and was standing beside him as he watched Nick bend to kiss her goodbye. It was like a one two punch when Slade turned to him and said, "I hope you get over this white knight thing you have before he's raising your daughter seven hundred miles away."

Rossen turned to look at him and Slade continued, "Come on Rossen, your theory of letting her finish growing up was commendable, but you don't have the right to force her to do anything. And if you don't soon let her make some of the big choices she wants to make, you're going to regret it for the rest of eternity. The old adage, 'If you love something set it free, and if it comes back to you it's yours, and if it doesn't, it never was.' doesn't have an addendum just for you that says 'and even if it does, you can't have it.' She's eighteen, not seven and she's had far more than her fair share of walking those hard miles. Cut her some slack. I'm telling you, if you don't, you're gonna regret it more bitterly than you've ever imagined, for the rest of forever."

"What are you saying, Slade?"

Slade made a disgusted sound. "I'm saying your girl just kissed a guy she doesn't particularly care about, just before he climbed into a Maserati to drive away. And if I don't miss my guess, that was just after he'd asked her to marry him. Again. Rossen, what she really wants is to stay here and be with you. Are you honestly too much of a bonehead to see that in her eyes?"

Rossen turned to look out the window again with a sigh. "Maybe I am."

Slade walked back out the door.

Chapter 24

Monday morning Rossen and Mimi helped Kit pack her bag into the back seat of her car, and he searched her eyes before she drove away. For days he'd been trying to figure out what he should be doing in his life as far as she was concerned, and he was more mixed up than ever. When she looked back at him with those startling blues, he honestly didn't know what she wanted from him, and he was confused as to what was still in her best interest at this point.

She didn't cry when she left, and he walked back into the house wondering if she was slipping away from him. She only had two more weeks of school before the end of the semester. Maybe over the long Christmas break he could figure out what to do. He knew he couldn't live like this for much longer. He went in and called Treyne's cell phone to remind him to make sure she had someone with her all the time.

That night before he went to bed, Mimi was at his feet in his room, playing with the little girl she saw in the full length mirror. After a few minutes she'd plastered it with her tiny, slobbery hands, but she was having a great time giggling at the little girl reflected there. He put her down in her crib and went to his own bed thinking about what Slade had said about Nick raising his daughter.

Deep in the night he woke up from a dream that devastated him when he became fully awake and understood what it was. Mimi was a beautiful child of eight or ten years old and she was still there playing in his mirror, talking to the girl reflected there. When she looked up at him, she asked, "Daddy, why do I still have to play all by myself?" He got out of bed to go and stand by her crib and look down at her sleeping so peacefully there in the dark. He knelt beside his bed praying for wisdom and peace, to know best how to take care of this beautiful, sweet, little daughter.

It wasn't even a week later that he was working quietly in his office with Mimi Star playing there beside him in the playpen, when a song came on the radio about a little girl dancing at her parents' wedding. It told of how the band that was performing, watched this little girl celebrate because her dad was finally marrying her mom. Rossen listened and watched Mimi and had never felt so guilty in his life.

****

That week Naomi flew to Tucson for the trials. The slimy foster father and his wife were convicted of almost every one of the charges and Naomi flew home secure in knowing that this guy would never harm another child, and in fact, would probably be in prison until he was an old, old man. The judge had postponed sentencing, saying he wanted to meet Kit and her daughter before he finalized his decision, so Naomi came back to Wyoming and returned to Arizona with Kit and Mimi Star and Rossen in tow.

Kit had no idea what was going on and didn't think Naomi even understood why the judge wanted to see her. When she walked into his chambers carrying Mimi, he stood up and came around his desk and shook her hand. He looked into her eyes and watched Mimi for a second and then with a sigh, leaned back against the edge of the desk and rubbed the back of his neck with his hand.

"I'm sorry to drag you all the way back to Arizona. I imagine it's a place you never wanted to see again. I just had to see for myself if the system was as bad as it appeared from the court documents. After meeting with you, I can see that Ms. Rockland's representation was indeed accurate."

He sighed again. "Miss Star, I'm sorry to the bottom of my heart for what you've had to endure at the hands of the State of Arizona. It didn't take me thirty seconds to figure out that that man was not fit to have a dog in his custody, let alone a young woman. He'll never be around another child, but that is of no help to you and what you've been through. I can see you've made the best of a bad situation, and that you've chosen to overcome the wrongs done you and love this beautiful child. I'm proud of you for your selflessness.

"Under the circumstances, I'm choosing to subvert the wishes of the drug investigators here. This man's motel was confiscated by the authorities because he and his wife had been manufacturing drugs. I am going to award the proceeds of the sale of that motel to you. It could never be enough to right the injustices done you, but it's a start. Honestly, a large portion of the proceeds had to go to cleaning up the hazardous materials, but the balance is yours, along with the rest of the money he had in his accounts. You'll find all of the information here in this file. Ms. Rockland can see to the transfers for you and help you select a trustee to handle the lion's share of it until you are twenty one. I suggest you hire a professional to handle investing it for you.

"I also want you to know that I have personally asked for the resignations of those who handled your casework and am, in fact, pursuing criminal action for some of those involved. I can't promise to fix the system, but I can promise you I'm going to try. No one should have to go through what you have in your short life." He handed her a large file folder and ushered them to the door. "Once again, please forgive me for dragging you here. I'm so sorry, and I hope this in some small way can make up for your troubles. You've become an extraordinary young woman, in spite of it all, and I wish you all the best in the balance of your life."

The four of them stood outside the door of his chambers looking at each other. Finally, Naomi said, "Oh, my."

Rossen took the folder and looked inside and then repeated her sentiments. "He just awarded you almost seven hundred thousand dollars. He's right, it can never make up for everything, but that's a lot of money."

As they walked down the hall, Naomi said almost to herself, "I wondered why he wanted to meet the two of you in person."

****

The last week of the semester Rossen and Mimi went to Logan to stay for a few days. He hadn't called and when Kit came home from classes Monday evening to find them in the living room, her face lit up even as tired as she looked. She hurriedly changed her clothes and apologized about having to leave on a date and Rossen knew as she left and kept turning around that she wished she could stay home instead.

He wondered if he had, in fact, pressured her too much to do things like date, to enjoy this season of her life. She'd hardly even looked at the poor guy. She was home two hours later, and then she and Joey and Treyne went to do something with their family home evening group.

The rest of that week as he hung out and watched her around campus, he was appalled at how much she was trying to do in the five day period. She hadn't even had to fit a trip to Wyoming in on Wednesday to come home and see Mimi like she had been all fall. And she hadn't been back to LA for almost three weeks. Her life had probably been even crazier.

She had dates every night that week, and even one for lunch as well, and she worked out with Joey and Matt in the mornings and then with Matt again on Thursday before her date that night. Rossen watched her do her final project in her sculpture class and then she had finals in Spanish and music. For some reason she'd also gone to take two other tests that he didn't know what they were for and she passed off another belt with Matt. Rossen had finally gotten to meet him and was almost glad he hadn't known much about him before. When he realized what good friends they were, he knew he'd have been miserable wondering about the two of them these last months.

When Friday afternoon rolled around, Matt brought her home around two thirty. They sat in his car talking for almost an hour. When she finally came in, she was sobbing and walked through the living room to go into her room and close her door, without even talking to Rossen or Mimi. She came out twenty minutes later and began loading a couple of duffle bags and some boxes out to put them next to the front door. Then went into the kitchen and started to empty the fridge into a box too, crying all the while.

She never approached Rossen and he had no idea what to do about her. When she went into the bathroom and started loading stuff out of drawers into yet another box, he finally put Mimi in the playpen and went in and literally forced Kit to stop and pulled her into a hug. She just continued to cry, and when he couldn't stand it any longer and asked her what in the world was wrong, she began to sob all the harder. Joey came home about then and looked at the two of them standing in the bathroom with Kit still sobbing against his chest.

Rossen looked over Kit's head at Joey and

mouthed the word, "Help,".

Joey came up close and asked, "Was Matt by any chance here recently?"

He nodded, "She talked to him in his car for almost an hour before she came in here and has been like this ever since. Why?"

Joey hesitated, "I just saw him and he doesn't appear to be much better. I wondered if this was going to happen." She pulled Kit away from Rossen's embrace long enough to ask, "What's going on, Kit?"

Kit looked up with misery shining from her teary eyes and cried like her heart was broken and said, "Oh Joey, he asked me to marry him." Her face crumbled and she buried it against Rossen's chest again.

Joey wrapped her arms around them both. "Oh, Kit, I'm so sorry." Rossen was incredibly lost. As if she sensed this, Joey paused in rubbing Kit's shoulder to explain, "This is the fourth one this week, and this one matters. Matt is her closest friend here. I kept trying to tell her he was in love with her, but she didn't believe me. I was afraid this day was coming."

Kit pulled away from the two of them to continue tossing toiletries into the box almost with a vengeance. Rossen looked on until the drawer was empty, then took the box from her and took it to the front door, too. Eventually she had everything she intended to take and had settled down to only intermittent tears. Mimi stood at the edge of the playpen watching it all with her two fingers glued to her mouth. Rossen started to load the pile by the front door to the bed of his truck and when

Treyne came in, Rossen asked him if he would mind driving Kit's car home instead of riding with Joey.

When everything was loaded, Rossen coaxed Kit to come to the truck and helped her and the baby buckle in, and drove away. A few blocks down the street, he saw Matt standing on a porch watching them drive by and he silently cussed him as the tears started once more. Rossen didn't dare even ask her anything for fear she'd melt down again. The only time they even talked was when he stopped at a drive through to order her dinner. She finally fell asleep forty five minutes into the drive and even then, every once in a while she gave a little hiccupping sob.

Chapter 25

They were home and he'd helped her unload and unpack, and she'd gone to bed, before it finally dawned on him that he'd just helped her completely clean out her college apartment. He sat straight up in bed, realizing for the first time she'd just quit college and he had helped her! She'd been so upset that he hadn't thought a thing about it when she stripped her closet and emptied the bathroom drawers.

How had he not seen this coming? He got up to pace the narrow confines of his room, then went next door into the game room to pace some more. He looked up at the speed bag and was sorely tempted, resisting only because he knew he'd wake the whole house. That little! He didn't even know what to call her in his head. Thinking back at some of their recent conversations, he began to understand that she had been planning this for a long time, maybe even since the very beginning.

He went back to bed, but couldn't sleep for thinking of all the things he was going to say to her in the morning, when he explained very succinctly, that she was heading back to school in January. He fell asleep somewhere along the line and when he woke up he was surprised to realize he'd slept way in.

When he came into the great room, everyone was already there eating except Kit. She was rushing back and forth from her room to the front porch carrying her suit bag and luggage and purse and what all he wasn't even sure. He'd momentarily forgotten she was flying out to LA early this morning. Mumbling under his breath, he followed her back to her room and as he walked by, automatically picked up Mimi Star as she was reaching up from her crib, saying "Dah-eee." Kit went to step past him at her door and he reached out to stop her, saying, "Kit, slow down for a second, we need to talk." She looked up at him, and he realized she must have cried a good portion of the night. She wasn't in a very good mood this morning either.

"What?" She almost barked it at him. Whew! She was *really* not in a very good mood this morning!

He fell into step beside her as she marched back out to the front porch with her purse and a carry on. She set them down near some shoes and a leather rope case that were sitting there, turned on him and snapped, "I'm kind of in a hurry here to catch a plane, what do you want to talk about?"

She was in such a temper that he had to work to keep from cracking a smile. He'd never seen her quite like this. Without sugar coating it, he said, "Well, for starters, you're not quitting school already."

He was ready to do battle, but he wasn't anywhere near ready to handle the temper she turned on him. After staring him down for a long second, she said almost slowly, "You *big, fat, boneheaded jerk*! Don't you *even* try to tell me what I can and can't do! I have done everything you asked and then some! I have gone off and left my daughter! I have dated more stupid, pig headed, chauvinistic, egotistical men than I ever want to see again in my life! I have earned sixty two credits this semester, sixty two! I've gone without sleep, I've driven and flown thousands of miles. I've turned down marriage proposals from five different men, one of whom I completely trashed! I have sung in front of millions of people and worn high heels to do it! I've gotten a purple belt in Karate. Except for taking statistics, which I didn't have the right prerequisites for, I've been through your whole list *to the letter*! I have done everything you asked me to, just to keep you happy and I'm done! Nothing is good enough for you! I'll be eighty and still be a child to you!"

She barely paused for breath, then went on, "I am going to California today, and I'm going to get through this concert, and then I'm going to come home and hold our daughter and sleep for a week! I'm going to bask in being settled down! I'm going to revel in it! Do you hear me? I'm going to build my own house this spring, and plant a garden barefoot, and ride a horse until I can't even walk, and then I'm going to sit on the porch in a rocker and watch our little girl play, and when she's tired of that, we're going to go swim in the pond, and then while she naps, I'm going to work with my clay for as long as I want.

"I don't have to go *anywhere* I don't want to; with

anyone I don't want to be with! I am not going to keep dodging being kissed by guys I don't want anywhere near me! I am not going to have any more awkward conversations with handsy men about why I'm an unwed mother, but still a nice girl! I am not going to drive away from here in tears ever again! And I am certainly *not* following any more of your stupid rules!

"In fact, do you know what you can do with your stupid rules! You follow them if you want to! And you and I can grow old, *single*, in two houses across the bench from each other, watching Mimi play by herself as an only child! *You* can insist that she always have her mother's last name, and *you* can explain to her on Father's Day why she doesn't have one.

"You do that if you want to, but count me out! I'm going to love whom I love, and tell whomever I want that! I am not going to try to carefully control how I feel anymore! I am sick and tired of your stupid rules, and being bullied by you because you think you know what's best for me better than I do. You can sit at your computer and pretend that we don't mean anything to each other if you want, but I am *not* gonna play the game anymore! And I am NOT going back to school next month!"

As she finally wound down Rossen was speechless. He couldn't even begin to process a comeback. She walked around him and began to throw her bags into the back of her car. She picked up his leather rope case that was laying there on the front porch with her stuff and put it in, too. He took it back out with just the barest hint of a smile on his face.

The second he smiled, he knew it was a mistake. It only made her madder than ever! She threw some more stuff into the car and he finally took her hand and pulled her to look at him and said, "Easy Kit, settle down. What did I do to deserve this? What is it that you want from me?"

She jerked away. "You really don't want me to answer that. It would be against the stupid rules!"

He reached for her arm again, exasperated. "Then give me a hint, Kit!"

She spun on him. "You want to know what I want from you? Try emotional honesty! Try commitment! Try respectability! Try *physical intimacy*! Try any of the things that most couples who love each other like we do, have! Ope, sorry, broke the stupid rule! Can't talk about anything that matters between us!" She climbed into her car, slammed the door and peeled out on the snowy gravel road, sliding sideways and sending snow flying all over his pant legs as she went.

He just stood there watching her car disappear over the hill. Mimi looked at him with big eyes, her fingers still in her mouth and started to laugh. "Oh, you think it's funny do you? I thought so too, and that was a big mistake. I never shoulda cracked that smile. And she still got away with my rope. Daddy has now graduated from just plain bonehead to big, fat boneheaded jerk." He shook his head, amazed at all the things she had said. Said? Yelled at the top of her lungs!

Slade came out onto the porch to stand beside him. "Who was it that said hell hath no fury like a woman scorned?"

Rossen shook his head again. "You've got me. But he had that right. And I haven't even scorned her. Holy Canoli!"

"Did she just say what I thought she did?"

Rossen shook his head one more time and laughed. "Yeah, I think she did."

"Maybe you'd better go to California."

****

Kit was mad until almost the very end of the concert that night. She'd started to mellow out slightly beforehand while a stylist had been doing her hair, until she'd looked up to realize she now had a brilliant pink section woven through it! Then she was angry all over again. She sent the girl packing, almost in tears, with Kit hoping that whatever she'd put in wasn't necessarily permanent.

She only lightened up when she sang the old Bonnie Tyler song, "Holding Out For A Hero". Nick had asked her to sing it as a tribute to all the families that had been willing to let their loved ones donate organs. She started the song still ticked off, but somewhere in the middle, she thought about Rossen and all the things he was forever doing for her, and by the end of the song her anger was gone.

They sang two last songs and did a couple of encores, and then she went back down into her dressing room, suddenly weary to the bone. There on the dressing table in front of the mirror was a beautiful bouquet of all kinds of wildflowers. She bent down to drink in the fragrance. It reminded her of high summer back home on the ranch. She wondered why Nick had switched from the roses he always sent.

She was just looking at her hair, wondering how she was going to get the pink out before church the next day, when Nick spoke to her from the doorway. "Hey, you rocker chick, what did you think of your first real concert?"

She looked up at him in the mirror and smiled. "Hey, Nick. Thank you for the flowers. They're beautiful. The concert was great! You were right! It is the ultimate rush and I loved it. I'm sorry I was so irritable before hand."

He laughed. "No problem. You're a kickin' guitarist when you're hot! I'm thinking I'll tick you off before every concert!" His tone softened. "You quit being mad in your hero song. Were you thinking about me?"

She turned to look back at him and then looked down. "Honestly, no. I'm sorry."

He shrugged. "I figured it was him again. It's okay. He's too nice a guy to even be mad at."

Kit felt guilty when she answered, "I used to think that, but this morning I'm afraid I was as mad as I've ever been in my life. I probably said a few things I shouldn't have." She could feel herself blush and he laughed at her.

"That bad, huh? Maybe it's a good thing. At least he knows you care enough to be passionately angry."

She gave him a tired smile. "Oh, I imagine he knows that."

He turned to go out the door. "I'll have the car wait in case you want a ride back to your hotel."

Confused, she asked, "Why would I not want a ride back?"

This time it was his smile that was a little tired. "Because the flowers weren't from me."

She watched him turn around and walk away and was wondering what he meant, when Rossen came in to stand nonchalantly against the door jamb just like Nick had. He almost looked like a California pretty boy in his cowboy boots with his matching leather jacket. Their eyes met and held while they both tried to figure out what to say. He finally broke the silence, "You were great tonight." His voice was gentle, but there was something in his eyes that was far from tame.

She suddenly found it hard to breathe and wished she hadn't been quite so forthright with him that morning. Almost shyly, she said, "Thank you. I've been worrying about when I'd have to face you after my tirade. What are you doing here?"

The light deep in his eyes intensified and she glanced away. In a voice that was almost velvet, he said, "Being emotionally honest."

Her eyes flew to his again and she felt almost a little panicky at what she saw there. Hesitantly, she asked, "What about the rules?"

He smiled. "All rules are off when you're dealing with somebody with pink hair."

She put up a hand to touch it. She'd forgotten about the wild streak. "It was not my idea, I promise. It would never have made it there if I'd been paying attention to the stylist and not thinking back on our conversation this morning."

"Conversation. That's an interesting word." He walked into the room and came to stand behind her and put his hands into her hair. "Actually, I think it's hot. I think you should leave it there."

She looked up at him in the mirror wondering who this man was who had taken over Rossen's body. "Leave it there? Can you just imagine Gladys Maggleby tomorrow?"

He laughed. "She's been saintly since that incident last winter. She's probably dying for a good head of rocker chick hair." He put his hands through it and then put his fingers on her neck to stroke her skin and softly said, "It's actually going to be very nice to have all the rules off. I hate them, too. I think we should keep the pink hair forever."

She was still staring at him in the mirror, her heart beating thunderously in her chest. He slowly bent his head, watching her eyes in the reflection, then ever so gently placed a lingering kiss on the side of her neck below her ear. His breath on her skin gave her chills to her toes. "What are you doing?" Her voice was low and almost husky when she finally got the words out.

He looked back up at her reflection. "I'm kissing

your neck." He went back to nuzzling her and she turned around to look directly up at him.

"What's going on?"

He put his head down and spoke as he nuzzled her skin again, "You were good enough to struggle through my list for me, I figured the least I could do was work on yours for you. This is the physically intimate part, at least as physically intimate as we can be before we get married." He paused to kiss the other side of her neck and then looked back up. "I'd like to ask you about that, but I'm a bit intimidated. You've already turned down five other guys this week, and I really don't want to be the sixth."

She was looking at him like he'd lost his mind and she honestly wondered if he had. She'd never seen this side of him before. Nervously, she accused, "Now you're lying. You know I'd marry you tomorrow if you wanted."

He stood up to look down into her eyes again. "Tomorrow's incredibly tempting, but I want you forever, so we have to wait until you can go through the temple. Does that mean you'll marry me?"

"Does that mean you're asking?"

He put both hands on her shoulders and then moved one to brush her lower lip with his thumb. "Kit Star, I love you. Would you marry me and be with me forever and ever?"

She was still looking at him, her brighter blue eyes searching his deep blue ones in wonder. "Yes, of course I'll marry you. I'd be honored." She looked down. "I love you too. I always have. You know that."

He tipped up her chin to face him as he slowly lowered his mouth to hers. She'd waited so long for this kiss. He had too. He hugged her tighter and she moved closer to him as it lasted, the warmth of his firm mouth making up for all the wasted months.

His low groan as he finally pulled away to hold her close filled her with sweet heat. He touched his chin to her forehead. "I've wanted to do that for forever."

She leaned back and looked up at him. "Then why did you make us wait so long?"

He pulled her back into his arms again. "I had to Kit, and I'm sorry you felt bullied, but I'd do it again if we had to start over. I had to." He stepped back to look down at her. "You were too infinite of worth to short change. Look me in the eye and tell me the last year hasn't been important to the woman you've become?"

She tried to meet his eyes and finally looked down. "You're right. You always are, darn it! But what's so different about tonight than all these past months? Why can we finally show our feelings now?"

He gave her a sad smile. "Lots of things. Watching you kiss Nick goodbye was the hardest thing I've ever done. It was awful! The other day he accused me of taking away your agency. And every single person I know, you included, has called me a bonehead."

He paused to kiss her again and then admitted, "But mostly I just knew the raging female I saw this morning was all woman. There was nothing childlike about her." He smiled at her as she looked guilty and then he sobered. "I love you, Kit. And I can't live without you, temper and all." He pulled her close to kiss her again. This time she kissed him back with all the pent up need of the last year.

Finally, he raised his head and his voice was husky as he said, "Come on, honey, we should go. Let's get you back to your hotel. I have a room there, too. Our flight is early in the morning." He paused to kiss her again, and at length added, "And we need to leave plenty of time to do your pink hair."

Epilogue

Ten weeks later, one year to the day from when he'd baptized her, Rossen watched Kit and Mimi Rockland walking across the lawn of the Salt Lake Temple, the spring flowers around them a riot of blooms. Their white dresses showed off their dark hair to perfection against the brilliant emerald of the grass and the gray stone behind them. He was just thinking how lucky he was to have two girls worth far above rubies, when Mimi turned to try to walk toward him with toddling steps as she called out happily, "Dah-eeee!"

The End

About the author

Jaclyn M. Hawkes grew up in Utah with 6 sisters, 4 brothers and any number of pets. (It was never boring!) She got a bachelor's degree, had a career and traveled extensively before settling down to her life's work of being the mother of four magnificent and sometimes challenging children. She loves shellfish, the out of doors, the youth and hearing her children laugh. She and her fine husband, their family, and their sometimes very large pets, now live in a mountain valley in northern Utah, where it smells like heaven and kids still move sprinkler pipe.

To learn more about Jaclyn, visit **www.jaclynmhawkes.com**.

Author's Note: My mother, who just happens to have delivered eleven children, of which I am number five, was horrified when she read this book and Rossen touched Kit's pregnant tummy. And she wasn't just slightly horrified. She was absolutely certain that those incidents should be removed because they were completely inappropriate!

She also considered this book as "moving way to fast in their physical relationship". At first, I laughed and said, "Mom, they never even kiss until the very last page. C'mon. How is that fast?" It didn't matter. Because of the unusual circumstances, Rossen, who to me was the most saintly guy on the planet, was a bit of a player to my mother.

I still kind of chuckle at her, but the bottom line is, I guess we all have our own morality yard sticks. With that in mind, to anyone I've offended, please forgive me, because after all, this is a romance. Stuff like kissing happens occasionally in romances. And while it isn't the main story, I happen to think kissing is one of the most vital activities of earth life, and I don't intend to stop writing about it, or enjoying it, anytime soon. Sorry, Mom.

Plus, I'm willing to bet that even my dear, sweet mother has been kissed once or twice. At least that's my dad's story. Yeah, they've been busted a couple of times. And she does have eleven kids—that's a bit incriminating, I'd think! Don't you? Bless her heart.

Anyway, just don't tell her how much kissing is in the third book! Of course, we all know that Sean is the rebel of the family, so what can we expect? (But then, so was my dad and my mother seemed to like him a little. This is him, so you'll understand why.)

Sean Rockland definitely turns out to be the most perfectly, dreamily romantic of the family so far. I love the dancing in the night wind in the woods scene! And in all honesty, I like the kissing parts. Call it a character flaw if you will.

Teasing aside, I hope you enjoy Sean and Lexie in *Once Enchanted.* They are fun! They're just hard headed enough to make you laugh before you sigh at the end. They have been one of my favorite books to write, Jaclyn

Peace River Rockland Ranch Series #1 excerpt

Woodland Hills, California

Her running horse could be heard long before she appeared out of the mist. In the half light of dawn and the wisps of fog drifting off the river behind the track there was first the cadenced hoof beats and then the horse's rhythmic, even breathing. Finally, like an obsidian ghost appearing through a veil, the great black horse materialized and raced ahead, his gait so smooth he seemed to barely touch the earth with each massive stride.

She rode as if she was part of him, their motion fluid, his black mane streaming past her face in the wind to whip against her jockey helmet. He appeared and blew past in a matter of seconds, then disappeared again into the mist where the track curved into the distance. For a moment there was again his breathing and hoof beats, until these too faded into the half light, and it was as if the sleek ebony spirit flying down the track had never been.

Flagstaff, Arizona

The sweet sad strains of *'This is Where the Cowboy*

Rides Away' came on over the PA system as the lights started to come back on in the grandstands. Slade Marsh and Rossen Rockland listened from behind the bucking chutes where they were packing the last of Slade's bull riding gear. The rodeo was over and the last of the fireworks had faded from the night sky leaving only the sulfurous smell and the mess the local youth groups would clean up first thing Monday morning.

It was the last night of this rodeo, and for both of them, it had been a profitable weekend. Together they'd taken first place in the team roping, and Slade had also been in the money bulldoggin' and riding bulls. It had been a good rodeo, but now Slade was tired.

He zipped the duffle bag closed and stood up, stretching tired muscles. There was dust on his jeans from where he'd landed in the arena dirt after his ride, and his black cowboy hat would never be the same after being stepped on by a nineteen hundred pound Brahma bull. At least the bull had only gotten the hat. He'd been aiming for Slade.

They stopped to untie their horses from the outer rail and headed back across the rodeo grounds toward the trailer that was home to them on this rodeo circuit. Leather reins in hand, they paused when they realized a street dance was starting up in the area directly ahead of them. Giant speakers that had been set up on the lawn chose that moment to emit a series of crackling static and then throbbing country music. Their horses were veterans of enough rodeos that all they did was twitch an ear and wait to see what the two cowboys would ask

Jaclyn M. Hawkes

them to do.

"We're old, Rossen," Slade stated it matter-of-factly. Rossen simply turned to look at him with one eyebrow quirked as Slade went on, "We are. Just look at us. Saturday night, good music, beautiful girls under the stars. And what are we doing? Trying to figure out a way to get past this crowd without being seen, so we can go home, put on some liniment and go to bed. It's true. We're old."

Rossen grinned. "You may be old at twenty-seven but I'm still only a whippersnapper at twenty-six. I'm in my prime."

Slade had to work not to limp. "My backside hurts. Actually, most everything I own hurts. I gotta quit riding bulls."

"Better your backside than your head." Rossen laughed and added, "Backsides are optional, heads aren't. Although Jesse probably wouldn't agree. You're right. You'd better quit riding bulls."

Slade groaned and said, "Jesse. Now you can see why we're avoiding the dance. It'll be a meat market. Let's try going through the south parking lot and cutting through the warm-up arena."

As they trudged across the lot, Rossen said, "Someday, Marsh, we're gonna meet some girls we actually look forward to being with."

"I just hope we're not too old to enjoy them."

Rossen chuckled. "Hey, we enjoy girls. Sometimes they make us laugh."

Slade answered in a voice devoid of energy.

"Sometimes they just make us tired."

"Sheesh, you're negative. I have half a mind to drag you back to that dance just to perk you up." They skirted a row of cars waiting to exit the parking lot, their horse's feet clip-clopping on the pavement.

Shaking his head, Slade said, "Can't dance tonight, I smell like a cow pie."

Rossen let out a laugh. "I gotta teach you to be more selective on your landings."

"How 'bout if you just teach me to stay on until I can jump down nice and easy?"

"How 'bout if I just teach you to stay off the bucking stock?"

They reached their trailer next to the row of stalls where they kept their horses, then tied them up to start stripping their saddles and bridles. After brushing them down and getting them settled for the night, the men headed back to the big six horse trailer with living quarters.

Rossen went in to see about scrounging up a late dinner while Slade loaded their gear into the tack storage, then settled his tall frame on the trailer step to take off his spurs. Rossen's head appeared inside the screen door. "Nuked pizza okay?"

Slade sighed. "After I learn to dismount bulls, I'm gonna learn to cook."

Journey of Honor (excerpt)

He pulled up and got off his horse and was just about to speak, when he heard the sound of a cocking gun. The wagon flap moved and the barrel of a pistol appeared, followed by Giselle's head. When she realized who it was, she dropped the muzzle of the gun and took a deep breath, then whispered with her accent. "Oh, Mr. Grayson, you frightened me. I thought you were Henry Filson. What are you doing?"

That's exactly what he was asking himself just about now. "Uhm, you're not going to believe this, but I've come to see if you would consent to marrying me." He put up a hand. "It's just to be able to get you away in the morning, and we'll have it annulled when we get to your valley. It's either that, or stay here and deal with Filson and a trial, and waste more time getting started west."

She looked totally confused for a minute, and then said, "Just a moment." Her head disappeared back inside the wagon cover and he could hear her whispering quietly to someone. Then a bare foot and lower leg appeared through the flaps. He realized she was getting out.

He went forward to help her down and she turned to look at him with big eyes in the darkness. She was wearing a nightgown covered with a long robe and her hair was loose and hanging around her shoulders. She was even prettier than when she'd been all dolled up, and he questioned again to himself what in the world he was doing, while he waited there to see if she was going to laugh or cuss him.

He was completely amazed when she looked up at him in wonder and asked in a soft, sweetly Dutch voice, "You'd do that for me? Really?"

He didn't know what to say to that. He'd never experienced anything in his life that would help him figure out what to do in this situation. Finally, he just said, "Uh, yes. I would. But honestly, it's not being totally unselfish. Without you and your grandparents, we can't leave either until we find someone else to take your place. The army won't let trains of less than twenty wagons start out."

He paused for a minute and then decided that being absolutely forthright was in both of their best interests. "I give you my word to be a gentleman. I wouldn't expect anything other than your help in getting underway. You needn't worry."

She laughed a sweet laugh at him in the dark and said with her intriguing accent. "Worry? You have just taken a huge load of worry off of me! I don't doubt that I can trust you. I knew that the moment I saw you on the hotel boardwalk. And I fully intend to help all the way across this great journey. I will be glad to. I am more grateful to you than I can say right now. I would love to marry you to get started in the morning. I would be thrilled!"

For a second, he thought she was going to come right up and hug him. Just when he felt relieved that she didn't, she actually did. Just as quickly, she pulled back and looked up at him with a sober face. "Tell me what you need me to do."

Still a bit shaken, he simply said, "Be ready to go into town a little before sun up. We'll meet with the sheriff, get married and be back and ready to leave at first light."

All she did was look up at him with those wide eyes and say, "Okay." With that, she turned around and climbed back into her wagon without a backward glance at him. He walked away in the moonlight in a stupor. He got clear back to his own wagon before he remembered that he'd ridden his horse to hers and he had to go back and get it. Gathering his reins, he was turning to go when she poked her head out again.

Feeling slightly sheepish, he said, "Sorry. Forgot my horse."

The Outer Edge of Heaven (excerpt)

Luken Langston pulled his pickup truck into the parking spot in front of the bunkhouse and shut off the engine in the lavender gray light of dusk. Opening the door and stepping out, he stretched his tired back and reached back in for his leather work gloves and the rope that lay coiled on the seat. He slapped the rope against his dusty pant legs and boots and breathed deeply of the evening smell of river bottom and beef cows. To some that may have been a questionable smell, but to him it was home in its purest essence and he loved it.

His stomach growled and he wondered if there was any real food in the bunkhouse fridge or if he'd have to either settle for junk, or head back up to the main house before crashing tonight. He'd been up since four thirty that morning and was too tired to go for food, even though he'd skipped dinner. Maybe there was some fruit left, or some milk. Fo lived on milk, so there should be some. Or maybe that was backward. His boots sounded loud on the wooden porch boards as he took the two steps.

He tossed the rope onto one of the hooks inside the door of the bunkhouse, threw the gloves onto the shelf above it and reached to unbuckle his chaps. Hanging them beside the rope on the hooks, he pulled his shirt off over his head in one single motion. He dumped it into the laundry hamper next to his bunk as he kicked out of his boots and spurs, grabbed clean clothes from a drawer and headed for the shower.

Thirty seconds later, he decided a hot shower was the greatest invention known to man and resolved to sleep right there under the pounding, steamy spray. This had to be the purest form of heaven.

The need to sleep there cooled with the last of the hot water and he got out, dried off, and wrapped the towel around his hips as he stood at the sink to shave. The aftershave he slapped on helped to wake him up enough that he decided he would go in search of real food, even if he had to go up to the house. It had been a grueling evening.

He usually let the hands have Sundays off except for the barest minimum of feeding chores, but this afternoon he'd had a whole herd of heifers go through a break in the fence and get into a grain field. It had been a pain rounding them all back up, moving them alone, and then repairing the fence. The field would never be the same, at least not this year.

Slipping on a clean pair of jeans, he walked out of the bathroom, shirtless and bare footed. He was halfway to the fridge when there came a light knock and then the bunkhouse door opened. A beautiful stranger with blonde curls and long legs stepped inside and called out for Fo. She didn't see Luke there in the half-light and came in several more steps, calling as she came, then abruptly pulled up when she finally saw him. Both of them were speechless for a second and then she stammered, "Oh, I'm so sorry. I didn't know there was anyone else in here. Please forgive me."

The Most Important Catch (Excerpt)

North Carolina

As their meeting with the coaches ended, Robby Robideaux stood up and moved toward his friend Jason to touch base about what time they were going to be leaving for the airport in the morning. He absent-mindedly accepted a courier envelope a waiter held out to him, slipped a finger under the seal, and opened it as he turned back to his conversation. "Seven forty-five? That should be long enough to make it through security, if we only have carry-ons. I'll pick you up." He glanced down at the papers he'd pulled from the envelope, swallowed a gasp, and hurriedly shoved them back inside. *Holy Toledo!*

He looked up, hoping no one else had seen the suggestive photos of a woman with far too few clothes on that he'd pulled from the seemingly innocuous express envelope. Geez, these things usually came in heavily perfumed pink letters or in elegantly wrapped packages and he knew not to open them, but this one had taken him by surprise. He'd expected business correspondence this time.

Jason looked at him sympathetically, and Robby rolled his eyes and shook his head as he bent to retrieve the piece of paper he'd dropped in his hurry to hide the pictures. What were these women thinking? Didn't they listen to the news at all? Just this week there were two reports of women who had been assaulted by professional athletes. Not that he was that kind of a guy, but these women didn't know that. They didn't know him from Jack the Ripper! Were there no nice girls left in the whole wide world?

He checked to make sure the plain paper he was seeing didn't feel like a photo before he turned it over. It was a note and he would have just shoved it back in as well, except that it only said five words that literally jumped off the page at him. "Meet me on the balcony."

The hair on the back of his neck stood on end as he resisted the urge to even turn his head to glance at the balcony overlooking the main dining room where he was standing. Even the fact that he was a 240 pound All-Pro football player didn't stop his dread at the thought of another stalker. He hated this! How had she even known he was going to be meeting here? And, what courier service had delivered this to him?

Stepping to his left where he was far enough underneath the balcony to keep anyone above from seeing him, he set the note carefully on a table beside him, knowing it would be dusted for fingerprints, and pulled out his phone. This meeting had been only head coaches, their staff, and a handful of the most senior players. He glanced at his phone as he went to call security. He never let anyone near his phone, but he still wondered if someone had managed to plant something in it again to track him and listen in on calls. It seemed absolutely paranoid, but it had happened to him twice before.

His suspicions were confirmed when he'd no sooner asked for security than there was a disturbance on the balcony above him, then glass shattering and the sound of a women's heels rushing out the back. He ran a hand through his hair with a sigh, hoping this was just a one-time fluke. The last thing he needed right now was another psycho female.

Illinois

As the heavy metal doors shut with a clang behind her, Kelly Campbell squinted in the brightness of the late afternoon sun. She turned to glance at the austere tan building she had just left. It was only a psychiatric hospital, and she was a nurse, not a patient, but sometimes that building felt more like a prison. She took a deep breath and tried to rid her nose of the nasty institutional smell of commercial disinfectant, but even the thickness of the air here in Chicago wasn't enough to kill that odor.

She rolled her shoulders and headed for her car, wondering if this was really all there was. She'd spent years getting her RN and finding what she thought would be a fulfilling career, but just two months of this job was beginning to make her question if she'd made a mistake.

At first it hadn't been too bad. She knew helping these mentally ill patients was a worthy work, and when one of the seemingly sharp, young doctors had started asking her out, it had been a rush. But it was a short lived one. Dr. Peter Holmes was handsome, and for a short while she'd thought he was completely charming, but now she was beginning to wonder. There was something strange going on here at this facility, and it involved him. She just hadn't figured out what it was yet.

To buy these or any of Jaclyn's other books, please visit spiritdancebooks.com or call 1-855-648-5559